Gael Harrison was born in Malaysia but was
qualified as a primary school teacher and sper
west coast of Scotland. She has worked in Vi
and has recently returned from Australia. She
up children and her home is in Edinburgh.

Other books by Gael Harrison:
The Moon in the Banyan Tree
The Highland Games

WHERE THE
GOLDEN
ORIOLE
SANG

GAEL HARRISON

Gael Harrison

Edinburgh 2012.

SilverWood

Published in 2012 by SilverWood Books
30 Queen Charlotte Street, Bristol BS1 4HJ

www.silverwoodbooks.co.uk

ISBN 978-1-78132-064-8
Also available as an e-book
e-pub ISBN 978-1-78132-065-5

British Library Cataloguing in Publication Data
A CIP catalogue record for this book is available from the British Library

Set in Sabon by SilverWood Books
Printed on responsibly sourced paper

For Mabel

Acknowledgments

Thank you to Marie and Bakar in Kuala Lumpur, who joined me in my search for Malaysia's past. Together we went on a journey to rediscover the people, tastes, and smells of the rubber estates of long ago. Also I want to thank Kate Blackadder for her time and patience in reshaping the manuscript. But most of all my thanks goes to John, who never lost faith in me and who gives me the confidence to go on.

Glossary of Scottish and Gaelic words

Beinn – Mountain
Blether – Idle or foolish and irrelevant talk
Brae – Hill
Burach – A mess, a state of great untidiness and confusion
Cannae – Can't
Ceilidh – A social gathering or a formal evening of traditional Scottish social dancing
Crottle – A type of lichen, used as a dye
Dae – Do
Doot – Suspect, doubt
Dreich – In reference to the weather, when it's cold, damp and miserable
Eilidh – Scottish form of Helen, Scottish Gaelic for "light" (pronounced as 'ay-lee')
Hae – Have
Gey – Very
Lochan – A small loch
Manse – Minister's house
Midden – The waste disposal area or bin
Thon – That
Whit – What
Wynd – A narrow path or alley snaking through buildings, sometimes linking streets at different heights up or down hills

Glossary of Malay words

Amah – Female servant (Also used as a name)

Assams – Sweet/sour pickled plums

Attap – Thatched roof of palm leaves

Ayam – Chicken

Banyak – Very

Bukit – Hill

Bulan – Month

CTs – Communist terrorists

Chantik – Pretty, beautiful

Chepat – Hurry

Chichak – A small lizard

Chuchi – Clean

Cheongsam – Chinese dress with mandarin collar

Gula Malacca – Dessert made with molten brown sugar on sago with coconut milk

Gunner (drink) – Mix of ginger beer and ginger ale with a dash of Angostura bitters

Hantu – Spirits

Ikan bilis – Dried anchovies

Jalan – Road

Jaga – Guard

Kaboon – Gardener (Also used as a name)

Kafan – Simple white cotton shroud

Kampong – Native hamlet or village

Katis – 1/3 pound or 617 grams
Kebaya – A traditional woman's blouse usually worn with a sarong
Kedais – Shophouses
Laksa – Prawn and coconut soup
Lalang – Coarse Malaysian grass
Murtabak – Indian stuffed pancake made with bread flour
Nasi goring – Stir fried rice laced with prawns, chicken, onions, chillies and vegetables
Nasi lemak – Coconut milk rice with anchovies, peanuts and chilli sauce
Parang – Machete
Satay – Kebab style meal comprising chicken or pork with accompanying peanut sauce *Lagi satu* – One more
Selamat jalan – Have a good trip
Songkok – Cap in the shape of a truncated cone, usually made of felt or velvet
Stengah (drink) – Whisky and soda
Terima kasih – Thank you
Tolong – Help or please
Tabik – (1) Greeting, salute given in greeting, (2) Hello, good morning (afternoon, etc.)
Tuan – Sir or mister
Tuan besar – Manager or boss
Ubat – Medicine
Satu, dua, tiga, tiga belas – One, two, three, thirteen

Prologue

Anna's face was a picture. Her brows were creased into a V whilst her tongue waggled along her upper lip. She adjusted the stamp album that served as her desk. Imagining herself as a secretary, she crossed her legs, pulling her skirt tight like the pencil fashions she'd seen on *I Love Lucy*. Today she was engrossed in colouring the invitations on which she had printed in bold letters: EVERYONE WELLCOM. She was quite proud of the effect of alternate shades of pink and purple. Below the letters she had drawn a picture of a swing suspended between two flame trees. Anna looked up crossly as a voice interrupted her.

'Where I put these crates, Anna? I think too close and BOOM! You daddy not happy with me Santosh, maybe his head fly off.'

'Put two on one side here,' the purple pen arced to the right, 'and two over there. They have to see the act. We can't have the audience miles away, you know.'

Santosh shook his head, not at all convinced that this was a good idea, but as the son of the Indian gardener and the best friend of the 'Star of the Show', he dutifully put the four beer crates in position.

Anna carried on colouring. Today was different. Today was the day of *The Great Flying Trapeze Act*, when she and Santosh would amaze the assembled audience with a dazzling display of daring deeds. After practising this routine for at least five days, she felt that they were now ready for a public performance.

Anna stood up and went to inspect the seating arrangements. Walking carefully, her toes pointed outwards and her back straight like a ballerina, she viewed the position of the crates and then tugged one of them a little closer to the proceedings.

'Now I shall swing,' she announced, 'and you must practise the fearless "running past whilst blindfold" act. I'll count and you must go when I say. First I'll do a few swings, like this,' and she pulled on the chains and was propelled forward, 'and then I'll stand on tiptoes and put out my leg and hold on with one hand. Right,' she swivelled around, her voice rising to a screech, 'it's your turn. Don't run too soon. I'm going to start counting any minute. Just close your eyes for now. We'll just pretend that you've got the bandage over them. Are you ready, Santosh? Come on, come on! One, two, three, Go!'

PART ONE

Chapter 1

2001 – Druimfhada, Scotland

It was only an old tin box on a worn rug. Photographs and flimsy envelopes had spilled and scattered on to the faded pattern. The heat from the single bar electric fire was causing the corners of the pictures to curl, and was making her nose twitch. Emanating from the carpet she recognised the faint odour of dog, long since dead. This, she thought, was her legacy. She was lucky. Some people only get an urn of ashes or a newspaper notice. At the sudden squall of rain lashing the window the woman looked up, only to see the vast sweep of moorland dominated by the smudged shape of the sombre mountain, a landscape where deer ran free and wildcats roamed the bracken.

'For goodness' sake, Aunty Molly, is this why you asked me to drive all the way up here for, to look at a battered tin box?'

Responding to her aunt's phone call last night, Anna Maxwell had left Edinburgh in the morning. She always enjoyed the journey north to the Highlands, and to the accompaniment of fiddles and Gaelic tunes, she took the Forth Road Bridge over the shimmering expanse of black river estuary. Soon the city skyline receded in her rear view mirror. Cows and sheep dotted the windblown fields of Kinross, and when the pastoral grazing lands fell behind her, the scenery changed to brown peaty rivers, sodden glens and villages rising to the higher plains where mountains glowered under heavy caps of menacing clouds. Nearing her destination, she turned towards the small hamlet where whitewashed cottages huddled beneath the Beinn. This was Druimfhada, where once she had been a child.

Anna looked at the box and glanced back at her ancient relative, sitting in a crumpled heap, small, round, and lost in her stained orthopaedic chair. She was eyeing her niece expectantly.

'Well, dear,' she began, but then got sidetracked, struggling with the chair's remote control gadget. A soft humming sound like a lost bee floated from the contraption, and the chair-back propelled forward, pushing Aunty Molly with it. 'Well, dear, the last time I had a clear-out, I put your poor mother's things together and put them in that tin. There's stuff in there that came from your granny's as well; I just gathered up the photographs and letters from her cupboards. Oh now, there's a thing: all your bits and pieces are in there as well, even the letters you sent when you first went out to Malaya, right from the time when they took you away – you couldn't have been more than seven years old. It seemed only right that you should have them, and what do I want with all that clutter when I'll soon be over the dyke myself?' She was referring to the stone wall surrounding the bleak cemetery, the final resting place for those who lived in the scattered villages and townships in this remote part of the Scottish Highlands. Those who had lived as neighbours in life often found themselves in neighbouring graves.

'Oh I don't know,' Anna replied, 'you're made of stern stuff; how many times have I heard about your imminent departure for the ultimate journey?' All the same Anna could see how frail the old woman had become, and she tried to calculate just how old she was. She couldn't be much under eighty-five, she thought. 'How are you keeping?' she asked gently.

'Och, I'm still alive, dear, as you can see. Archie from down the road comes in every day to check I'm all right and to drink my whisky.' Molly's eyes twinkled, making light of her disability. The paralysis from the stroke she'd suffered meant she was unable to get about as she had once done. 'Anyway, what about yourself, it's news of you I want to hear.'

'Actually I'm at a loose end. October is a time when I always feel restless; the garden is dying and the nights are getting longer, so I'm glad you phoned.'

'And what about Duncan?'

'He's away in Thailand but he promised he'd come and see you when he gets back.'

'Well tell him not to bother bringing me any more ornaments, my home help has enough to do without polishing more elephants.' She fixed her beady eyes on the sideboard, frowning at the offending group of souvenirs. Anna laughed, bringing her attention back to the interrogation.

16

'And what about the boy? How's Jason?'

'He's busy and happy; well, the last I heard.'

Anna had a sudden vision of her tall son leaning against the kitchen door frame, his mouth pulled into a stubborn line. His words came back to her: 'You can't make me go to university, Mum. I want to travel and work with my hands, not sit behind books or a computer all day.'

'He's still down in the south of France working with his cousin. He's doing some carpentry work, building chalets, I think. You know what he's like, not the greatest communicator in the world!'

'And your dad, how's he?'

'Fine…'

'Such a grand-looking man,' Molly sighed dreamily. 'I can still see him now coming through that door, laughing and full of fun. He was always at me, you know, trying to put snow down the back of my jumper and what not.' She suddenly became aware of the present, and pulling herself upright, she pointed to the tin box. 'Take it back home with you, Anna, and sort out what you want.'

'Does it hold any secrets?' Anna asked, her mouth twisting into a wry smile. 'There's always such an air of mystery whenever I mention the past.'

'Och lass, I don't know, you know your father just moved on after your mother passed away. He put his grief behind him and just got on with his life.'

Anna leant over and opened the box, its lid and sides decorated with scratched and once colourful pictures of a smiling family enjoying a now illegible product. 'For goodness' sake, what a collection! The same old photographs and God only knows what else you've stuffed in here over the years. Do you remember how I loved going through it all when I was young?'

'I do, lass, and you always wanted me to tell you stories of your mother.'

'Well, my father never did. He was so busy living in the present; he acted as though she'd never lived, as if she was a taboo subject.'

Molly gave an unnecessary cough, as though embarrassed by events of long ago. 'I know, dear, I suppose it's the Scots in us, we like to keep our business private.'

'Shall I make some tea?' Anna cut into Molly's reverie. She felt impatient suddenly and didn't want to hear the same old stories about her father, about how grand he was and so much fun. It was her mother's history that interested her. She felt unsettled, and was glad of the opportunity to fuss about with the kettle and mugs and putting the drinks on the table. She sipped her tea and took one more look at the bleak shape of the mountain before kneeling down to investigate the contents of the box. Inside were hundreds of photographs, the older ones in sepia, others in black and white, and a few later ones in colour. Their sizes ranged from the tiny squares proudly produced by ancient Brownies to more formal studio prints with a stiff backing.

'Look at this one, Aunty Molly, is this my mother when she was a child?' She handed her a small picture.

Molly squinted through her glasses to focus on the old photograph. 'Aye lass, it is right enough, she'll be the one on the left. She always had such bonny hair!'

The young girl looked about ten years old and she was holding hands with a small friend, her eyes infectious with laughter. Anna picked up another, a portrait of some children sitting on two benches, taken in the classic form outside their school door. It depicted the cropped hair and uniform bleakness of this particular genre worldwide. The teacher was dressed in a long black skirt with a wide belt, her hair pulled back off her face in the style of the times, but Anna was drawn immediately to the child in the middle of the front row. She was wearing a knitted Fair Isle jumper, and her blonde curly hair and wide grin seemed at odds with the dark hue of the sepia. Anna reflected, a touch wistfully, that the only person who could have helped her unravel the stories behind the scenes depicted was gone, for only a mother knows the intricate web of families. She wanted to piece together her dead mother's life but saw only a jigsaw of photographs. Who could these children in Edwardian gymslips and coquettish bows be? Who had taken the time to photograph the deer stalking party at rest on the hill? Spidery writing scrawled dates of another age and she tried to sort the pictures into piles that might have been connected somehow. Anna pulled a strand of hair from her face and stretched her arms, releasing the stiffness of her shoulders. Her long hair was loose today; normally it was tied back, but now she pulled a long curling wave forward and studied the soft mingling of silver and chestnut threads. Warmed by the fire, the lines caused by the stresses of the past fifty years seem to smooth themselves out as she sat by Molly's feet, just as she had done so many times as a child.

Looking again at the photograph of her mother as a ten year old, Anna exclaimed, 'Gosh, Aunty Molly, I was about the same age when I first came to stay with you; do you remember when they first sent me to boarding school in St Andrews? The six years I spent there were the most miserable of my life. I can still see Mrs Innis, the housemistress,' and sitting up straight, she mimicked the schoolmarm's reedy voice. '"This is school, Anna, not a home, just school. Don't expect any more than that and you will be happy here".'

Molly cackled. 'She was a right old bat, that one, I do remember her. I didn't want to leave you; you looked such a poor wee waif standing there.'

Anna looked down at the photos in her hand, but it was not the blurred images of old relatives she saw; instead she pictured herself on that first day at school, a thin girl with long braids with navy blue ribbons. 'I know I had to go to boarding school, but it was the way it was done, shunting me out of their lives because his new wife came first. You have your own fond memories of my father, I know, and you make excuses for him, but I wish I could understand why he sent me away.'

'Aye, it wasn't a very good time for you, but never mind, you came through it. You're a survivor, lass, and we had some good times when you stayed here with me in the holidays.'

Anna leant over to squeeze Molly's hand. Her banishment from Malaysia, or Malaya as it was then, remained her own unique experience, still impossible to explain. During her school years, Druimfhada and Aunt Molly were the only source of warmth she experienced, but even within that affable environment she was unwilling to travel beyond her own private world. It was not until many years later when she met her husband Duncan that she was finally able to talk about the past. Now, looking down at the old tin box, she wondered if its contents might provide a link with those who were gone.

As she succumbed to one of her many daily naps, Molly's head fell forward on to her chest. Gently Anna eased the glasses from the old, worn face, noticing the broken arm so inelegantly repaired with

Elastoplast. Outside the small cottage, blustery gales scoured the moors, the sound reverberating down the chimney. The rolling hills matched the dun colours of the pictures spread around her. Golden bracken and peat-sodden marshes mirrored the autumn sun as it set over the black looming shape of the Beinn.

The peculiar smell of candlewick and polish pervaded the air as she entered her room, the smells of a bedroom that is spare: clean, cold and waiting. Anna opened the wardrobe and saw the dresses that had once belonged to her mother. They still hung on red padded hangers as they had done since she was two years old. As an adolescent, she remembered burying her face into the silks to recapture her mother's essence. Each year she would put them on, and each year the folds and fabrics slowly enveloped her developing figure. From the ages of four to twenty-four she had stood in front of the mirror and viewed herself in the beautiful silks of another age. Only in photographs had she seen them on the woman they'd been made for. There were oriental satins in shimmering shades of green and silver that nipped the waist. Dresses of net and black velvet fell to the floor in opulent swirls. The white wedding dress felt cold and stiff in comparison, a conical shell that sparkled with pale pink sequins. Anna closed her eyes, and breathed the essence of the fabrics, inhaling the perfume that lingered across the years. She tried to imagine her mother on that snowy day in February. The bridesmaids had worn yellow, as though heralding the golden life that was about to come. As a bride, Eilidh had been the fairy-tale princess whose beginnings had been so humble.

That night in the spare room, Anna switched on the bedside light and snuggled beneath the satin quilt. She reopened the tin box and pulled out a batch of letters tied together with a piece of tartan ribbon. She remembered the postage stamps of the old Malaya and recognised the childish writing on the envelopes, but she had completely forgotten the contents, and as she unfolded and read her early compositions, she couldn't help laughing at the forthright abruptness of her younger self.

Dear Aunty Molly,
Please rescue me at wunce. I HATE it her and want to go home.
Please come soon. I will wait at the gate we will get a BOAC
plane.

Anna opened another and it would seem she had settled down a bit.

Dear Aunty Molly,
Daddy nearly died today. He walked into a hornet's nest and
his face blew up. It was reeely red and nobbly. He fainted on
the toilet and broke his cheek. The toilet broke as well. He had
to have 2 jabs and 6 stitches. I have a tortoise and he is called
Wilson and I gave him papaya and he pooed red poo all over
Amah's room. Aunt E was reelly MAD.

Dear Aunty Molly,
I have a swing and I have been training the gardener's boy to be
a trapeeze artist like me. He won't do it blind fold. It would be
much better if he did. I am not aloud to climb trees and Cookie
has to spy on me. When are you coming to get me?

She compressed her lips and looked away, trying to breathe deeply
and calm the rapid increase in her pulse rate. Anna glanced down at her
silly letters, and seemed almost to remember writing those words. It was
like looking at the framed photographs and seeing the dresses with the
net petticoats and the smiles that hid painful mental scars. She put the
letters away for another day, and then her eye was drawn to one written
in an adult cursive style in violet ink.

Bukit Bulan, Malaya, May 1956
My dear Molly,
As I write I am still shaking from the shock of the events of
yesterday. It must be one of the most terrifying days of my life.
I don't want you to tell Mam and Dad, as I know they will just
worry more. We were driving back from KL with the car loaded
up with food from the Cold Storage and Anna was asleep on the
back seat. The roads were mostly deserted, just the occasional
boy herding cows or goats, and the Malays in the kampongs that
we drove through were dozing in the afternoon sun. I cannot tell
you the fear we felt as we approached a tree that had come down
across the road. It was even more ominous that there was no

21

one about. Alex slowed down and we tried to listen for anything unusual, but there was nothing. Maybe the silence should have warned us, as normally there are people who take advantage of a fallen tree for firewood. Only insects could be heard, and I felt as though I was watching it all in slow motion, for suddenly from out of the jungle two Chinese soldiers emerged on each side of the road. Well, Molly, I have never seen anything like it; Alex just threw the car into reverse and we roared backwards in a frenzy of blind panic. The CTs, the communist terrorists, for that's what they were, came straight after us, and a bullet skimmed the bonnet just as Alex swung on to the grass verge in a sharp u-turn. We raced back to the police station at Taman Minyak to tell them what had happened. I was so sick afterwards from the shock and sheer terror. Amazingly, Anna slept through it all! I shudder to think what might have happened if we hadn't got away from them. Anyway, we eventually arrived back at the estate, but I can't tell you how much I'm looking forward to getting home to Scotland. Will this Emergency never end?

Anna put away the letters and turned off the light. The wind continued to howl over the moors, trying to uproot the already bent and twisted trunks of the rowans and alders, and the rain splattered in gusts against the windows. It was as though, for the first time in her life, she had heard her mother's voice. Words that felt like whispers had flown through the years in a stream of violet ink.

The following morning, Anna squinted at the deepening grooves around her eyes then parted her hair into three thick ropes and proceeded to plait it into one long queue. She braced herself to face the chilly day.

Molly looked up when her tall niece entered the room. The old lady was sitting by the window with a magnifying glass held over the newspaper. She adjusted her glasses, peering through the thick lenses in her usual critical way. 'Aye, it must be all the walking you do that makes you as slim as when you were a girl. Not like me, I get all excited if I can just make it through to the kitchen on my Zimmer.'

After giving her aunt her planned morning itinerary, Anna left the cottage and drove over the desolate landscape, the autumnal colours glowing bronze and gold in the morning sun. Eventually she came to Glengrianach, the small town that had been her first childhood home. She passed the railway station with its little row of cottages, the shinty playing field, the old castle ruins and the river that had been her playground as a child. Out of the town, the road curved past fields with wet sheep and horses dressed in muddy raincoats. The great bulk of the Grampian Mountains framed the sky as she encountered a sombre stone dyke surrounding a bleak cemetery. Anna parked the car and walked through the heavy iron gate, leaving behind the rolling landscape of dead bracken and gorse for neat rows of granite headstones adorned only with small stone vases to hold seasonal flowers. She couldn't help reflecting on the contrast with the colourful graveyard cities of France and Italy, where statues, memorials, angels and portraits, together with dizzy selections of gaudy plastic flowers, always gave her the uneasy feeling of being a voyeur of some decadent orgy. Not so in the Highlands of Scotland. The teachings of Knox and Calvin had the austerity and purity of the cold, rough stone, and the sough of the wind seemed to carry their simple message to God-fearing souls. Standing alone, surrounded by four grey walls, she read the inscription on the headstone she had sought:

EILIDH MCINTYRE

1929–1956

DEVOTED WIFE AND MOTHER

The wind whisked up the dead leaves and swirled them around the graves; the only other sound was her footsteps crunching on the gravel as she walked back to her car.

Chapter 2

February 1956 – Malaya

Eilidh McIntyre stood in front of the full-length mirror and looked critically at her body. The scar that cut across her belly was fading to a dark pink, a permanent reminder of the difficult birth sixteen months ago. Her prominent collarbones were as skeletal as her ribs. She stepped closer and seemed to be swallowed into the dark hollows of her eyes. Eilidh realised there was no need to suck in her cheeks, for the roundness of her girlish face had taken on the angular structure of her bones. She could feel the spasm returning and the wretched cough jarred again through her lungs. 'Oh Lord!' she cried, 'I can't stand this any more, why won't it stop?' Turning towards the door, she called out, 'Amah, are you there? Can you come up, please?'

The Chinese servant padded up the stairs and shuffled into the bedroom. Frowning at the violet shadows beneath her mistress's eyes and the hollows beneath her cheekbones, she observed, 'You not look well, Mem.'

'I'm so tired, Amah, I can't finish sorting these clothes. Please take Anna when she wakes up, I need to rest.'

'Yes, Mem, I help, I look after Anna. You don't worry.'

Eilidh lay down and watched the ceiling fan slice through the torpid air. A *chichak* raced across the ceiling and paused, suspended upside-down, secure in the knowledge that its suckers would keep it safe. She closed her eyes. Noises filtered through the open window; the rhythmic snapping of the shears as the bamboo hedge was trimmed, the persistent chatter of the cicadas in the verdant tree canopy. She could smell the wax polish that Amah used to buff the wooden floors. She felt under her pillow for the cotton handkerchief and held it to her mouth as her body was wracked with painful spasms. Sweat glistened on her forehead and she wiped the red spittle from her lips.

'Mum Mum Mum!' Anna was awake and had pulled herself up but now she was tired of entertaining herself. 'Mum Mum!' she demanded.

Amah deftly straddled her on her hip and proceeded down the stairs to distract her with the doings of the kitchen, the cats and the dog. Sinbad, so named for the piratical black patch that encircled his right eye, looked up, mournfully aware that his peaceful snooze was over. The trio set off to the garden and Anna screwed up her eyes under the glare of the fierce sunlight to concentrate on the new discoveries she would make in her little world. The garden of rough grass sheltered nasty biting ants that weren't content to stay outside and paraded to every nook and cranny of the big white bungalow, the home of the Manager of Bukit Bulan Rubber Estate, his wife and small daughter. Canna lilies were planted in geometric patterns within the lawn, and orchids were being cultivated in pots lined with coconut husks, the long untidy roots dangling in mid air and the delicate flowers wantonly emerging in colours and shapes that defied any orthodox design. Down under a tree off the driveway, bricks lay in an untidy heap, and string had been carefully pegged out to form a perfect circle. Some clods of turf had already been dug out. Anna laughed and wriggled to free herself and explore the new construction project. It was to be a little paddling pool with a fountain.

'No, too dirty for Anna,' said Amah, turning back towards the house.

Sinbad sniffed about excitedly, his mouth wide and smiling, his ears flapping and his tongue dripping great globs of saliva. His ears perked up at a rumbling sound coming from the black circumference of the trees, and into the bright sunny garden roared the dusty Land Rover. Alex McIntyre pulled up beneath the porch canopy and jumped out. He was a tall lean man with muscular arms and wide shoulders. He was deeply tanned and wore beige knee-length shorts above woollen socks that were a mess of grass seed, and walking boots thick with dried red earth. He kicked them off and padded into the cool, dark cavern of the hallway and through to the bright room that was the spiritual heart of the house, the room that should have held Eilidh. The doors and windows were wide open to capture the slightest breeze. The sunlight shone on chintz-covered rattan chairs, and the pictures on the wall echoed the colours and tones of the Persian rugs. Magazines, sewing, and abandoned embroidery were piled on one side of the settee and baby toys were scattered in the playpen, a blue and white bear and a squashed monkey keeping guard.

'Dad Dad Dad!'

The excited babble distracted him and he grinned and took his blonde-haired daughter from Amah. 'Hello, you little rascal, what have you been up to this morning?'

'Daddy dig?' Anna asked hopefully.

'Not now, Daddy has to eat lunch but we'll dig later. Are you going to help me?' His brow crinkled as she patted his face and he looked over her silky head to Amah.

'Mem very tired, *Tuan*. Mem cough, Mem sleep, Mem no eat.'

Alex nodded, but his eyes lost the look of anticipation and he walked through to the dining room and put Anna into the high chair beside him. Together they ate cottage pie while Sinbad lay drooling on the step outside the French windows.

'Now are you going to feed yourself, or am I going to help you?'

'Anna can. Spoon, Daddy!' she demanded and proceeded to chase the peas around the plate.

Undeterred, Alex fed the contents of the bowl into the little girl's mouth until she'd had enough and sent much of it flying back in little volcanic eruptions. Peas were scattered around the legs of the high chair and rolled over to where the dog and the ants waited.

After checking on his sleeping wife, Alex stretched out on the rattan sofa, clasped his hands over his chest and slept. His high cheekbones and sharp nose made his face appear gaunt, and his eyes seemed to have receded deeper into his skull, making it almost corpse-like. Two lines had etched themselves into his forehead. Around his closed lids the normally deeply grooved laughter lines had faded, leaving a trail of silvery threads. Sinbad slumbered, slumped against the cool stone wall outside, and soon the rubber estate took on the guise of the Sleeping Beauty's palace. Anna's eyelids flickered and closed as she lay beside Amah, and the bottle of milk that she'd been sucking gradually slipped from her grasp. Only the dark jungle that encircled the bright paradise of colour continued to stir. It was the hottest time of the day. The sun was at its height, the gardeners had retired to their shacks at the back of the house, and the rubber tappers, whose day had began at two in the morning, were back in the labour lines, the name given to the housing for the Tamil workers. Everyone slept.

This was Malaya in the 1950s. Thick virgin rainforest ran down the spine of the peninsula, but the forests to the west had been cleared, and in their place acres and acres of rubber trees had been planted with seeds imported from South America, set out with mathematical precision in lines that, like the Mona Lisa's eyes, followed you whichever way you looked. The rubber boom had reached its heyday during the two world wars, and now the big companies were experimenting with a more lucrative product, palm oil, using seeds imported from Ghana. Many estates now had two crops growing side by side, and adjoining factories competed for air space to disgorge the reek of smoked rubber and processed palm nuts. Roads had been built to link the major cities to the capital, Kuala Lumpur, which thrived in an age of postcolonial grandeur. State buildings echoed the splendour of Morocco, but elsewhere the architecture favouring traditional red tiled roofs was more Portuguese and French than oriental, the legacy of various colonial settlers throughout the centuries.

From the air it was almost impossible to see where the jungle gave way to the rubber, and totally impossible to see the bright oases of colour that were the gardens cultivated by people from foreign lands, uprooted and desperately emulating the homes they were so homesick for. In reality, the houses they had left in the northern hemisphere could never match the colonial spaciousness that they inherited when they arrived in Malaya. The bungalows were airy, with wooden floors, sweeping staircases and high ceilings. Many had verandas and French windows that led out to emerald lawns. Flame trees, hibiscus, bougainvillaea, frangipani and lime trees were seen in every garden, and butterflies of every colour and description visited these flowering trees and shrubs. Golden orioles warbled their songs every morning, and when the sun set, flying foxes soared over the treetops. Gibbons and rhesus monkeys collected in the trees, and cobras and pythons slithered slowly and silently around the dark shadows of the bamboo hedges when they sensed the presence of chickens corralled for domestic consumption. But it was not only creatures of the jungle that crept through the undergrowth, silently, with intent to kill: the Malayan Emergency, the guerrilla war being fought against the British and Malayan administration by the Malayan Races Liberation Army, continued, with deadly results.

Eilidh learned of the many incidents of murder and mayhem in the daily newspaper, the *Straits Times,* and she and Alex listened intently to the English news bulletins. She'd read of how, after the surrender of the Japanese on 12 August 1945, Malaya had reverted to British rule, and in January 1946, the British announced their plan for a Malayan Union, but this was abandoned and replaced in February 1948 by a new agreement for a Federation of Malaya. The communist leader, Chin Peng, had other ideas and in March 1948 initiated armed conflict with the aim of bringing communism to Malaya. The State of Emergency was declared on 18 June 1948 following the murder of three British rubber planters, and a long and brutal campaign of civil unrest, disruption and terror followed. Conversations at the Golf Club and the Selangor Club were peppered with accounts of planters ambushed and killed on lonely roads as they went to collect the weekly wages from the bank, of native workers intimidated into supporting the guerrillas, of wives and children murdered whilst alone on the estates, of officials brutalised for supporting the British. Eilidh knew the fear of being alone with her small child and just a few servants when Alex was away from home. How many times had she wished she were safe in Scotland, far away from this land where hatred and menace seemed to lurk behind the swaying grasses of her tropical garden paradise?

Eilidh woke to the sound of laughter. She pulled on her shorts and a cotton blouse, and running her fingers through her close-cropped curls, she went down the stairs and stood framed in the archway leading into the sitting room. Alex was lying on his back with Anna held above him, flying her like a little aeroplane as she laughed into his eyes. 'I can see your tummy,' he said and he lowered her over his face and blew a raspberry on to her naked midriff. She let out more giggles and was propelled upward again.

'Hello, you two,' Eilidh said sleepily as both pairs of eyes swivelled towards her. She grinned and came and rescued Anna, then flopped down on the leather pouffe at her husband's side.

'Well, sleepyhead, do you feel any better now?' Alex's brow crinkled in concern. 'Do you want some lunch, shall I call Cookie? The cottage pie was very good, but I think this one fed most of the peas to that bad dog.'

When she shook her head, he asked, 'Are you not hungry at all?'

'No, not really,' and she shrugged resignedly, 'I couldn't eat a thing, but I do crave some lime juice, my mouth is so dry. How about you, do you want some?'

He shook his head and watched as she leant over and rang the bell on the carved side table.

'One fresh lime juice please, Cookie, with some ice, and put some rose hip syrup in a cup for Anna.'

'Yes, Mem.' Cookie nodded and went out. He was immaculate in white trousers and white shirt. He and Amah had worked for Europeans for the last twenty years and were thorough and efficient. Whereas Amah was amiable and liked to chatter, only occasionally would Cookie's face light up and he would display his wonderful set of gold teeth.

Eilidh turned back to Alex. 'Dorothy is coming round this afternoon with Lucy, we'll have tea then. Sam said he'd call in on his way back from the club and I suggested they share some supper with us. What do you think?'

'Sounds good to me, but I won't be back till around five as Angus Robertson is coming over with a load of seeds.'

'Bring him back for something to eat as well! Poor Angus, he must be fed up being on his own so much, now that Elizabeth and Jonathan have gone back home.'

'Good idea, he'll grab the chance of some company. And that means,' he leant over to Anna, 'we'll just have to dig our fountain tomorrow.'

'Anna dig?' The child's face lit up with expectation and she made for the door.

'Come back here, young lady, we'll dig tomorrow; today you have Lucy to play with!'

Alex stretched and yawned, then standing up he beat his fists on his chest like a baboon and howled. Anna laughed up at her daddy and pursed her lips as she watched him stoop and kiss her mum's forehead. Dutifully, he placed a gentle kiss on the soft rosebud mouth so generously offered. Turning back to his wife, he shook his head and his eyes betrayed his sense of worry. 'As I said, I'll be back around five. Are you sure you're all right, Eilidh? I wish you'd eat something.'

'Cookie is making scones; I'll have some with Dorothy.' She stood up and moved into his arms and he held her close, feeling the sharp bones of her shoulders digging into him. He ran his hands down the knobbly vertebrae of her spine. They felt so fragile. They reminded him of a sea shell he'd once found on the beach.

Tiny tendril arms encircled his leg. 'Bye bye, Daddy.'

He laughed and kissed his wife, then picked up Anna and blew one more raspberry on her tummy before handing her back to Eilidh. 'See you both soon,' and he was gone.

Eilidh lay on the floor, resting her back on the pouffe and watching her daughter piling her coloured blocks on to her tummy. 'Come, sweetheart, Mummy has to get dressed and so do you.' Slowly they climbed the stairs and began the foray into the cupboards for dresses. Anna was dressed for the fourth time that day, this time in a lemon smock with pale blue embroidered butterflies. Eilidh slipped on a floral skirt of wild jungle flowers in deep purples and royal blues, and changed into a white sleeveless shirt. She traced her lips with a red lipstick and dabbed some Blue Grass behind her ears.

'Pretty ladies,' she said to Anna.

'Pity lady,' Anna mimicked and together they went to await their guests for tea.

Later that evening, as the sun fell dramatically behind the black canopy of rubber, Eilidh left Amah to supervise the two girls splashing in the bath. Wearily she stretched and closed her eyes. Just for a moment she stood on the landing and her eyes followed the shining wooden banister as it curved its way down the stairs. Cookie was crossing the hallway out to the veranda where Sam and Dorothy were laughing at some anecdote Angus was sharing. He's such a nice man, Eilidh thought, and it was so sad that his wife had taken their son away to school in Scotland. She was due to return but then changed her mind because she couldn't bear to leave her little boy to the mercy of boarding school; he was only eight.

'There you are, Eilidh!' Angus boomed while taking a beer from the tray that Cookie offered to him. 'Are the mermaids enjoying their bath?'

'They are, Angus. Amah has everything under control. Don't worry, Dorothy, we'll be able to eat our lamb chops in peace.' She turned to Cookie, 'Please serve up when you are ready.'

Eilidh sipped from her glass of water and relaxed. Dorothy was flushed from her second gin and tonic, and her dark eyes were sparkling in the candlelight. She was a striking woman and Eilidh marvelled at her friend's latest fashion trend, a dramatic Cleopatra hair style which framed her elfin face. In contrast to his petite wife, Sam was big boned and red faced, and he was laughing heartily at one of his own jokes, this time about the terrorists.

'Well, Angus, you know a thing or two about these commies, always sneaking about in the dark. Too bloody scared to come out and fight.'

'Aye,' said Alex, 'it's very easy for them to attack isolated estates and tin mines from their jungle hideouts. I just wish Chin Peng and his cronies would call it quits and leave us in peace.'

Angus sighed and his face turned serious. 'Well, if we can believe the *Straits Times,* the British, Commonwealth and Malayan forces are managing to quell the insurrection. The new jungle fighting techniques developed by the British are proving successful. And General Briggs' plan to interrupt the flow of food and weapons, medical supplies and information, from sympathisers and Chinese immigrants to the communists is resulting in the resettlement of hundreds of thousands of people, mostly Chinese squatters, to new villages where they're given ownership of their land.' He took a sip of his drink, before continuing, 'They will get education and health care as well as protection from the communists. A brilliant hearts and minds strategy giving them self-respect and better living conditions, well so they say in the paper.'

Not wanting to hear about the conflict, Eilidh walked inside and placed a recording of *South Pacific* on the radiogram. She smiled as the music flooded the veranda. Distracted from his tirade, Angus suddenly stood up and burst into song: '*Bali-Ha'i* may call you…Ah, what music! I used to sing in the local opera back home; did you know that?'

'No, I didn't!' laughed Eilidh, looking at her guest with renewed interest. She took in the twinkling blue eyes that dominated his rather flushed face. Gravity seemed to be pulling his sagging jowls down towards his equally generous neck, and the liver spots gave the impression of an ungainly rash. His hair, the colour of creamy buttermilk, was sparse on top but grew long and curled over his once white collar. As Angus prepared to launch forth into another recital, Eilidh summoned her guests: 'Now come on all of you, Cookie has prepared a feast for us.'

Walking into the dining room, Alex ran his hand along his wife's shoulders. 'How are you feeling, Eilidh, are you all right?'

She smiled up at him, her eyes bright. 'We're blessed to have good friends, my darling. Their company does me more good than all the medicine in the world.'

September 1938

Dust motes floated in the golden September sunshine streaming through the net curtains into Eilidh's bedroom. Her blue satin quilt was piled high with her school pinafore and various discarded cardigans. The only chair was strewn with books and a wet towel had been carelessly flung over the back. An ancient wardrobe filled the space at the end of her bed and it was into its tarnished mirror that Eilidh was gazing this morning. She was tucking her unruly head of blonde curls beneath one of her mother's aprons. She now put her arms into the sleeves of a peach silk dressing gown. She preferred wearing it back to front for it then gave the illusion of being a long, smooth dress. Solemnly she reached for her Bible and, pleased with the effect of the flowing fabrics, she marched sedately out of her jumbled-up room singing, 'Here comes the bride, here comes the bride.'

'Eilidh!' Hellen Matheson shrieked up the stairs, completely destroying her nine year old daughter's fantasy. 'It's Saturday morning and I have to get on. Would you stop your tomfoolery and get yourself down here and help me to make the jelly. I hope you've tidied up that midden of a room like I asked you?'

Eilidh scowled but backed into her room, muttering under her breath, 'I tidied it on Tuesday; no one else has to tidy their room on a Saturday...'

Crossly, Eilidh pulled off the dressing gown and wrapped her kilt around her slim waist.

'And what's all this I'm seeing now, my good apron draped around your head? Well that can come off at once.'

'I hate my hair; I want long hair, why can't I have long hair and plaits like Daisy and Morven? You scrub it in the sink every Friday night and it all frizzes up in front of the fire, and now look at it. I look like a silly moppet.'

Her mother looked back at her appraisingly. She took in the slender frame of her young daughter, the round face with the high forehead, the wide mouth and the spray of freckles across the nose. The eyes were bright, like opals, flashing green and blue depending on the reflected light. 'You look fine to me, lass. When I was your age I ranted and raved about my hair being as straight as thon poker by the fire. Nothing would give it a kink. All my tantrums must have been heard by the Lord God himself for he's certainly blessed you with a head of curls.' Affectionately, Hellen pulled the apron off and took her daughter's face in her hands. 'Lift those eyebrows, Eilidh Matheson! Now try and raise the corners of your mouth, there's nothing that spoils a bonny day as that of a sulky face. You can help me and then you can take yourself off and enjoy Saturday. There's a sheep and cattle auction over there at Market Stance, why don't you call for Daisy or have you two fallen out again?'

'Och I don't know, she's got Morven now, and it's just horses, horses, horses. It's not fair.'

Hellen passed her the chopping board and Eilidh started peeling and slicing a banana. She then took over stirring the lemon-flavoured pieces of jelly into the boiling water. Meanwhile her mother prized open a tin of pineapple chunks.

'I'll put these in and then it can go out on the window sill. It should set in time for our dinner. Now, if you finish that, I'll go up to the butcher's and get us some sausages.'

'OK, Mam.'

Shortly after her mother had left, Eilidh stepped out of the house and looked up the street. All the houses in the row were identical, and each owned a shed and a bit of grass at the front for playing and drying the washing. She could see over the fence to Glengrianach railway station where she made out the figure of her father in his station master's uniform, strutting along the platform. The overnight train from London to Inverness was due any minute, and sure enough she could feel the vibrations of the approaching train. The piercing whistle and great clouds of steam and the screeching of brakes locking onto the shiny rails invaded the quiet of the once silent station. Doors opened and were slammed shut. Mail bags were thrown onto the platform, and parcels hurled into the guard's van. To the blast from the guard's whistle, the train puffed and panted and lugubriously chugged its way forward and the cacophony of noise and frenzied commotion faded away into the distance. Eilidh called out to her dad and waved before turning and heading away from her street and meandering up to the farm at the edge of the village. She was in no hurry so decided to walk along the bank of the river. Above her the alder trees clustered in shades of orange and yellow, and hazel trees were full of their autumn harvest, their nuts falling in a profusion of ripeness. Eilidh looked up as she did every morning to the solid mass of rock that dominated her village. The crags and crevices seemed to play in the shadows of the scudding clouds and suggested a million pictures to her already fertile imagination. Today the mountain was suffused in sunlight and the roofs of the village lay clustered beneath its palette of autumn hues. Eilidh loved the colour and feel of the scarlet berries adorning the rowan trees, always abundant at this time of year. She pulled off several heavy bunches and scattered them onto the ground for the starlings that were eyeing her from the branches around her. Further along, again her progress was hindered for she could not resist stopping to savour the abundance of brambles, greedily sucking the purple juice and watching them burst on to her fingers. Wild rasps left over from summer grew alongside, but Eilidh took care to search for the small white worms that lay buried in their flesh before popping these morsels into her mouth. She took her time walking out to the farm and the shinty playing fields, slashing at crackly brown bracken and the tall plumes of golden rod with a stick as she passed by.

It was coming up to the stalking season. Each year the landowners from south of the border, who owned many of the Scottish estates, came and took up residence in their big houses. Her grandfather and uncles acted as gillies, assisting with the horses and stalking, and finally the shooting and butchering of the deer. Eilidh knew that these Highland herds had to be culled but it still made her sad. Sometimes at night or in the late afternoon she could hear the stags rutting and baying on the mountain – the brave roar that marked the eternal cycle of life in the wilderness areas of Scotland. Instinctively they called for mates, and fought each other for domination and possession. The rumbling and the clashing of their horns seemed to reverberate around the lonely glens and hills.

Nearing her destination, she quickened her pace for she sensed the excitement, the sounds and the smells and the hustle and bustle of the market, the clopping hoofs of the sheep, the lowing of the cows, the snuffling of the pigs, the indignant moo or grunt as a sharp switch on a rear end made an obstinate creature move on. She recognised some of the men, leaning on gates and enclosures as they inspected the animals before they were herded into the auction ring. Many wore brown overalls and had pencils stuck behind their ears, some carried clipboards and others wore deerstalker hats and plus four-style tweed trousers. To avoid the collie dogs that had a tendency to slyly nip the back of passing ankles, Eilidh decided to get out of their way and find a viewpoint where she could see what was going on. She clambered on to a dry stone dyke and sat astride it, looking down at the men gathered around the pens. The auction was already underway. The rapid pace at which it proceeded always mystified Eilidh; a discreet nod or a raised eyebrow or even the twitch of a nose would signify a bid and the auctioneer would talk at such a speed that it seemed as though a foreign language was being spoken. Gavels were struck and clipboards were ticked as purchases were confirmed and the livestock changed hands.

A thin boy with a dusty cap on his head stood surveying her, a look of interest in his deep-set eyes. 'What do you think you're doing up there?'

'I'm practising for when I get a horse.'

'Aye, and when will that be then?' The boy took in the thin legs and tartan kilt, and sloppy green cardigan.

'Well, I won't actually get one, but I might be allowed to ride the ones over in the dell, if Daisy Sinclair talks to her uncle. He's got about twelve and he says we can exercise them.'

'I went on a horse once,' the boy told her, 'but it took off at a hundred miles an hour.'

'Were you racing?'

'Aye, a race is what you'd call it, but all on my own,' and he kicked a stone and sidled closer to where she sat astride the wall. 'Donald, he's one of my brothers, gave it a whack on the backside, and I just had to hang on. Bloody thing threw me into a bed of nettles.'

Eilidh looked at him with new respect. 'So I take it you're not up here with the Clydesdales?'

'What? You think I'd go near one of those beasts again? No way, I'm just up here delivering a load of tatties.'

'So, where do you come from?'

'I work on a farm down in Perthshire. See there! That's my big brother Donald, the one I was just telling you about; he drives our truck.'

Eilidh kicked her legs against the rough stone of the wall, and wondered how she could get down without this boy seeing up her kilt. The stones were jagged, her thighs were numb. She needed to move. When he turned to walk away, she took the opportunity to jump. The day was warm and she decided to leave the smells and noises of the cattle market and made a beeline back along the road, over the railway crossing and up the street to the sweetshop. Eilidh liked the displays in the brightly lit window. There were two rows of glass jars bearing promising-sounding names: Soor Plooms, Humbugs, Chocolate Éclairs and Dolly Mixtures. On the shelf below were Flying Saucers, Liquorice Laces in red and black, mouth-watering chunks of coconut macaroon, fudge and tablet. The door bell jangled as she entered the shop and Eilidh made straight for the counter, further deliberating on the best way to spend her pocket money. Her head tilted to one side, she screwed up her eyes to read the names on the jars; Black Jacks were good, but then so were gobstoppers and penny chews.

The sweet shop proprietor raised her eyebrows expectantly. 'Do you not fancy the Lucky Bag today, dear, or what about the sweetie necklace that you had last week?'

Eilidh's face was intense as she finally came to a decision. 'I'll have the liquorice and sherbet please, Mrs Wiseman.'

The woman breathed out and accepted the pennies before handing over the sherbet. 'Bye bye, dear, you go and find somewhere nice to enjoy it.'

Feeling the sun warming her back, Eilidh decided to retrace her steps along the river. She cut through a field and clambered over a rickety fence, where she found the perfect spot beneath a clump of alder trees. She plopped herself down to watch the water gushing over the boulders in the river. From far away she heard the lowing of cattle and the sharp barking of a collie. Slowly she bit the black liquorice straw and licked the end before dipping it into the white sherbet. She closed her eyes, savouring the sharp tang of the sherbet popping on her tongue. She rolled on to her stomach, and with her legs bent up behind her she studied the tedious progress of a wasp struggling over the terrain of broken twigs and grasses.

Her mind wandered to her best friend, Daisy. They had been

inseparable until Daisy's uncle had moved from Inverness, bringing his daughter Morven with him. Morven was also nine and could ride the horses and had jodhpurs and a hat and a whip. Daisy spent all her time with her cousin now, and the pair talked non stop about horses. Eilidh was just about fed up with it. She also suspected that Daisy was quite giddy about her other cousin, Morven's big brother. John was sixteen and had started work in a grand hotel in Pitlochry. He was tall and gangly, and wore a blazer when he was not in tweeds. He was quite different from the boys she knew from her school. John had a polish to him that came from attending school in Rannoch Moor. He played rugger and talked about 'chaps' and 'hols'. He saw himself one day as being the owner of a string of hotels across Scotland. Eilidh thought he was a bit too grand for his own good, and didn't like the way he held forth when he was regaling her and Daisy. Unfortunately Daisy was very impressed with his grown-up mannerisms. Eilidh was lost in her thoughts while she monitored the wasp's painfully slow journey, not helped in any way by her poking a blade of grass at its antenna.

'So, it's you again! What are you doing this time?' It was the lanky boy that had talked to her at the Market Stance.

'I'm wondering where this wasp is going, that's all.' Eilidh shielded her eyes with her free arm. The other was propping herself up on her elbow.

He dropped down beside her. 'I remember what pests they were at school. The teacher used to have a jar with some jam in and the wasps would crawl in, then she'd put on the lid. Mind you, I won't have a wasp problem this year; I left school in the summer.'

Eilidh squinted at him, her arm shielding her eyes. 'Why? Why did you leave school?'

'I had to because I'm fourteen now,' the lad continued. 'My father can't keep all nine of us; he can't afford to feed us and buy uniforms and shoes. Me and my older brothers live in a bothy attached to a farm. It's better there, because at home, some days we only got half an egg and a bit of bread and jam.'

Eilidh looked at him, a little in awe of such poverty. She'd never had to do without food.

The boy went on, 'We're farm labourers. My father is too. He's still got the five younger ones at home, and they're still at school. My brother Tam ran off to be a soldier; he was fed up with eating jam sandwiches and wanted to drive tanks and stuff. I quite fancy going myself one day.'

Eilidh bit off a piece of the black liquorice and handed it to him. Suddenly she felt very benevolent. 'Have you a name?' she asked.

'Alex McIntyre, and you?'

'Eilidh Matheson.' She tipped the tube of sherbet into her mouth, and immediately spluttered as the grains lodged in her throat. She struggled to a sitting position and he gently patted her back.

'Careful,' he laughed, 'I think you need some help with that,' and he tipped the remainder down his own throat.

Five years later, the world was still at war. British Pathé newsreels kept the small Highland community abreast with the happenings in London and Europe. At first there were many volunteers but then as the war progressed all able-bodied men were summoned to don the khaki and fight for king and country.

Eilidh, now fourteen, was still at school but she was lonely, for her friend Daisy had left school and gone to work in a riding school in Perth. Today, Eilidh ran home from school to drop off her books and pick up an apple. She stepped out of the warmth of her mother's kitchen and a fresh gust of wind whipped up her curls as she took her bike from the shed. It was a changeable spring, where one minute the day was full of promise, the next it was as cold as mid-November. She could feel splatters of rain as the clouds scudded past. Pulling her hood up tight over her head and hunching her shoulders against the biting chill of the unseasonable weather, she headed away from the village and out towards the open fields to watch the shinty practice. The nightly broadcasts on her father's wireless brought the war closer and she was afraid for her small village. Eilidh didn't think Mr Hitler would bother with a wee Highland glen but she knew that the boys she'd grown up with would soon be called up to fight. Cycling to the edge of the shinty field, she passed behind a prickly whin bush. The yellow buds of broom were about to burst and she caught sight of a bird's nest safely hidden amongst the thorns. Three greeny-blue eggs nestled in the soft down.

'Those are starlings' eggs,' a voice informed her.

Eilidh nearly jumped out of her skin, causing her to wobble on her bike. 'Where did you come from?' she gasped, then whimsically, 'I know you, I've seen you before.' Squinting at the boy in front of her, she let out a laugh and her mouth opened into a wide grin, 'You ate my liquorice sherbet!'

It was indeed Alex McIntyre, grown taller and thinner, but he still had the wicked smile and the twinkle in his eyes that she recalled from the dusty lad she had met five years ago.

'Why aren't you in the war fighting the Germans?' she asked, indignantly.

'I'm not in the war fighting the Germans as you put it because our boys need to eat and what would happen if all our land workers down-tooled and took up a gun, eh? Us farm workers need to keep the tatties growing and the cows fit to give milk. Deliveries have to be sent to the cities. I'm not exactly idle, you know. I'm up here delivering seed potatoes for planting this year…but God, it's a cold wind. You'd hardly credit it was May. Poor wee birdies will have a bad spring for their introduction to the world. Come on, let's get away from the bush before the mammy bird attacks us!'

Eilidh glanced back at the field and wheeled her bike around. Falling into step with Alex, they strolled past the tinkers' tents which were pitched by the river. The two young people shouted 'Good day!' to a girl, not much older than themselves, who sat cowering over her fire. A blackened kettle was hanging above the burning embers. Two ragged children stared back, a defiant, belligerent look in their eyes.

'My mam used to threaten they would take me away if I was bad,' Eilidh laughed. 'They come here every year and that lassie's mother's been coming hawking round the doors since before I was born. She wheels an old-fashioned pram and asks for woollens in exchange for pegs and scrubbing brushes.'

Alex waved to the little group of tinkers and said, 'Aye, we meet them every year as well in Blairgowrie. Same ones come and me and my brothers pick the raspberries alongside of them. We've had some famous battles with those rasps; you can imagine the cheek that flies with those berries! Again in the autumn we see them at the tattie picking. The farmers know those people are like gold dust. They couldn't bring in the harvest without them. As for us, all the money we earned went straight into my mother's apron, and we were then given a penny each for ourselves. Everything went on shoes and clothes for the school. It couldn't have been easy kitting out nine of us, and I can tell you we were hard on our clothes! I'd often meet some travelling folk in our school, though they only stayed the winter months. I remember one year my three older brothers and myself met up with two tinker lads and we pulled a prank on a farmer. We made all his Aberdeen Angus cows cross a narrow burn over to a neighbouring field, and all the neighbour's Friesian cows cross to the other side. We thought we were the greatest cattle rustlers of all time.'

'What happened when they found out?' asked Eilidh, her eyes round with shock as she tried to imagine the scene.

'Och! The police came knocking and my father rounded us lads up, didn't know who was guilty so skinned us all alive. "It's no us, it's the tinks!" we shouted, but he just beat us harder!'

Eventually they reached the wall where Eilidh had been practising her horse riding skills when they had first met. 'Whatever happened to your career as a horse woman?' he asked mischievously.

'I did get to ride with Daisy and Morven sometimes but now Daisy's gone; she's made riding her career and lives in Perth. I'm going to stay on in school and then hopefully go to Inverness College.'

'What will you learn there?'

'Oh, goodness knows; home economics they call it, though it sounds much the same as what my mam teaches me every day. Here we are, by the way. This is my home.' She looked at him shyly. 'Why don't you come in and meet my mam? Dad's working at the station, but I'm sure you'll get a cup of tea, if you want?'

Alex nodded and followed her into the small kitchen. Hellen Matheson looked up from where she was frying the eggs and gasped in surprise at the sight of the visitor.

'Mam, this is Alex McIntyre, he's about to go back on his lorry down to Fife. Can you give him a sandwich before he goes?'

The mother looked at the young man. She took in the tall, thin frame, the prominent, high cheek bones, the skin pulled tight across the sharp features, the green deeply set eyes. He was the colour of a hazel nut, his brown hair parted at the side, his clothes dusty and worn. Beside him, Eilidh, with her wild blonde curls and her smart grey gabardine, looked like a princess by comparison. Very different from the lads she usually takes up with, Hellen Matheson thought with a sniff.

Chapter 3

Scotland

The summer of 1952 was hot, so hot that rivers ran dry and boulders that had previously sheltered shy brown trout lay grounded and reeking of ancient river smells. Exposed and vulnerable, the snails slithered down into the mud to escape the black-eyed crows. Alex McIntyre lay on his back in the sun. The aromas of the earth rose around him and he relished the soft spring of the heather at his back, like a gift of nature, just made for contemplation and reflection. Blaeberries grew purple and fat; his fingers were a testament to their sweetness for already they were red and stained from the juice that ran like syrup from his lips. Far off in the distance he heard the pop of a gun. It was the season for the beating of the heather and the shooting of the grouse. He let out a sigh of contentment. Life was good.

Alex was home at last. Three years had passed since he had left the patchwork fields of Scotland, and it was with a sense of deep satisfaction that he listened again to the cry of the lapwing hurling its way across the open fields where the corn lay ripe and yellow as butter. Oh, how he had missed the fresh breeze and the puffs of cloud chasing each other across the sky. After the stifling heat of the tropics, he relished the lazy wind sighing over the heathered hills above White Hills Farm. A broad grin spread across his face as he thought about his arrival at the farm that morning. After driving over the rough cobbles and parking the car that he had hired especially for his leave, he had strolled about looking for any of his old workmates who might not be out in the fields. He spotted some men outside the cowshed.

'Aye aye, Murdo, grand day!'

'Alex McIntyre! For God's sake, lads, see what an ill wind's blown in. Look at you man, with your fine motor and your swanky jacket and posh brogue shoes, you must be raking in the money in that far flung place. Is it a Rover?'

'Aye, but it's not mine. Got the sleeper up from London, then I hired the car in Edinburgh. Gets me about. So how are you lads? Looking gey fit and relaxed…I doot you've been hiding in that byre having a sly fag.'

Murdo, Geordie and Alan Mutch had gathered round the car, kicking the tyres and feeling the car's soft leather upholstery. They obviously wanted to sit in it but were mindful of what was sticking to their boots.

'Whit dae you drive over there in Malaya then?'

'Well, I've got my own personal transport but the chain keeps coming off; I sometimes get to use the boss's Land Rover though. Are we going to stand here and blether about cars all day, lads, or are you going to tell me how the farm has managed to stand without my great input?'

'Ach away you go, Alex, whit's there to tell. Turnips grow, coos eat them, and my back is just about broken from spending my days bent in the wind, sun and snow. What else is new? Tell us aboot Malaya. Do you have to plant them rubber seeds yourself, or do you have coolies for that? Grand it must be to be ordering folk around. Maybe I should think o' going myself?' Murdo leant back on the shiny Rover and let out a sigh.

'And the lassies, Alex?' asked Geordie, winking lewdly. 'Dae ye get time for the lassies?'

'Och aye,' Alex laughed, 'always hae time for the lassies!'

'I hear they have Indian lassies working on the estates…now that's what I could do with here…a few buxom black-eyed wenches that will just do my bidding. No' like the coarse strumpets that we have aboot here. Full of lip and ready just to tease the trousers off a bloke then go crying to the meenister.'

'Listen to him!' broke in Alan Mutch, 'the only thing he gets to cuddle on a dark night is a coo, and don't go denying it, lad!'

Alex enjoyed the easy camaraderie so readily rekindled with his former workmates. The ribald chaffing and joking continued, but there was also a new sense of respect, for although it had only been three years, something had changed in Alex.

He sauntered up to the house of his benefactor and friend, Lord Greystone, the landowner and farmer who had given him the opportunity to change the course of his life.

'Alex! Goodness me, what a surprise, come away in, come in, lad. Margaret! Set another place for lunch would you please, we have a very welcome guest. How long are you back for?'

'I've got six months' leave and it won't be a day too long. I can feel Scotland just seeping into me. It's grand to be home again.'

'I'm sure it is! Now come in here and we'll have a wee dram together and you can tell me all about your exploits and adventures.'

They walked through to the book-lined study and Alex sat down in a winged leather armchair while Lord Greystone poured generous measures of a ten-year-old single malt into two crystal glasses, and added a little water to each. He passed one to Alex and they clinked their glasses together before nosing the peaty aroma and savouring the smooth flavour on their tongues.

'Now tell me, what is the situation out there in Malaya? I listen to the news and I read all I can. I hear tell there are still some terrible slaughters going on and those commies are just not letting up. Are you yourself in any real danger or is it like everything, just blown up for effect?'

'No, sir, it's not blown up at all, and yes, we are in constant danger. We're armed at all times and I don't mind admitting there are many occasions when I don't like driving around the estate on my own. Some of the rubber runs right up to the jungle and even the crack of a falling branch can make me draw my pistol. There have been a lot of nasty incidents close to home. Having said that, Malaya's a fantastic country and I'd not be missing the experience for anything. Mind you, the conditions and climate can be pretty tough and it's often quiet, but I settled into the new way of life fairly quickly and the long evenings have given me time to learn the languages.' He took another sip of his whisky and with a mischievous glint in his eye, let forth a tongue-twisting torrent in the Tamil tongue.

'My God! What in the name of the wee man did all that mean?'

'I think I could keep you guessing on that one, sir! But I'll let you into my party piece. It means: ninety-nine-thousand-nine-hundred-and-ninety-nine!'

'Ha ha, very amusing, you had me going there, lad! Well, I'm very pleased that you've adapted to it all so well. Now, that sounds like Margaret serving up the lunch, so let's pour ourselves another dram and we'll go through and continue our conversation. Say it again, Alex. Margaret, will you just listen to this!'

Later, after a plate of lamb stew thick with onions, Alex took his leave with a promise to return and made his way back to his car. Lord Greystone returned to his study and reflected on the change he'd seen in the lad. Gone was the gangly youth who had dug potatoes, who had braved the whiplash of cruel sleet at dawn whilst venturing out to the steamy cow byre. The boy had gone, and in his place Alex had become a man with money in his pocket, a smart tweed jacket, and with a confidence in his step. He had also talked eloquently about the political situation and Lord Greystone was glad that the lad had made such a good beginning and was to be promoted to a manager. He wondered if he would be considering a wife on this home leave, and if so, would it be that Fiona lass he was sweet on before he left?

After leaving the farm, Alex drove a short way up the hill above the parklands and pulled on to the verge. Replete after the congenial lunch with his former employer, he got out of the car and walked up into the heather and gorse that grew wild and rough and unsullied by human habitation. He had a lot to think about and to be grateful for. Stretched out on the rough cushion of heather, he put his hands under his head and stared up at the sky. How could he have predicted the winds of change?

It was Lord Greystone who had recognised his capabilities and consequently had recommended him to the rubber company that had offered him a new way of life. Alex knew that as a lad, he'd had no expectations for any future other than that into which he'd been born. The war had come; his formal education had ended at the age of fourteen. It was the way things were; he knew of no other. The war had caused no outward signs of drama, no bombing or loss of life in his immediate farming community. The countryside continued to fulfil the need of providing food for the shattered cities, so Alex had followed the farming tradition of centuries, his life ruled by the cycle of the seasons. His early years had seen him pay a harsh apprenticeship to the soil as a farm labourer, his days spent in hard physical labour, his nights either in the cramped confines of a tied farm cottage, shared with his large family, or in the farm bothy with other young workers like himself. There were early mornings and late nights of arduous toil. There was the tending of the beasts, the ploughing of the fields and the preparation and sowing of the soil. There were stone dykes to be built and repaired. Hot summer days saw him weeding drills of turnips for winter animal feed, and the long summer evenings saw him courting a series of farm girls. Autumn and winter were the toughest and harshest times; the hard frozen earth did not give easily; the cold driving sleet cut into his eyes when he ran from barn to outhouse.

It was on such a cold winter's day, three years previously, that Lord Greystone was taking tea in his drawing room with a visitor from London. Lord Greystone owned a sizeable number of shares in a company operating in the Far East. According to his visitor, the demand for rubber was increasing, meaning that shares were likely to rocket. As a consequence, Fergus was saying, the rubber companies were advertising for more men to train as planters in such far flung posts as Borneo, Sumatra, Indonesia and Malaya. It was then that Lord Greystone looked out of the window. He observed the lean figure of his ploughman hunched against the wind, making towards the barn. He knew he was one of a number of brothers, and he knew that he was a hard worker.

'Do you know, Fergus?' he said as he raised his cup and with it pointed out to the barn, 'I think I know just what I might do...'

At twenty-five, full of energy and with no responsibilities, Alex jumped at the opportunity to travel to Malaya, a land that he had never even heard of. 'I'm going to run my own rubber estate,' he boasted to his younger brother Callum when he got home.

'Aye, right, and where the hell is Malaya?'

'God knows, but I'm sure there'll be plenty of Asian lassies lined up at the airport just waiting for me to arrive. What about it, do you want me to put in a word with his lordship?'

'Nah,' replied Callum, 'I'll let you go and be the big explorer. When you come back you can tell me what it's like and then I'll think about it.'

Alex went to see Eilidh several times in the months before he left for Malaya, grabbing every chance to go north, delivering farm machinery, wooden crates or barley seed, in the hope that he would see her again. He liked the idea of her waiting for him, standing rooted amongst the heather, her life stilled until he could claim her. He said nothing, he promised nothing; instead he asked if she would write to him. Then he packed up his cardboard suitcase, supervised by his mother, who made sure that he had plenty of clean underwear and socks with no holes in them.

*

Alex became aware of footsteps trampling up the path to where he was lying. A sharp whistle cut into his reverie.

'Aye, man, grand day to be sunbathing. Here, Roy! Sit down here, sit down, or you'll feel the sharp end of my toe on your rear end!'

An old fellow, in plus fours and wearing a deerstalker hat, stood above him, leaning on a shepherd's crook carved out of what looked to be deer's horn.

'Hello yourself,' Alex replied amiably, sitting up to greet the old man. 'That's a fine dog; you have him well trained.' The border collie sat alert, watching both men with keen eyes and waiting for its next command.

'Aye, he's a good companion.'

'Why don't you sit down here, and take the weight of your legs for a while? The name's Alex McIntyre, by the way.'

'Well well, I've heard of you, lad, you used to work hereabouts didn't you, down at White Hills? I've been shepherding all my life, retired now of course, knees are not what they were, but it's grand to be out of the house on a day like this. They call me Harry MacGilvery.'

The old man settled himself down on the heather and squinted at Alex as though trying to remember what he had heard about him. 'You went off to plant rubber trees, did you not? So tell me, what's it like out there in those foreign parts? How many years have you been away?'

Alex lay back on his elbow and studied the leathered features of the old shepherd, the sharp nose and high cheekbones, the piercing blue eyes staring from deep-set sockets. Alex thought he was very like his own father, having the same characteristics, though Harry MacGilvery did not have the height of McIntyre senior. Harry fumbled with a tobacco pouch and brought out a stained black pipe. He commenced the ritual of stuffing tobacco into the bowl, lighting it with a match and sucking, then repeating the lighting and sucking until the flames took hold and the tobacco glowed red. Soon the rich aroma surrounded their two heads like a soft grey cloud. Meanwhile the dog, sensing he was going nowhere for a while, lay down by his master's side and closed his eyes.

'It was three years ago I set off,' began Alex, 'with three other lads from about these parts. As green as the grass, we were, never even been to Glasgow. All done up to the nines in our woollen suits bought specially

46

with money we were advanced. We flew to the capital of Malaya, that's Kuala Lumpur or KL as we call it, and nearly died of shock when we got off the aeroplane. The heat just came up and nearly knocked us over. I was scratching under my arms all the way in the taxi and when I eventually got my shirt and vest off, I saw I'd come out in red weals under my arms and across my chest. You should have seen that heat rash. I thought I'd caught something terminal just by being in the place. My mother had insisted I wasn't to go without my vest. Dear me! She was nearly the end of me and that's the God's honest truth.'

Harry chuckled and puffed at his pipe, clearly enjoying the picture that Alex was painting.

'We were met at the airport by a big Scotsman, Angus Robertson. He took us to a shop called the Cold Storage and told us to stock up with all the food we needed and we didn't have to pay a penny, or a cent I should say, until pay day at the end of the month. What a time we had. We got corned beef, and beans and tins of sausages, and we bought a case of beer between us. It lasted nearly a month as we used to share it. A bottle between two. The four of us were assigned to different rubber estates and we each became one of two or three assistants to the manager and there we learnt the ropes. Assistants have to share a bungalow to live in. It was all pretty daunting at first, but we soon got the hang of it and gradually we were given jobs to do on our own.'

'My word, lad, it sounds a grand life. So were you near to Kuala Lumpur?'

'No, we're a good fifty miles away and we're dependent on the estate car taking us in when they go for supplies or the payroll or things like that. On the estate we each have a bicycle and we get around on that. We're surrounded by jungle and to be honest I didn't see anything but trees for months on end. We ended up eating local fish and rice most days, and wondered if we'd done the right thing leaving all this behind.' Alex pointed in a grand sweep to the beautiful panorama of fields that lay below them.

'I suppose you're back home looking for a wife now?' the old shepherd asked, giving Alex a knowing wink. 'You cannae beat a good Scots lass, and I should know, been married for over fifty years to my Janet. Not too many complaints from my side, though I doot she would have a different story if you were to ask her!'

Alex grinned at the old man. 'Aye, you're right about that and I do have a lass in mind. Mind you, those Malayan girls come in quite a selection box. Indians, Chinese and Malay, with their black eyes and pungent perfumes and skinny wee bodies dressed up in all the colours. They make our heads spin every time we go to KL, looking at you, daring and laughing all at the same time. You never know where you are with them!'

'So,' said Harry, 'you've come back to find a Scottish wife, and then what? Back to being an assistant, and what will the new wife say about sharing a house with the other men?'

'No, I've done all that. I've served my apprenticeship and I've mastered two languages. The powers-that-be in London seem to think I'm ready to manage my own estate now, so I'll be starting on a new estate in February.'

'My! That's a grand holiday you'll be having, six months, plenty of time for courting! Well, come on, Roy, Janet will be looking at the clock. It was good meeting you, Alex, and the best of luck to you, son!'

Alex shook his hand and watched the old fellow's stooped form walk back down the path, the dog at his heels. He leant back once more and let his thoughts drift over the events of the last few days. Many of his colleagues had been writing to their sweethearts back in Liverpool or Surrey with the hope that they would come back as their wives and share the long, isolated and often dangerous postings with them. When Alex was given this home leave, he first made his way to see his mother and father. Leaning on the stone wall surrounding their house, he regaled his brothers with stories of his life in that far-off land. Callum was the only one of his brothers that showed a genuine interest in Malaya and it was not too hard for Alex to persuade him to leave his life as a farm labourer. He made the necessary phone calls to enable his brother to get an interview. Today though, he had other business to attend to. He knew where his heart lay, so with all his obligations completed, he decided to waste no more of his precious time. He got up and stretched, then made his way back to his car and took the road north, winding up through the Scottish Highlands to a small village that he had visited once before when he was just fourteen and then returned to periodically over the last ten years. He had never forgotten the blonde tousle-haired girl sitting astride a stone wall.

Chapter 4

Scotland

Eilidh tugged the brush through her heavy curls. She had let her hair grow longer since leaving school and now it fell to her shoulders in soft waves. Not that anyone could admire it, she grumbled, scraping at the flyaway wisps and covering the entirety with a fine net in the manner required for students of the College of Domestic Science. For three years she had been drilled in the arts of cooking, sewing and keeping a house: 'To do this well,' the principal continually lectured, 'girrils must have a neat and tidy appearance. Hair must not be flaunted like that of a glamour girl.' Her own short-clipped locks stood as a touchstone of perfection. 'Long hair must be pinned and rolled so that no contamination can enter the food.'

Eilidh had survived the principal's daily lectures and nothing could suppress her sunny nature. Giggling on the telephone to her old school-friend one day, Eilidh described the fierce wardens who supervised the girls in the hall of residence. 'They're obsessed with cleanliness and godliness. If they had their way we would all look like old matrons. We have to creep in and out and sign a book so they know we're all safely tucked up in our beds and alone. God forbid if a boy is seen around the house! Left to them, I think the only houses we'll be looking after are those designed for spinsters and old maids!' Outside the public call booth Eilidh could see a line of girls queuing up for their turn to ring home. 'I have to go, Daisy, will tell all next time! Cheerio!' She climbed the steep stairs of the residence and lay back on top of her bed, carefully hanging her feet off the bottom of the counterpane. John Sinclair had come back to Glengrianach, and she had been seeing him for a few weeks. Now assistant manager of a hotel in Perth, he was even more self-assured and his easy grace and eloquent tongue made her laugh. Eilidh was enjoying

49

a new sense of sophistication. She knew there was a world outside the Highland glen and she felt a growing restlessness when she watched the films that were coming out of Hollywood. She ached to be like Ingrid Bergman, to wear dresses of silk that swished around her naked legs. She longed for the exotic. Her imagination was fired by the idea of a sunset over the minarets of Cairo, or elephants walking in the waves on yellow beaches in Ceylon. There was a world outside that beckoned to her, and she knew that if she waited long enough it would claim her.

Eilidh and the other girls from her year, their hair long and curled in glamorous styles, graduated from the college with their diplomas and a blessing from the principal: 'Do well, girrils, take what you have learnt here and be good managers in life, wherever it may lead you. Remember that a girril will always be able to hold her head high if she runs a good, respectable establishment, whether it be a hotel, a hospital or a home. I wish you all well.'

The ensuing months were frantic. Job offers and interviews filled her days. Decisions on where to ply her newly qualified skills were argued out at home with her mother and father. Hellen was determined that her daughter should not go too far away. 'I know of a good hotel that might take you on as a housekeeper and it's only up the road in Druimfhada.'

But Eilidh was distracted. Standing in her bedroom, she fingered a pair of nylon stockings then threw them on to the bed. Her dressing table was a mess of powders and bottles. She'd got nothing to wear; she scowled, scanning the shelves of the wardrobe in despair. There was only that ancient tweed skirt and three worn-out jumpers. How could she enjoy her newfound freedom dressed in those old dusters? Just then she heard the door bell ring. Who could be calling at this hour? She heard her mother screech up the stairs.

'Eilidh! A visitor for you.'

It was John Sinclair. Grabbing her skirt she wriggled into the boxed tweed and sat down on her bed to pull on the stockings. Her fingers felt like wooden clothes pegs as she struggled with the sheer nylon and the clips of her suspender belt. What jumper could she wear today? He'd seen them all and she felt such a poor relation. Oh dear, she thought, it was fine being treated like a lady and eating in grand restaurants but she needed to get work to pay for some new clothes. Last time they'd gone walking, he'd taught her how to shoot grouse, and she'd fitted in well with his sophisticated friends who were also clad in tweed. It was all very well for him with his fancy car and stuffed wallet, but now he was talking about going dancing. She needed to do something, and quickly.

'Eilidh! What's keeping you? John's here; he's waiting for you.'

'Just coming, Mam, two minutes.' Eilidh dabbed some scent behind her ears, then studied her finished appearance. Passable, she thought, considering. She'd finally chosen a burgundy blouse with white stitching round the collar, and thrown a white cardigan over her shoulders, just as Deborah Carr did in the film she'd seen last week.

John stood up when she entered and Eilidh was pleased to note his glance of appreciation. 'At last!' he laughed. 'Your mother warned me you might be another hour so I've accepted her offer of a cup of tea.'

Eilidh sat down on the sofa and patted the cushion. 'Come, sit beside me. What do you want to do today?' She fidgeted with the buttons on her cardigan. 'Did you want to go somewhere special?'

'That depends on you,' he said enigmatically. 'I have a proposition for you; maybe it's good that your mother can hear it at the same time.'

'Are you sure?' Hellen Matheson's eyes were like saucers.

'As you know, working in the hotel business I get to meet lots of people.'

'Yes?' Eilidh looked at him expectantly.

'Well, I heard of a family in need of a nanny. I thought of you and wondered if you might be interested?'

'A nanny,' scoffed Hellen, the wind rushing out of her sails. 'I'll have you know, she's a graduate of the College of Domestic Science. She's qualified for much higher things than childminding.'

'If you'd let me finish,' John said gently, 'the family in question is quite well-to-do. I think this job is more than just childminding. They're looking for a responsible person to care for the children as well as run the household when they're away in London.

'Who is this family?' Eilidh asked.

'You'll have heard of Hamish Potts, the Conservative MP?'

Eilidh and her mother exchanged looks. 'Of course,' Eilidh said.

'Well, the job would be looking after his three boys.'

'How old are they?' interrupted Hellen.

'The eldest is five,' John counted them out with his fingers, 'the next is three and the youngest, Ian, is one. You'll be living in their house in Perth; it's a lovely old stone building with a walled garden, and there are other members of staff so you would get some afternoons off. That's the part I like; it would be a lot easier for us to meet than it is at present.' He took a sip of his tea while he let his words sink in.

The next few months slipped by. 'I love my job,' Eilidh told her friend one afternoon as she watched her preparing the horses' feed, 'but my goodness, I get so tired sometimes, it feels as though I'm the boys' real mother.'

'You're as good as,' commented Daisy, 'those folks are lucky to have you.'

'Mr and Mrs Potts alternate between London and Perth but they prefer to leave the boys in Scotland with me when they're away. Mrs Potts has to attend parties and functions with her husband; she's so busy, she hardly ever sees them. At least this way the boys can stay in their own home with me and we can do nice things every day.'

'I think you quite like it when they're away. I don't know where you get your energy from, making a fuss of looking at daffodils and singing them all those silly songs.'

'I care for them, really I do; they're so easy to entertain. They're happy whether they're sailing boats, flying kites or just kicking a ball around.'

'And John?'

'Yes, I'm happy, I have a job with children that I dote on, and I have a man that dotes on me…I just wish he wasn't so tied down with the hotel. He doesn't seem to want to go anywhere else; he won't even go away for a holiday. I don't know if I would make him happy in the long term. I'm too restless I think; there's so much of the world I want to see.'

'But you like being with him, don't you?'

'Of course, why wouldn't I? We do such lovely things, but I don't know, I think I want more…' and she fell silent, watching a stallion snuffle the bar of his enclosure. Subconsciously she put her hand into her raincoat pocket and fingered the blue airmail that she'd received that morning and had read and reread until she could quote it by heart. She smiled as she contrasted her excitement on receiving the letter from Malaya, from a man she barely knew, with her feelings for a man who had her in his sights as a wife. Somehow she could never tell Daisy about Alex. She kept him in a secret place in her heart; he was someone who had always been there, a spirit that answered her own. Silently she counted the years; three gone already since he'd said goodbye. Would he come to her when he returned home? Would he be married already? Would he still like her?

It was August, the honeysuckle sweet and growing profusely around the fence and over the front shed in her small home in Glengrianach. Eilidh had been given six weeks' holiday, as the Potts were taking their annual vacation in Cannes with friends who had a resident nanny. Ian, the youngest boy, was sickly with a persistent cough and they felt that some warmth might be the answer to his malaise and his unhealthy pallor. So it was that Eilidh was in the kitchen with her mother, wiping dishes, when the knock came on the door. Hellen Matheson gasped at the sight of the well-dressed stranger. Could this tanned, gaunt man in the immaculate tweed jacket be the same dusty lad who had stepped off a farm produce truck all those years ago? Eilidh dropped the dish she was holding. Her eyes wide with shock and her mouth gaping in surprise, she could barely register who it was in front of her. 'Alex!' she screamed. 'You could have warned me; look at you so handsome and smart, and here's me in my old clothes!'

Alex swept her up into his arms and held her tight. 'At last,' he whispered into her hair, 'you don't know how long I've been dreaming of this moment.'

It was almost time for Alex to return to his post in far-off Malaya. There was no question in his mind of leaving his beloved Eilidh behind and there were no doubts in hers about leaving her job or family or country. The year was growing to a close. Skeletal trees like lonely soldiers marched across the wintery skyline. Pale lemon sunlight glimmered through the gusting clouds as Alex tramped behind Eilidh along the path leading to the manse. On the banks of a lochan they saw a bleak house framed by the foreboding mountain backdrop.

'Gey lonely place to live,' commented Alex. 'You'd have to be desperate to make your way up here in your hour of need.'

'Mrs Gordon, the minister's wife, left him two years ago. She couldn't stand the place. Too remote for her, I suppose, coming from Glasgow as she did. She only lasted one winter, which I must admit was pretty harsh, and she couldn't stand being cooped up in the house all day. There were all the usual rumours of course; you can't stop people's tongues wagging. They say she ran away with the postman! He was often the only company she got, poor soul, so I suppose she took to giving him tea,' Eilidh gave a little laugh, 'no doubt as reward for cycling up this brae delivering the church periodicals!'

'So he's on his own now, Reverend Gordon?'

'Yes, he is, all alone rattling around in that big house. But wait till you see him! Can you imagine what he might look like?'

'He's probably a wee mouse of a man. Maybe a bit bent and screws up his eyes when he looks at you. Is he about seventy?'

'No, you are so wrong! Try again!'

'Well, I don't know…a right sanctimonious sort with a thin face as long as a poker and a funny English way of speaking.'

'Well, you're going to be surprised; I can't wait for you to meet him. He's like a lanky stork with legs as thin as broomsticks. On Sundays he makes such an entrance into the church. He wears a long robe and as soon as the vestry door opens he rushes in at a great rate with the cloth billowing out like a black cloud behind him. And then his hands start waving and pointing. It's not folk he should be lecturing; he'd be better employed conducting the cars in the High Street!'

Alex laughed at the picture she was painting and so was not too surprised when the door of the manse was opened by the tall figure of Reverend Gordon himself. He was everything that Eilidh described and more. He was drunk. His eyes were rolling and he was swaying unsteadily on his stilt-like legs.

'Come in, can I offer you a double room or a twin bedroom?'

Eilidh started to giggle. 'Actually, Reverend Gordon, we've come to ask you if you'd be so kind as to marry us at the beginning of February!'

'Oh…Oh, I see, my mistake, I thought you were walkers that wanted Bed and Breakfast. I get quite a few lost souls up here! Ha ha ha,' and he chortled at his own joke. 'Ah, I see it's you now, Eilidh, come in, come in.

Will you have a sherry or maybe a wee dram and then we can talk about your plans. This must be your young man; I don't believe I've seen you at church on Sunday?' He admonished Alex with a questioning look, but his eyes reeled up and he staggered over to the table.

'No, sir, you have not, but I've made a good study of the Bible. I have a lot of time in the evenings so I've made good use of it and I've read most of the Old Testament already.'

'Have you indeed? Well, I am impressed. Where do you hail from and what do you do with yourself?'

'The name is Alex McIntyre, sir. I come from down Perthshire way. My family are all farm workers, as indeed I was until I was given the chance to go to Malaya to learn how to be a rubber planter.'

'Indeed? Now that is interesting and I'll want to hear all about that, but as you can see I am a little preoccupied this morning. You'll be wondering why I'm at the bottle so early in the forenoon?' and he started laughing again. 'Don't normally have a tipple until at least after twelve but these old biddies I visit are always bringing out the sherry.' He leant over to Eilidh to dramatise the effect: '"You'll just have a wee one with me, minister?" It's the least I can do to keep them company, and it passes a lonely hour or so for them. Now let's go through to the kitchen where it's warmer. I have the Raeburn on in there; the rest of the house is like a graveyard. Ha ha ha! Oh forgive me, full of the jokes. Now sit yourselves down here at the table and I'll just charge the glasses with a wee drop of Glenfiddich. Well now, lass, what will you have? I think I have a bit of sherry here in the cupboard, left over from the New Year, though which one I don't know, ha ha ha!'

Eilidh nodded and watched him pour.

'*Slainte!*'

'Good health, sir.'

The wedding date was set for the beginning of February in the church at Druimfhada.

'I have charge of both parishes so I can assure you that everything will run as smooth as silk, though between you and me, I'll only be responsible for the actual marriage part. I know full well, Eilidh, that the rest of the proceedings will be commandeered by your mother.'

Eilidh smiled in agreement, and they both shook the minister's hand.

Waving goodbye, the young couple took their leave from the manse and made their way back across the moors to Glengrianach.

'I'm glad we've decided to marry in Druimfhada,' Eilidh said. 'Most of my relatives live there anyway, and John will see us proud with his new hotel.' She walked with a skip in her step, her head buzzing with plans for her approaching wedding. John Sinclair had taken her rejection badly at first, but once he saw that she had made up her mind, he gave in gracefully, then ambition prevailed over his rebuff, and, with the help of his father, he bought the local hotel in Druimfhada.

Alex walked a little ahead of her, lost in his own thoughts. He tried to imagine Eilidh in Malaya. Would she be happy with him there? Would she miss her family? He worried that the loneliness of estate life might drive her crazy and she would leave him, like that minister's wife today. He knew that he had come back into her life and turned it upside down. He remembered the shock and excitement he had seen in her face the day he'd burst in on her in her mother's kitchen, and how gratified he felt when she'd immediately broken off her relationship with John Sinclair. With a girl that clearly adored him, Alex felt that at last his life held some purpose. He turned round to watch her plodding along behind him, her silvery curls bright in the weak winter sun and her cheeks red from the cold wind.

Eilidh returned to her young charges in October. She was nervous about breaking the news that she was to be married and would be leaving for her new life in Malaya.

'Malaya!' Mrs Potts cried, 'But that's wonderful, Eilidh. Who is this man that has stolen you away from us?'

'His name is Alex McIntyre. I've actually known him for ages and we've been corresponding these last three years. He came home on leave last August and we sort of picked up the threads.' She coloured slightly, feeling embarrassed talking about her private life with her employer.

'Awful for us, I shall miss you more than you know and the boys will be devastated, but children are resilient and you've been such a wonderful nanny to them. We'll all remember you but you must write, do you promise?'

'Of course, and please send me photographs of the boys as I shall miss them too. Especially Ian, he's such a brave little chap and he's had such a bad time with that chest infection.'

It was with a heavy heart that she said her final goodbyes. With moist eyes she heard her heels clipping along the pavement as she walked away from her first and only employment. Three years of domestic science had stood her in good stead, for she had been able to practise all that she'd been taught, and now the next adventure would be her own house and family.

So the year ended and the villages of Druimfhada and Glengrianach stoked up their fires and set their tables to offer traditional welcomes to friends and neighbours and to drink a toast of health and happiness for the coming year. Eilidh and Alex smiled into each other's eyes at the toll of the bells bringing in 1953.

'Are you all right, lass?' Eilidh's father stood peeping in at her bedroom door, his voice full of concern. A man of few words, he nevertheless felt the same sense of imminent loss as his more ebullient wife. His gaunt face was creased with worry and two deep grooves had etched their way down on either side of his nose and mouth to his chin. Even in the house he had taken to wearing a flat tweed cap, like a hairpiece, to conceal his balding pate.

'I'm fine, Dad, what could be the matter?'

Davey Matheson cast his eye around his daughter's room and thought to himself that nothing much had changed. There was still the burach of her clothes and belongings all over the bed and floor. 'I doot that woman at the college would have something to say if she saw this, lass! She'd have that diploma off you right smart!'

'Och, Dad, where can I put it all?' She clambered over a shoe box on the floor and put her arms around her father's neck. 'Thank you, Dad. You and Mam have been great organising everything. When are the cars coming tomorrow?'

Breathing deeply and giving her a squeeze, Davey said, 'They'll be here at two o'clock. That should give us plenty time to get to Druimfhada, mind you with this snow I hope the plough gets out first. There's a bad forecast on the wireless. Well, let me know if I can do anything.'

After her father had quietly left, Eilidh sat down and surveyed the room she had occupied since she was a child. She saw the same sparse furniture and the small window which overlooked the drying green.

Tomorrow she would dress in all her new finery and stand in front of the same ancient mirror that had reflected all her growing years.

'Eilidh!'

She heard heavy footsteps clamber up the narrow stair and her door was abruptly pushed open, letting in a rush of cold air. 'Molly! Look at you! You're like a snowman. How did you get past Mam looking like that? Come here, there's a towel here somewhere and we'll wipe some of it off. You can't sit down until you're dry.'

Her cousin looked a picture of health. Her face was as bright as a rosy apple and her eyes blue as cornflowers. Her dark curls tumbled out of her woolly hat and she shook her scarf at Eilidh, smattering the snowflakes over the floor. 'I'm here,' she trilled, 'I don't think we'll get the chance to wear our Cinderella slippers tomorrow, have you seen the snow outside? Oh my goodness, we'll have to wear our wellies under our dresses.'

Later that night, when the house was silent and Molly was asleep in the spare room, Eilidh slid out of bed and pulled back the curtain. The street light caught the snowflakes in its yellow glow. She watched them falling one after the other, perfectly formed feathery puffs, only to become one with the great sweep of snow that already covered the entire town and countryside. In the filtered light she could see her wedding dress hanging on a red padded hanger from the picture rail. Below it was the box containing the veil that was as fine and beautiful as anything she had seen. The white shoes were still cosily wrapped in tissue in their box. Eilidh stretched over to where her new underthings were laid out; soft, flimsy bits of silk and satin that ran through her fingers like water. Her mother's words came back to her. 'You'll need something old, something new, something borrowed and something blue.' Mrs Ross had lent her a white ermine stole to put over her shoulders, and Molly had given her a pale blue ribbon to tie her hair back under the diamante tiara. Picking up her great grandmother's pearls, she let them nestle in the palm of her hand, perfect and smooth, with their own lustre, shining in the saffron light of the street. 'Those pearls have come down through the generations to you,' her mother had told her, 'so when you wear them, feel all the love and folly, wisdom and laughter that came from the women that wore them before you. That is your legacy. Each would have suffered and cried, laughed and endured the rough road that life can sometimes lead you, but they would all wish you happiness, Eilidh love, as I do now.' Tears had come then and mother and daughter had sat quietly, fingering the small, perfect strand of pearls, culled from a Highland river.

The snow that had fallen during the night had frozen and the world was packed in a glistening time freeze.

'Get up, Eilidh! It's gone nine and we have to get ready. Bessie Miller is coming at ten to do our hair and we both have to get washed and the kettle is on. And we have to do our nails.'

Molly was a tornado bustling about organising the household. Davey Matheson was relieved to take a walk up the High Street to get the newspaper. He wanted news on the roads and to find out what time the snow plough had been out. He worried about the cars coming from the south through the Drumochter Pass and he hoped it would be open and the roads clear.

Hellen Matheson took leave of the girls and she too escaped the turmoil that was her house. The door bell hadn't stopped, as neighbours constantly dropped in with silver-wrapped gifts. The display on the sideboard was growing, with canteens of cutlery, pillow slips, butter knives and fish forks daintily displayed on beds of red velvet. She pulled her scarf tightly over her head to hide the curlers that Bessie had painstakingly put in an hour ago. With her ankle boots inelegantly zipped up the front and her old brown tweed coat, she knew she was a far cry from the image of the mother of the bride. 'Have you got the flowers ready yet, June?' she asked at the florist's, 'and did you remember the white carnations for the button holes?'

'Aye, Hellen, of course. Don't you fret. I can see you're up to high doh, come through here to the back and have a cup of tea with me, I can see you need to sit down!'

Hellen gasped when she saw the bouquets, all glistening and fresh. She bent over to smell the wax-like lilies and white roses in a cloud of baby's breath. The bridesmaid's bouquet was smaller but was like a burst of sunshine. Yellow roses and a few early narcissi were entwined together, the stalks bound up in a wand of silver foil. Beside them was the flower girl's posy, echoing the colours of the bridesmaid.

Hellen was glad that Alex's family were coming, although she knew that not all of his brothers would be there. His elder brother Donald was to be his best man and his wee daughter Lilian was to be the flower girl. Hellen was just a little apprehensive about meeting her new in-laws and hoped she and Mrs McIntyre would get on well.

'Oh, Molly, do I look all right? Will I trip on my veil?' Eilidh stood poised in the middle of the sitting room. It was time to go. The cars were waiting, and the neighbours had all come out and were anxious to see the bride and wish her well. Snow clouds were gathering again, dark and heavy, looming over the craggy tops of the mountain.

Molly looked at her and saw her cousin as though for the first time. Eilidh's face was misty behind the white gauze of the veil, but her eyes were bright and soft with just a hint of cosmetics to enhance her brows and lashes. Her lips had been painted a soft pink. Bessie had worked wonders with her hair, for the unruly curls were now swept back from her forehead and left to cascade on to her shoulders. The beautiful white dress fell smoothly to her feet and in her hands she held the bouquet of virginal lilies and roses.

'You really are beautiful,' Molly whispered, 'now here's your dad. I'll be waiting for you at the church. Let's hope the road is clear and we can all get there in time.'

And so it was on that cold, crisp, wintry February afternoon that Eilidh and Alex were married. The snow glistened over the Grampian Mountains, turning the normally desolate, lonely landscape into a picture. The portal of the tiny church framed them as they stood and smiled for the photographer. Eilidh held her bouquet and a single silver horseshoe intertwined with sprigs of white heather. Alex stood proud in his dark suit, and Molly and Lilian in their yellow gowns completed the idyllic tableau.

John Sinclair had set up the hotel dining room with long trestle tables covered with white cloths and swatches of Black Watch and Royal Stewart tartans. Dried heather was placed in small bunches at each of the ladies' seats. The bridal party sat along the top table and from her place Hellen Matheson was able to keep an eye on Alex's mother, a striking woman dressed in an olive green coat and a domed hat to match. She had an air of formality about her, no doubt from being ill at ease in a room full of strangers. Hellen vowed to spend some time with her after the food and speeches. As for Alex's father, she thought he looked even more out of place. He was fidgety and clearly uncomfortable with the fancy food and overheated hotel. Tall and thin with stooping shoulders, he made a rather sad picture in the hired suit that was too short at the ankle, and his big hands were exposed to well beyond the wrist. By contrast, Davey was sitting frozen with fear at the thought of saying the few words he had prepared. He'd smartened up quite well, she thought, and she was surprised that he still managed to button up the one and only suit he possessed. And what a relief to see him without that awful bonnet on his head for once!

A glass chinked and the best man was on his feet and the speeches had begun. Donald McIntyre regaled the world about the accomplished girl his brother had just married. He praised her looks and her diploma in domestic science, and hoped that she would also have the recipe for domestic bliss.

Then it was Davey's turn. He stood up, his hands shaking with the bit of paper he'd scrawled on at the railway station. Looking down, he realised that he didn't have his glasses so was unable to read the words. The guests stared at him expectantly. His mouth went dry and his face coloured red. Eilidh looked up at her dad and smiled at him encouragingly. Holding her gaze and looking only at her he began, 'Hellen and I thank you all for braving the snow to be with us today for our only daughter's wedding. Alex, if she gives you just a fraction of the happiness that she's brought to me, you are a lucky man. You are going far away across the sea to a strange land, Eilidh, but never forget your roots, lass. You are a Scot from this land of mountains, lochs and heather, and as I was told last night, the great bard Rabbie Burns slept in this very hotel and no doubt he would have had the right words and the right songs to serenade you. I can't do that, but I hope you will always carry the spirit of our country in your heart wherever you go. So now I ask you all gathered here today to raise a glass to my daughter Eilidh and her grand new husband Alex, and haste ye back, my bonnie lass!'

Hellen sniffed and wiped the tear that was coursing down her powdered cheek. 'Sentimental old fool, who would have thought he had so much to say?'

The accordion player and fiddler started up with a medley of tunes while the room was cleared. The dancing soon turned hectic and it was as well that John Sinclair had arranged for glasses of beer and lemonade to be circulated, for the faces grew redder as the partners whirled and screeched and shouted 'Hooch!' and then let ladies fly to be caught and whirled again.

Eilidh pounced on the minister when she saw he was retreating towards the bar, his white handkerchief mopping his wet brow. 'Come on, Reverend Gordon, you can't deny me a dance. And thank you for getting us through the service. Alex and I were both so nervous and the church was so cold my knees and teeth were knocking and chattering at the same time!'

'You're a bonny bride, Eilidh, and I'll be happy to dance with you, but just let me have a wee refreshment first.' He winked and put his hand into his jacket and pulled out a silver flask. He poured a measure of whisky into a glass of lemonade and drank it back as though it were water. 'That's better! Now I'm ready.'

His long legs propelled him faster than the other dancers and they overtook the more sedate steps of her new mother and father-in-law. Eilidh was in danger of flying off the slippery floor as he enthusiastically swung her around the room. At the end of the dance she was relieved to escape, so she made her way to one of the adjoining lounges and found two old aunties sitting either side of an open fire. Both were relatives on her father's side and had made the journey especially from their home on Lewis in the Outer Hebrides.

'Oh look, sister, it's Eilidh! Well I couldn't believe it when I saw you today, dear, walking down the aisle on Davey's arm. I said, "Is that Eilidh?", for the last time we saw you, dear, you were just a wee thing. Now you're all grown up and a married woman. Come and sit with us and tell us how you are and where you found such a handsome husband. We've been on the lookout for one of those for sixty years but believe me they're hard to come by!'

The other sister cut her off then and pointed out, 'We brought you a hen for your wedding, dear. It was Peggedy Ann and I reared her myself.'

'Was?' interjected Eilidh.

'Well, yes, I told the kitchen staff to just add her to the plates. We brought some eggs as well. We weren't sure how fresh yours would be. I carried them in my basket all the way on the ferry and the train to get them to you. Oh here! I nearly forgot the tweed. We brought you a nice bit; here it is, bonny heather colour. Maybe you could get a skirt and jacket made up in that far-off place you're going to?'

Eilidh was touched and took the gift that was offered to her. 'Do you want some tea or anything?' she asked politely.

'Tea!' They looked at each other aghast. 'For goodness' sake!' and they resorted to their own Gaelic tongue for the stream of expletives that followed. 'Did you hear the girl? She wants us to travel all this way to sit in a church that nearly froze the tears from our eyes and now she wants to give us a cup of tea!' They started to laugh in a giddy way.

Eilidh could see they were well on in their state of inebriation.

'Gin, lass, gin. That's what we like, and look here. See what we bought in that toffee-nosed shop in Perth...' She fumbled in her handbag, and then pulled out a blue packet, 'French fags! Now that's what we like, gin and French fags!' They both lit up and settled back in their chairs, looking like a pair of Wally Dugs on either side of the fire, with a glass of gin in one hand and a smelly Gitanes in the other. Soon the air filled up around them and Eilidh quietly took her leave.

Outside the blizzard continued and the Drumochter Pass was closed and the snow plough was out clearing roads for nearby villages. Inside the hotel, however, there was light and laughter as the two families and their friends intermingled and cemented the union with good whisky from the nearby distillery. Reels and Strathspeys saw the colours of the wedding finery weave together as gaily as a piece of Scottish tartan. Old and young danced together and the night passed with little care of the icy wind that sculpted the frozen snow into drifts.

Three days later Eilidh stood wrapped miserably in her woollen coat, her blonde curls blowing in the icy wind. Her father held her close to him and she felt the rough tweed of his jacket against her cheek and smelt the smoke and saw the small nick on his throat where he'd cut himself shaving. She then squeezed the frail form of her mother.

'It's so far away, so far away. I might never see you again,' Hellen Matheson sobbed.

'It's only for three years, Mam...it isn't so long and I'll write, I promise,' and then, her eyes blurred with tears, Eilidh was gone.

Alex stared ahead and let her weep while he negotiated the icy road banked high with snow on either side. They drove on in silence, both lost in their own thoughts. The glistening mountains sparkled in weak, wintry sunlight. Stags were down as far as the fences, lonely black forms driven down by hunger. Sheep pawed the ground, their woolly coats dirty in contrast to the pristine whiteness of the fresh snow. The miles slipped by and Pitlochry, Dunkeld and Perth marked the distance away from the little house in Druimfhada.

Hellen and Davey Matheson were bereft. They stared at the fire, then at each other. There were no words.

Eilidh's whirlwind wedding was over. She sat nervously strapped into her first class seat in the BOAC Comet. An airhostess leant over with a tray containing a bottle of champagne and two chilled glasses.

'Welcome aboard, madam, I hope you enjoy the flight. We shall be stopping in Rome, Cairo, Bahrain, and Colombo, then finally in Kuala Lumpur. Is this your first time visiting Malaya?'

'Yes, and my first time flying. I thought it might be bumpier than this, but it's really quite calm, like an armchair high in the sky! I feel quite guilty sitting here when you are so busy!'

'I am busy, madam, but I wouldn't do anything else. It's a job in a million. I'll have three days to relax and explore the streets of KL, and just last week I watched the sun rise over the Coliseum in Rome and I've ridden a camel in the deserts of Oman.'

'Gosh, your life sounds so exciting. Well, this is such an adventure for me; I never thought I'd be whisked away to the Far East!' She took her glass and looked into Alex's eyes.

Unobtrusively the airhostess moved away and left the young couple to themselves. It was clear that they were newlyweds and she was determined to give them first class service.

'What have you enjoyed the most about your leave, my darling?' Eilidh laughingly enquired of her new husband.

'Hmmmm, that's a difficult one. I shall have to think about that. I might give you an answer when we leave Colombo!'

'Stop teasing, Alex!' Eilidh cried. 'Was it the wedding? Or was it our trip to the north of Scotland? Or maybe it was when we cooked tatties on that funny fire you made down by the river and ate them mashed up with butter? Oh I could think of it all for ever, we've had such a wonderful six months.'

'Yes, and by now Callum will be settled into his estate. I'm looking forward to meeting up with him and the others again. And to answer your question, my darling, the best part for me was when I heard the organ music start. I was standing there with the sun shining through Daniel or Jeremiah's head in the stained glass window, and old Mrs Shaw was thundering through her set pieces at a great pace and I was wondering how long you would be. Just for a minute I thought you might have had second thoughts and run away with another of your suitors, then suddenly I heard the wedding march and all the hairs rose on the back of my neck. I could feel you walking up behind me and when I turned to look, the gold from the window hit your hair and you were like a shining angel and your eyes as misty as a glen full of dewdrops, just as they are now. That was the best bit, Mrs McIntyre.'

Tears of happiness glistened in her eyes as they drank their champagne and squeezed hands, and later they slept and the long hours passed until at last the plane roared across the tarmac, burning rubber as it braked to a shuddering halt in front of Subang Airport.

For the previous six months, Eilidh had listened avidly to Alex's stories about her new home, but nothing could have prepared her for the heat and humidity that engulfed her on her arrival. 'I can't breathe, it's like an oven. How am I supposed to breathe?' she gasped.

The long flight had left them both exhausted. Eilidh's transition from the airport into the bustling cacophony of noise and energy that was Kuala Lumpur was a brutal assault on her senses. She stared wide-eyed at Indian ladies wearing saris of purple, saffron and scarlet, demure Malays in sedate *sarong kebayas* and tiny Chinese women in figure-hugging *cheongsams*. She smiled shyly at Indian men whose grins split their faces from ear to ear. Smells of intoxicating spices and acrid frying overwhelmed her. Ushered through the crowds by their porter and gripping her husband's hand like never before, she climbed into the back of a black-and-yellow taxi. There she sat, her back drenched in sweat whilst their car jolted into the noisy throng of traffic grinding through the streets, her head constantly swivelling in amazement at the scenes being enacted around her.

Drawing up at the Railway Hotel, Eilidh gaped at the sheer opulence of the building's design. Its creator had attempted to rival the Moorish designs of Marrakech. The sweeping staircase led up to bedrooms as large as banqueting halls. Eilidh gasped at the sumptuous proportions of their room, their bed like a small island lost amidst the shadowy colours of cream and ochre that covered the walls and ceilings.

'Oh my, this is too much! Is this all for us? It's big enough for four families!' She hugged Alex and ran to the bathroom where there was a huge tub with clawed feet, and a mirror with light bulbs around it. She ran the bath taps and the room was engulfed in swirling clouds of steam. Revelling in the luxury, they bathed and slept and woke and ate pineapple and drank English tea and dozed again.

As the sun gave way to inky blackness, they dressed in their evening clothes and Eilidh giggled at Alex's clumsy struggling with the hooks and eyes of the new dress he had bought for her in London's Regent Street. She preened and looked over her shoulder into the mirror and saw her elegantly transformed self. 'I could be Ingrid Bergman after all!' Her dress fell in swirls of creamy chiffon with a net shawl that dipped around her shoulders like a cowl. As she walked, the full skirt swung, revealing a flower design in muted greys and reds.

Coming down the stairs, Alex was aware of eyes turning towards his vivacious young wife and he squeezed her hand, delighting in her enthusiasm. They ventured outside to the night that had brought forth street vendors selling their wares on the pavements, their children sitting on the edge of the monsoon drains that ran alongside the busy streets. Walking beside Eilidh and listening to her gasps and exclamations, Alex saw again the wonders of the East through her eyes. Shop houses ran together in concertinaed terraces with red tiled roofs and colonnaded walkways. Shops selling bolts of cloth, carpets and ironmongery were teeming with customers and the streets were a hotchpotch of cars, bicycles and trishaws. Confusion reigned. People ate and gossiped and everywhere there was colour. Eilidh was completely transfixed with everything she saw.

Alex hailed a taxi and they drove to the Selangor Club. 'This is the place everyone heads to when they come into town. You can be assured of a good meal and it's very pleasant sitting out on the veranda away from the hustle and bustle of it all. You'll meet all sorts of folk: planters, tin miners, army; a good place to rendezvous as they say in France. Here we are, now you just go on up and I'll settle the fare.'

Eilidh stepped out of the car and looked at the black-and-white splendour of the Tudor-style club house presiding over a huge expanse of green *padang*. She walked up the stone steps and gratefully entered the air conditioned vestibule. Immediately she was struck by the elite atmosphere, hushed and still carrying the overtones of colonial rule. Alex joined her and together they made their way to the cocktail bar. On their entrance, three young men stood up and came to greet them. They were all smartly turned out in slacks and white shirts and ties.

'Callum!' Eilidh cried, 'It's so lovely to see you. I must say your suntan's improved since I last saw you!'

'By God, Eilidh, look at you; you look good enough to eat. Come here and give your brother-in-law a hug.'

Eilidh giggled, and when he released her, she looked expectantly towards the other two men standing awkwardly at the bar.

'These two dubious characters are my fellow assistants,' Callum gestured towards them, 'Jack Dunbar and Michael Parrish.'

'I'm very pleased to meet you, Eilidh, I'm Jack.' The taller of the two men stepped forward.

'And I'm Michael,' the third man said, 'the only Englishman in the trio but a friendly face nevertheless!'

'It's good to meet you at long last, I've heard so much about you both.'

'Nothing good, I hope,' replied Michael.

Focussing on Jack, Eilidh registered an arresting face, olive hued with a bluish shadow on his lip and jaw. His black hair was slicked back, and his dark brows contrasted startlingly with his blue eyes. His nose was aquiline and for a moment she was mesmerised by his full and sensually formed lips. When he spoke his Scottish accent was mild, and just by listening to him she guessed his formal education hadn't stopped at fourteen. This man was cultured and at odds with her husband and his brother. She blinked when she realised he was grinning at her, and smiling back she absently tossed a stray curl behind her ear.

'I hear you've been visiting my neck of the woods near Dundee,' he said.

'Yes, I used to work in Perth when I was a nanny to the Potts' children.'

'Oh, I've heard of him, an MP isn't he? I did a bit of politics when I was at university.'

'Politics? How does that connect with Malaya?'

'No, no, my degree is in agriculture; my dad has a farm in Ainsley Kirk. He wanted me to go back and help him once I'd graduated, but when it came to the crunch, I decided to see a bit of the world before settling down to a life of soil and toil. I can tell you, he was not amused.'

'So much for all his fancy learning about politics and so on, all he has to do here is dodge the bandits and throw darts at the *chichaks* of an evening,' muttered Callum.

'Life can be very dull on the estates at night!' explained Michael.

'Doesn't sound much fun for the *chichaks* either,' laughed Eilidh. 'What are they anyway?'

'They're little lizards, some people call them geckos. You'll be seeing plenty of them in the house.' Callum leant closer to Eilidh and added, 'Though I wish to God he'd do the same with cockroaches; they are my worse nightmare.'

'You always were a lousy shot, Callum,' Michael added.

Eilidh laughed, taking in the tall, athletically built Englishman in front of her. His sandy hair was severely cut and somehow he carried the air of an errant schoolboy. Surreptitiously she glanced at his shoes, idly wondering if he wore matching socks.

'Shall we go through to the dining room?' Alex suggested. 'Did you reserve a table, Callum?'

'No, afraid not, the three of us don't usually eat here, it's beyond our budget. We usually just go to The Dog for a steak and a couple of beers.'

'The dog?' asked Eilidh.

'The Spotted Dog, to be precise.' Michael informed her. 'It's got a long bar but is strictly off limits to ladies, I'm afraid.'

'Oh?' she said, her eyes wide with interest.

'You're not missing much,' laughed her husband, 'just a lot of language best kept for men and beasts!'

They made their way through to the dining room, taking their drinks with them. The tables were clustered around a small area of parquet flooring. In the corner a band was playing a selection of light classical and romantic pieces.

'How do you like your new life, Callum?' Eilidh asked.

'The work is grand, I don't mind that at all,' he said, leaning back in his chair. 'I don't even mind the early mornings, in fact I quite like the estate at that time of day, but I just can't get used to the 'roaches. Horrible things with oily-brown bodies and long, wavy antennae. I try and annihilate them with the newspaper, but they just refuse to die.' Eilidh looked horrified as he went on, 'They even run over my head on the pillow, greet me in the morning from inside the sugar bowl, or fly at me from the bristles of my toothbrush.'

'Ugh,' she shuddered, I'd no idea. I was only prepared for spiders and snakes.'

'Och, you've no need to worry, you'll have Cookie and Amah to take care of you, and the gardeners. Don't you worry your pretty head about my phobias.' He clinked his glass with hers, 'Welcome to Malaya, Eilidh!'

She smiled back at him, and she saw in her new brother-in-law all the features of her husband but rearranged in his own unique way. There were the same green eyes, brown wavy hair, and wicked grin. Whereas Alex had an angular face, his sharp features reflecting his caustic wit and boyish sense of fun, Callum was rounder and had a stockier build. His characteristics favoured their more buxom mother with her fleshy cheeks, and he had about him a gentle, lazy manner.

Eilidh sipped her drink and felt the condensation on her glass. She listened to the clink of ice cubes and felt the soft chiffon against her bare legs. Could this be her, could this lady with satin high-heeled shoes, with diamonds glittering in her ears, really be her? She closed her eyes for a moment and tried to conjure up the face of her mother. She pictured her leaning against the sink, her face lined and her grey hair cruelly held by a tight hairgrip above her forehead. She was weary and bent, and although not very old, she favoured dark clothes with no adornments, and Eilidh's heart ached for her loneliness. Then she thought of her father and his heartfelt speech at her wedding. She knew that she had left a great space in their lives, and for one small minute she felt regret but then she gave herself a shake. She squeezed her eyes and came back to the present. Looking around her now, she knew she was beginning a wonderful adventure and she leant over and smoothed her husband's sleeve, and when he turned their eyes met and they smiled.

Dinner was served formally by white-jacketed stewards. The menu was extensive but the four men all chose steak and chips. Eilidh perused the fish and salads but finally selected an exotic-sounding dish, Chicken Maryland. Dessert was tinned fruit with tinned cream. As they sat on savouring the dark aromatic coffee, Eilidh heard the plaintive sounds of Acker Bilk's *Stranger on the Shore.*

'Oh, can we dance, Alex? I'd so love to dance to this.'

Self-consciously Alex frowned, but his friends urged him on. He downed his brandy, stood up quickly and held out his hand.

'Not a bad-looking pair,' remarked Jack Dunbar. 'I think Alex has come up trumps with his choice of wife. We'll just have to wait a few years yet before we can find such a cracker.'

The music changed and Alex hummed softly into Eilidh's ear along with the music, 'Mmm mmm, I'd love to get you, on a slow boat to China...'

The next day the newlyweds left Kuala Lumpur in the company car. Eilidh's head was swivelling around, looking at the various landmarks as they drove out of the capital.

'It's about fifty miles to the estate and there's not a lot to see on the journey,' Alex informed her. 'We'll come back to KL soon and do a tour and I'll take you to the Lake Club; it's bonny up there.'

'I see what you mean, Alex,' Eilidh agreed as they left the built-up areas. 'It's just all rubber trees now. Can we stop? I want to see the actual stuff coming out of the trees.'

'You'll see plenty of that on the estate and I don't want to stop until we get back. I've explained about the political situation and look up ahead, there's one of the check points I told you about.'

The car slowed and came to a halt. Two Malay soldiers approached the car. 'Where you go?'

'Bukit Bulan, close to Taman Minyak,' Alex replied.

The soldiers grunted and indicated that the barrier across the road should be raised.

'Oh my goodness, did you see their guns?' Eilidh exclaimed, her eyes wide with fear.

As they drove along endless miles of lonely road, Alex pointed out estates whose occupants were already familiar names to Eilidh. 'That's the Bathgates' place; I think you'll like Dorothy, she hasn't been here long either. Sam's a good bloke, I play golf with him.'

Eilidh nodded, but she was still tense after the check point and she was afraid of the ominous blackness that lurked within the trees beyond the sunlit road. The Emergency was on everyone's lips, and she had listened with growing unease to the men last night at dinner. The newspaper at breakfast this morning was full of the latest stories of guerrilla warfare.

At last they came to a sign that formed an archway over the entrance to a red laterite road bordered by rubber trees on each side. It read 'Bukit Bulan Estate'. The road wound around hills and through valleys, but there was no view, only acres and acres of dark, forbidding forests of rubber trees. Local superstition had allowed termite hills to remain untouched by the roadsides and these had been decorated by Indian garlands of white jasmine. Some female rubber tappers were making their way back to the labour lines after the second cutting of the day, women whose bodies were completely covered as protection from the biting insects, only their smouldering dark eyes peering out of the swathes of cotton. Then at last, out of the gloom, the car drove into a garden of light.

Eilidh's mouth opened and she gasped. 'Oh! How beautiful! It's so beautiful!' She saw green lawns, brilliantly coloured shrubs and flowers, and a white house covered by red roof tiles. Was this to be home?

Cookie and Amah and the three Indian gardeners came out to greet them as the car pulled up at the entrance.

'Welcome, Mem,' the Chinese servant with gold teeth smiled. 'Welcome to Bukit Bulan Estate.'

Although Alex had just returned from home leave, he was still entitled to a week of local leave and so decided to introduce Eilidh to Port Dickson and the Malacca Straits. It was to be their private honeymoon, away from the servants, where they did not have to dress for dinner or entertain friends. It was a time to linger, to walk with fingers interlaced, to marvel at the new and to hold each other in the moonlight. It was the true seal of their new life together. The little bungalows were close to each other and each had a small veranda with a table and two chairs. It was only a short walk to the beach and there in front of them stretched the blue ocean of the Malacca Straits. The sand was golden and only faint, dying bubbles of spume remained of the last great wash of the sea as it gushed on to the shore. Eilidh ran down and felt the water rise up over her ankles and she laughed and splashed, then plunged into the clear, warm waters. Lying on her back she felt the cushion of water hold her body effortlessly. She stared up at the thin cobwebs of cloud. Her thoughts drifted, and fragments of words and faces ran through her mind in no clear direction. She was at one with herself and her body felt part of the great mass of water. Lazily she swam, and then she rose with the swell of the waves and felt them tugging her towards the shore. She felt nothing, no pain nor fear, just an exhilarating feeling of the present, of this wave, and then the next. Soon she felt the sharp shells under her feet and she knew she had been effortlessly cast up with the rest of the ocean debris and deposited at the tidemark. Alex came and sat with her and they watched the sea sweep and cover their feet. Away in the distance, ships sailed like black silhouettes on the sharp line of the horizon, and they heard the thud of the engine as a fishing boat edged close towards the shore.

'I love you!' She turned to smile at her brand new husband and in return he drew her to him and licked the salt that was already drying on her shoulders.

'Siesta?' he grinned suggestively, then taking her hand he pulled her to her feet and together they ran laughing back to their room.

Already the sea was sucking at the sand where they had sat; a great wave washed over their imprints and within minutes no trace remained of their existence.

That evening they ate dinner by kerosene light. The meal was simple; just two plates of the local speciality, *nasi goreng*. The stir-fried rice laced with prawns, chicken, onions, chillies and vegetables was guaranteed to scintillate a palate not accustomed to spicy food. Eilidh looked radiant, her skin already tanned, and she caressed Alex's hand that was resting on the shabby table cloth. Outside the night had fallen like a black curtain.

After Alex fell asleep that night, Eilidh reflected on the changes that had occurred in her life. She had been propelled from a frozen winter in Scotland to a land that assaulted her senses, where smells spoke to her of food and perfume yet sometimes made her gag and retch at the vileness of rotting garbage and long-dead animals. She would often smile as she splashed in the palatial bathroom on the estate, where she showered or luxuriated in deep baths, scented with sweet-smelling oils and cubes of lily of the valley. She remembered how her mother had rejoiced when the indoor lavatory became a feature in working-class homes. No longer had they to take themselves down the garden path to the little shed on bitterly cold and snowy nights. She recalled the relative comfort of washing in a tin bath in front of the coal fire, and later sitting with a mug of cocoa and hugging her hot water bottle. Sleep eluded her and she drifted back to Glengrianach and saw again the lupins and wild irises growing out of the marshes by the river bank. Smells, she thought, how evocative they can be. Here she could smell the kerosene from the lights, and the brackish smell from the river, yet somehow she was transported back to a Highland village! How could that be? Was it really only four weeks since they had left Scotland?

The months slipped by and the next summer in the Highlands of Scotland turned to autumn and then again to winter. A parcel arrived at the railway cottage and Hellen Matheson sat down to cut the string and pull open the paper. Her husband Davey had already left for work so she was alone. The fire crackled in the grate and her hand shook as she touched the parcel that had been prepared with so much love. She opened the album, and there on the dark pages was a mixture of small black-and-white snaps and a few in glossy colour. She was able to see her daughter's life as though it was a film unfolding before her eyes. Suddenly she was transported from the worn-out sofa and the threadbare carpet to a land where she saw Eilidh laughing and posing against a background of impossible images. Turquoise oceans edged with feathery palms, and a house that looked as though it had been designed for royalty.

'Oh my!' Hellen took off her glasses and wiped her eyes and glanced at the framed wedding photograph on the sideboard. She turned again to the album and saw Alex bent over yards of material, presumably sewing hems on the new curtains. She squinted and could make out peony blooms on the fabric. She looked past him, and trying to see the features of the house, noted the high ceilings and cane furniture, a long sideboard, pretty lamps and oriental rugs. 'Hmmm...very grand,' she sighed. There were pictures of Eilidh in dresses of every colour as she posed before going out to parties. Here was one of her stretched out on her tummy in the garden with a rifle over her shoulder, her elbows balanced on a leather pouffe and her eye trained along the sights. More pictures showed the arrival of a white puppy with a black patch obliterating one eye, and two adorable kittens. Eilidh looked so happy. Other photographs featured the house and servants and garden, and then there was a different composition. With a garland of temple flowers around her neck, her daughter was sitting in the middle of a group of beautiful Indian women wearing saris. She was holding an Indian child on her knee. Presumably the workers, Hellen thought. Finally she opened the accompanying letter.

Bukit Bulan, November 1953
My darling Mam and Dad,
Each time I write, I find it so hard to tell you everything so I thought this time that I would see if the photos would help me. You can see how our house has become more homely with curtains and carpets. Alex and I chose them at a wonderful bazaar in KL. They are from Pakistan and Persia. The black panther was shot on the estate; we had the skin cured, and it is quite a wonderful feature with its glossy coat and vicious teeth. Alex says that there is little danger of more as the jungle clearing is now complete. The worst threat we have to face now is the wild pigs that have been known to charge and attack the tappers (the Tamil work force). Sometimes we have to attend celebrations at the temple, so Alex and I go along and are treated like royalty and are given platters of rambutans, mangosteens and lychees. Such delicious, exotic fruit. We sit on a little stage wearing garlands, and after some speeches, Alex thanks everyone in fluent Tamil and then we have our photographs taken.

We had a terrible experience last week as a local contractor came to Alex at six-thirty in the morning begging him to bring his camera and take a picture of his son. Alex went along, and found that the boy had died in the night. The tragedy was that the family had no photo of the child, so they'd dressed him up in shorts and a clean white shirt, propped him up on his father's knee and the family gathered round and Alex duly snapped. The

74

poor boy was then laid out ready for the funeral.

The women here are so beautiful and when I saw where they lived I couldn't believe how they could achieve such a transformation. Cement boxes specifically built to house the labour force with just a hose for washing (but at least they have running water). There is a school, and a 'dresser' who although not a doctor as such, is still very competent, almost like a medical student. Our man is Mr Fernandez and Alex has great faith in him. I have had an irritating cough and have been feeling very tired. Mr Fernandez gave me some ubat (medicine) but the trouble with small things in the tropics is that they seem to take so much longer to get better.

Anyway, I have taken to the women and their children, and sometimes Sinbad and I meet them on our evening walk. I cannot recognise them when they have their work clothes on, as these completely cover up their lovely faces.

We see a lot of Callum, Michael and Jack; they play golf with Alex then come back for dinner with us afterwards. It's quite lonely for them, for until they serve three years they are not permitted to marry and their salary is fairly minimal. They also have to make do with bicycles in order to go about the estate. At nights, Callum says they play cards and listen to Jimmy Shand records on their gramophone players!

Alex has been teaching me to shoot. I have become an expert and can demolish quite a few beer bottles in an evening. The men have to keep their rifles ready at all times. The Emergency is a constant source of worry to us all.

Never a day goes by that I don't miss you or think about you, but although I am sometimes homesick I do love my life here. There is a bird called the golden oriole that wakes me up every morning, and with that as my alarm clock, how could I be unhappy!

With all my love to you both, Eilidh

Chapter 5

February 1954 – Malaya

'I'm dying, darling…Oh God, I'm so sick.'

Alex looked down at his once vibrant, beautiful wife and shook his head.

'It's the brandy, I told you not to have that last one. I'll go and ring Mr Fernandez. Here, sit up and I'll run a cool bath for you.'

Looking blearily around her, Eilidh grimaced at the debris of last night. The bachelors and Sam and Dorothy Bathgate had come over to Bukit Bulan for dinner, followed by much singing and definitely too much drinking. Eilidh vaguely remembered demonstrating a Highland Schottische. 'Oh God!' she groaned again and burrowed her head under the pillow. Her discarded dress lay in a heap of green satin and the dressing table was cluttered with lipsticks and discarded pearls. With supreme will she arose from her deathbed and started to clear her things away, but as she checked the water level in the bath, she felt the overpowering need to retch yet again. 'Never, never, never again,' she muttered resolutely as she lay in the cool water and immersed her hair. She surfaced and opened her eyes. On either side of the taps sat a cat, each resembling perfectly symmetrical ornaments. They stared at her haughtily, their yellow eyes impassive, but as Eilidh flicked water at them, they seemed unperturbed and just raised a paw and licked and groomed where the offending droplets had landed. 'Oh to be a cat,' she sighed. She hauled herself up and reached for a towel before slipping on a red checked housedress. 'Oh I can't bear this, it's too tight; it must be all that rice Cookie keeps serving up. Her body heaved, and she turned back to the toilet as the nausea rose again.

'Good morning, Mem, please let me feel your pulse and look at your tongue. I see, yes I see. Hmm, well, it is a very happy thing I have to tell you…because I can tell you now that you are expecting.'

Alex stared at Mr Fernandez. Eilidh stared at Mr Fernandez.

'What?' they both said in unison, 'but the brandy?'

'No brandy just now, dry biscuits will be enough and maybe a cup of tea. Never you mind, my wife was just the same all nine times. Sick, sick, so sick! Morning, noon and night but you will see, everything will be fine. Just tea and biscuits and no brandy, no no no!' Shaking his head from side to side, he went about packing up his medical bag and scurried over to the edge of the room. 'Now don't you worry, madam, everything is normal. You will have a bouncy baby soon enough. Have a jolly good day! Goodbye now.' He left, leaving behind the echo of his laughter as he cheerfully told Cookie and Amah the delightful news.

'But what about tests, what about proper doctors, what about hospitals? Alex, I'm scared. What about the ambushes? I want to go home!'

'Ssssh…Everything will be fine.' Alex held her and patted her back and listened to her wailing somewhere down in the middle of his chest. 'We'll go to KL tomorrow and see Dr Davidson at the Bungsar Hospital and he will confirm everything. Do you think you might be?' he grinned conspiratorially.

She smiled weakly and sniffed. 'There certainly have been lots of opportunities lately!'

Waking up the next morning and before she had even opened her eyes, she felt the wave of nausea rising and she ran to the toilet bowl and retched and retched until she thought her insides were coming apart. She coughed and the pain scythed through her chest. Staggering back to bed and laying down, she wondered how on earth she could travel in a car feeling like this. Amah heard her distress and brought tea and a cracker biscuit and helped her to eat a little and then to bathe and dress. The food stayed down, and when Alex returned from his morning rounds of the estate she was ready for their journey.

Dr Davidson sat across from them. He was not smiling. Eilidh had undergone two hours of tests, which she thought a little excessive for the confirmation of a pregnancy in a twenty-five-year-old woman. They had had to wait for the results, so to pass the time they had driven away from the hospital to the Selangor Club, where they sat on the veranda to watch the cricketers playing on the *padang* in front of them. Friends came and went, some stayed and had tea or orange juice, but still the couple sat, filled with inertia and foreboding.

Now they faced the doctor, an imposing man in his late fifties, with an egg-shaped head and eyebrows that seemed to be permanently raised. Half-moon glasses that dropped to the end of his nose revealed penetratingly blue eyes. He spoke now with the clipped tones of the English upper class. 'Eilidh, I have to inform you that you have contracted tuberculosis...'

'What?' interrupted Eilidh, 'What did you say? What about being pregnant? That's why we're here; you must have made a mistake.'

The doctor cut in. 'It is very advanced and I am certain you must have had it for more than a year, in which case you must have contracted it in Scotland. Do you know if you had any direct contact?'

Eilidh stared at him. She felt woozy, the room was going black and cotton wool was taking over her brain. Her lips were numb. Suddenly her eyes rolled back and she slumped forward. Alex caught her and together with the doctor lifted her and laid her on the consulting bed. Her face was ashen. Dr Davidson called to a nurse to fetch some water.

'Eilidh,' Alex patted her cheek. 'Eilidh, do you hear me?'

Her eyes fluttered but the room was still reeling and faintness was threatening to engulf her again.

A Chinese nurse came into view. 'Mrs McIntyre, come along, I have you, take a little sip, there there...'

The room was so still; slowly she opened her eyes then closed them again. She felt Alex's fingers take her hand. She wanted to be close to him, to shut out those ominous words. She wanted to lie on a wave and feel herself being rocked. Instead she floated on the memory of her honeymoon days at Port Dickson. She remembered walking with the waves lapping at her feet, lying back on the sand and staring up at the silvery clouds spread like wisps of smoke across the bluest of skies. She remembered the feeling of life never ending and her future going on and on and on. Now, with hot tears running down her cheeks, she knew that her footsteps would indeed be washed away forever, just as they had been on that beautiful day by the shore when the tide rose and ebbed and erased all trace of their existence.

On returning to Bukit Bulan, the distraught couple parted at the bottom of the staircase.

'I shall just bathe and change,' Eilidh said, and turning to Cookie, 'just heat up some soup please.'

The following morning, Alex arose before six o'clock and drank his coffee, strong and black. As was his habit before departing the silent house, he dealt the cards for a game of patience. Then, ready to face the day, he sat on the porch and laced up his walking boots whilst Sinbad looked up at him expectantly. 'Not today, boy, you can't come with me today,' and with a quick tug at the floppy ears he stepped outside just as the first rays of the morning sun were filtering through the tree canopy. Two miles down the road he stopped the Land Rover to talk to his Indian contractor to discuss the planting of newly germinated seeds. As they spoke, the rubber tappers emerged from the gloom of the trees, laden down with their buckets full of latex. The truck used to transport the white liquid was waiting to take this load to the factory for processing into rubber sheets. The contractor nodded his head at his boss's instructions, and with a wave, Alex drove away in a great swirl of dust.

Instead of going to the office he turned down one of the dark tracks between the rubber trees and bumped along until he came to a clearing where the process of grafting the new tree shoots would take place. He left his vehicle and walked towards the sunlight, narrowly avoiding entanglement in a giant web that had been spun across the track. The sunlight caught the threads and turned them into slivers of silver with droplets of dew suspended like an exquisite piece of fine lace. An enormous black spider, wider than the span of his hand, was spread across the top right-hand side where she patiently waited for what looked like a man's head to be her breakfast. Carefully Alex ducked down and left her to trap something a little easier to digest. He sat on a boulder that had not yet been cleared by the workers, and put his head in his hands, his mind in turmoil. TB, tuberculosis, consumption; they were words that he associated with flu and pneumonia, or with people who lived in slums or those who were malnourished. Memories of his own illnesses were limited to the mumps and measles of his childhood. The more dramatic ailments were those that were whispered over fences between neighbours as they hung out their washing: influenza, pneumonia, scarlet fever and the horrific tuberculosis that often plagued the poor, those whose lives were lived out in damp, overcrowded rooms, and where nourishment consisted of the most pitiful of diets. He associated it with the hushed voice of his mother relaying some choice piece of gossip, raising her eyes to heaven and proclaiming, 'I doot she's no long for this world.' He could hear her voice describing some poor soul, 'eyes that glittery and face flushed the colour of a scalded bum.' Those were the poor she spoke of. His Eilidh was strong and fit, and had eyes that sparkled when she presided over her dinner parties. Although Alex's learning curve had been steep, neither his new status nor his study of the native languages had prepared him for the profound blow he was dealt when he learnt of the life-threatening illness engulfing his vibrant young wife. He was angry at the injustice and he riled at the wisdom of Dr Davidson's advice. 'This climate is not good for her. The heat is oppressive and the humidity is not helping her lungs to get the necessary ventilation. She will need constant nursing. The pregnancy will take its toll on her body so if you want to save your wife and your unborn child she will have to go home.'

Alex could not sit still; he stood up and cursed and kicked out at the rock, frustrated and angry. Marching back into the rubber, he walked through the hushed darkness of the orderly rows until he came to the natural forest that had not yet been cleared. Gingerly stepping into the damp perimeter, he felt the lushness of the grasses pulling at his socks, his feet crackling the carpet of dead leaves. He strode forward and felt the sharp hooks of a fallen branch tear at his flesh. The leaves were massive, maybe the length of two men. He looked up and saw the parent tree, its smooth girth towering into the sky. Alex felt reduced and vulnerable, and although his own height dwarfed the millions of crawling creatures that ran beneath his feet, he doubted that he was a match for their ferocity and purpose. The seething battalions of army ants marched relentlessly in ordered lines of destruction, but those threats he could see. He knew there were other threats equally ferocious, but hidden, watching him closely to see what his intentions might be. He could hear the shrieks of monkeys, the calls of birds that harmonised in a raucous, often melodious duet, and the never-ending cacophony of music from the cicadas. Warily he retraced his steps to the clearing and climbed into the Land Rover. He drove fast to the office and curtly nodded to his clerk, Mr Cecil. He went straight to his desk and dialled Dr Davidson's number at the hospital in Kuala Lumpur. 'Instead of going home, could she not go the Cameron Highlands or to Fraser's Hill...you said she would need nursing, well... why can't we do it there?'

Mr Cecil was busy preparing invoices, making piles of paper and clipping everything neatly on his desk as he watched Mr McIntyre telephone several numbers and talk animatedly and with growing good humour. He would have to have a chat with Mr Fernandez later to see if he knew what the boss was up to. Alex put down the receiver after the last call and stood up.

'I'm going home for breakfast, Mr Cecil; make sure that site for grafting gets properly cleared. There are still too many rocks lying around.' He looked distractedly down at his boot and felt the tenderness of his toe where he had given the boulder a mighty kick.

The Land Rover roared into the driveway and Alex screeched to a halt under the porch and kicked off his boots. 'Eilidh!' he roared. 'Where are you? It's all arranged!' He came bounding into the lounge in his stockinged feet. 'You're not going home, you'll stay here and you will get better!'

Immediately, Eilidh responded to his rush of energy and sense of purpose. Her eyes began to sparkle. 'Alex, what's happened? What have you done?'

He was grinning from ear to ear and she felt fizzy bubbles of excitement rise in her tummy. His mood was infectious. 'Bacon and eggs, toast, marmalade...just everything please, Cookie,' he instructed the white-clad servant who had appeared silently and who now nodded apprehensively.

He looked from one to the other and then said quietly, 'Mem, you eat?'

'Yes, Cookie, toast and some tea, thank you.'

Cookie nodded, then collected the filthy boots and retreated to the back of the house. He too was bemused. Last night, when the young couple had returned, the atmosphere was black. Mem's eyes were red from crying, and after a meal eaten almost in silence, they retired and the house was soon plunged into darkness. There was no Scottish music playing, no laughter; there were no orders for beer or brandy. Cookie and Amah had speculated about what could have happened.

For the next six months Eilidh lived in a bungalow in the Cameron Highlands. It was a white Tudor-style cottage, with pink and white roses in the garden, mirroring the English chintz fabric on the loose covers of the chairs inside. She was cared for by Rokiah, a Malay nurse from the Bungsar Hospital, who cooked for her and administered the drugs that were necessary to combat this granulomatous inflammation that was widespread in her upper right lung lobes. The nausea of her pregnancy along with the cough that brought up red blood droplets, compounded by the constant feeling of tiredness, made her an ideal patient. She had no resistance and she obeyed all the instructions from her doctor. She slept, went for walks in the chill mountain air, read books and sewed. Rokiah made fruit jellies to entice her to eat, and slowly, as the weeks went by, she saw her belly round. 'I look so funny,' she laughed at Alex, 'I look like a snake that's swallowed a chicken!' The nausea left her and she started to gain weight. Finally she knew that she would to be well enough to bear a child.

Alex visited her every other weekend. The drive up was tortuous and dangerous around sharp S-bends with a sheer drop to the side. The road had no safety barriers and many vehicles had already plunged over the edge, taking their passengers to an untimely death. Sometimes Alex got out of the car to look over the precipice, thoughtfully surveying the thick expanse of forest. Within the latticework of leaves, towering walls of bamboo sheltered the hideouts of the omnipresent communist forces that were still trying to take control of the country. Snipers and ambushes were a constant daily threat, and as he looked, he felt the same sense of vulnerability that he had felt when alone in the jungle. He could sense the unseen hostile eyes upon him. He thought of his young wife and the game of roulette they were all playing. It all seemed so random; a stray bullet, a killer disease. Life was just a game of chance. It had been chance that had brought him to Malaya in the first place; a chance meeting, a word, an opportunity and an escape. And now the roulette wheel was spinning again.

Jack, Callum and Michael often accompanied him on these weekend trips. They grabbed the opportunity of a ride up in the car, and sharing a set of clubs between them, they made use of the golf course that had been sculpted into the rolling hills and flats. Eilidh loved it when her dashing visitors arrived to entertain her with their jokes and gossip of their escapades. Later she would write long letters home to her parents who, on reading her words, would be transported into a world of scorpions and six feet-long snakes that lived in the roof cavities of the bungalows. She would tell them of the slithering sounds and surprised squeals that would be the only indication of the presence of these unpaid rat catchers.

On one such evening, Jack was leaning back listening to Michael describe his recent adventure with a cobra that he'd killed as it had been entering the hen house. His head was resting on the sofa and his shadow was cast on the white behind him. Eilidh tuned into Michael's enthusiastic depiction.

'I was just drying myself off after a shower,' Michael began. 'It must have been around five in the evening when I heard the most god-awful row coming from out the back. Well, I threw a sarong round my middle and dashed out to the *amahs*' quarters. I could see there was a great kafuffle coming from the henhouse. By this time the light was fading and I saw Kaboon streaking across the grass, the whites of his eyes all lit up as though he'd just seen Ganesh, the elephant god, he was that excited. He was babbling away and when he caught sight of me he yelled out, "Quick, *Tuan*! Run get rifle quick shoot Bang Bang!" His eyes were nearly popping out of his head. "Snake, *Tuan*! Big snake!" I asked him what was wrong with his *parang*; these gardeners normally dispatch a snake pretty damn quick, either thwacking it with a stick or grabbing it by the tail and smacking the head against the wall, so what did he need my rifle for? Well, the noise was reaching fever pitch. Overhead the monkeys were shrieking hysterically, some blasted dogs were woofing their heads off, and the hens were going cackle-crazy. By the time I got back with my pop gun, I felt quite bemused by the image I must have created; not quite the intrepid hunter with pith hat from the comic books, more like your debonair Englishman in flowered sarong about to defend the honour of a few feathered friends!' Michael sipped his drink, grinning idiotically as he painted a less than heroic picture of his masculinity. 'But by God, when I saw that bloody great serpent I just cocked the rifle and blasted. Skin and blood all over the place, not to mention feathers. What a mess; the python was in ribbons. It must have been fifteen feet long and thick as a young tree; definitely not a beast you'd want hand-to-hand combat with. The head had been poking through the wire mesh of the chicken run, so Kaboon just sliced it off and left it for the chickens to peck at. He slung the rest of the corpse over his shoulder like an old fire hose. Later on I saw him and Hassina slicing it up. I imagine they had a great feast of curried python for the next few days.'

'Did it not put the hens off laying?' Eilidh speculated.

'Not them. My girls are reliable as clockwork; stout hearts they have! I did get Kaboon to reinforce that wire mesh though, and he is very vigilant now about patrolling the back fences.'

Eilidh rose and ruffled Michael's hair. 'I think you were very brave. I remember seeing a python that had been killed on the estate and I was horrified at the sheer size of the beast. I certainly wouldn't like to have one come uninvited into the house. Ugh!' It was then that she turned and her eyes rested on the silhouette of Jack's head on the wall. Cold fingers of fear tiptoed up her spine and for no good reason that she could fathom, except perhaps the story of the slow-moving constrictor that had wrapped its coils around her imagination, Eilidh felt a premonition. She felt afraid. She'd been so caught up with Michael's oratory that the return to the present suddenly made her aware of their predicament in this dangerous land. 'Is that all we are?' she said quietly. Her thoughts drifted as she stared into her glass. 'Just shades and transient shadows? People who come after us will never even know that we existed. Look at Jack, so real and solid, and yet his shadow is as fleeting as a moonbeam. When the sun rises, it'll be gone. Just like all of us. One day no one will know about us and our remains will end up covered with moss, chickweed, grass or nettles. Our names once chiselled in stone will be obscured by weeds and eventually the wind will erode even the stonemason's marks.'

'Steady on, old girl, what brought this on?' Michael looked at her, concern in his eyes.

'I'm afraid. I'm so afraid of what I know is going to come to pass.'

'Eilidh?' Jack asked, his eyes dark and questioning, 'What is it, you seem so far away?'

'I don't know. Come here, I want to squeeze your hand. Reassure me that we are all here now…I don't want anything to change. I wish we could always stay just as we are.'

Michael tried to reassure her. 'I think you must be spending too much time alone. It's about time you were back amongst us and having us all round for a nice, tasty dinner. Are you seeing spooks up here, or is that Malay woman Rokiah filling your head with spirits, or *hantu*, as she calls them?'

'It was your shadow, Jack. I just felt how transient we all are, and a sense of foreboding. I can't explain it.' Eilidh sniffed and blew her nose.

'Well, I'm certainly more than a flickery shadow on the wall, lass, believe me!'

Alex shook his head and looked at the domestic tableau as though from far away. Again he thought of chance. How lives can be changed by a word, or a look. Something so small can have a huge repercussion and lives be changed forever as a consequence. He too had felt her fear, understood her very understandable feelings of mortality, and he looked at them both, the black silhouettes created from the soft light emanating from the cream shade of the table lamp. He shuddered and thought of the term she had used, 'transient shadows', and wondered if it was a premonition.

Returning from the kitchen carrying a tray with an ice bucket and soda water, Callum was totally unaware of the previous exchange and subsequent undercurrent. He settled himself back into his chair, his glass recharged. His mind was still dwelling on Michael's conversation about the snake that had been shot to bits, and he chuckled at the memory. 'Aye,' he said, 'best thing for them, for if you've ever looked one of those things in the eye you just don't want to do it again.'

The tension seemed to disperse and Eilidh smiled at her brother-in-law. 'Tell them, Callum, tell them about the fright you had,' and as he started his own story, she travelled back with him to the morning last year when he'd arrived at the house visibly shaken. It had been only ten thirty and Alex wasn't home. Callum had driven over from the neighbouring estate, his face white, his eyes wide and staring. He'd marched straight into the house, for once without taking off his boots at the door.

'I need a whisky, Eilidh, give me a whisky!'

Cookie took the order without comment and shortly brought back the drink in a crystal glass on a silver tray complete with embroidered cloth.

'Whisky, *Tuan*.' He withdrew a little, but stayed close enough to hear what the drama was about.

'A bloody great king cobra rose up out of nowhere!' The whisky disappeared down Callum's throat. 'The boss gave me the use of his Land Rover for the day as I had to check D division and it would have taken several weeks to get there by bicycle. I was juddering over the potholes when a bloody goat leapt out in front of me. I skidded to avoid it and the Land Rover got stuck in a ditch. I revved and revved but the wheels wouldn't grip, so I went off into the rubber to see if there were any fallen branches or suchlike. A couple of tappers came to see what I was up to – stood gawping at me as I lugged half a tree in front of the wheels to give some traction. Suddenly from out of the ditch came a huge cobra. I thought I could scare it off with the branch, but as I moved, the bloody thing reared up. I have never seen such a big one. Black as the devil! The hood was extended and it swayed, unblinking, our eyes locked together, for what seemed like hours. Its whole body was arched up level with my head, just a few feet away from my face. It was at least ten feet long.'

'What did you do?' cried Eilidh, her hand rising to her throat.

'What did I do? Absolutely nothing! I was frozen rigid with fear. I'll tell you this though, I just about wet myself. Then one of the gawping tappers yelled at me and as I turned round, the bloody thing spat at me and then it took for off. Look where it got me on the shoulder and chest!'

'Oh my God! How terrifying; I'm so glad you are all right.'

Cookie came forward and took the empty glass.

'You very lucky, *Tuan*, snake spit make your eyes no see. You very lucky man. You need more whisky?'

'Yes I think so, that's definitely a good idea!'

Now in the safety of the little bungalow, Callum shivered at the memory as he saw himself again, eye-to-eye with such a deadly killer. The others let out admiring sighs at the incident he'd endured with such fortitude, and as the clock ticked, more stories were recounted, and more drinks consumed. Eventually they retired to their own rooms, but sleep eluded Eilidh. Her head span with the stories and images and she was already composing a letter with all the details to send home to her parents.

Eilidh continued with her regime of pills and nutritious food, and as the months slipped by, miraculously her cough became less severe and her handkerchief was no longer spotted with blood. Her nights passed without the wretched fevers and when she looked in the mirror her cheeks were filling out and the haunted look had gone from her eyes. 'I love these strawberries,' she wrote in one of her letters to her mother; 'imagine having strawberries and vegetables straight from a garden surrounded by acres and acres of tea bushes.' Other planters and their families befriended her and she would stroll down to the golf club and sit there in the late afternoons. When the temperature dipped she would snuggle by the fire with a warm cardigan draped over her shoulders, sewing by the yellow light of a standard lamp.

One weekend Eilidh was putting the finishing touches to a small brown felt monkey.

'He should have some bananas in his hand,' Alex suggested as he rummaged in her bag for bits of yellow and green felt.

'Look at me, Alex,' she giggled, 'sitting here sewing monkeys, with my huge tummy. Imagine if I had gone home, we would have been apart for so long and I wonder if I would have got well in cold, wet Scotland? I often wonder who it was that might have infected me; do you think they are as lucky as me to be able to convalesce in such a wonderful place?'

Dr Davidson had explained how a person could be infected with TB for years and yet could remain perfectly healthy. She could have breathed in the germs anywhere. She remembered her young charges in Perth. Could Ian, the youngest son, have been ill too? He'd always been pale and sickly. She recalled how Mrs Potts insisted that the family spend their annual holiday on the French Riviera for warmth. Perhaps that was how she had become infected. The disease would have taken hold quickly, but the symptoms would have been disguised as she adjusted to the tropical climate. She'd not been alarmed by the loss of appetite, the weight loss or the cough; these things in themselves were not so unusual. She'd just been so distressed that the diagnosis had coincided with the discovery of her pregnancy. There had been plenty of time for reflection but now she felt confident that she'd be able to deliver a healthy baby and put this nightmare behind her. She was ready to go home.

On her last morning in the Cameron Highlands Eilidh slipped out, for she wanted to be alone to savour the last few moments and gaze over the rolling hillsides of citrus-green tea leaves cascading down to the valleys. Her eyes took in all the shades of green that seemed so intense and emerald when close up, but as her eye drifted to the horizon the colours blended and only a smoky haze joined the heavens. 'It is just so lovely,' she sighed, soaking up the panorama before her eyes. The morning dew made her feet wet as she inhaled the cloying perfume of the white magnolia flowers. Her hand automatically smoothed her tummy and she could feel the helter-skelter of limbs as the baby did watery somersaults, causing her bump to undulate. It wouldn't be long now, she thought, and smiled down at the pattern on her dress. She breathed in the perfume of a rose and caressed her cheek with its downy petals. She felt sensual and dreamy, far removed from the upheaval going on indoors. It was time to go home to Bukit Bulan.

Alex drove carefully down the long, winding road and Eilidh felt the heat begin to smother her as they descended from her highland retreat. They chatted about neighbours and news of the Selangor Club until they reached the archway proclaiming Bukit Bulan Estate. Cookie and Amah, Sinbad, and the cats were all waiting in the porch. Cookie gave her a dazzling smile, and Amah held her hand and patted her bump. Sinbad barked and the cats rubbed against her legs. She was home.

'I had forgotten,' she said. 'It's so sunny and so beautiful, but so hot! It's so good to be back with you all again.'

Alex put his arm around her. 'You will feel better after a cool shower and a siesta. It's grand having you back!'

It was October. Eilidh lay back on her pillows, her hair wet with perspiration. She was dressed in her blue satin nightdress that she'd bought especially for her stay in the Bungsar Hospital. Around her, the room was bedecked with roses from the Cameron Highlands, orchids from her garden and baskets of beautifully arranged flowers of every hue. She looked down at her newborn babe lying in a bassinet beside her and saw the miniature face pucker, lost in its own dream world. She wanted to touch the tiny tendril arms and legs that were as vulnerable as chicken bones, but her own body ached whenever she tried to stretch, for her stomach was swathed in bandages, the wound held together by her doctor's intricate stitching with surgical thread. So she contented herself by gazing at her baby's face and tried to fathom the miracle that had created this little girl. The birth had been difficult, the labour long and the threat to mother and child had been grave. Alex had been given an ultimatum at one critical moment; he had to choose between his wife and the child. Dr Davidson had eventually made the decision for him. Eilidh was too weak, so an emergency Caesarean was performed.

Eilidh recovered well in the hospital. 'I'm getting stronger every day,' she told her visitors one afternoon. 'I feel just wonderful. I feast on sweet papaya and mangoes for breakfast and the nurses bring me cold drinks made from freshly squeezed limes. They're so delicious; I just can't get enough of them.'

'It's Guinness you should be drinking,' Alex advised. 'That's what my mother swore by.'

'I heard Sweetheart Stout is a good one too,' offered Jack Dunbar knowledgably.

'Ugh!' Eilidh screwed up her nose. 'You know I hate Guinness and all those sorts of drinks.'

'Mother had nine of us,' Callum reminded her, 'and I'm sure the real reason she drank the Guinness was to forget. I wouldn't blame her for that either,' and he winked at his brother.

Eilidh shuddered. 'I can scarcely imagine drinking even a glass of brandy right now, let alone any of your suggestions. I'll stick with my lime juice, thank you very much.' Then she was interrupted, for they all looked round at the nurse who had just entered the room.

'Time for visitors to go, please.'

Later that evening, Eilidh asked the same nurse to help her walk out to the hospital garden. With the Chinese woman's assistance, she limped haltingly over to the edge of the hill on which the hospital stood, and she looked down over the city of Kuala Lumpur. She asked for her baby to be brought to her, and standing alone under an ancient banyan tree, its aerial roots hanging almost to the ground, Eilidh looked out over the mismatched roofs and took in the kaleidoscope of colours as the tropical sun set in a scorching band of crimson. She looked into the face of her sleeping child and said, 'I want to call you Anna.'

Chapter 6

April 1956

Alex leant back, tossed the ball into the air and whacked it hard into his opponent's corner. 'Ace! Game, set and match!' he shouted, leaping about with his racquet and running over to Jack to shake his hand. 'Rehydration therapy is called for! Your round, I believe!'

The two men wiped the sweat from their foreheads and necks with small hand towels that gaily proclaimed 'Good Morning' in bright red letters.

'One gunner and one shandy please,' Jack ordered.

They glanced around the club house and saw some golfers come in.

'Aye aye, Sam! Good day, was it?' Alex called out.

'Not bad, but I got stuck in the rough at the sixteenth and then made it to the green with a five. Shall we see you Sunday for golf and curry tiffin?'

'Aye, you will that; I tee off at eight o'clock, partnered with my brother this week.'

Alex and Jack perched on their stools and gazed out at the undulating fairways of the golf course. The district club was the heart of the planter's social life. It catered for golf, tennis, snooker, bridge and, of course, a lot of drinking.

'It's been a good day,' Jack said as he relaxed over his drink. 'I enjoyed the exercise after that drive into Taman Minyak.'

'Aye, that journey's pretty nerve-racking, isn't it?'

'They wouldn't believe it at home, would they? An armed police escort just to collect the payroll from town.'

'It's very different here, that's for sure, but it's a challenge. Without these bloody bandits, it would be very near perfect,' he paused and looked into his glass, 'except for Eilidh's poor health, of course. I wish there was a way to make her fit and well again.'

'I know, it's a terrible worry for you. Anyway, how is the wee bairn? I haven't seen her for a while.'

'Anna's fine, a real bundle of mischief; she's getting to the stage when she wants to rule the roost. Which reminds me, I can't stop too long; I should get back to Eilidh or she'll have the wooden spoon out.' Alex drained his glass and stood up.

'Just have one more with me before you go. I can't face going back to that cramped bungalow just yet.'

'Is it getting you down, Jack?' Alex sat down again and turned to the bar boy; 'Two Anchor beers, please.'

'Aye,' Jack frowned then looked up, 'you know yourself how three men living in close proximity can irritate each other, to put it mildly. It gets a bit strained sometimes. Look, I'm hoping to get an acting manager's job. I've done three years as assistant on minimum pay now, and you're going home on leave in October. Would you put in a good word for me? I'm sure the London office would upgrade me sooner if I had some experience as acting manager.'

Alex blew the white froth from the top of his glass before sucking in the cold beer and wiping his mouth with the back of his hand. He registered the personal appeal and the look of hope and expectation in his friend's eyes. Apart from the fact that Jack was thirty-two and unmarried, Alex realised he knew very little about him.

'Why not? I'd be more than pleased to assist if I can. When we're stuck out here on our own, we need all the help we can get. I'll see what I can do, Jack.'

Alex recalled Eilidh's words the other night as Jack pedalled away from their house: 'Why doesn't he have a girlfriend? He's so good looking and such a catch; there are so many girls in KL who would give anything for a date with him.'

'Have you any plans for when you go home, Jack? Is there anyone special or does the bachelor life suit you?' Alex winked, remembering the dusky ladies of the night that made life more exotic for a lonely fellow.

Jack raised an eyebrow and flipped over a beer mat, then flipped it back again. His tall frame was slouched over the bar. His normally well-groomed hair had fallen forward and his jaw was dark with the day's stubble. He raked his hand through his hair, his blue eyes twinkling and a half-smile forming as his face lit up. 'Aye, there is someone as it happens and she's a cracker! She's got the reddest hair and fieriest temper in Scotland. She writes me these long newsy letters that I can barely decipher for all the swirls and loops she uses.'

'Oh? You've certainly kept her pretty quiet.' Alex sounded bemused.

Jack let out an embarrassed laugh and grabbed a handful of peanuts. Between mouthfuls he confessed, 'If I so much as looked at another woman, I think I'd feel her wrath even at ten thousand miles' distance!'

'Well, you are a dark horse! And does this firecracker have a name?'

'Her name is Estelle; once seen, never forgotten!'

'Well, well, well! We'd better drink to your lady of good fortune. Two stengahs over here! To the lovely Estelle!'

The sun had set but the sky seemed reluctant to give up its mauve and lilac hues as Alex thundered along the driveway to his house. The brakes squealed as he lurched to a halt. Seeing Sinbad barking and running in circles near a flowerbed of canna lilies, Alex headed over the grass to see what the dog was getting so excited about. Through the half-light he made out the shape of a scorpion in the act of full defence. Its tail was raised over its head with the bulbous sting poised to attack. He had seen them before in the jungle clearing when the men were burning back the brush. The creatures would commit suicide by bringing their tail over and stinging themselves between the eyes rather than burn to death. Alex was feeling quite light-headed after the beers and whisky and soda, and watching the scorpion, he didn't hear Eilidh approach him from behind. She had Anna straddled on her hip. She lifted her hand and slapped him hard across the face.

'Ow! What was that for?'

'How could you? You are so selfish. You leave me here all day, worrying myself to death each time a tree splinters or a monkey screeches. I'm going frantic for fear that something has happened. You know I'm sick and now...' she broke off and started sobbing.

Anna clung to her mother, too shocked to react, but as the realisation dawned she too started to wail.

Alex shook his head. 'Eilidh, what is it? I'm here now, I'm sorry. I got carried away at the club; I know I should have called. Have you heard something?'

'It's Tim Bradley from Bukit Timor; he was shot dead this afternoon.' She started to weep.

'Oh God,' Alex looked up at the now black sky, 'Oh my God...why him?'

Sinbad left his scorpion to its fate and was now staring up at Eilidh with devotion. Slowly the little family made their way back to the house.

'Sssssh,' Alex whispered into her hair. 'I'm so sorry; I got talking to Jack and...I just didn't think.'

'I was so afraid, Alex. If anything happened to you what would I do? And Anna? We need you. Oh poor Norah and the boys, it's just too awful.' He handed her his handkerchief and she blew her nose, then looked up all red-eyed. 'You were gone all day and you had all that money.'

Alex thought back to the news broadcast on the radio that morning. The Alliance Party led by Tunku Abdul Rahman wanted immediate Malayan independence. How would he control the communists? How would it affect the British nationals? There was much talk in the Selangor Club and on the estates about the new face of Malaya. Now Tim Bradley was dead. Tim, who only the other evening had stood up and proposed a toast to a new Malaya. Who would be the next victim of this senseless war? Alex knew that Eilidh had every reason to break down and express her fears in a hysterical rage. 'Come,' he said, 'give Anna to Amah and sit with me. I'm hot as hell after the game of tennis I had with Jack at the club. The reason I was late back was he decided to tell me about his girlfriend in Scotland. To be honest, I was quite intrigued!' Talking softly he led her through to the kitchen where Cookie was getting a plate ready for Anna's supper. Alex kept his voice gentle as he continued with the inane news of whom he had seen at the club. 'Saw Sam come in at the eighteenth, he'd had a good round, and I see on the fixture board I'm playing with Callum tomorrow; we tee off at eight...' Gradually Eilidh allowed herself to be soothed by his deep monotone and she felt calmed by his presence. Later that night, lying side by side on the crisp cotton sheets with the fan ruffling the gauze of the mosquito net, he reached for her hand. 'Eilidh, perhaps you should go home early with Anna and spend some time with your family before I come? It's dangerous here and you do need special medical care. You can't go on like this and I can't bear watching you suffer.'

'I know,' she sighed, 'I know, I know all of that. I'll ring Dr Davidson tomorrow and arrange to see him. I'm so scared Alex, I'm so scared when you're out of my sight. When the phone rings, do you know that we all run for it, Cookie, Amah and I? Whoever answers it immediately nods and smiles to the others to reassure them that this time it is all right. These are such frightening times.'

Grim faced, Alex looked into the darkness and held her to him.

A week later the couple drove to the hospital in Kuala Lumpur. After the consultation, Alex took her to the Selangor Club where they sat on the veranda sipping fresh lime juice. Eilidh wore a loose-fitting emerald-green dress. She got up and walked to the ladies' powder room and sat in front of an oval mirror. She drew back as she confronted her reflection. Her eyes had sunk into black hollows. Her blonde curls were hanging limp and her face resembled a skull. Her hands shook as she took out the bottle of pills that she'd just been given. It had been decided that she would not go home to Scotland but instead would go to Fraser's Hill and undergo the same rest therapy that had helped her last year; the heat and the noise were just too much for her. Another new regime, another separation from Alex; why had she contracted such a debilitating disease? She took a small rolled-up face towel from the tray and ran it under the cold tap. She bathed the sweat from her face and neck then reapplied her make-up. She powdered her pale cheeks and applied fresh lipstick. Brushing her hair, she surveyed the wan image in front of her. 'Oh dear,' she sighed, 'it will have to do.'

When she rejoined Alex on the veranda she saw he was sitting with Angus Robertson. She leant over and gave the older man a small peck on his hairy cheek. 'How are you, Angus?' she smiled cheekily. His gruff, authoritarian manner always transported her back to the schoolroom.

'Good! Good, in fact as right as rain; lovely to see you both again!' He rubbed his hands together enthusiastically at the prospect of enjoying a pleasant meal in their company. 'Why don't you both join me for a bite to eat so that we can catch up; Coliseum all right for you?'

'Yes of course, we're both starving, aren't we, Alex?' Eilidh replied, feeling his bonhomie lift her spirits.

They looked at their watches, finished up the remains of their drinks and then wandered down the front steps of the club. A steward whistled to Angus's driver, who pulled up in his Ford Zephyr. Alex and Eilidh followed them through the thronging streets, dodging bicycles laden with every type of produce and colourful ladies carrying huge cotton bundles on their heads. Arriving at Batu Road, they settled themselves into the bustling restaurant and ordered beer and made their selections from the grimy menu. Waiters festooned them in snowy white bibs in preparation for the impending feast, huge glasses of chilled beer dripping rivers of condensation appeared before them, tantalising aromas permeated the air, and they chatted and drank and looked around at the other diners until, at last, the sizzling platters of steak and chips arrived. Eilidh, who had previously felt ravenous, pushed her plate away after only a few mouthfuls, and looking across the street, she focussed on a billboard advertising the latest Tamil film. A voluptuous Asian beauty was draped in a fluorescent orange sari; her black plait snaked across her ample bosom while her lovesick suitor leered at her with lascivious bedroom eyes. Eilidh grinned to herself at the seductive images, and turning back to the table, she tuned into the men's conversation. Angus was discussing his golf fixtures, but inevitably the conversation turned to the latest murder. Tim Bradley had already been buried.

'You know that Norah and the boys are going home next week, don't you, Angus?'

'Aye, what an appalling business; those poor wee lads, so young to be losing their father, and Norah is just devastated. Tim and the policeman with him didn't stand a chance. It seems they were tricked into stopping when they turned a bend and saw a mangled bicycle and a man lying bleeding in the road. It looked like a hit and run accident, but when they pulled over to assist, the CTs who'd been lying in wait opened up on them from both sides of the road. Cut them to pieces then fled with the payroll. Bastards, I hope they rot in hell. There's been a massive search going on for the perpetrators, but as usual they seem to have just melted away into the jungle. The tapper lying in the road had been badly beaten, but the shots alerted his workmates and now he's in hospital and pulling through, so I believe. He told the police there were four terrorists involved in the attack.'

'Oh God, how much longer can these people terrorise and kill and maim with impunity?' Eilidh shuddered at the thought that it could so easily have been Alex who'd been lured into the ambush. 'Why is it so difficult for our troops to find Chin Peng, Angus? Besides, I thought there weren't so many guerrillas left in the country now?' She felt feverish and wiped her brow and neck with her napkin. Suddenly overwhelmed, she just wanted to lie down in a cool place.

Alex looked at her anxiously, wondering if he shouldn't just take her back home to rest.

'Unfortunately Chin Peng is a grandmaster of guerrilla techniques. Don't forget how he organised the Chinese resistance groups into an army to fight the Japanese.' Angus put down his fork but waved his knife in his schoolmasterly fashion. He was all set to launch into a full lecture about regiments and military strategy and the latest line in politics that the governments of Malaya and Britain were advocating, but he could see the droplets of perspiration on Eilidh's forehead and upper lip, and the concerned frown on her husband's face, so he lowered his knife and said gently, 'It's just a question of time, my dear, just time, I don't think it will last so much longer.'

'We have the Ghurkha regiment as well as the Malay and the British and the Commonwealth troops; why can't we defeat them?' she persisted.

'We are, dear; the tide is turning now, thanks also to the policy of cutting off support from the squatters.' Once again waving his knife like a conductor's baton as though to give emphasis to his words he added, 'Chin Peng has been counting on support from China and the USSR. He thinks that world opinion will force Britain to give Malaya her independence, and then he will move in and raise the red flag.'

Alex nodded in agreement and took a long drink from his glass.

'Well, even if we do win it's too late for poor Tim, isn't it?'

'I know, lass. It could have been any one of us, but the Emergency is nearly over, thanks to our soldiers living out in the jungle for months on end playing the guerrillas at their own game. They are winning and these tactics have forced Chin Peng to move his headquarters to Thailand. You are right, I believe there are only a few hundred guerrillas left in the country now.' Having failed to stab anyone during his lecture, Angus finally laid his knife to rest and looked about him, waving to a waiter in white who was hovering nearby to take more orders. 'I'll have a jam omelette and a black coffee please. What would you two like?'

Alex and Eilidh opted for ice cream and the talk turned to less serious subjects.

Finally as they left the Coliseum and stepped out into the afternoon sun, Angus kissed Eilidh on the cheek and asked her, 'What now, lass? What are your plans? You've got to get yourself well and strong again.'

'Fraser's Hill for three months,' she laughed. 'I want to fight my own battle and be well enough for our leave in the autumn.'

'Good for you, Eilidh. I wish you all the very best, and God go with you.'

Angus strode over to his car and waved at the young couple before instructing his driver to head back to his estate. Arriving back at his bungalow at sundown, he wandered over to the radiogram. He selected a recording of *South Pacific* and took the whisky that his Cookie brought to him. He turned the volume up high and listened to *Some Enchanted Evening*, and lay back in his chair and closed his eyes. The wind rose outside in the pitch-black of the tropical night, the bamboo tats on the veranda started to thrash about, and suddenly the shriek of the telephone jarred into his reverie. 'Hello! Angus here, who's that?' but the line went dead, another wrong number. He sang as he padded up the wooden stairs to his bedroom, 'Once you have found her, never let her go...' The rain started pounding like thunder onto the roof, the thin gauze curtains blew up and Angus dashed over to lift the mosquito-proof blinds in order to close the windows. Huge gusts of rain blew into the room and he was soon soaked as he struggled with the task in hand. As he leant out to catch a window the garden was illuminated by a flash of lightning that zigzagged out of the heavens. The lights in the house went dead as the generator died. 'Buggeration,' he muttered, but continued pulling the windows in and securing the catches, then pulling down the blinds. Another crack of thunder tore the sky apart. 'Cookie!' he called out. 'Always here except when I need him,' he grumbled. A gust of wind pulled a window from his grip, forcing him to lean out further, his soaked shirt sticking to his body.

As the sky lit up in another metallic flash he saw them. Crouching down behind the bamboo hedge were maybe three or four dark shapes that didn't belong. He caught the glint of metal as it mirrored the storm and he knew he should fetch his gun, but instead he stood frozen. The thought occurred to him that these shadowy figures might be the same ones that had killed Tim Bradley. He wanted to keep an eye on their movements but at the same time instinct told him to arm himself for the violent confrontation that was sure to come. Releasing the window he moved like a shadow across the room to retrieve the loaded revolver he kept by his bed, then with the heavy weapon in his hand he returned to the open window. Great waterfalls of rain were pounding the garden and it was only when the lightning again lit up the skies that he could make out the shapes of bushes and trees. Where the hell were they now? The drinning sound of the deluge on the roof masked all other noise and he never heard their footsteps as they entered the building or the creaking as they climbed the stairs. As they burst through the door, he spun round, wildly determined to take some of them with him, but before he could fire a single shot, a hail of bullets smashed into his chest. The noise was deafening in the confined space and the impact hurled him against the wall where he fell slumped in a sitting position, his head flopped on to his chest.

Downstairs, Cookie had already ushered his wife out of the house and into the servants' quarters, two rooms constructed of palm leaves lashed together with rattan. Wild eyed, he pushed her under the bed and gripped his master's rifle with trembling hands. He guessed the fate that had befallen his boss, but he clutched at the hope that the storm might deter the murderers from searching the outhouses for the servants. Another crack of thunder heralded the storm's gathering momentum. Hearing muffled voices and sloshing footsteps in the waterlogged garden, he knew the terrorists were desperately looking for them, and backing against the wall he cocked his rifle and pointed it at the door. Unrealistically he hoped that the feeble lock might deter the intruders, but under a barrage of furious kicks accompanied by cursing sounds in staccato Cantonese, the rattan door rapidly burst inwards. As the black form strode through the opening, Cookie fired point blank into his face and the body crumpled before him. The slumped figure lay twisted on the floor only inches from the bed and Cookie stepped over him in a futile attempt to re-secure the door, unaware that his white uniform shone out like a ghostly beacon in the dark garden. Silently the other assailants moved out of the shadows and, raising their long *parang* knives, they darted into the dark, cramped space. Cookie's eyes were wide with fright and before he could fire another shot the first knife slashed down on his shoulder and another hacked ferociously into his head. In blind agony, he turned and lurched back into the hut. He stumbled over the body of the man that he had shot, and as he fell, the blade of a third knife plunged into his back and he screamed and his eyes filled and his lungs coughed up great mouthfuls of blood. He lay with his eyes open, and as the lightning lit up the sky once more, his wife from her hiding place saw a fine network of gossamer threads cover his pupils. She had seen his passing.

The shack fell silent after the intruders had melted away, and Amah lay motionless beneath the bed, paralysed with fear. The rain had finally ceased and the jungle night was long, only drips from the overhanging trees disturbing the sinister silence. Were they in the main house, ransacking and stealing food and ammunition? Would they move on before dawn? She remained still, the hard wooden floor cutting into her hipbones. At fifty-five she was thin and her body had stiffened in the unnatural position. Mosquitoes droned around her ears and she could hear the scurry of rats approaching the bodies. The blood seeped into the floorboards in black, inky pools and she could smell the foul odour of the dead guerrilla. She knew she should wait until it was light before running to the Tamil labour lines for help, but she needed to get out; her body was in shock and she could feel great waves of nausea overwhelming her. She tried to wriggle out from her safe cocoon but it was difficult with the two bodies obstructing the narrow opening and she felt revulsion in touching them. Her husband's eyes were open and staring, his head had a great open slash and his blood had congealed into a black and sticky mess. Slithering like a snake, she pushed and pulled her body out of the narrow space and squatted down and vomited amongst the blood and wreckage. She stood up and warily made her way out of the smashed door opening. Dawn was just breaking, the sky looked clean and fresh after the night of rain, and somewhere morning birds were chattering. Peering nervously around her, she turned towards the perimeter of the garden, her only thought being of escape.

'*Ai Yaaa!*'

A high pitched scream pierced the air, and turning she saw three men advancing towards her. In terror she ran, weaving through the rubber trees, careless of any kind of caution as her pursuers gained on her, and expecting at any second the retort of the rifle or the crack of gunshot from the revolvers that she knew would prelude her death. But the crashing of running feet through leaves and the scream of monkeys overhead convinced her that death would not be instant. The rifle butt thudding into the back of her head felled her; her eyes rolled up as she pleaded for instant unconsciousness, and for a few seconds she saw only the blackness of space. Aware of ripping cloth and listening in dread to the sound of belts being unbuckled, she writhed as her legs were wrenched apart and then her body was torn and the flesh from her most private parts ripped with the assault. She kept her face averted and her eyes squeezed shut. Opening her eyes again and with hot tears flooding her cheeks, she saw yet another face, ugly and distorted with animal lust as he grunted into her and when he withdrew he looked down at his blood-smeared member and cursed her. Her ravaged body was roughly turned over and her buttocks pulled apart and she screamed, fierce pain engulfing her as she was pounded and impaled. Standing again, her attacker viciously kicked her hip, and she retched into the mushy compost of dead leaves, her body on fire, burning rivers of agony running in place of blood. She heard the sound of belts again and recoiled in fear, but the orgy of sadism was over and now the thugs approached her with their *parangs* and the brute that had started the rape slashed his knife deeply across her throat, enjoying her pain.

The new day had begun, the bougainvillea bloomed vibrant after the night's soaking, and the birds of the garden sang and whistled in the hot sunshine. Black-spotted butterflies chased each other around the lime bushes. At ten o'clock Angus's assistant, Michael Parrish, cycled up to the manager's bungalow, concerned that Angus had made no appearance at the office at six o'clock as usual. Perhaps a bad hangover; he knew he'd been to Kuala Lumpur yesterday and according to Eilidh and Jack had been in fine form. Michael walked into the bungalow, surprised to find the door open but nobody about. 'Angus! Where are you, Angus?' he called as he cast his eyes around the deserted rooms, 'Cookie!' He walked through to the kitchen, where by this time bacon and eggs should have been under preparation. Instead the kitchen had been ransacked and remains of tins and ham and bread had been left, as though a party had taken place. Ominous silence met him, so he walked back into the main dining room and looked at the unfinished glass of whisky. He made his way up the stairs, prickles of fear creeping down his spine. 'Angus! Are you there? Angus, where are you, are you OK?' He looked into the bedroom, and at first didn't see his boss. The bed was smooth and had not been slept in; the polished wooden floors were glossed to a sheen, but one window was open and the floor was wet from the night's rain. Then he saw him. Angus was sitting slumped against the wall beside the open window, his head bent as though he was resting, but the bloodstained shirt confirmed his untimely end. He had been shot several times in the chest at close range, and where he'd slid to the floor, his blood had smeared down the wall and puddled around him. 'Oh, Angus, you poor bastard,' Michael whispered. He went closer and touched his hand, but he already knew that it would be cold. Running downstairs he called 'Cookie!' but he was aware that there was little chance of a reply. He knew that being a servant of the British imperialists would merit a violent end. He picked up the telephone and dialled the number for the Port Swettenham police. The sergeant assured him that they would be over instantly. He then dialled the estate office and told the staff there what had happened. Finally he called Alex McIntyre. 'Hello, Alex, I have terrible news. It's Angus. I know you were with him yesterday. He was murdered last night, shot dead in his house. I'll wait here until the police arrive...no, there's no sign of the servants or anybody else. I'll go and investigate outside now...yes, would appreciate that. I'll see you shortly...soon as you can.'

Michael met the estate staff as they came up the driveway in a cloud of red dust. They had commandeered a latex lorry and now they jumped out in their freshly pressed white cotton shirts and shiny black shoes.

'Oh this is a terrible, terrible thing! I cannot believe what you are saying. All this time and now this Emergency is nearly over and poor Mr Robertson is shot dead. What a commotion for our office. There will be a pandemonium when the police get here, all the questions, who saw this and who saw that?' How could anybody see anything with all that rain? Oh my golly gosh!'

'Come, Mr Lopez, we'll wait here until the police arrive.' Michael went back to the kitchen and looked out of the window towards the servants' quarters, partially hidden by a large clump of bamboo. The silence was ominous but he knew he'd have to investigate, so he opened the mesh door and stepped out into the sunny garden. As he came around the tall, dense wall of fronds and spiky leaves, he saw the broken door and the sad latticework wall that had crumpled under the violent attack. He approached carefully, climbed up the two wooden steps and saw the chaos within the shadowy interior. Cookie was face down on the floor, his white shirt stained red, his head turned as though he was sleeping. Michael could see the great gash in his back and the ghastly wound to his head. Then his eyes turned to the body of the Chinese youth, part of his face shot away, his army fatigues soaked in his own and in Cookie's blood. From outside he heard a commotion of people shouting and the Tamil voices of the tappers coming up the side of the garden. Mr Lopez answered them, and called to Michael.

'*Tuan,* quickly, come with us. Another body has been found in the rubber.'

Later that evening, Michael sat with his friends Jack, Callum, Alex and Eilidh in the McIntyres' bungalow. He had finished recounting the details and was leaning over his whisky as the horrors of the day engulfed him. He remembered the irony when the police had started up the generator in the early afternoon and simultaneously the radiogram's turntable, interrupted the previous night, continued its rotation under the needle arm. They had all started with alarm when, from Angus's deserted lounge, the rich tenor voice resumed singing *Some Enchanted Evening.* Michael swallowed his whisky and blinked hard.

Angus's funeral service was held in St Andrew's Presbyterian Church in Kuala Lumpur, but those of the congregation who wished to attend the burial had to drive to Batu Gajah, a short distance from Ipoh which was a hundred miles north of Kuala Lumpur. The road took Eilidh and Alex through native *kampongs* where the pace of life had not changed for hundreds of years. Brown houses built on stilts nestled in clearings off the road and fencing of woven bamboo gave a certain feeling of privacy to the homesteads. Windows were framed with gaily coloured curtains, dusty orange cats slept on the wooden steps, and batik sarongs hung over makeshift clothes lines. Old men sat in the shade of the verandas smoking their native cigarettes, picking their toes, and watching the traffic speeding past the grazing buffalo with a purpose completely beyond their comprehension.

Eilidh gazed at the scenes around her. She was used to the jumble of *kedais*, the shophouses, advertising 'Singer Sewing Machines' and 'Beauty Shop Inside', marketing their wares and trades in Chinese characters or bold English lettering. Passing a restaurant, she glanced at the food piled up behind small screens and at steaming cauldrons of curry sauces to accompany *biryani* or *roti* breads. She watched a group of children crowd around a bicycling vendor selling lurid pink drinks in plastic bags. She thought of the goldfish she used to take home in the same way, long ago when she was little. She had grown used to the easy tolerance practised in Malaya, where food customs illustrated the intertwining of the three races throughout the centuries. Northern Indian and Malay cuisine provided the wonderful spicy vegetarian curries that both races now relished, and the hot curries of the Tamil Indians were served next door to the Cantonese or Szechuan delicacies of China. Malays formed eighty percent of the population, and their mosques with their geometric roofs and crescent moons on top stood proudly in town and village centres. Religious toleration was made easier as there was a careful segregation of the two races. The Malays lived in their *kampongs*, and generally lived from the land, planting, growing fruit, and raising chickens, whereas the Indians lived on the rubber plantations as immigrant labour. Their temples with magnificent florid carvings of Ganesh and Shiva grew up amongst the rubber and oil palm fields where the worshippers had easy access. The Chinese tended to live in the cities, where they dominated the retail trade and business, and their temples depicting dragons and pagodas with gentle Buddhas rose high, showing their exotic carvings amongst the city roof silhouettes.

'Do you see how the landscape is changing?' Alex pointed to the gouged-out earth on either side of the road.

'What is it?' she asked. 'What's happening here?'

'This is tin mining country and home to many Australian and American miners. The tin dredgers make a real mess of the landscape; can you see them over there where those craters are filled with water?'

Eilidh craned her neck towards the excavations. 'I see them; the water is a luminous shade of blue.'

'Aye, well the miners have to get out the ore that's lying in the milky depths. I came up once to visit Joe Butler, an Australian who's been here for years. He gave me a grand tour. But it's even lonelier here, as the men don't get down to KL as much as they'd like.'

Eilidh squeezed her eyes shut.

'What is it, darling? We're nearly there.' Alex took his hand off the wheel and patted her thigh.

'I'm sorry, I just thought of Angus, so lonely on his estate. I'm glad he had a good funeral though.' She wiped her eyes. 'So many people, and the singing was wonderful!'

'I know, I know. I can't believe that this time last week we were having lunch with him in the Coliseum, and now here we all are about to bury the poor man. First Tim and now Angus…it's just too much, what is the point of it all?'

On arriving at Ipoh, they drove straight to the club, a replica of the Tudor-style Selangor Club building in Kuala Lumpur, and Alex strode over and shook hands with Michael, Jack and Callum who had arrived earlier. Eilidh went to look out over the *padang* and saw the tall, slim monoliths of limestone mountains towering around the town. They shimmered in the afternoon sun, their shapes reminiscent of a watery Chinese print, and in the distance more mountains formed a purple backdrop to the great forests of unclaimed land. Eilidh looked down at the emerald perfection of the *padang* and watched the native *kaboon*s tending the flowers and shrubs around the club house. She almost forgot why she was there as, hypnotised, she watched the rhythmic movements of their hands clad in leather gauntlets pulling out the razor-sharp *lalang* grass.

'Come along, Eilidh, let's have some tea, we shall have to make a move to Batu Gajah soon. The burials are to take place at four o'clock.'

She blinked; she had been miles away, her thoughts drifting from Angus to Tim and to the young soldiers who would also be buried this same afternoon. Angus's poor murdered servants had already been buried in their native Chinese cemetery near their hometown of Telok Anson.

*

104

Nearly thirty cars formed a procession for Batu Gajah, where soldiers stood on duty directing drivers to park further down the hill. Thus it was that they entered the cemetery in a procession, and following the tradition of nearly every culture in the world, they paced behind the coffins to the allotted land where the graves lay dug and open. God's Little Acre at Batu Gajah was the designated burial ground for rubber planters and tin miners but in the last twelve years, new mounds of earth had appeared and small stones marked the graves of the soldiers killed in the Emergency. This afternoon the assembled group watched as the three soldiers were interred first. The commanding officers stood and saluted. The Reverend Andrew Thompson in his black clerical robes conducted the burial service. The three young men were aged only nineteen, twenty and twenty-one, all ambushed and shot in the jungles on the Perak Pahang border. Then the company moved to the last waiting grave. Alex, Callum, Michael, Sam, Jim and Alan walked forward and took a silken cord and slowly lowered Angus's body into the earth. Eilidh's eyes filled with tears as she listened to the familiar words, 'Dust to dust, ashes to ashes, the Lord giveth and the Lord taketh away, blessed is the name of the Lord.'

Looking up at the darkening sky, she thought of Angus's wife and small son so far away in Wick on the northeast coast of Scotland, where the North Sea pounded and seagulls soared on swirls of spray, where waterlogged fields rolled down to the craggy coast and the sheer drop of the scree-lined cliffs fell harshly into the swirling waters of the cruel sea below. She imagined her walking alone, looking out to a horizon that hid the images of another world that had murdered her man. She imagined her windswept hair and her sense of loss. It was not his native land that would hold his bones, or a cold granite stone that would commemorate his life; instead as the sun set over the dark shapes of the coconut palms, Angus was lowered into a piece of ground whose perimeter was planted with yew trees and whose entrance was marked by an archway that was a replica of the ones that led into the rubber estates.

As the sun set, the sky held the faint whispery tones of pink and lilac, and the skeletal shapes of the frangipani and hibiscus fell into black relief until tomorrow when the sun again would mirror their brilliance and send its heat falling like molten bronze into this isolated garden. Angus and these three young English boys from Devon and Cornwall would become part of the soil that was Malaya. Eilidh's eyes lifted and looked beyond this oasis towards the virgin forest, so close she could see the creeping, stifling weeds, ferns and mosses. She could hear the shriek of monkeys, and she imagined the black, soft, moist humus beneath the colossal tree trunks and she shivered at the thought of the snakes, scorpions, ants and centipedes crawling, working and reproducing in the hot putrefying weeds. She shook her head and her eyes focussed on the ferns and juicy creepers that were insidiously commandeering a fallen branch on which white and purple orchids had flowered. A Ghurkha soldier came forward and raised his bugle to his lips. The soldiers stood to attention and held a salute as the Last Post was played. As the notes died in the air, the mourners turned and made their way back to the gates. Alex laced his fingers through hers and silently they walked to their car.

Eilidh was listless as she watched Amah pack up her clothes that lay strewn across the bed. Since Angus's funeral, she had been jumpy and irritable and had grown paranoid. Fear gripped her like a physical force and was triggered by the snapping of twigs in the garden or the crack of a branch splintering in the forest. The noises of exploding rubber seeds sounded like bullets, and the scream of monkeys brought about spasms of uncontrollable trembling. Fear was eating into her soul, and TB was eating into her body. She knew that she had to go to Fraser's Hill or to the Cameron Highlands again, and they had decided on the former. She was terrified of leaving her husband, and fretted each time he left the house. 'I can't leave you here alone and I won't go away without you. Oh, darling, please come with me,' she begged every night, but Alex knew it was impossible.

It was June of 1956. The political situation was stabilising and the Emergency was not so much of a threat in Selangor as it was in Perak, Pahang and Johor. With the shift of power going to Tunku Abdul Rahman, Malaya was on track towards independence and would indeed become a country truly for the Malays. Still there were reports in the *Straits Times* of planters and tin miners being murdered, and when Eilidh read these, she became hysterical with fear. She stared out at the rubber trees and listened for Alex's Land Rover and kept Anna inside. Although there had been no further attacks on their personal friends and in spite of

106

Alex's reassuring voice, she could not regain her peace of mind.

'You have to go, my love, and you have to go soon,' Alex said gently, sitting beside her as she lay on their bed, unable to eat and unwilling to talk.

'I want to be with you,' she whispered.

He held her shoulders as the cough returned and racked her body until she was sick, and then he lowered her back on the pillows, his face crumpled in concern. She lay gasping, her eyes black and staring, until finally her breathing eased. He sponged her brow with iced towels as Eilidh fell into the uneasy sleep of one in the clutches of fever.

At last the car was packed and Alex waved cheerily to Cookie, raising his eyes to the sky as though the two men had a conspiracy. The drama of the morning, of getting Eilidh and Anna packed into Alex's Zephyr, together with Rokiah and all the toys and the pushchair was quite a feat. Amah hugged Anna, who struggled to be free and instead had to make do with stroking her arm as she was placed on Rokiah's knee in the back seat.

Eilidh smiled wanly and squeezed Amah's hand. 'Goodbye, please take care of *Tuan*, it won't be too long.' Sobbing quietly, she looked out of the window, only to be met by Sinbad's big brown eyes, so questioning, so trusting, his head playfully cocked to one side. 'Oh God, darling, please just go.'

The drive to Fraser's Hill was long. The road with its spiralling bends closed in on them and the jungle seemed to creep towards the road as insistent, insidious tendrils and broken branches edged forward. Soon they rose up into the milk-covered mists. They had missed the storm that had sent heavy curtains of water down in a huge wash and now the air was fresh and the luxuriant foliage dripped and at last they emerged triumphantly at the summit.

'Oh, how quaint!' Eilidh exclaimed. She took in the fairway of the golf course and the cluster of slate-coloured stone buildings that formed the nucleus of the small hill resort. It was like an English village. 'And there is the village clock,' she said, and laughed at the small touches that someone had added to make this place reminiscent of a home so far away.

Alex drove past the golf course and turned into the driveway of a small bungalow. He parked and they all got out, stretched and looked around them. There were dahlias of a red that was almost black, scarlet gladiolas and clashing orange marigolds and ferns that were taller than the roof. Their fronds were ancient and primitive and framed the sky just as they had done when dinosaurs walked the earth. Pitcher plants or 'monkey cups' nestled in the jungle area at the back of the house, and creeping mimosa opened its tiny leaves provocatively, inviting a hand to stroke the downy pink flowers. Eilidh never tired of touching the leaves just to watch the coy withdrawal and sharp snap of the leaves. 'You are a tantalising flirt,' she told the plant, and withdrew her finger quickly but snared it on a sharp thorn on the fragile stem. 'You are also a brute,' she scolded, sucking her index finger.

While Rokiah unloaded all the paraphernalia into the house, Alex lifted his daughter into her pushchair and set off down the road. 'I need to stretch my legs after that drive,' he shouted to Eilidh. 'You'll get on better without us in your way. Come on, Anna; let's see what we can find down this road, maybe some kangaroos?'

Standing barefoot in his slacks, his left hand stuck in his back pocket and his hair still damp from his bath, Alex dialled Eilidh's number.

'Hello! Oh, Alex, I'm so glad you called; I've so much to tell you...'

Listening to Eilidh's chatter, Alex signalled to Cookie to bring over a chair. He stuck his legs out in front of him and picked up the framed photograph of his wife and daughter.

'It's been such a long time without you, Alex, two months already, but I am getting better. The cough is not so bad and there's no more blood, but let me tell you what happened today. I actually accompanied Rokiah and Anna on one of their walks, and now I understand why they take so long. Anna is determined to inspect every single item of interest that she comes across and today it was a puppy; such a sweet thing. Well, she wanted to take it home and made such a fuss when Rokiah carried it back to the shack we'd just passed. She seemed determined to find a pet, and ran off into the jungle after a skinny tabby cat. You should have heard her, "Pussy, Pussy, come to Anna. Come, Pussy!" We had to chase her into the jungle; it was all quite creepy and dark and I thought she might have been scared, but not a chance! She found a caterpillar, a huge thing with black and white spots and a bristle of spiky hairs along its back.

Rokiah screamed, "*Ai Ya*! Hairy caterpillar, no good! Make Anna itchy!"
So the poor little girl had no pets to take home.'

'Is she being good with Rokiah now?' Alex managed to get a word in.

'Oh no,' said Eilidh with feeling, 'not at all, she's terrible. Rokiah is at her
wits' end. You know how Anna isn't used to wearing any clothes at home,
well apart from her singlet or very light dresses, but here she's expected to
wear shoes and cardigans and oh dear,' she laughed, 'she just tears them off
and tosses them into the bushes. When I'm sitting on the veranda sewing
I can hear them from about a mile away. Rokiah is scolding, and Anna's
voice is laying down the law, "No shoes…Anna no shoes!"'

Alex laughed, picturing the antics of the trio in their mountain retreat.
He was reassured by the optimistic tone of Eilidh's voice. She was getting
better.

On a lazy August afternoon during one of Alex's visits, Eilidh made a
suggestion to her husband. 'Darling, I feel so well, and Anna is thriving
here, please let's leave and we can have a couple of weeks together at Port
Dickson. She would love the seaside and Dr Davidson is very happy with
my progress.'

They were sitting in the garden of the Red Cross bungalow looking
down over the panorama of hills below them. The air was sharp, and the
mist lay in pockets of the tree canopy and was draped in wisps over the
tall branches of the trees. Alex could see the colour in his wife's cheeks
and her quick smile, and he grinned as she chattered and interspersed her
stories with her girlish laugh. It was agreed that that they should go to
Port Dickson in September, before they flew back to Scotland.

'Jack will be acting for me whilst we're away; he's very keen to get
recognition and an estate for himself. I told you about Estelle, didn't I?'

'Only that he had a girlfriend in Scotland; is it very serious?'

'I think they're engaged; they'll probably marry when he goes back
on leave next year.'

'But that's wonderful, darling, maybe we could visit her when we go
back, what do you think? I'm sure he's told her about us. Shall we do that?'

'Yes, we may do, but right now I think I shall put on my new hat, and
take my two best ladies for a walk.'

With Anna again ensconced in her pushchair, he proceeded at a leisurely pace down the winding road, chattering to his daughter as they went. Eilidh took the camera from her sewing bag and ran to catch up with them. She looked down into the viewfinder of the box camera, and tried to capture her dashing husband, but just as she clicked the shutter he pushed his hat to one side and crossed his eyes.

'Oh no! Why did you do that?' she giggled as he encircled her in his arms and they continued on their walk.

Eilidh lay on her back in the sea, floating on top of the waves. The ocean rocked her, its timeless motion mirroring the very life force that pulsed and echoed the rhythm of eternity. She felt languorous and sensuous. Her skin was sleek and slippery. She ran her hands over her breasts and down over her hips. A smile played over her mouth as she remembered the night before. Alex had come into the washroom of the little government rest house and had laughed at her attempts to wash herself with a plastic dipper and a dragon pot full of cold water. She had gingerly poured water over her knees and shivered, then watched as he undressed and poured a dipper full of water straight over his head. He'd started to laugh with his eyes screwed up tight and then promptly filled the container and splashed her. She moaned now at the memory of the slipperiness of the soap and his strong hands as they massaged and caressed her sunburnt body. 'Oh how lovely this all is!' she said aloud to the sky, and as she focussed above her, she saw two trails of white condensation across the blue expanse where minutes before a jet aeroplane had flown. She heard her daughter laughing on the sand and watched her pointing up to the sky.

'Long legs, Daddy, look at the birdie with long legs!'

Eilidh pushed through the breaking surf and her feet felt like leaden weights as the sand and pebbles sucked her down. She struggled up to the hard compacted sand of the shore.

'Are you OK?' Alex looked up at her.

Eilidh grinned and rumpled his hair. 'I'm more than OK!'

He was digging a huge hole for Anna who was squealing and shouting instructions.

'Deeper, Daddy, dig deeper!' Anna jumped into the hole and as she disappeared, they both pretended to walk away. An outraged howl made them turn as an angry little mud ball struggled to get free.

'Well, what a change from when we arrived,' said Alex as he jumped back into their rapidly filling swimming pool.

Only a week ago when Anna had seen the beach and the shimmery blue Straits of Malacca for the first time, she'd yelled at Rokiah, 'No No No!' and waved her arms around like a miniature King Canute, trying to command the sea.

'Take out the plug, Rokiah! I don't like it.'

'You crazy little girl!' Alex had said as he scooped her up and walked down to the ocean.

She'd eyed the waves suspiciously and touched the receding tide then run away as the water chased her up the sand. She'd been like a curious kitten, unwilling to leave this new toy, but equally unwilling to give in to it. Now she loved it, and patted the sand and lay stretched on her tummy. She wore herself into sleepy exhaustion running in and out of the water and collecting buckets full of pebbles and shells. Even though she was partially covered by a baggy T-shirt and floppy hat, her skin had turned nutmeg brown.

'What's this?' she demanded when she brought back the bleached remains of a cuttlefish.

'It's the fish's backbone, sweetheart,' said Eilidh.

Anna looked at it solemnly. 'And where is its front bone then?'

'I don't know,' Eilidh laughed, planting a big kiss on her salty cheek.

Now their golden holiday was nearly over and on the last night Eilidh walked alone along the sand. In a few weeks they would pack up and fly back to Scotland where they would stay for five months. She was excited about returning. It would be October then, Anna would have her second birthday and Eilidh would hopefully qualify for the operation to remove her right lung. Her only hope of a better life and a second baby would be to get rid of this debilitating disease. The sun dipped and she stood motionless. Only the wash of the waves could be heard. A red ragged rip like an imperfect scar cut along the ocean as the light source disappeared and the sun finally dipped over the edge of the horizon.

A robin danced on the window ledge and then flitted off to hop expectantly around the stationary form of an abandoned garden fork.

'Oh, Molly, it's so cold here in Glengrianach, I'd forgotten just how raw this weather can be. Look at it, the sky is full of snow.' Eilidh, adorned in her blue satin nightdress, leant against the headboard in the spare room of her parents' house and sipped her tea.

Molly was admiring the shimmering spread of silk dressing gowns in all the colours of the rainbow, brought over from Malaya as gifts from the East.

'Have whichever one you fancy. I gave a pink one to Isabelle Sinclair and a lime-green one to Estelle. She's the fiancée of one of our assistant planters. Oh, Molly, you should see him! His name is Jack and he's a real handsome hunk. I have to remember I'm a respectable married woman when he comes round. He's so dark and swarthy, almost Italian looking with eyes the colour of violets. But you mustn't breathe this to a soul...' Excited as a schoolgirl, Eilidh lowered her voice. 'Estelle let slip that they were secretly married! Imagine! She'd drunk a few too many and probably didn't remember saying anything, but Alex and I agreed that we wouldn't tell. Isn't it exciting, and so romantic?'

Molly grinned, feeling the contagious energy emanate from Eilidh, just as she always did when she was around her effervescent cousin.

'Come on, Molly, I have to get up; what colour are you going to choose? Personally I think the purple or the scarlet. Both would look stunning with your dark hair, in fact I think you should have both. Right, that's all arranged! Oh listen, there's my mam bawling up the stairs. Nothing ever changes!' Eilidh called back, 'Just five minutes, Mam, I have to change, don't start fretting yet.'

Molly picked up the tweed suit that was hanging over the chair. 'Is this not made from the material from Lewis that your aunties gave you at your wedding? It's such a bonny colour; did you get it made up over there?'

'Yes, it's so easy. You choose the style you want from pattern books, or the tailors can copy anything that's already been made. I copied this one from Worth. Look! It's all beautifully lined and everything. I've had dresses made, and evening gowns. Oh, I wish you could visit. It's like a magical fairytale world, and it's the best place to have a baby. Anna can play and Amah takes care of her if I'm resting.'

'But what about all the shooting and murders? You wrote such terrible things about the Emergency.'

'Yes, I did. We've had some terrible frights and lost some very good friends. I get sick with worry when Alex is out, especially when he's collecting the money for the wages.' Eilidh folded up the gowns and carelessly dropped them back into her suitcase. She went on, 'But the incidents are less frequent now and there's a big political movement advocating change so we all, that is the rubber and tin mining communities, are more optimistic for the future: including me. That's why I've decided to have this operation. I want another child, Molly. The doctors told me that my lung is too diseased, but if they remove the damaged section, then I will be as healthy as you. It's been so hard struggling with these negative feelings of mortality every time I have a relapse, but this should put an end to all that.'

'You're so brave, Eilidh, I'm glad the doctors are so confident.'

Hellen Matheson shouted up the stairs for the second time, 'Are you two girls coming down today? I've made some scones and the kettle is on. Alex and my favourite little girl in the world are sitting ready to tuck in.'

'Coming, Mam. You start, Molly, but leave one for me!' Eilidh made a face at her cousin. 'You see, nothing changes; she nags me as though I were still thirteen. Hasn't she noticed that I'm a mother too?' She rummaged in her case and pulled out a navy blue turtle neck sweater and a matching pleated skirt. 'You go and placate her while I slip these on. Do you know that since she looked after Anna while we were away on the West Coast, she has managed to spoil her silly and undo all my good work over the past two years?'

'That's grannies for you,' laughed Molly. 'Indulge her, Eilidh; you'll be gone soon enough.'

Eilidh's spirits were infectious the day she registered into the Torn-na-Dee hospital in Aberdeen. She chattered nonstop, giving Alex instructions about Anna's bedtimes, and what magazines to bring when he visited the next morning. She had insisted that Molly stay in the hotel with her parents. 'Please, Molly, you know what Dad's like, he'll go for his solitary walks and poor Mam will be climbing the walls with all sorts of imaginary worries, and I know the hospital frowns on children coming into these wards with all these nasty TB germs, so please keep everyone calm for me.'

Molly looked into her cousin's eyes, searching for any fear about the operation that she was about to undergo, but there was none. 'I'll take care of them, don't you worry; you'll be out before you know it, and if I have my way that little minx of yours will be worn out from all the walks I'm planning!'

Now it was time, and Eilidh gripped Alex's hand as two gowned attendants wheeled her through the corridor. She felt vulnerable as she woozily looked up at her husband's face. 'Don't worry, my darling, I'll be fine, we have so much to look forward to. Take care of Anna for me.'

He squeezed her hand and then bent down to kiss her cheek. He watched the lift doors close and he sighed. Suddenly he was alone.

For the next three days, Eilidh lived in a hazy world of lights and shadows. Nurses tended her and gently administered the drugs necessary for her recovery. Through it all she was aware of the strong hand that held hers, and she struggled to let him know that she knew he was there, but it was an effort to move her fingers and so her hand lay inert in his. On the third day, she was aware of his voice, the low rumble of familiarity as he talked about Malaya and home. But Eilidh was confused; what was he talking about? Home was a river, and a mountain and wild starlings and rowan berries. I want to go home, she thought, and she struggled to mouth the words, but none came. I want to go home, please take me home. Alex looked down at the limp hand in his own. Then he felt it – almost imperceptible. Did he imagine it, the tiny flicker of movement, rather like the dying flutter of a moth's wing?

Chapter 7

2003 – Scotland

Anna struggled with the heavy iron gate, the strap of her bag falling off her shoulder as she finally managed to secure the catch. She was conscious of the silence, disturbed only by her footsteps crunching on the gravel as she walked back to her car. For a moment she turned and looked back at the desolate cemetery. Through the gate she could see the green grassy coverlets on the graves; it was as though she was saying farewell, yet again. She drove back over the moors to Druimfhada and was reassured to see the tall chimney of the distillery and the huddle of workers' cottages nestling around it.

Thankfully Anna drew up to Molly's house, and shutting out a sharp burst of wind and rain, she peeped in at her aunt and felt a rush of affection for the old lady slumped sideways in her chair, the good arm protectively cradling the one rendered useless by the stroke. She might be paralysed down one side, Anna thought, but she's lucky she's got all her other faculties and her memory is as sharp as a tack. Anna decided to make some coffee, so quietly made her way through to the kitchen. She gazed out at the dark shapes of the hills, rounded and threatening, the heavy clouds making the day feel like evening. She contemplated the stormy sky and thought of the graveyard that she had just left: Eilidh McIntyre, Devoted Wife and Mother, the stark grey dyke, the granite headstones, the cold that seeped into the very bones of the living.

Anna took her coffee through to the bedroom and once again opened the lid of the tin box. She rummaged beneath the loose photographs and pulled out a black and silver album. Opening the cover she saw a picture of a bassinet lined with white *broderie anglaise* and a sleeping baby wearing only a nappy. Carefully turning the pages she saw the child in the arms of first one proud parent and then the other. The images changed as the newborn metamorphosed into a little girl with silky white hair and a sturdy brown body. On a blanket laid out on rough jungle grass, the child was playing with a blue-and-white teddy and a brown felt monkey holding a bunch of bananas. Anna's eyes quickly scanned the picture. She was not so interested in the child but more so in the woman who was laughing and holding her. Another showed the same pair but this time the mother was getting a soaking from her toddler who was knee deep in a fountain. Could this be the great feat of engineering that she and Alex had made with their own hands? Anna glanced up as the rain lashed the windowpane, and then turned to the back of the album. A folded piece of paper adorned with violet ink was tucked into the back cover. Inside the letter was a loose photograph of herself with her dad. Wearing black shorts and long white socks, he was pushing her in an old-fashioned pushchair. On his head he wore a hat placed at a rakish angle and he had a silly expression on his face. Written on the back were the words: Your granddaughter and son-in-law, my husband (unfortunately!). Anna smiled. Her mother looked and sounded so happy. Looking back at the album she peered closely at the pictures towards the end of the book. Eilidh was so thin. What had happened to her in that short time? Anna picked up the sheet of paper and read the letter.

Christmas 1955, Bukit Bulan
My darling Mam and Dad,
The house is so quiet now after all the excitement. Anna is asleep and Alex is having forty winks on the sofa (too much brandy I think). We had the most wonderful day and Anna really enjoyed her first proper Christmas. After all, last year she was only two months and slept through most of it! This year she sat amidst the biggest pile of wrapping paper and laughed and laughed at the antics of the cats as they dived in amongst all the tissue. Her lovely presents were forgotten as she watched their high jinks!

The blue-and-white teddy that Uncle Callum gave her last year sat next to her in his own cane high chair during the Christmas dinner! Callum, Jack and Michael came and joined us for the turkey feast and we had such a good day. Our little lady was given some jewellery, a gold charm bracelet from

Callum, and a gold heart locket from Jack. Michael gave her a rocking horse and Alex and I gave her a little trike that she's been pushing all over Cookie's polished floors! Tomorrow we are getting together with our neighbours, Sam and Dorothy, so Anna will have fun learning to share her toys with Lucy!

As usual at this time of day, I think of you, and miss you and wish we could all be together. I long to see you again. Alex has promised that we may be able to go back to Scotland next autumn. My cough has returned and I've been feeling tired, but perhaps it's because of too many late nights and parties.

Goodnight my dears and all my love for now and for the bright new year ahead!

Eilidh

Anna registered the year that the letter had been written: 1955. Looking at the grain on the wardrobe door, she let out a sigh. It was not so difficult to calculate. Eilidh would be dead by the following Christmas. Anna closed the album and put it back into the box. She realised how cold the room was, and shivering she decided to go back and make some more coffee to warm herself up. She tiptoed past her aunt but the old lady opened her eyes and smiled sweetly.

'Well, well,' she said, 'what are you creeping about for? You won't catch me sleeping during the day. I hope you're going to put the kettle on and mind you empty out that old water that's been sitting in it. I can't abide foosty old water, and whilst you're there…'she paused and her blue eyes twinkled through her pink plastic-framed glasses, 'what about a wee dram? Shall we have a wee dram as well, you know, just to cheer us up!'

Anna shuddered involuntarily and went instead to her overnight bag and pulled out a small bottle of Courvoisier she'd purchased for just such an occasion.

Molly, suddenly full of life, rattled out her orders. 'Just reach in and get the bottle of malt from the sideboard. Oh! I see you're having a brandy!' Her eyes lit up with mischief, as though she was a conspirator in a midnight feast. 'Aye you will have that, just like your poor mam, but for me, there's nothing like a good drop of Scottish whisky. I've sworn by it all my life, good for every occasion.' She reached for the sticky glass at her side and passed it awkwardly with her good hand. 'Just put a wee drop of lemonade in with it, dear.'

Anna poured the drinks and sat opposite her enjoying the warmth emanating from the electric fire.

Molly chuckled. 'You've been at that tin box again, haven't you? And you're always raking around in that wardrobe looking at those dresses. I don't know, they've been hanging there for almost fifty years. I suppose you'll be trying them on again in a minute. What a lassie for dresses! Ever since you were a wee thing, it was: "Look at me, Aunty Molly! Do you like this one?"'

'What happened, Aunty Molly, why doesn't anyone ever speak about her? My dad never mentions her. There's always this black wall of silence. She died of TB and that's all I know. Please tell me what happened? How can a woman of twenty-seven vanish? Didn't her life make any impact on anyone?'

'Och, it was sad right enough. Your poor dad was just heartbroken and everyone felt it was best just to let things be. After she died he didn't know what he was going to do, and your granny and granddad begged to have you and so he let you go. He was in no fit state to look after you on his own in Malaya, and the times were dangerous.'

'Didn't they know she was dying?'

'No! It was a great shock. They came home on leave in the summer of 1956 I think it was, and had a grand old time, driving here and driving there. She had the TB right enough but the doctors said she'd be fine if she kept taking the pills.'

'So why?'

'Och, I don't know pet. She wanted more children I think and the doctors in Aberdeen suggested removing the damaged lung. Then she would be rid of the disease and be strong enough to have another baby. It was her; she volunteered to have the operation.'

'So she had it cut out?'

'Aye, that's what they said. I remember going with you and your granny and granddad to Aberdeen. It was the Torn-na-Dee Hospital; it catered for the TB patients in those days.' Lost in her thoughts, Molly picked up her glass and sipped at her whisky. 'I remember Eilidh waving to us as she went up the steps. So bonny she was. She had on a heather-coloured tweed suit and the snow was thick on the ground.'

Molly blinked back the years, suddenly unaware of Anna sitting in front of the fire. It was so easy these days just to drift into the past where her loved ones waited and all their voices floated across her memories. The clock ticked, and the rain continued to batter the window. It was only four o'clock, but the afternoon was already dark.

'And then what, Aunty Molly?'

'She died, pet…'

'Yes, but how? Why?'

'The operation went as well as could be expected. She was wheeled back to her ward and your dad sat with her for three days but she didn't regain consciousness. Only once, he said, she squeezed his hand, but then on the morning of the second of December she was gone.'

The room was quiet except for the ticking of the clock on the mantelpiece. Anna swallowed, her throat tight, and she looked over to the window. The wind continued to howl and the rowan tree pattered against the side of the house. She felt engulfed by a black sadness.

Molly resumed her story as though recalling something from yesterday. 'He came away from the hospital looking like a ghost. His eyes seemed to have fallen back inside his head. When he got back to the hotel he was met by your granny and granddad and I thought your granny's heart was going to break.'

'Oh God, what a dreadful shock.' Anna swirled the remains of the brandy around the glass. 'I suppose they'd all been told that it would work out well?'

'Aye, it was something she wanted to do and she did survive the operation, but it was the complication afterwards that she wasn't strong enough to fight. Aye, it's all chance in this life. You have to live your life to the full while you can, lass, that's all you can do, for you're a long time dead.'

'So she was buried in Glengrianach?' Although she'd heard this part of the story many times, Anna could see Molly's eyes still held that far away expression and she needed to come to the end of her narrative.

'It was a bitterly cold day with snow and hail cutting into our faces. The church was packed. There were even people standing on the pavement outside. Faces from all walks of life, everyone she had ever touched was there. Daisy and her cousins Morven and John Sinclair, he was her first boyfriend, and a whole lot of other school chums. I've never seen such a big funeral. There were folk there that had travelled up from Edinburgh and Dundee and a lot of folk I didn't know, friends of your dad. It's funny but that was the first time I saw Estelle. She was all in black of course, but what hair! As red and curly as leaves at the end of an autumn storm. I asked who she was but nobody seemed to know.' Molly drained her glass and put it on the little table in front of her.

'Estelle was at the funeral?'

'Och, lassie, it was all such a long time ago, why are you so interested now?'

Anna shrugged. In truth, she wasn't sure but she did feel that Estelle held the key. She knew there were untold secrets with links to her own dark place and just maybe she would find answers. Hopefully the contents of the tin box might throw some light on the past and she might finally understand why she'd been ostracised so suddenly and so completely from her home and from her father. She continued to sip her brandy; the fire was hot, the outside storm raged on, yet she felt quite removed. Instead she thought of pain and wounds and scar tissue. Everything fades in time, but sadly, and Anna did know this from bitter experience, the knowledge of what caused the pain lives on. She put her glass down, and stretched her neck in a circular motion, relieving the tension in her spine. Eventually she said, 'I need to know, Aunt Molly, I just need to know – everything.'

The following morning Anna left Druimfhada and drove west over the well-worn roads towards Kyle of Lochalsh. She had promised Aunty Molly that she would try to call in again on the return journey. This time her mission was to visit a family she'd known since she was a child. They used to own the hotel in Druimfhada that had hosted her parents' wedding on that snowy night in February 1953. She drove through the desolate glens where the great mountains soared high and sombre, where rivers gushed and water was turned upwards as the waterfalls suffered the great gusts of the autumn gales. Driving past the welcoming sight of the Cluanie Inn, she saw the mountain ridge outlined against the sky and she could make out each of the seven individual summits. Stags and deer were huddled in the protected enclaves of rock. She turned a corner and there ahead of her were the soaring points of the Saddle. It made her feel so insignificant, yet glowing with the familiar excitement of being back in this wild landscape that she so loved. What did it all matter anyway, Anna thought. Tin boxes and untold stories; life was so fleeting, people's needs basically so biological. The passing on of similar genes just continued the same storyline and each generation created its own truths. Would she have been a different person if her mother had lived? Would Eilidh's guidance have affected her? Would she have made different choices? She did know one thing: She knew that if Eilidh had lived she would not have left her daughter to suffer alone.

At last Anna arrived at Catriona's house, only to be nearly knocked over by a Great Dane.

'Down, Juno! God, Anna, it's years since I saw you last. Don't worry about her, she loves visitors. Worst guard dog I've ever had. Come here and give me a hug.'

Anna stood swaying in her friend's arms, smelling the peat smoke on her Icelandic jumper, and looking down she became aware of the dog's face staring up at them, eyes as big as wet almonds and lolling tongue dripping with expectation. 'She's beautiful, how long have you had her?'

'I got her from a rescue home. She'd been caught up in a messy divorce and was traumatised so I brought her here. Nice and peaceful here isn't it, Juno, my lovely black lady? But come on, come in, how do you like the house? It's just me and my dad; he's gone to Inverness so we'll have some time to catch up before he comes back. You know what he's like, once he sees you he'll be wanting to relive his past and be off down memory lane and we won't get a chance to speak. Come on, let's go in and sit by the fire. Do you want some coffee? Let's put the kettle on.'

Anna leant over to pat the large head and pull a floppy ear. 'I'll be just behind you, I have something to show you,' and she went back to the car to collect the tin box.

'What have you got there?' Catriona asked, pushing magazines and papers aside and placing two steaming mugs of coffee on coasters that must have come from some Middle Eastern country.

'Aunty Molly gave it to me. She thought it was about time she had a clear-out and I thought we might have a look together.' Anna placed the box on the table and lifted the lid.

Immediately the pictures spilled out and Catriona picked up a small black-and-white photo. 'Look at this one! Oh my goodness, Anna, what are they wearing!'

The clock ticked away the hours as the two women sifted through the photographs and exclaimed at the old Highland pictures. In some, Catriona recognised her own mum and dad, and she picked up a photo of Eilidh and Alex standing together with them on the shores of Loch Duich, the very same loch that could be heard lapping at the bottom of Catriona's garden. Anna peered at the writing on the back; it read: October 1956. 'How funny,' she said, 'here we are in the same place fifty years later.' She squinted at the picture and could make out the majestic outline of the range of mountains named The Five Sisters of Kintail.

Later that afternoon when John Sinclair arrived home, he looked at the same photograph and whistled through his teeth. 'Aye, she was a bonny lass. She was always so full of fun. Did you know I used to take her out myself when she lived in Glengrianach and then later worked in Perth all those years ago? I had hopes for us, but she had her heart set on your dad. I admit I was a sad man at their wedding.' He paused, seemingly miles away, then he looked at his daughter. 'Just as well really or else I would never have met my own lovely wife, Isabelle, God rest her soul.'

Catriona smiled. She had heard of their courtship many times.

'Eilidh and Alex stayed friends with us all the same,' John went on. 'They came here on holiday in the autumn; I think it was about 1956. We had some great ceilidhs; Eilidh just loved to dance. Then in the mornings they would go walking in the hills. They left you with your granny in Glengrianach for a couple of weeks whilst they toured about. I remember Estelle came with them that time. She only stayed a couple of nights before getting the bus back down south. That was when Estelle told us that she was married. Poor thing.'

'Married? What do you mean? What are you talking about?' Anna suddenly became alert.

'Well, you know she'd been married before she married your dad?'

'No,' she replied, looking at him accusingly. 'I only know she and my dad married after my mother died. But that was because Estelle's fiancé was killed in Malaya in the Emergency. It was rather romantic really that they both got together.' She hesitated before continuing, 'He's always been very protective towards her.'

John poked the fire, and as though speaking to the flames he said, 'His name was Jack Dunbar.' He made a business of picking up the bucket and shaking on some more coal. The fire hissed and blue swirls of smoke puffed back into the room. He sat back in his chair and made a bridge of his fingers on his chest, enjoying rekindling the memories of days gone by. 'We didn't have a television in those days to entertain us. Instead we would meet up in neighbours' houses; someone would play the fiddle and sometimes we would do a dance. The singing was the best though, and what nights we had with Donald Murdo and Alistair the Goat! The hairs would stand up on the back of my neck when Kathleen Morrison sang *The Mountains of Kintail*. What a beautiful song. You never hear it nowadays.'

'But what about Estelle?' Anna persisted, wanting him to get to the point.

'Well, we'd had a few to drink, and she was dancing a military two step with Willie the Post. Such lovely red hair she had.'

'Go on,' Anna prompted, a touch impatiently.

'Well, let me see, Willie was teasing her and saying how he would like to run away and marry her, and she said well that would be fine, but she was married already!' John let out a laugh at the memory. 'Your mam and dad couldn't believe it. It seems she was married in secret and wore her ring on a chain around her neck. Her husband wasn't permitted to marry you see, because he was only an assistant in those days.'

'Well I never, that sounds very clandestine and romantic, but why did nobody ever tell me Estelle was married? Did Aunty Molly know?'

The old man shrugged and stroked his chin. 'I couldn't say, lass, though I think she might have done. Eilidh and she were very close, always laughing and talking. You know what you girls are like when you get together!' He sat back, smiling at the pictures unfolding in his mind's eye.

Anna looked down at the photos, but sifting through them she could find none of her stepmother. 'How strange that there are no pictures of Estelle.'

'There was a right to-do when Jack was killed and then it came out that he had a wife!'

'I'll bet there was!' Catriona smiled at her friend before getting up

123

and patting her dad's shoulder. 'All this hot passion that went on in your day, you'd think you could have been more tolerant of us when we were young!'

'Maybe it's what I knew that made me worry about you!'

Anna turned her attention again to John Sinclair and asked, 'Where did they go after they left you on their Highland holiday?'

'Well now,' the old man stared down at the rug for a minute, 'let me see, they put Estelle on the bus back to Glasgow, then they drove over to the Isle of Skye, I think that's where they went. I remember standing with Catriona's mother and waving them goodbye. I didn't know that would be the last time I'd see Eilidh. I went to the funeral of course and I held a cord at the burial. God, what a day that was; cold and snowy, everyone bundled up in black coats. The cemetery was frozen and I remember looking about thinking what a sea of sad faces. Your poor father was like a corpse himself.'

After John Sinclair's disclosure about Estelle's previous marriage, the talk drifted from Eilidh's funeral to the death of Jack. It was as though a mantle of cobwebs had been pulled over Anna's box of memories. The light that was Eilidh had been switched off and somehow the sealing of her coffin meant the sealing off of her life. Anna understood that the past was over, but in order for the living to go on, there was a need for the closing of metaphorical doors. She had come to terms with all of that when going through the angst of the teenage years but there had never been anybody willing to answer her questions; there was only a litany of set phrases designed to appease her curiosity. Now suddenly she had found out that Estelle had been married before. Would it have made any difference? Why such a mystery?

Lost in his own reveries, John perused the piles of photos that Catriona passed to him.

Anna couldn't contain herself and reverted back to her forthright self. 'What did happen to Jack? Do you know?'

The old man frowned, as though unwilling to be drawn in. 'A tragedy, lass, that's what it was, just a terrible tragedy.' He looked into the fire. 'I only know that he was shot and that he's buried out there in some graveyard that was set aside for the rubber planters. Your best bet,' he turned to look at Anna directly, 'is to ask one of your dad's old cronies who was there at the time. I presume Alex doesn't speak much about those days, what with the stroke and all that?'

Anna turned away, to avoid his eyes. 'No, he can't.' She glanced down at the dog stretched out in front of the fire. She tried to imagine the hospitals and the police inquiry that must have figured in the drama of long ago. She could visualise the twitchy lace curtains that hid all the gossipy, well-intentioned worthies of the small Scottish town where he came from. But was Jack Scottish? She had no idea. Surely someone must have been privy to the confidences of one of the main players. How could such a furtive relationship have remained so? Something happened that had a direct impact on her life and no one had thought to enlighten her with any information. She did appreciate that much of what happened back in the 1950s might not have been appropriate for a young girl's ears, but surely in later years, someone could have pieced the parts together for her.

Could there be a connection between Anna's own troubled conscience and her stepmother's secret marriage? After all these years, Anna still remembered the feelings of being unworthy, of being a disappointment to her father and to Estelle. The tin box seemed to have prompted an independent inquiry. She felt just a flicker of excitement, as though a symbolic boulder had been moved and as a result she felt a growing sense of optimism. What more would she find?

It was late afternoon when Anna eventually took her leave from Catriona and drove back through the glens to Cluanie, the wind whipping up the spume of the water along the shores of Loch Duich. The autumnal colours were dun and murky. She took in the slippery boulders that formed a sentinel around the tide mark, where only crottle and wild mussels hung on in the face of relentlessly surging waves.

She was confused and upset at John's revelations. She felt that he had been evasive. He'd told her that Estelle had been married to Jack but he would not divulge anything else, only that Eilidh had died and that Jack had been shot. Why did no one speak of it all? She drove on straight past Aunty Molly's. The old lady had made her mother real. She had related stories of a golden life, and had given her the letters to read, letters written in violet ink. Some other time she'd want to hear about the life of her mother as a girl but for now her heart seemed to be full of heavy stones. Anna had wanted to touch and feel Eilidh, to find and understand the woman who had worn the dresses. She wanted to know how her own life might have been had her mother lived. Instead, in spite of all the years that had passed, she still felt a keen loss and a continuing sense of abandonment.

Approaching the Spean Bridge, Anna fiddled with the radio and tuned in to Classic FM just in time for the thundering chords of the finale of a Rachmaninov symphony to come to its shattering conclusion. Then she felt the familiar warmth steal over her as the ripples of Smetana's *Vltava* quietly began its metaphorical journey through Czechoslovakia. She hummed along with the music, her mind leaping with the stream trickling round the rocks before passing a colourful gypsy wedding.

Unconsciously her thumb fiddled with her own wedding ring. What would Duncan think of her quest? He, who lived for the present and yet was always in pursuit of the past; he, who spent his days unearthing treasures and shipping home the exotic artefacts from distant shores to their shop in Edinburgh. She pictured his face, his deep brown eyes, hooked nose and hair that was now silver at the temples. How she loved his slow, considered way of speaking before finally answering a question, so typical of the West Coast Highlander. He was passionate about everything, yet so down to earth and cynical. Anna could just imagine him now, poised on a hilltop with his eyes screwed up and narrowed, focussing into the binoculars. 'Well, if it isn't a capercaillie, look at that! And still with its winter coat on!' Although he hailed from a small, tight-knit community on the Morven peninsula, the couple had chosen to marry in far-off Thailand. Two friends they knew in Phuket had witnessed the signing of their names in the register. It was a good choice. No relatives. Oh my goodness, listen to me, she thought, I am still bitter, even after all these years. Most of the time, she had been quite clever at hiding the sense of abandonment she experienced as a child: the loneliness in boarding school, the desperation and need to feel like other girls, the covering up and the lies to explain the dramatic exclusion from the family, the summer holidays that were only perfunctory visits, the isolation in an already isolated community. Still, today was a breakthrough. She twisted in her seat, relieving the pressure on her back, and felt almost optimistic. Well, well, well! She smiled in spite of herself. So Estelle had been married before! And who was this Jack? What did it all mean?

Chapter 8

August 1955 – Ainsley Kirk, Scotland

Estelle Williams rushed about, smoothing the candlewick bedspread for the hundredth time and checking her face in the mirror whenever she rounded the dressing table. She'd pulled her hair down into a clasp at the nape of her neck but the bright red curls sprang free each time she moved her head. She ran to the window to look at the empty street.

'You're wearing out the carpet,' Jess, her younger sister muttered from the adjoining twin bed. 'Just be patient for once in your life.'

'It's all very well for you, lying there in a heap of bedclothes without a care in the world, but supposing he doesn't come? Supposing Mum and Dad find out where I've really gone this week?' and she ran again to the window. 'Supposing Fiona calls from Inverness when I've gone and they find out that I'm not really visiting her?'

'Supposing, supposing, supposing! Stop it, Estelle, just calm down.'

'I think I've got everything, and you will cover for me? Do you promise, Jess?'

'Oh for goodness' sake, this is really annoying me now. You're only going away for a few days, what's the big deal?'

Sighing deeply, Estelle sat down by her case and tapped her long fingernails on the handle.

'Stop that,' Jess snapped, 'just take a deep breath; he'll be here in a minute.'

Estelle stood up and smoothed the indent from the bedspread and then leant towards the mirror and tried to tame another flyaway curl back behind her ear. Oh Jack, she thought, where are you? Please don't have cold feet. She looked at the framed photograph of him beside her bed. He was wearing his graduation robes from the University of Aberdeen, the most handsome man she had ever seen in her life. For the

127

last year-and-a-half they'd been a couple, even though he'd spent most of those in far-off Malaya. How she'd cried and even once slapped him in rage when he told her he wanted to be a rubber planter. 'How can you? What's wrong with you?' she wailed, choking back the tears. 'You have everything here, your dad's farm, your friends and your family, not to mention me. What about me? Don't you love me at all?' But he did go, and she had no choice but to carry on with her life, working at the bank, living with her parents and going out at weekends with her sister and friends. There was a certain mystique however, having a boyfriend who was not only glamorous to look at but was not afraid to work in a country at war with the communists. Letters flew across the continents, and Estelle kept the pile of blue airmails tied with a green ribbon. Each word was memorised and soon she grew familiar with the people and estates that made up her fiancé's life.

It had come as a surprise when a month ago she heard of the sudden death of Jack's father. The news spread around the village and Estelle's heart almost flipped with anticipation for she knew Jack would have to come home! She paid no heed to the rumours circulating about what would happen to the large Dunbar property, and after making a perfunctory visit to Jack's mother and shedding a tear or two for her loss, she galloped home in a fever, knowing that Jack would be returning on the next available flight.

And now, the funeral was over and Jack had arranged with the lawyers for the farm to be sold. His mother had moved in with her sister to a small cottage on the outskirts of Ainsley Kirk. After settling these family matters he'd taken her for dinner.

'Are you still my girl?'

'You know I am.' She'd taken his hand across the table and kissed each of his finger tips.

'I can't wait, Estelle, I don't want to wait any longer.' His tanned face accentuated the blueness of his eyes.

Lowering her lashes, she was uncertain if he was suggesting a room in a hotel, and if he was, she knew she would certainly agree to go. His presence was making her weak at the knees.

'Marry me now.'

'But...'

'We can keep it secret for the next eighteen months until I get promoted, then you can come out and join me as my wife. What do you say?'

And she'd said yes! It was the most wonderful feeling in the world. She'd spent the days and nights since walking on air, singing love songs and dreamily washing plates twice. Her family put all this romantic nonsense down to Jack's return, having no inkling of what was really on the girl's mind. Now, it was all arranged and only her sister knew the true significance of Estelle's elation. The couple were going to Perth today, the registry office was booked and in only two more hours she would be Mrs Jack Dunbar, but where was he? Oh please don't let him have changed his mind. Estelle was on the verge of tears when at last the sisters heard the soft purr of an engine and Jack pulled up outside the council house.

'He's here,' shrieked Estelle, 'come and give me a kiss, Jess, and wish me luck.'

Jess reached beneath the bed and came up holding a posy of red roses. She stood up and hugged her sister and handed her the flowers. 'Go on now, have a wonderful time. I'll be thinking of you at two o' clock!'

Estelle Dunbar stood at the side of the loch laughing at her elegant husband balancing on a boulder in the water. 'Come back, Jack! If you fall in, that jacket will be ruined!'

'And what about me, do you not care about me? Is it just the jacket that you are worried about?'

'Well it is a beautiful jacket!'

He jumped nimbly over the rocks and took her hand and ran up the loose shingle. 'Come on then, Mrs Dunbar, we'll have to buy you one as well, so that when I leave I'll know that you are as well turned out as your dashing husband!'

He enclosed her in his arms, crushing her small frame against the rough texture of the blue Harris Tweed. They had been married for only four days, the ceremony quiet with just two witnesses to sign the register. Now they wandered hand-in-hand past glorious pastel-shaded lupins standing to attention like multicoloured swords. They manoeuvred around prickly gorse bushes, the yellow flowers emitting an aroma reminiscent of coconut. Tramping cautiously past clumps of stinging nettles, they emerged upon open land where sheep and horses grazed together. Assailed by yet more overgrown vegetation, they waded through a sea of frothy cow parsley. August saw the mountains blazing purple with bell heather; the rivers ran full with trout and salmon. It was a honeymoon of magic. They sat eating venison and beef in quaint hotels and slept in rooms with wallpaper depicting regimented patterns of strawberries. They lay in such places marvelling at the silence and the clear skies, and the awesome thing that they had just done.

They took the winding road north to Inverness and it was there that they saw a small jewellery shop nestling under the castle beside the fast flowing River Ness.

'I would like a gold chain please,' Jack asked the assistant.

'And I would like a gold heart locket,' Estelle added.

The plump lady wheezed and bent over the tray and produced the trinkets. She placed a fine chain into Estelle's hand, where it slithered into a ball.

Jack looked at it and said simply, 'It will do. Now let us see the lockets.' He deliberated over two and finally selected one that opened to hold miniature portraits. 'Do you like this one?'

Estelle's head tilted to the side, 'I do,' and she smiled.

'Very well, we'll take this one please.'

Their selections were packed into little red boxes and a white paper bag.

They stepped outside and Estelle laughed. 'You are the most efficient shopper I have ever seen! Is that how you always choose?'

'Come here, I want to hold you. I want us to remember this moment. Let me look at you. I am going to look at your eyes and your skin and listen to you laugh, and then I shall buy my beautiful wife a warm woolly coat for the winter!'

The next morning they drove west and sat by Loch Ness in the ruins of the old Urquhart Castle. The waters lapped at their feet and they waved to some men on a fishing boat chugging round the headland. Estelle wiped her face as the wind whipped up the spray.

'It's only for eighteen months, Estelle, maybe less if I am promoted before that, and then you will be with me forever.'

She looked down at the simple wedding ring on her finger and knew that she could wear it there for only four more days. Their marriage was secret, he had violated his contract; not even his mother knew what they'd done. She knew that when they returned to Ainsley Kirk she would wear her ring on the golden chain he'd bought for her and it would hang hidden alongside the locket containing his beloved face. 'Come on, my darling, let's get going, we have a ferry to catch!' she shouted, not wanting to linger in such a melancholy frame of mind.

They continued through the valley of Glenshiel where the high peaks of the Kintail Mountains towered above them and the sun cast dappled shadows on slopes lush with ripe bracken. Sheep huddled at the foot of tall Scotch pines and overhead the golden eagle soared, defying man to climb the rocky peaks. At Kyle of Lochalsh the rain resumed, and eventually they made the ferry crossing to Kyleakin and drove on to the island. Skye lay under a blanket of cloud, midges plagued them and the drizzle seeped into their coats. Hotel waitresses with stringy hair and a sour attitude served them with unimaginative meals. 'They're not going out of their way to attract customers,' Estelle grumbled after requesting a bread roll with her soup. 'There's no bread till Wednesday, that's when the ferry comes from Mallaig,' had been the surly reply.

Jack's optimism and good humour helped to distract Estelle from her downward spiral of misery. The days were slipping by and soon they would have to part, but he was determined to enjoy this stolen time. By contrast, his new wife seemed to enjoy her depression and instead of seeing the beauty of the towering grandeur of the Cuillins looming out of the mist, she complained that they would have been better seen on a sunny day after a good meal.

'You are not a poet, my love!' Jack laughed at her, and wrapped her in his arms and felt the silky curls and knew that his heart was breaking.

In the early hours before dawn of their last day, Jack eased himself out of Estelle's embrace and made his way to the window where he pulled over a chair and sat gazing at the outline of rocks on the shoreline. Only the wash of the tide broke the silence of the sleeping village. He sat holding his head in his hands. If Estelle had woken she would have seen her husband bent over in grief, his father's memory suddenly present in the room like a great yawning absence. Images clearer than any photograph pasted into the family album overwhelmed him, as though the older man's voice, sharp and crusty, was calling to his dogs across the brow of the hill on a summer morning. He could almost hear the peewits crying out, before circling and diving, full of the joy of being alive. Jack's brow creased, remembering the pain he'd caused his beloved father. He could see again the look of bewilderment on his face when he announced he was going to the University of Aberdeen.

'Why, for God's sake, what more do you need to know to run this place? It's just a waste of time, I need you here now. It's enough that you can read and write and count, it was enough for me and your mother and we haven't done too badly.'

Avoiding his father's eyes, Jack looked down at the tiny shoots of green battling through the hard clods of earth, rough and uneven from last autumn's ploughing. The panorama of fields stretched ahead of him, as far as the eastern hills and down to the woods to the west. His father had farmed these fields for a quarter of a century and saw the farm as his legacy to his son and future generations. He'd said, and Jack would never forget his words, 'What can be more important than the land?'

It was his mother who persuaded old Ian Dunbar to relent. Always the mediator between her strong-willed husband and equally stubborn son, she paved the way for Jack to have his three years of academic pursuit. At that time neither parent could have foreseen the change of direction that would eventually take their son to the Far East.

Sitting in the gloom of the hazy street lamp, watching smoke-like tendrils of mist rise from the sea, Jack cringed inwardly at the memory of those turbulent few weeks before his departure. He turned from the window, hearing a long sigh as though Estelle was dreaming and stirring in her sleep. He couldn't believe he was married and sitting here in this small hotel on the Isle of Skye. From cycling through the jungle on laterite roads, and smelling the acrid aromas of curry rising in clouds of steam, his eyes now focussed on the sucking pull of the cold tide on this remote Scottish beach. Memories were lingering in his mind and he was unwilling to let them go. It was an indulgence, he thought, like revisiting old friends. But that was the past and he preferred looking to the future. I wonder what's next, he thought, what does fate have planned for me in these next few years? And what of Estelle? He'd met her by accident, literally. He sat back in the chair and let the images play like a film show in his head, and as he had done on many a lonely night on the rubber estate, he conjured up the day he'd bumped into her. He was home for the summer break after his second year in Aberdeen, and was in the village of Ainsley Kirk running errands for his mother. Laden with boxes, he didn't see the young woman, also heavily laden with parcels and heading straight for him like a red meteor. The impact was dramatic. The collision was head on and boxes and parcels fell about in all directions.

She'd started to wail as she tried to find one particular parcel, 'Oh look what you've done, you great clumsy oaf! Could you not have moved over? My clock, my beautiful carriage clock! I got it from my granny and was just getting it fixed and now you've broken it into a million pieces!'

'Excuse me,' retorted Jack indignantly, 'I think you've got the wrong end of the stick. Have you never heard of looking where you're going? You were the one charging down the street as though on a mission to annihilate my shopping.'

He looked at her appraisingly, and his annoyance melted as he saw the comical side of the situation. She stood there in front of him, angry, flashing eyes and a head of red curls. Her skin was white and as smooth as clotted cream. His eyes ran down her petite frame clad in a summer dress, the colour of a warm green sea. A bright orange scarf at her neck contrasted wildly and set off her furiously coloured hair.

'Look, I'm sorry. Maybe I should have seen you. The least I can do is help you pick up the parcels; why don't you come and have a pot of tea with me at that shop across the road?' She continued to look mutinous, but he persisted, his voice deep and persuasive, 'I'm sorry about your clock, why don't you let me look at it and we'll see what can be done?'

'Oh very well...I suppose I've got half an hour to spare,' she scowled ungraciously.

Jack grinned at her as he knelt on the street. 'And do you have a name?' he asked gallantly.

'Estelle Williams,' she replied, and her voice took on an air of importance. 'I work in the bank on the High Street, you know, and I only have an hour for my lunch break and we've wasted ten minutes already.'

'We'd better get going then,' he said briskly. 'I'm Jack Dunbar, by the way.' He held out his hand and smiled in what he hoped was a beguiling manner.

Estelle hesitated for just a second before placing her long thin fingers into his smooth palm.

'My father has Rollings Farm,' he informed her as they crossed the street together, 'just a mile out of town.' Immediately her green eyes flashed, weighing up this piece of information, as though registering him in a *Who's Who* guide of the area. He chuckled at how transparent she was and went on, 'I'm at university at Aberdeen, home for the summer though.'

'Oh, are you not going to take over your father's farm then?'

'Who knows? I probably will eventually, but I prefer to let the future take care of itself.'

Now looking over at his sleeping wife, Jack thought of their subsequent courtship. His last year at Aberdeen had been tumultuous, combining cramming for his finals and placating an impatient Estelle. Their relationship that year was akin to a firecracker, with frenzied meetings that left them both weak with unsated passion. When at last the graduation ceremony arrived, both father and girlfriend smiled conspiratorially at each other. Ian Dunbar wanted his son and heir back in his rightful place on the farm, whereas Estelle wanted to start a life of perfect wedded bliss. Jack looked to his mother for respite, and saw her eyes wet with tears.

'Oh come on, Mother, come here!' and he encircled her in his arms.

'You know I'm so proud of you, son, you look so clever and handsome in your black gown and mortarboard. I can't believe you've graduated with honours from such a grand university.' She looked back at the exquisitely carved stone façade of the Marischal College. 'You must do what you want to do, my boy. Take your time, don't make any hasty decisions.'

'Thank you, Mother, it means a lot you saying that, because there is something I want to do first.' He walked with her a little apart from the other two and said, 'You know I'll always come back to the farm, and I will be there if you or Dad ever need me, but Dad is still in his prime. He's as strong as a Clydesdale and I reckon he'll go on for years. It's Estelle that I'm worried about. Do you think she'll wait for me?'

'She loves you, dear, we can all see that, but what is it you're planning to do? I'm very intrigued.'

'Not now, Mother, I'll tell you and the old man, but all in good time.'

*

134

Massaging his forehead as though trying to erase a persistent pain, Jack recalled the day he'd told his father of his plans of going to Malaya. They'd been up in the north field checking the fencing. All had to be secure as Ian Dunbar had just purchased a mighty Aberdeen Angus bull at considerable expense.

'It has to service all our stock and then be hired out to the neighbouring farmers at a price. I think it should be a grand investment.' His father looped his thumbs behind his braces and stuck out his chest, 'I'm a lucky man having you come back to me after your sojourn at the university.'

Jack stood firm and in a level voice told his father, 'I'm going to Malaya, Dad. I've signed up for three years as a rubber planter's assistant.'

'What! You've done what? After all I've done for you, after building up this farm for you, you're going to throw it all away? Is that what all my sacrifice and hard work has been for? I never thought it would come to this.' The tirade that followed made Jack fear for his father's health, for the old man raged at what he saw was a premeditated act of defiance on his son's part. No words could soothe his wrath, and for the next few days the two men lived in stony silence. It was the father that relented first, overcome by curiosity and much persuasion from his long-suffering wife, and the matter had ended as all arguments did in the Dunbar household, with a grudging harmony brought about by her subtle diplomacy.

Jack's throat felt tight as his memories took him to the day of his departure for Malaya, the subsequent years spent as the assistant on Bukit Bulan Estate, and the close relationship that he'd formed with Alex and Eilidh McIntyre. His life in the tropics seemed so far away. His inner thoughts returned to the bleak winter parklands, the collie dogs running over the furrowed fields, and his father's face, hardened by the cruel North Sea winds. He could see the blue eyes, the steady gaze, the lined indentations that cut deep into his cheeks from nose to chin. Now he was gone, buried in the cemetery at Ainsley Kirk, and with his passing the opportunity to marry Estelle had presented itself. He recalled the image of her saying yes, so demure in the restaurant, chastely looking at him from under those long feathery lashes. But after the meal the firecracker returned in all her glory and Jack marvelled at her audacity when she pulled him off the street into a narrow passageway and literally flew into his arms, covering his face with hundreds of kisses, and immediately began setting out plans for their secret wedding.

Estelle stirred again in the bed, and he could see her arm searching for him in the empty space where he'd lain. Silently he padded over and climbed in again beside her. He pulled her into his arms and started kissing her softly on her eyes and down the curves of her neck and shoulder. Then gently and rhythmically he caressed her soft, velvety breasts.

All too soon the honeymoon was over and Jack returned to Malaya. The months slipped by but it was no comfort for Estelle to know that she had a husband on the other side of the world. Only her sister knew her secret but she was a poor companion. Meanwhile Jess had started dating Bob Brown from the Ironmonger's and had few thoughts for anyone other than herself and Bob. Estelle had little opportunity to voice her fears about the troubles in Malaya, so lonely and forlorn all she could do was worry. Now it was Christmas and she found herself resenting other couples, so happy and carefree, window shopping and laughing with the expectation of being together. On a frosty Saturday morning she walked down the street, wrapped in her navy Harris Tweed coat. Her high heels clicked on the pavement and her gloved hands held the silk scarf at her throat. Her ring was warm on her chest. She had just been to the post office where she had sent a small package to Jack. It held the locket that he had bought for her in August.

Ainsley Kirk, Scotland, December 1955
My dearest Jack,
I am sending you this to give to little Anna for Christmas. I know it was a gift from you to me but I already have the golden ring for eternity. It is enough. Give the locket to Alex and Eilidh's child and in this way you will have a part of us in your day to day life. I want you to watch her grow and see in the months that pass a time when I shall be with you and be able to share your life.

I saw your mother on the street last week. She is looking well and politely asked after my health!

Take care my dearest Jack. I pray for you and think of you every single day. I send a kiss with all my love, Estelle

*

Another year passed, and Jack and Estelle wrote regularly, the blue airmail letters crossing the ten thousand miles that separated them. They kept abreast with happenings in their lives and Estelle soon became familiar with the news and gossip that Jack took pleasure in recounting. She was looking forward to meeting Jack's friends, the McIntyres. They were due on leave in October and had promised to look her up. Jack had insisted that she must pretend that they were only engaged to be married.

Bukit Bulan Estate, October 1956
My beloved Estelle,
I am writing this sitting on the veranda with a cold bottle of beer. Cookie and I are here on our own. Amah has taken a well-earned rest now the family has gone back to Scotland. She has returned to her kampong near Taman Minyak. I have Sinbad at my feet. He is staring at me with his big, sad eyes, yet his ears are cocked and his tail is wagging; he imagines that I shall take him for a walk. I will of course but not just yet.

You should be with me, my darling. The sun has set, and over the rubber trees you can see the flying foxes swooping in the dusk. I normally shoot them because they're a nuisance and eat the young palm nuts, but with the recent murders of Tim and Angus Robertson we are all a bit sensitive to the sound of gunfire. I'm so happy that you have met Alex and Eilidh and little Anna. I know that Eilidh will be a good friend to you when you eventually come out. I have been keeping busy, going to KL a couple of times and I play golf every Thursday and Sunday. Otherwise my days are fairly routine and I'm getting to grips with running an estate.

Christmas is approaching fast. Last year you sent the locket. This year I want you to send me a picture of yourself. I need to look at you and see the freshness of your face. We have been married for fourteen months and I miss you more than you can imagine. Tonight I look out at this garden and try to picture you here. It drives me insane with longing.

Yours always, Jack

Chapter 9

April 1957 – Malaya

Eilidh's death affected not just Alex, but Callum, Michael and Jack as well. Each man felt the deep loss of her vibrancy and joy. The house she'd shared with her husband and baby daughter took on the air of an empty carapace. When Alex returned in April after his home leave, he looked about the rooms in dismay. He expected to hear Anna's cry from upstairs, a footstep, Eilidh's voice. The days drifted by and he threw himself into his work, but when he returned she was there. The bungalow, the pools of light falling on the Persian rugs, the rattan recliner, it all brought her back. 'Beer, Cookie, bring me more beer!' and he slumped down in his chair to savour the cold, bitter taste. Only the fan and the sharp croak of a bullfrog broke the silence. He looked around the pleasant room and saw all the treasures she'd insisted on buying. He knew he should clear some of it away. Leaning over to a carved nest of tables, he picked up a lacquer box and immediately his mind seemed to shimmer with an image of the sea and a market stall that had caught her eye.

'Oh look, Alex! It's so beautiful; I can keep all my needles and thimbles in it.'

'More rubbish, more things to dust and insure and pack up when we go. You can't take all this nonsense with you, Eilidh,' he'd growled.

Christ, he thought, look at me, sitting here drinking beer every night, drowning myself in misery. She'd be so ashamed of me. Squeezing his eyes, he tried to shut out the pain of his loss. The rumble of wheels on the driveway jerked him back to the present and he saw a jeep pull up at the porch. It was Dorothy Bathgate.

'Alex, how are you? I heard you were back and I just wanted to say...' It was then she registered his face and the object in his hands. 'Oh my dear,' she said gently, 'perhaps I can help?'

Alex nodded, 'I can't do it. She's still here with me, I can feel her. I thought I could clear out some of her things but I get stuck over each trinket. I see her face everywhere I go, she's in every room.'

'It's natural, Alex, you've suffered so much. I could help pack up some of her things if you want?'

'Would you mind? I can get the contractor on the estate to make some boxes up. I want everything to go. I just need to put the pain away.'

Dorothy walked over to him and put her arms around him, 'Don't worry, Alex, you're not alone. I'll come back tomorrow when you're at work, and Cookie and Amah can help me.'

Dorothy spent the next few days folding clothes and boxing up Anna's toys and Eilidh's precious ornaments before packing them into wooden crates for shipping home to Eilidh's parents in Glengrianach.

Alex wandered amidst the debris, lifting up pots of lotion and perfume from the dressing table, sniffing the familiar scent. 'Alex! We must buy more hangers. Look at all my dresses, and where shall we put your shirts? We'll hang your trousers in the spare room!' Now rows of empty wooden hangers hung dejectedly alongside his clothes which he'd duly reinstated into the master bedroom. Downstairs the lounge became a Spartan place of rugs and cane furniture. No feminine fripperies, no toys or magazines littered the coffee tables. The light that was Eilidh had gone out.

'It says "Drinks and Curry Tiffin", so what do you think? Free booze and a decent meal, and old Roger's a good sort. It's this Sunday and we've all been invited.' Michael Parrish sat down with the invitation in his hand and looked over at his two housemates, Jack Dunbar and Callum McIntyre.

'Do you think Alex might go as well? It's four months now since Eilidh's death, he might be glad of a diversion to take his mind off things.'

Jack shrugged and continued cleaning his rifle. 'He'll go for the beer, if nothing else.'

Michael padded through the house in his socks which were thickly coated in grass seed. Hassina brought in a pot of coffee and he waited until she'd refilled their cups before handing her his socks. She nodded her head and withdrew silently.

'I hear Rog has his planting adviser here for a visit. That would explain the sudden burst of entertaining!'

'I could do with a good curry,' Callum said indistinctly through a mouthful of salted peanuts. 'Alex won't take much persuading to join us, that's for sure.'

'Come on, Jack, leave that wretched gun alone for five minutes, the bullets will whiz through the barrel without you pulling the trigger at this rate, you've put that much oil in it.'

Jack and Michael were back sharing the house with Callum, after both assistants had spent some time as acting managers. Michael had been covering for Angus after his death, and Jack had enjoyed his stint of running Bukit Bulan for Alex whilst he had been away on leave. It was hard returning to assistant status after their spell of management, and they found the atmosphere stifling. The years were dragging on, and they all desperately wanted their own estates to give more meaning to their lives.

When Sunday arrived, Alex drove over to collect his brother and Jack and Michael. All four men were dressed in white shorts and white Aertex shirts, black shoes and long white socks. Michael settled himself in the back with Callum. 'OK old boy, on to the curry!' He wound up the window as the car purred over the red laterite roads, sending up rolling clouds of dust. The estate road meandered beneath the shadows of the tree canopy. The blue sky above was completely obliterated from view. They travelled over hills and round deep ravines until they joined up with the main road heading south towards Kuala Selangor. Alex drove fast and with calm assurance, taking the bends with skill. The countryside slipped past, and apart from the odd herd of bullocks, the road was deserted. At last they came to Anak Kamsiah Estate, and when the estate road eventually led them out of the gloom of the rubber and on to the driveway of the manager's bungalow their eyes had to adjust to the lush green lawns that swept down from the imposing two storey house. The driveway curved around a tall bamboo hedge that shielded the swimming pool, complete with a native attap palm hut bedecked with rattan bar and wooden sun loungers.

'Oh yes, this would suit me very well,' Michael laughed. He could just imagine himself relaxing after a hot sweaty day, spreadeagled on a lilo in the middle of the pool and drinking an ice-cold beer.

The four men clambered out of the car and, stretching their long legs, they strolled over to the porch.

'Hellooo!' It was Freya, Roger Grant's young, vivacious and very attractive wife. They looked up towards the welcoming, cool interior and she clattered down the steps in her high heels, clutching a flute of champagne. 'Hellooo! So good of you all to come, you must be gasping. Lovely to see you, Alex. Oh God, it's so hot out here. Come in and have a drink, lunch won't be too long. Lots of people you know.' Freya was gay and vibrant and as she talked she presented her smooth flushed cheek to each of the men, then she clattered back up the stairs in a cloud of lemon silk.

'Well, let's go,' grinned Michael and he led the way into the house. There was a bee-like hum of conversation interspersed with a raucous laugh and then Roger tottered over and amiably greeted them. He too held on tightly to his glass, half full of gin and tonic.

'Good to see you, lads, just you make yourselves at home, drinks over there.'

Alex walked over to the table that ran parallel to the back wall and asked the white-clad Chinese servant for a beer.

'Aaaah, I needed that! That is so good!' Alex gasped as he took a long draught from the chilled glass, his eyes closing in pleasure at the instant cooling effect. Turning round, he found himself looking into the pale, watery eyes of his host. Beside him stood a small, wiry man, totally bald and peering through a tight-fitting pair of round spectacles. There was an air of the comic duo about the pair and Alex suppressed a laugh as he looked at them over the rim of his glass.

'Alex McIntyre, Andrew Cruikshank, my planting adviser. Alex is over at Bulan, you know?'

'Pleased to meet you, Alex. I think we did meet before at Angus Robertson's funeral. Bad business that. Hope you travel with guards when you do your payroll run? Still risky, even though the troubles have died down somewhat.'

'Yes, sir, we still keep all arms in good working order.'

'Good man.' He patted Alex on the shoulder. 'Sorry about your loss, Alex. TB is a terrible thing. Please accept my sympathy.' He coughed to cover his embarrassment at the personal turn of the conversation. 'Very good then,' and he cleared his throat as he glanced around the room, 'I was actually hoping to have a word with Mike Parrish, he came with you did he not?'

'He did, sir, I see him over there, and if I'm not mistaken, he's regaling those ladies with stories of his attempts at sailing off the coast of Cornwall!'

Andrew walked over to the group just in time to hear Freya say, 'You'll have to teach us next time we go to Port Dickson. I would love to learn,' and she giggled as she drained her glass. Seeing the planting adviser, she took off to the kitchen to supervise Cookie and give orders for lunch to be served as soon as possible. She was definitely feeling the effects of too much alcohol on an empty stomach. The other ladies moved away, leaving traces of Chanel and Joy in their swish of silk.

'Hello, sir, how are you? We heard that you were paying a visit.'

'I'm very well, Michael, very well indeed. Rubber prices are on the increase and with this new Malayan government, I think we may be heading for a period of stability. When I'm through with the accounts here at Anak Kamsiah, I'm going on to Sungei Harimau Estate. How are you getting on with Gilbert Dawson?'

'All right, sir, he's a good man. He's done a fine job since Angus was killed.'

Both men sipped their drinks as they looked around the room. The name of Angus Robertson was on both their minds. The memory of the bloody murder was still fresh in everyone's memory, especially Michael's as he recalled that horrendous morning when he'd found the body of his manager slumped against the bedroom wall.

'We're very pleased at the way you stepped into the breach until Gilbert took over. I know your three-year probation is up but head office in London has put your name forward for consideration for another acting manager's job while Ian Hancock is on leave. I've talked it over with Roger today, and we want to transfer you to Bukit Hijau Estate. It'll be very close to Anak Kamsiah Estate so Roger will be able to keep an eye on you. What do you say?'

Michael's mouth spread into a wide grin and then he took hold of the older man's hand and shook it vigorously. 'Thank you, sir, that's excellent! Excellent news, thank you!'

'We have a lot of faith in you, Michael. I'll be sending you the written contract this week but I imagine you would be in Bukit Hijau by the beginning of June.'

Roger rejoined the pair and his eyes twinkled as he shook Michael's hand. 'Well done, old boy! We shall be neighbours. Freya! Freya come here for a minute and stop dashing about like a giddy filly. Young Michael Parrish here is coming to our neck of the woods. Get me another gin, girl; must have another before tiffin, what?'

'Oh, Michael, that's wonderful news!' exclaimed Freya, struck by the disparity in the appearance of the three men in front of her. There was her elderly and already tipsy husband with his generous paunch, wide baggy shorts and thin freckly legs. She saw his pale blue eyes and blotchy scalp with a faint covering of baby-fuzz like orange fluff: She sighed deeply. She moved on to the small figure of the planting adviser. His whole manner exuded earnestness, and one's attention was drawn hypnotically to his too-large eyes which were magnified by his thick-lensed glasses to look like gobstoppers: Hmmm, he reminded her of a cartoon character. Her gaze then moved to the third man. Michael's tall frame epitomised youthful energy. His broad shoulders and floppy dark brown hair gave him a debonair look and his eyes twinkled, full of fun as though he was about to say something outrageous: Yes, this man was interesting, without a doubt. Her eyes were drawn to his mouth and she smiled at him, and in return he grinned enigmatically, sensing something she hadn't yet identified. She realised the three men were waiting for her to speak so she quickly coughed and cleared her throat. 'Yes, that's wonderful! I'm so happy for you, Michael. I'm looking forward to getting to know you better. You must come and swim; after all you'll be living just down the road.' She couldn't look into his eyes, choosing instead to study her empty glass. 'Oh,' she shrugged, 'the responsibilities of a hostess, I must go and see what's what. Lunch will be ready very soon!'

'I suppose you've heard the news?' Alex asked Jack as the two men spooned chutney and *ikan bilis* on to the side of their heaped plates.

'About Michael? Yes, I just heard. He's like a kid with all the conkers. Good for him though, he's had a tough time after that business with poor Angus. Funny, he was just saying how he'd like a swim in that pool in the garden; no doubt Freya will be inviting him over, lucky bastard.'

'Aye and I'll just get myself another beer,' Alex muttered, sidling over to the bar.

Jack watched him, a line of concern between his eyes; the man was never without a drink these days. Ach, it's none of my business, he thought as he helped himself to another *puri*. Clutching his plate and cutlery wrapped in a paper napkin, he made his way over to the lounge and made himself comfortable on a rattan chair. He placed his beer on a linen coaster beside him and inhaled pleasurably as the aromas of the different curries wafted up like a spiral ribbon of spicy mist. Sighing deeply he looked over at the ladies gossiping like a flock of silky butterflies and he imagined his own beautiful wife sitting there amongst them. Her image was etched on his mind; he could conjure her up at will and suddenly he was back in Scotland: Estelle was laughing, her head thrown back, her red curls soft around her face. She was framed by a regiment of tall multi-coloured lupins growing by the loch.

'Hi, Jack, do you mind if I join you?'

'Of course, Dorothy. Where's Lucy?'

'She's having a nap, thank goodness. She had a swim earlier and Cookie gave her some soup and a banana and now she's sleeping. At last I have a chance to eat!'

Jack chuckled. He enjoyed her company; she never quizzed him about his private life or made jabs about him looking for a wife. They ate in companionable silence, and when they'd finished, Aminah, the Malay *amah,* cleared the plates quietly and efficiently. She loaded her tray and smiled shyly. Jack stared for a moment at her purple-saronged figure weaving its way through the various groups of people before disappearing through the swing door into the kitchen.

'You look like a satisfied sahib,' Dorothy laughed.

'I am that,' he grinned, leaning back in his chair and stretching luxuriously.

It was a very good curry lunch, everyone agreed as much. It was an occasion that would be remembered by everyone as an oasis of peace, a tranquil moment just before a storm. The guests chattered or discussed business or tennis or golf or their families. The children enjoyed the freedom of a lazy afternoon. Fans turned; beer and gin and champagne provided the social lubrication to guarantee a convivial atmosphere. Roger and his pretty young wife were relaxed and uninhibited hosts and everyone had gone home a little drunk and full of bonhomie. After the pots and glasses were washed and glinting in the moonlight of the kitchen, the servants finally retired and the house creaked in the silence. The night reclaimed the gardens; only shadowy shapes suggested the clumps of canna lilies and lime bushes and the tall silhouettes of the flame trees.

On the balcony of Freya's bedroom, Roger stood with his arm around his wife's slender shoulders. 'I don't suppose...?'

'No, dear, not tonight.'

'I thought...maybe you're right, bit tight eh? Not tonight.'

He retreated, leaving Freya alone. Involuntarily she shuddered. She stood framed in the doorway for a few more minutes, her eyes looking but seeing nothing. Finally she too retreated and slowly unzipped her dress and let it fall in a shimmer of soft whispers at her feet.

Over the next few days Jack went about the estate in a gloom. His usual suave demeanour was gone and he felt agitated and angry. In the house a growing sense of claustrophobia engulfed him and every little thing irritated him. He knew he had no right to feel so black; after all, his wife was not dead. Admittedly she was thousands of miles away and hadn't written for a month, but it was no excuse to justify this spiralling depression. Living in close proximity with Callum's infuriating habits, his paranoia about noises and possible attacks, his maudlin fits of drunken grief at the unfair death of Eilidh and the subsequent loss for his brother, Jack had had enough. He found he resented Michael's promotion and his constant bloody good humour. 'I'm off,' he announced at breakfast on Friday. 'I'm off to KL.'

'Why today, Jack? Why don't you wait until tomorrow and we'll all go? I know I could murder a mixed grill at the Coliseum.' Callum patted his belly and licked his lips theatrically.

'I have to go. If I don't I'll be murdering more than those bloody *chichaks* you try to nail with your darts, and that includes you, you great clown.' He turned on his heel and jumped on his bike and pedalled off down the track to the estate office.

'I suppose he'll get in with Alex, he usually goes to KL on a Friday.' Michael finished his coffee and stood up. 'I have to inspect the weeders over at G Division. One thing I won't miss about being an assistant is that rickety, bone-crunching bicycle. Only a month or so and I'll have my own Land Rover!'

Callum bit noisily into an apple and stood up and winked at the waiting wash-*amah*, 'OK, Hassina, *tolong chuchi*!'

Jack wasn't in the mood for the Selangor Club, so after eating a steak at the Coliseum with Alex, he decided to stroll along Batu Road then down a lane at the back of Chotirmalls. Finding himself in Little India, he wandered aimlessly, entranced with the goods spilling chaotically over the pavements. He inhaled the throat-catching odours of the acrid curry spices and paused in admiration to watch as a plump Indian, wearing only a white sarong pulled tight below his overhanging belly, pounded and kneaded a lump of elastic dough. The man's head seemed to nod from side to side as though he was holding his own private conversation, yet his body was at one with the moving ball of flour, water and oil. He stretched it and pounded it until its shape changed into a flying saucer soaring above his head then he would bring it down with a slap on to the surface and beat it into a ball once more.

'*Murtabak, Tuan?* Very good *murtabak*, very good I say!'

Jack nodded, 'Why not?' He stood mesmerised as the rice dough was stretched like a pancake, wafer thin, by those beguiling nimble fingers. He watched as the maestro sprinkled a handful of minced beef and smeared it over the surface. Then he took a fistful of chopped onions, so translucent they fell like a spray of seed pearls over the meat. Finally he broke two eggs and with his fingers he mixed the yolk and white in swirls over the entire surface. His hands still flying and his fingers performing their magical manoeuvres he folded the dough into circles, then thirds, and then layered the edges into a compact parcel. He scooped the package on to a greased griddle balanced on burning charcoal and fried it methodically. Finally he took down a ladle and spooned some curry gravy into a small bowl.

'No, it's not for now,' Jack shook his head. 'I'll eat it later.'

The cook nodded his head sideways, and poured the curry sauce into a plastic bag and secured it tightly with a green rubber band. The *murtabak* was chopped into edible pieces with a cleaver, then wrapped first in cellophane and finally covered with brown paper.

'Thank you very much, *Tuan*!'

Jack paid him and walked away with his purchase, not yet sure where he was going or what he was looking for. He found himself walking to the small Presbyterian church of St Andrew. The whitewashed facade of the unprepossessing brick building had seen so many gatherings in recent years. The last happy occasion that he could remember was Anna's christening. Alex and Eilidh had stood at the top of those steps and posed for photographs. He remembered how painfully thin she was. He refused to think of the memorial service that marked the closure of her life for all those who knew and loved her here in Malaya. He felt his eyes pricking as he remembered how Alex had been unable to deliver his eulogy. He'd begun bravely and read shakily from his piece of paper, 'We met when she was nine; she was sitting on a stone wall...' then his voice had broken and he'd sat down. It was Callum that came to his rescue and talked about Eilidh's brief life amongst them all. Jack reflected again on the tragedy. It was as well they didn't know what the future held for them, he thought, for fate has a funny way of writing its own story. Wandering through the churchyard, he noticed the fallen blossoms of the frangipani lying scattered on the grass, casualties of the thunderstorm earlier in the afternoon. He smelled the heady fragrance and bent to pick up one of the waxy flowers. Sitting himself down on a bench, he surveyed the scene around him and as he did so often, tried to focus on Estelle to imagine their life together.

'Excuse me, *Tuan*. I see you before!'

'No thank you.' Jack stood up, annoyed at the persistence of men, women and children constantly peddling everything from torches, food and now even their bodies wherever he went.

'No, *Tuan*, you know me?'

'I said no, I don't know you.'

'*Tuan* Jack, it's me, Aminah, from Anak Kamsiah Estate. I work for Mem Freya.'

'Oh! God, I'm so sorry. Aminah, of course! What are you doing here?'

'I just come back from Johor; I went to visit my family for one week. I go back, but no bus till Saturday. Why you sit here?'

'I don't know,' said Jack. 'I thought it would be quiet but those birds are making enough noise to wake the dead.'

'Oh *hantu*, *Tuan*! Malay people believe in ghosts and spirits, and you sit here in a church garden! Not good place. Better go in case dead people wake up.'

'Yes, I suppose I'd better go; it's getting dark any how.'

'You stay in KL, *Tuan*?'

'Yes, that was my plan; what will you do?'

'I have to stay. My bus no go until tomorrow. I feel frightened now. I don't like *hantu*.'

'Come on, I'll help you, give me your case. Good God! What's in it?'

'Just some food prepared by my mother,' she giggled, holding her hand in front of her mouth.

Jack looked down at her. She did look different. He tried to remember her at the curry tiffin, but only vaguely remembered a purple sarong and a demure girl with a great ability for balancing a lot of plates on a small tray. This girl was clad in a pink sarong with a lacy *baju,* a loose top, and her hair was tousled and rapidly escaping from her plait that had obviously started the day in a severe queue down her back.

'Come, I'd planned to stay at the Rex Hotel, we'll get you a room there as well, it's not far. It's good and clean and you'll be quite safe there.' Jack strode on as the girl struggled to keep up with him.

'*Tuan*, I cannot,' Aminah faltered.

'Of course you can. Come along, I shan't eat you, what a silly girl.'

The Rex Hotel was very plain, despite its grandiose title. The decor was minimal, with a reception desk, two upright chairs, and a corridor that led to a shady interior, presumably inhabited by the owner's family.

'Good evening, Mr Chong. I would like two rooms please; this young lady has missed her bus, so I shall be responsible for her.'

'Very good, Mr Jack, two rooms for one night, yes? You want dinner, Fanta Orange, *nasi goring*? I can get you anything.'

Jack turned to Aminah and smiled reassuringly, 'Fanta?'

'Yes, thank you, Mr...Jack.' She kept her eyes lowered.

'I'll have a bottle of Johnny Walker Black Label, Mr Chong, and two dozen *satay ayam*. Now come along, Aminah, let's see these rooms.'

They climbed the stairs, Jack following the porter with vigour and Aminah more hesitantly, her eyes downcast. She was afraid that people in the hotel would think she was a bad girl. When they stopped in front of the room that was to be hers, she shyly looked up at the tall European man who appeared preoccupied with placing her suitcase on the bed and checking that she had a towel and soap. The bathroom was down the hall, shared by all the rooms on this floor. She looked at the simple bed, its clean white sheet with a folded blue counterpane placed along the bottom. The windows were closed and the blue gingham curtains were drawn. By the bed was a stained lacquer table that had seen better days.

'You'll be fine here.' Jack breezed back in after checking his own room and the bathroom. Now let's have a drink while we wait for the satay.'

Aminah sat quietly and stiffly on the edge of the bed. She felt awkward as she watched the drinks being poured.

'Aminah should be doing that, *Tuan*!'

'Yes, you should, but I'll let you divide the *murtabak* instead. Ah! Someone knocking on the door! That'll be the satay. Come in, come in. There we are, put it on this table and I'll draw up the chairs. What a feast, there's nothing like good Kajang satay, but this smells pretty good all the same!'

The chargrilled chicken satay was skewered on bamboo sticks and peanut sauce, cubes of compressed rice and chunks of cucumber had been placed in small dishes. Aminah gingerly dipped a piece of chicken into the sauce and put it and some cucumber into her mouth. Jack ate with gusto, dipping the succulent murtabak into the cold curry gravy and slurping it all into his mouth. He savoured the taste of the whisky, and as the liquor took effect he became effusive and happy. 'This is the best meal I've had in years.'

She looked at him shyly, seeing his long fingers curl around the pieces of *murtabak*. She looked up to his throat where the buttons of his shirt were undone and saw the dark chest hair curling up and escaping in soft twists. His face was strong, his hair as black as an Indian's, yet when he looked at her, she had to blink at the intensity of the blue of his eyes. They reminded her of the breast of the kingfisher bird. Of course his face was craggy like all Europeans, with wrinkles around the eyes, and the bones of his cheeks and nose were more prominent than the Asian faces she knew. The last time she'd seen him his hair had been brushed back off his brow, and she'd thought he looked very remote and distant, but today he was more rumpled and his hair fell on to his forehead and he appeared more boyish and carefree.

'You see, Aminah, you had absolutely nothing to fear. I can see you looking at me, wondering if I'm a monster.'

Aminah again raised her hand to her mouth and giggled.

Her eyes were bright and he looked into their black depths and Jack said quietly, 'All I really wanted was company.' A *chichak* made its tick-tock noise from the corner of the ceiling and he told her of the sport he and his friends played during the long, lonely evenings in the bungalow, throwing darts at the poor, unsuspecting lizards. 'The hunter is hunted, that's what it's all about; after all they eat the moths and I've even seen them go for a cockroach.'

'My sister and I used to play with grasshoppers. We would have special sports competitions and tie their legs together like a three-legged race. It was very funny.'

'Why did you leave your *kampong* and your family, Aminah? Was there no work in Johor?'

'Oh no, *Tuan*, my family are from the east coast, near Kuantan. That was where our *kampong* was. My father was killed by the communists. He was seen as a spy for the Europeans. After he was shot, my mother was very scared so she made us run away in the night. Me and my sister carried cooking pots and rice and tapioca and she carried bundles of clothes on her back and the small cooking stove. We ran through the trees, keeping off the main road, we were very afraid. Soldiers are not good to women and girls.'

Jack nodded, his eyes seeing the picture that she was describing. The story was so familiar. Just recently he'd heard of a sergeant who'd led his men into a clearing, newly deserted by CTs. There was even a pot of rice still cooking on an open fire and the sergeant went to help himself, but the whole place was booby tapped and the explosion cost him his hand. Jack took another sip of whisky and offered her some.

'No, *Tuan*, Malays cannot drink alcohol, you know that!'

'So how did you get away?'

'It was terrible. The police rounded us up eventually; we were very tired, and the jungle was dark, so we came out on to the path. They accused us of spying for the communists and didn't believe that our father had been shot. They put us on a bus and we were taken to Mersing where we were put in a cell with some other women. It was a terrible time. We lost all our belongings and my mother was slapped and punched but my sister and I were lucky, we were left alone. We stayed in that cell for nearly one month with rats and only a bucket to share with six others.'

'How did you get out?' Jack's eyes followed the movement of her hands as they replaced the glass on the table and resumed twisting the edge of the sheet.

'A lorry took us,' she said simply. 'One morning we were all bundled on to a lorry and driven south. No one told us anything. We were treated like animals, just given water and then taken away.'

Jack took her hand and smoothed the sheet back in place. He sighed and studied her face, so free of any signs of the ordeals that she must have suffered. 'So you ended up in Johor?'

'Yes, *Tuan*, an English policeman took charge of the lorry we were in and the authorities gave us work in a clothing factory. My mother is still there, she misses me but she has my sister. They have a small house and can grow vegetables. They sell some to a local *kedai*. It's not too bad.'

'And you, Aminah, why are you a domestic servant?'

'I learnt English at school and got a job as a rubber clerk's assistant. The same policeman met me one day and asked about my family. He suggested I work for *Tuan* Roger and Mem Freya. When they moved to Anak Kamsiah Estate I went too. It was very easy.'

Jack took the sheet that had crept back into her hands and smoothed it flat once more. This time he held on to her hand and examined her shell-pink nails, and then turned the palm over. He studied the lines. 'You are going to live for a long, long time! Look at that line.'

Aminah giggled and pulled her hand away, then stretched and took his hand and mimicked his action. She leant forward and studied his open palm.

'Well, what do you see?'

She looked up at him, her eyes unblinking, her face showing no emotion.

'I see nothing. I do not have your talents. Anyway you Europeans have too many criss-crosses. I cannot tell where they all go.' She released his hand and stood up and made to tidy up the debris of satay sticks and crumpled papers. 'Ants, *Tuan*, we must take these away.'

'OK, I'll take them, why don't you go for your bath?'

Aminah nodded and waited till he had closed the door. She looked again at her own hand, seeing the long lifeline sweep down her palm and into the folds of her wrist. She glanced at the door where he'd gone out and her eyes were troubled. Taking the thin towel, she walked into the bathroom. There was only a brown stone urn of water with a red plastic dipper. The terracotta tiles sloped towards a sluice opening that would wash into a connecting drain. Aminah shivered as she splashed the cold water over her shoulders and scrubbed her body thoroughly with the bright red bar of Lifebuoy soap. Later she lay naked on her bed, only covered lightly with her sarong. The *Tuan* was a good man. He had listened to her story and his silence had shown her that he understood what she had endured. She was drawn to him, his warmth, his eyes, his touch. Somewhere deep in her soul she felt him reaching out to her.

Jack lay on his back, his head cradled in his clasped hands. The thin curtains did not close and a shaft of moonlight lay like a silver sword across his body. He felt totally at peace. He felt no surprise when he heard the handle of the door turn. It was as though subconsciously he'd been waiting. He lay still and followed the girl with his eyes as she walked across the room and stood by his side and gazed down at his body. He sensed her hair, long and silky, and he longed to reach out and touch it but instead he waited. She released her sarong and leant over his chest. No words were spoken. He felt the soft butterfly touch of her lips followed by the wetness of her tongue as she caressed him in silence. Unbearable pent up longings rose and fell and overflowed in the darkness of the night, and as the moon deserted the sky and the new dawn awoke, the girl Aminah left the man who had penetrated her soul and had given her more than a night of true love. She carried away the seed of a new life.

The next morning when he awoke, Jack knew she'd gone. When he knocked at her door and looked inside, the little bed was as she'd left it. It looked as forlorn as he felt.

Michael Parrish's first weeks at Bukit Hijau saw him take the estate by storm. He was like a military general patrolling about and inspecting everything with the enthusiasm of a new recruit. He would be out in his Land Rover at dawn, criss-crossing the various divisions, determined to familiarise himself with the fields given over to tapping, grafting and planting. Most of the clearing had been completed and the estate was now operating with a good yield percentage. He checked out the tappers' housing, the school and the temple. The workers that were resident on the estate were all Tamil speakers, mostly descendants of those originally brought over from the Indian subcontinent. Some contractors were Chinese but they weren't living within the estate boundaries. Michael inspected the tappers and observed the buckets of latex being collected daily and then driven to the factory where they would be poured into metal trays and smoked in the ovens. He later checked the smelly rubbery sheets being hung out to dry in the sun. He stood with his clerk watching the workers baling up the brown sheets, punching the corners securely and loading them on to lorries, to be taken to Port Swettenham and Singapore for shipping. His Land Rover was constantly on the move and when it did pull up in front of the office, he would clatter into the open-plan room and spend two hours familiarising himself with the yield figures and rubber prices around the world. He and his clerk, Mr Perez, would peer over the finely printed ledgers and Michael would query every entry.

His Cookie saw little of him and twice he told Mem Freya when she'd driven over that the *Tuan* was not back yet. Invariably he would eat his breakfast closer to eleven than the more normal nine o'clock.

'Hellooo!' Freya called out one morning as he drew up in a cloud of dust. 'I came by on the off-chance and Cookie suggested I should wait for you.'

Michael's face lit up at the unexpected visitor. 'What a surprise. I hope you'll have some scrambled eggs with me?'

'No,' said Freya, 'I'll just watch, but I would like some coffee, please.'

Cookie nodded and gave Freya a side plate and knife, in case she might like some toast as well.

'It's been three weeks, Michael, and we haven't seen a sign of you.'

He looked at her sitting so comfortably at his table. His eyes slid over her girlish figure clad only in white shorts and yellow blouse. She was like a bright beacon lighting up the gloom of the dark interior of his house. Her long blonde hair was plaited and tied up around her head in the fashion of a German fräulein. He could feel his resolve to keep his thoughts only on his new job weaken. She was looking at him expectantly.

'Michael, did you hear me? We haven't seen you for weeks, too much work and you really will be considered a bore!'

'I'm sorry, forgive me, but it's been a high hurdle to jump, going from assistant to acting manager and I want to give it my best shot. Still, I think

I've cracked it now. Your swimming pool is a very enticing option, though. This heat is so oppressive, I sometimes feel as though I am walking into a wall of hot moisture.'

'I know. I simply cannot go out at midday. Instead I just lie under the fan, then go for a swim around four. I think we're building up to a storm; the monsoon is late this year. You must come over and have a meal with us tomorrow. I'm going to the Cold Storage in KL this afternoon; Roger has asked the driver to deliver some papers to the office in town, so I thought I would take the opportunity. Would you like to come over? Steak and chips at about seven?'

'Thanks, Freya, I'd appreciate that. It's been very quiet of late, I must admit. I've been hitting the sack at about nine, and up again at five.'

The two chatted easily as Cookie served Michael his scrambled eggs. Freya nursed her cup of black coffee between her hands, her elbows on the table. Between mouthfuls, Michael announced, 'There was a bad accident here two days ago; a wild pig gored a tapper woman, horrible business. I think we should have them working in pairs. It's bloody isolated in some divisions and I don't like it myself, walking through those trees next to the uncleared areas. I've taken to carrying a walking stick and singing hymns!'

'Hymns? How funny,' Freya giggled, 'I have an image of you, not as a planter but as a missionary with a pith helmet marching through the rubber trying to save souls! We had a man like that in Sumatra when I was growing up.'

'Sumatra?' enquired Michael, holding his fork midway to his mouth.

'Yes, my father was a planter there in the thirties. He was one of the first Dutch planters to go to Indonesia. His stories were amazing, of how they had coolies to clear the land, how estates were run like military operations with beatings for any worker that dared disobey the white man. Some of the white men should have been shot in my opinion. There was an element I think of the Wild West with accidents, deaths, drunkenness and murder. Wild men are always drawn to the wild life and most spent their nights drowning their sorrows and inadequacies in the bottle.' She paused to sip her coffee, then smiled over to Michael. 'I could tell you stories of those days. My mother's life as a planter's wife was very different to mine now. The war changed a lot of things, there's no doubt, and maybe in this case for the better.'

154

'So you met Roger in Sumatra?' Michael asked as he wiped his mouth with his white napkin.

'Roger was my father's assistant, just out from England, one of the few men then who had been to university. I was swept off my feet. He seemed so mature; he knew about books and music and he had seen cities that I had only dreamt of.'

'Romance in the rubber…And your mother?'

'They're both in Holland now. The war has changed so much in Europe but the Holland they remember has gone and I think they're finding life quite difficult after thirty years in Sumatra. When I was born, my mother was forty-three and my father was fifty-one; perhaps that was why I was drawn to Roger. Maybe I feel safe with older men!'

'That's some story, Freya, I had no idea.'

'What about you, Michael? What brought you to Malaya? Were you running away from some illicit love affair?'

'Certainly not!' Michael laughed into her eyes. 'I had a quiet, sheltered upbringing. The only illicit love affairs took place in my schoolboy head. I had a very different upbringing from you. I was born in rural Cornwall.' He started buttering his toast and layering a dollop of marmalade on top. 'I have three sisters,' he continued, crunching up the toast, 'all older than me, and my father works as a gardener and has his own allotment. I used to help him on Saturdays and I remember how peaceful it was working alongside him.' Michael looked down at his plate, as though considering whether to have some more toast. 'He's a calm, silent sort of man. Not at all like my mother and sisters, who never stop talking and planning and organising everything.' Michael smiled at his guest, obviously remembering their faces. 'Maybe that's why the old boy takes off to be amongst his cabbages and puff his Senior Service fags in his shed.' He poured himself another cup of tea and spooned in the sugar. 'Would you like some more coffee, Freya?'

'No, thank you, one cup is enough for me.'

'When I read the advert in the local Gazette about them looking for young men to go to far and distant shores, I jumped at the chance. My mother and sisters write every week and as you can imagine their airmail letters are full of instructions for my health and well being, even from across the oceans. I fancy my father would be here in a shot if only he were younger!'

155

'I'm sure they would be pleased to hear that you're still praising the Lord as you inspect your trees!' Freya laughed again at the amusing image he'd painted. 'Oh, look at the time, I really must go. You do have a late breakfast, don't you? Roger will be home for his lunch soon, then I'll have the car to go into KL, so sing well, and we'll see you tomorrow at seven!' She jumped into her little open-topped jeep and reversed out from the side of the house. With a wave and a shrill 'Byeeee!' she was gone.

Over the next few weeks Michael saw a lot of Freya and Roger. Their house was welcoming. Soft light glowed through yellow silk lampshades. Chinese porcelain and delicate jade ornaments twinkled on rosewood sideboards. Soft carpets and bunches of white orchids gave the room a sense of opulence. As he drank whisky from Waterford crystal and listened to the radiogram playing operas by Puccini, Michael's thoughts would wander back to his own empty house with just the few sticks of furniture and Cookie's plain cooking.

'I need a wife,' he sighed one evening.

'I'll say you do, old boy, but you can find your own!' Roger slapped Freya's rear end as she walked past his chair. She bent over and kissed his forehead.

'Do I have to go to Holland or Sumatra to get this vintage?' Michael laughed.

'Freya's mother is English, you know; the old chap met her in India. She was nursing there, quite the pioneer. When he got her back to Sumatra she immediately started a local hospital. Got so good I think she forgot to come home most of the time. Freya here grew up like a waif; spent half her life with the local kids.'

'It's true. Papa had me driving when I was eleven, and shooting. It was a terrible shock to be sent away to school and have to learn useless things like algebra and Latin!' She smiled to herself as though remembering her battle with conventional schooling. 'I was in England during the German occupation of the Netherlands, in a school in Kent. Papa and Mother were interned in Jakarta. They had such a bad time, and came out like skeletons, poor things. After it was all over, I got a passage straight away on a ship to Indonesia and our little family was reunited.' She sighed and sat up straight in her chair and fiddled with her plait, 'It was soon after that, I met Roger. He came out after the war in a new wave of planters seeking a new life and he became Papa's assistant. The next few years were hard for my father. He was tired and weakened by his ordeal. The war had left him a shadow of his former self; it was as though he'd given up, which I suppose he had for the way of life that he knew had gone, and poor Mother, although a survivor, never recovered her nerves. They tried to resume their life as they'd known it, but it was too much for Papa. After I married Roger, they returned to Holland and we got the chance to be transferred to Malaya. We were placed on an estate in Johor.'

'I'm glad they taught her to shoot, though, she certainly did her bit during the Emergency. Had the house all barricaded up down there in Johor. Remember the night I was away and those commies came into the garden?' Roger chuckled.

'I do,' replied Freya. 'I had rifles placed at four of the garden-facing windows, two upstairs and two on the ground. Cookie manned the downstairs and I was upstairs, and those guys had no idea how many of us were in the house! The rifles just cracked away, and they fled, but we hit two of them. A good night's work! Roger was with the commissioner of police in Malacca when it happened; he'd no idea that we were likely to be targeted.' Freya giggled and mimicked shooting the rifle on her shoulder. 'I wonder when my Latin will come in handy!'

Michael raised his eyebrows and regarded his hostess, realising that he had completely misjudged her. Previously, he had formed a very shallow opinion of her, seeing her only as an empty headed consort for a fairly wealthy middle-aged man. He shook his head and lifted his glass and drained it to the last drop.

'*Lagi satu, Tuan?*' Aminah appeared silently from behind his chair.

'No,' Michael smiled, '*terima kasih.*' He looked around and then stood and stretched. 'I must be off.'

Aminah smiled, but kept her eyes lowered.

'Come and swim anytime,' called Freya as Roger saw him out to his vehicle.

'I shall, thank you both, and good night!'

Roger put his arms around his wife and held her close. 'I love you; you do know that, don't you?'

'And I love you,' she smiled into his shoulder. She did love him, but as she closed her eyes that night with the sound of his breathing at the back of her neck and the heavy weight of his arm resting on her hip, it was Michael's face that she saw just before she slipped into a dreamless sleep.

It was mid-July. Michael lay in Freya and Roger's pool on the Anak Kamsiah Estate. He was floating on his back like a giant water spider. His body was lean and now a deep brown. Myriad ripples of translucent bubbles played around his spread fingers.

'Hellooo!' came Freya's familiar greeting as she threw down her towel, slipped off her sandals and dived cleanly into the pool.

'I thought it was too good to be true,' laughed Michael as he rubbed his eyes and shook the water from his hair. 'Just when I thought I was drifting off to sleep, along comes danger!'

'You should have been singing your hymns, then. I would certainly have been deterred.'

He ducked down under the water, and staying submerged, he swam away from her then circled back and rose like a cork from a champagne bottle taking her with him and throwing her up in a great rush of spray. '"Glory, Glory, Glory, Lord God Almighty!"'

She immediately swam back and jumped on his back, bearing down on his shoulders in an attempt to duck his head under the water. Her plan backfired as his back did not yield under her pressure and she was left standing with only her hands resting on his broad shoulders where she had placed them. He didn't turn or move; instead he covered her fingers with his. They stood and for a moment only the water splashed and tugged their bodies and he felt the smooth skin of her belly rub against his back and he was aware of her breathing on the nape of his neck. They pulled away and Freya laughed.

'Come, I have some lime juice. You should drink it before the ice melts.'

'Is Rog not joining us? I thought he was playing golf this morning and would be back for his swim as usual?'

Michael wrapped a blue-and-white striped towel around his waist and took the glass that she offered him.

'No, he had to cancel; he decided to attend the planters' meeting after all, so he left this morning for KL. I think they'll make a weekend of

158

it. Quite a few experts from London are due to visit to discuss palm oil production. I think they wanted to plan the itineraries for their visit. I suppose you would be interested in that?'

'Yes, I'll be interested in that all right.'

They lay back on the loungers and felt the sun's rays burn into the very marrow of their bones. Sweat collected in tiny bubbles and finally raced down the contours of their bodies. Michael watched as one little rivulet ran down Freya's arm. He reached out and touched it. When she turned to look at him their eyes met, and as the afternoon sun sank below the line of rubber trees and the colours of the day muted to the blues and indigos of evening, they both knew that he would not return home that night.

Freya brushed her hair back off her face. She secured the long mass of blonde tresses back with a rubber band. Her complexion was smooth and her Nordic blue eyes were bright in her tanned face. She selected a lime-green shift dress and stepped into the loose tube. Aminah came forward to help zip her up.

'This colour is good: makes you very beautiful, Mem.'

'Thank you, Aminah; I'm just going out with *Tuan* Michael. He found some baby wildcats that had been left by their mother. Maybe she'd been killed by bad men.'

'Better you take a box and old towels, Mem. Those cats are not like pets: can bite.'

'Good idea, can you get me something? I just want to brush my teeth. You look tired, Aminah, are you OK?'

'I'm OK, Mem,' Aminah smiled wanly. She had never felt so tired in all her life. She knew the reason, as well; it was four months since the night in KL and she was worried sick and not sleeping well, for fear of what her family was going to say. She could not think what to do. How could she have a baby and bear the shame of not having a husband?

While Aminah tidied up Freya's dressing table, and worried about her condition, Freya reached up to get her Dutch cap from the top of the vanity unit in the bathroom. Freya knew that what happened with Michael was explosive and wonderful passion, but she had no illusions of any romantic love. Both were level-headed individuals who had crossed the line into an illicit and exhilarating love affair. She was dizzy with excitement on one level, but she could also step back and keep her feelings well in reserve. As soon as she heard the crunch of the wheels on the driveway, Freya grabbed the box and towels and ran out the door and clambered into the front seat. The plastic was hot and burnt the backs of her legs and the smell of the idling engine made her cough.

'All set?' Michael smiled, and pushed the stick into gear.

'Let's go!' Freya waved to Aminah who stood on the top step waving goodbye to them. The Land Rover lurched over the rough back roads, past the lorry with the newly collected latex. Michael waved at the children who stood like soldiers at the side of the track and saluted him as he drove by. At last he reached a clearing where only rough logs and broken branches littered the forest floor. The noise of the cicadas was deafening as the sun burned in the heat of the mid-morning sky. He drove off the track and into some shade where he turned off the ignition. Without a word he jumped out of his side, and strode round and opened Freya's door. He pulled her to him and buried his face in her neck. She felt the wetness of his sweat as she encircled his body with her arms and they remained locked in an embrace that bridged the hours and days they'd been apart. When he finally reassured himself that she was there, he slowly kissed her and ran his hands over her body, rediscovering all the places that he could only dream about when he was alone. Passion overtook reason, and whether it was out in the midday sun, or hidden in a shady gully by twilight, both were willing to compromise on comfort for the wild abandon they achieved in their lust.

By the end of August, Freya realised that Roger was beginning to suspect. He had accepted the wild kittens, had allowed the gardener to build a small run for them, and had even accepted a role in their feeding programme. But after three weeks, they'd developed a voracious appetite for raw meat and had badly bitten the gardener's son as he attempted to feed them by hand. When the accident occurred, Cookie telephoned the estate office, informing him of the incident.

'Well,' growled Roger, 'get Mem Freya. Why are you bothering me, you know I'm at work.'

'I know, *Tuan*, but Mem is not here. She's out with *Tuan* Michael.'

'Very well,' snapped Roger, and stalked out to his Land Rover and roared back to the house in a pile of dust. On seeing the state of the boy's hand, torn and bloody, he inhaled deeply, his brows drawn into a fierce frown. 'That needs to be stitched, my lad, and you'll need a tetanus injection. You're right, Cookie, I'll take him straight away.' When he drove back to the house after the emergency medical trip, Freya was still not back. He sat in the lounge on his own and decided to wait her out. When at last she and Michael bounced into the house, almost like hysterical teenagers, he remained seated and calmly listened to their excited prattle.

'You should have seen it, darling!' Freya's face was alive with enthusiasm. 'It was thirty foot long! Imagine! I have never seen anything like it before!'

'A python?' Roger enquired, directing his question to Michael.

'A monster, biggest I've ever seen. We watched three estate workers put it into a bell-shaped cage. One of the guys said it had just eaten a goat, so it was probably feeling pretty sedated.'

'It didn't even struggle when the men lifted it up,' interrupted Freya, 'it just let them manhandle it without any resistance.'

'Poor thing was probably all set for a good sleep,' added Roger.

'Well, now it's going to KL to get cured, darling, and Michael said I could have shoes made from its skin. Isn't it exciting?'

It was, and their high spirits were infectious. Roger found himself offering drinks and hospitality as he normally did, but was aware of suppressing the feelings of disquiet that had come over him.

Sensing the tense atmosphere and realising that Roger must know, Freya resolved to put an end to this madness. She really didn't want to cause pain to her husband, and that night she invited him to her room and tried to reassure him that she truly loved him. As they lay together, Roger suggested they have a dinner party.

'Why don't we have a little get-together? I hear Sam Bathgate's sister is out paying a visit; she might like to meet our eligible bachelors!'

'Michael! I didn't hear you!' Freya clambered up from her knees, where she'd been sorting her record collection.

'No wonder, are you deaf?' He reached over and turned down the volume control, 'You and your operas! Is that Mozart?'

'Yes, *The Marriage of Figaro.* You're right, that's what's so good about living here, having no neighbours.'

'I came over for a pair of your shoes to take to KL to get copied. The skin has to be dried and cured of course, but as I was going in, I thought I could take them for you. I also miss you and had to see you. Are you avoiding me?'

'You're so silly! Of course not, but I've been busy. Cookie and I have been preparing menus for our dinner party. We had to think of things that would appeal to you men of simple tastes. Things have to be organised, you know.' She giggled flirtatiously and sat down on the sofa, 'Someone has to select the linen and organise the polishing.'

Michael stood at the edge of the Chinese rug, his normally cheerful face subdued. 'You have been avoiding me,' he said.

'I haven't, I just told you I've been busy.' Freya glanced around the room, aware that Cookie was hovering nearby. 'Beer, Michael? ' and he nodded. When Cookie brought the tray with glasses and two Anchor beers, Freya smiled and breezily said, 'Rest now, Cookie, we won't need anything else.' She looked at Michael over the rim of her glass. The afternoon was thick with an expectancy of rain, the sky dark, the atmosphere heavy.

'Where is Roger? I noticed the car is away but the Land Rover is still here?'

'Pay day,' Freya said simply. 'He and the two guards should be back around four. You have your beer and I'll run up and get some shoes.' She sprinted up to her bedroom, taking the stairs two at a time. When she returned, she took her beer, cold and wet with condensation and sipped the froth. The alcohol hit her stomach and almost immediately she felt the familiar ache she experienced when she was near Michael. 'I have missed you,' she confessed.

Michael smiled and looking around the empty house, he took her hand and pulled her towards the veranda. Outside the storm clouds were gathering, and they could hear the crackle of thunder and suddenly a jagged gash of splintering light seared through the sky, 'Come, run with me to the pool.'

As they ran barefoot across the rough grass, the rain started and balloons of water burst around them.

'Oh God, we're getting soaked,' Freya shouted.

'Come on, into the attap hut, you have towels there.'

They gazed out at the huge banana leaves bent over with the unexpected weight of water, the glossy leaves polished in the deluge as the sheets of rain swept down from the sky.

'It looks like a waterfall cascading from the heavens!' exclaimed Freya.

'I should sing a hymn,' laughed Michael.

'And I should sing an aria,' Freya giggled. They turned to each other and all of Freya's resolve and good intentions melted as he kissed her, the rain pounding a drumbeat on the decking outside. Later, although the storm had not yet passed, Freya realised that the afternoon was passing and Roger might soon be home, so she gathered herself together and urged Michael to be gone.

'How am I going to keep my hands off you when I have to sit so close to you at your party?'

'We'll manage; it might be fun,' and she smiled radiantly.

Candles burned and flickered on the laden table. Cookie served vegetables with silver service dexterity from a Noritake ashet. The polished wood of the extended rosewood table shone in contrast to the lace-embroidered place settings. Snowy linen napkins had been placed on laps and now guests were spooning ladles of casseroled beef on to their plates. The rich colours of the meat and roasted vegetables lay in a haze of steam. Dishes portraying patterns of Japanese cherry trees were passed like parcels from one guest to the next. Conversation was muted as Cookie now circled the table with wine. Splashes of red, so dark it was nearly black in the candlelight, filled each crystal goblet.

Diamonds glittered on throats and fingers that were tanned the colour of warm honey. The three ladies present wore dresses in delicate pastel shades. Presiding at the head of the table, Freya was a vision in dusky pink, her blonde hair tied back in a French roll, soft tendrils curling on her forehead. Dorothy's blue satin gown meandered down her body, the colour deepening from the palest of pale to the deepest of midnight. She'd allowed her wavy brown hair to grow long and it now fell to her shoulders, gleaming in the gentle light.

Lois wore a cream creation. Newly purchased in London, the sheer pearl silk fell like a veil over her body, highlighting her glossy dark bob. Lois could hardly suppress her excitement. Her trip to visit her brother

Sam was a transparent bid to find a husband. Now beneath lowered lashes, and with a demure countenance, she appraised the six elegant men seated around the table. Roger, her host, was listening intently to Dorothy whilst she chattered animatedly about their recent shopping trip to Malacca. He looked a kind man. A bit old, Lois thought, for his lovely wife. She turned to Freya who was chatting to Callum McIntyre, one of the four bachelors she'd met. He seemed a jovial type, happy and uncomplicated. His animated face was alive as he regaled his hostess with a story he'd heard on the golf course. Speaking with a pronounced Scottish accent, his wild gesticulations threatened Freya's precious crystal glasses. Her eyes moved round the table and settled on Jack Dunbar, a suave, good-looking man with piercing blue eyes. His black hair was brushed back, and in profile his face seemed carved from rock. No loose, fleshy folds or weakness of chin on him; his inborn aloofness gave him an aristocratic bearing. He'd been merely polite when introduced. Across the table sat Alex McIntyre, the one who had been recently widowed. Still grieving from the loss of his wife, his face was thin, his features sharp and his eyes cavernous. Deep lines creased his brow. Pain had engraved its mark on him. Although he'd smoothed his hair down, she could see the stubborn curl already breaking free and she couldn't help thinking how it softened his face. He seemed to be drinking heavily and was more focussed on his glass than on the present company. She noticed that when he looked at Freya, his eyes narrowed and Lois wondered at what she perceived to be open hostility. Next to her brother sat Michael Parrish. She knew he was from outside Penzance, and being from Ashburton in Devon herself, she felt drawn to him and was curious to find out what had propelled him to Malaya. She studied his hands as they twisted the stem of his wine glass. She felt the urge to lean over and smooth the blonde hairs escaping from his cuffs, just as one might stroke a well-loved pet. Although he'd shaken her hand warmly when they'd been introduced, Lois sensed that his mind was elsewhere.

After the meal ended on a glorious note of sherry trifle, followed by very good Stilton and rosy pink grapes, the guests retired to the lounge and a beautiful Malay girl made her entrance to serve coffee. Lois watched her as she gracefully placed the tray with the miniature cups and saucers by the table next to Freya. As soon as Freya poured from the pot, the maid glided over to each guest to deliver the cup and then proceeded to serve them with cream and sugar. She wore a purple sarong and white shirt. Her raven-black hair was pulled tightly into a chignon at the nape of her neck.

To an unsuspecting eye she epitomised all that was beautiful and graceful in the Malay race. But as someone who had known her more intimately and who had not seen her since their encounter in the stark, plain room of the Rex Hotel, Jack noted the mauve shadows beneath her eyes, the hollowness of her cheeks. He studied her back as she leant over to place a cup on a table. As she straightened he saw her figure from the side. There was no mistake. That would explain the loose white top instead of the more usual figure-hugging *baju kebaya*. He counted on his fingers; was it really four months? He looked down at his coffee and watched as he stirred in two cubes of sugar. He seemed fascinated and preoccupied as he studied the white grains dissolving on his spoon.

Alex continued to watch Freya as she played hostess. Sometimes he glanced over at Michael who had chosen not to sit, but instead was selecting a record from a pile on a table next to the radiogram. The guests looked up in surprise as the harsh, strident notes of the jazz broke into the subdued murmurs. The atmosphere immediately changed as the three ladies jumped up and selected partners. The couples danced, dipping and shuffling over the polished floors. Cookie quickly rolled up the circular rug to make way for the more exuberant stepping manoeuvres. Michael held Freya with the authority of prior knowledge. Dancing together, their feet and bodies seemed to move as one. Lois tried to keep pace with Callum but his eagerness featured more than his actual ability to keep the beat. Dorothy had asked Roger who now sedately steered her round the room in an elegant waltz, paying no heed to the music being played.

Alex did not drink coffee; instead he nursed another brandy and surveyed the room. He noted Jack standing near the tray of coffee, looking out at the swing doors to the kitchen. Alex downed his drink and gestured to Cookie to refill his glass. His anger, loneliness and frustration rose as he watched the lovely Freya throw her head and body back while Michael held her firmly, their hips joined in close familiarity. He drank deeply and continued to stare as the couple broke apart and walked back to their respective chairs. Seeing her glass empty, Freya walked over to the cocktail cabinet and Cookie poured her another gin, then slashed at the block of ice and handed her a sizeable chunk. Alex had sidled over and stood swaying close to the cabinet. Freya tensed and saw the cold look in his eyes.

'What's up, Alex? Did you want to dance? If you let me have a quick drink we could go for the Foxtrot if you like?'

'No, I'm no dancer.'

'Oh come on! I'll show you. I'm a good teacher!' She held out her hand, and took his.

'No, I said I don't want to.'

She continued to pull him and he yanked his hand away. 'Leave me alone Freya, why don't you get back to your lover boy? Old Rog is as drunk as a Lord, can't see what the whole district knows, his floozy of a wife is making a damn fool of him. Is it just Michael, or are you fussy?'

Freya gasped in shock and raised her hand to slap his face, the rage rising in her along with a sick sensation of fear. She'd forgotten that she still held the shard of ice that Cookie had just broken off. As she released her hand to slap his face, the ice flew with deadly accuracy and sliced the bridge of his nose.

The unexpected assault made him gasp, 'Argh!' He held his hands up to his nose and felt the warm gush of blood as it spurted on to his hands and stained his shirt front. 'Bloody woman, what did you do that for?'

Roger crossed the floor in an instant, and seeing him coming, Freya turned on her heel and ran from the room and up the stairs. Everyone stood stricken. Cookie dipped a linen napkin into the ice container and put some loose blocks inside then pressed the dressing on to the open wound.

'*Tuan* should go to dispensary, quite deep I think.'

'Yes, yes of course.'

Roger took control and went out and called the driver to get the Land Rover. Jack and Callum followed the procession in Alex's car. They would take Alex straight home after he'd been treated. Dorothy felt it was probably the time for them to leave also, so she and Sam ushered Lois to the door. Before driving off, Dorothy called over to Michael, 'Come and play tennis next week, we'd love to see you if you're free. We usually play on Tuesdays, around five.'

He leant over and kissed her. 'Thanks, Dorothy, I'd like that.' He shook hands with Sam and then turned to Lois. 'I'm glad we met,' he smiled rakishly. 'Goodnight now. I'll certainly be in touch soon.'

When the Bathgates had driven off, Michael looked up at the lit bedroom window that he knew was Freya's. Oh well, he thought, I suppose that's all over now. Alex must have found out about us and said something. Sighing resignedly, he stepped out on to the porch step and looked out at the dark garden. He knew it would be very unwise to attempt to see Freya now, so nodding to the maid Aminah who had come in with a bucket and a wet cloth to clean up the blood, and to Cookie who was now tidying away the coffee cups, he said, '*Selamat malam.*'

Both nodded and returned the greeting, '*Selamat malam, Tuan.*'

Michael climbed into his Land Rover and drove away. As he drove, he shrugged and with his eternal optimism he wondered where he'd put his tennis racket.

When Jack and Alex arrived back at Bukit Bulan, the house was in darkness. It was after midnight and the servants had already gone to bed. They'd dropped Callum off first at his bungalow and then proceeded up to the main driveway.

When they got inside Alex made straight for the kitchen and took out a bottle of Courvoisier. 'A snifter?' he enquired, holding the bottle questioningly out to Jack.

Jack nodded, but pointed instead to the whisky bottle.

They took their glasses through to the darkened sitting room and Jack turned on the switch of the standard lamp. He remembered Eilidh choosing the pink shade to match her new curtains, the ones that she and Alex had so painstakingly hand-sewed together.

'Well, old man, how are you feeling?'

'Bloody awful' admitted Alex. He smiled ruefully and then gingerly touched the white dressing that had been taped across his nose.

He pulled a face and crossed his eyes, and both men laughed, 'Ow! It is sore though. I don't know what came over me. That idiot Michael should have known better than to cavort with Roger's wife like that.'

Jack nodded; it was true, though he didn't know how Alex had found out. 'Jungle drums! Can't blame him though, I suppose.'

Alex sipped at his brandy and looked at Jack speculatively. 'Aye, secrets have a way of getting out.' He took a sip from his glass and continued, 'I've had my eye on you as well, Jack Dunbar. You're quite the dark horse, are you not? I also found out something about you.'

Jack swallowed, the blood draining from his face. 'Oh, now what could that be?' he asked, looking surprised and trying to read Alex's face.

'Well, it was during that last holiday we had in Loch Duich, near Skye, before Eilidh had her operation, and as you know we were with your fiancée, Estelle. I never told you, what with one thing or another, but she let slip that the pair of you were actually married.' He put the glass down and looked quizzically over at Jack in order to gauge the other man's reaction. Then he grinned, 'You guarded that secret well.'

Jack looked at Alex and slowly nodded his head. He sighed deeply. 'Inevitable I suppose; she didn't tell me that she'd told you.'

'Don't you worry, old man, it's just between you and me. She'd had one too many at a daft ceilidh, probably doesn't remember a thing about it. She just let it slip that she was a married woman. Eilidh and I never let on. Don't you worry,' and he drained his glass. 'Kills the pain, doesn't it?' and he staggered back to the kitchen and Jack heard the clink of bottles. He stared down at the dark green carpet and appeared lost in thought.

'Sorry, old man, stirred things up have I?' Alex put down the two bottles and unscrewed the whisky and poured a good measure into the other man's glass.

'Alex, I don't know what to do.' Jack breathed deeply, then leant towards his glass and took a swallow. He felt courage as the raw liquid burnt his throat.

Alex said nothing; he sensed that Jack would talk in his own time.

'I've made a girl pregnant.'

'You've what?' Alex was dumbfounded. Of all the things it might have been, this was an option he hadn't considered. 'What the hell have you been playing at?'

'I know, I know. I just found out.'

'Do I know her? Oh God, she's not someone's wife is she?'

'No. No! But she is Malay.'

'Not your *amah*?' Alex thought of Hassina's ocean-going hips and her attentive manner to the single men in her care.

'Are you mad? No, it's Aminah, Roger and Freya's *amah*.'

'Oh bloody hell, Jack, how on earth did you manage that?'

Alex had sobered up and his brain was rapidly thinking of all the ramifications of Jack's confession.

Jack went on and told his friend of the unexpected meeting in Kuala Lumpur and the subsequent events at the Rex Hotel. 'I haven't seen her since, well, not till tonight,' he added lamely.

'Well, there isn't much you can do except maybe give her money. Did you talk to her at all this evening?'

Jack smiled ruefully. 'I think you put a stop to all the evening's chit-chat with your dramatic accusations. Maybe in retrospect it wasn't a bad thing. Your diversion probably put a stop to more than just chattering.'

Alex looked stonily in front of him, recalling Freya's fury and the fear in her eyes at the thought of Roger confronting her.

'Estelle must never know, of course,' Jack added. 'Can I count on you to keep my confidence?'

'Of course, old man! Secret is safe with me.'

'Yet Aminah is a good girl.' Jack went on, 'I'll have to do something to help her. I'll think about that tomorrow when my head is a bit clearer.' He rubbed his eyes. 'Do you mind if I bunk down here for the night?'

'Be my guest. I need some aspirin; my nose is bloody sore.'

Chapter 10

1956 – Malaya

Time was just flying by, Freya thought as she plaited her hair in front of the mirror; three weeks already since the dinner party. She removed some pins from her hair and fixed the braids higher over the top of her head and blew out. Gosh, it was hot today. She surveyed the finished effect, feeling graceful and feminine. She picked up the silver-framed photograph on her dressing table and rubbed the metal, noting how tarnished it was becoming. The picture was of her and Roger on their wedding day. He might not be everyone's ideal husband, she thought fondly, but he was the man for her. Roger grinned back from the picture, his face strong and handsome, his hair brushed back from his forehead, and she smiled at the greying sideburns he had once thought so dashing. She saw him again as he was then, his maturity making him debonair and so tantalisingly attractive. He was a man that made everything complete; he added something; though she couldn't name what it was, but he made things look more interesting than they were. Freya turned to the laughing image of herself, not exactly demure, but, she reflected, still naïve and deserving of the white satin. Oh dear, she did hope the dust had settled. She was lucky to have such a forgiving husband. He seemed to have taken all the drama of the disastrous party in his stride. She remembered his words when he had come home after running the others to the clinic.

'Well, old thing, you seem to have rattled Alex's cage and God knows how many others'. It's lucky I'm a tolerant man and can handle my beautiful wife's flirtations. You're like a dazzling light out here in the rubber, and to be honest I can't say I blame these damn moths trying to get at you.'

She breathed out in relief; maybe he didn't know after all. He'd always given her freedom to develop her own friendships and she prayed he didn't suspect that she'd betrayed his trust. The last few weeks saw him rallying to her side, offering his continued support and devotion. She was a lucky woman.

'Phew, it's really hot this morning,' she said again, and began rummaging in her chest of drawers for her swimsuit. 'Aminah!' she called to her *amah* who was lackadaisically flicking the light fitments with her feather duster. 'Aminah, where is my orange bikini?'

'Down by the pool, Mem. I washed everything and put it with the towels in the cupboard down there. Are you swimming this morning?'

'Yes, it's so hot. Dorothy Bathgate invited me over to play tennis with Lois, but I don't think I feel like anything so athletic.' As she passed her maid, she gave her a perfunctory look and said, 'Are you all right?' before starting down the stairs. 'Have you got over that flu bug that's been making you so tired?'

'Yes, Mem, I feel better now, Cookie made me some chicken soup.'

Suddenly the clattering, juddering noise of a Land Rover rumbled out of the dark periphery of rubber and burst into the sunny garden, spraying stones and throwing up a red cloud of dust.

'Who on earth could that be?' Freya's pulse quickened. 'Could it be Michael?' She ran out to the porch, hoping and hoping that he'd come for her, just for one last time. Her resolve to forget him dissolved as the green Land Rover approached.

'*Tuan* Michael?' Aminah felt a spasm of fear for her mistress. *Tuan* Roger might come back, today was not safe, he was not away in Kuala Lumpur. She stood rooted to the spot, stroking the glossy brown feathers of her duster as though it were a live chicken.

Freya stepped out to the porch, her eyes wide with surprise when she registered who it was slamming the vehicle's door. 'Jack?' she smiled uncertainly.

'Hello there!'

'I'm afraid Roger's at the office, or maybe out on G Division; actually he could be anywhere...' She broke off, confused by this unannounced visit.

'No, I haven't come to see Roger specifically,' and he leant over to undo the laces of his work boots.

'Me?' Freya fingered the gold chain at her neck.

'Partly,' he replied. He stood up and made to come in.

'Please, come inside; I'm sorry, would you like some coffee or a cold drink? You've driven quite a way.'

Jack caught sight of Aminah, still standing frozen at the top of the stairs, clutching her feather duster.

'Aminah, can you ask Cookie to make some coffee, please?'

'Yes, Mem,' She made her way down the stairs and out through the swing doors to the kitchen.

'Well, Jack, to what do we owe this great honour? Come, let's sit through in the lounge; it's cooler there.' Freya walked through, leading the way, and switched on the fan before bending over to turn down the volume of the radiogram. A soft, rippling melody filled the air.

'Chopin?' asked Jack.

Freya nodded. 'Yes, I'm having a change from operas. I think Cookie is pleased!'

Presently Cookie brought in the tray with the pot of coffee and two cups, and a plate with a selection of biscuits on.

'Thank you, Cookie; that will be all.'

Jack waited until he had taken several sips of the strong black liquid before speaking. 'I'm imposing on your hospitality Freya; you must forgive me, but it wasn't until I saw things as they really are, the other night at your party...I realised then that I needed to take some action.'

Freya felt a hot flush suffuse her face.

'You mean Michael?' she asked, her eyes opened wide in fear.

'What?' Jack replied incredulously, and then slowly, understanding dawned on him. Never had he seen Freya so vulnerable. Her lovely face looked stricken, the cornflower blue eyes moist and imploring. Her fingers were distractedly shredding her paper serviette to confetti.

'Oh God, Freya! Relax old girl, I'm sorry. I'm an insensitive brute. As usual I was so caught up in my own worries I never thought how my words might have sounded.' He leant over and gently removed the torn napkin and took her hand. 'Your world is pretty secure, Freya; trust me, you've nothing to worry about.'

'Then what...what are you talking about?' she asked, removing her hand from his.

Jack took a deep breath. 'My business here today is with Aminah.'

'Aminah?' Now Freya really was shocked.

'Yes, Aminah; can you call her in please, Freya?'

Freya raised her eyebrows and walked through to the kitchen and asked Cookie to find her *amah*. In just a few minutes Aminah appeared before them, her eyes downcast.

'Mem?'

Before Freya could answer, Jack stood up and put his arm around Aminah, drawing her to the sofa to sit beside him. 'I am so sorry, Aminah, I didn't realise...'

'It's not your fault, it was me,' she raised her eyes and shyly smiled into his, 'don't you remember?'

'I do. Believe me, I do,' and he took her hand. 'But now I must help you.'

Now Freya understood. She'd been so preoccupied with her own passionate dalliance with Michael that she'd failed to notice her *amah's* uncharacteristic lethargy and sickness. She stood up. 'I shall leave you two; it looks as though you need to talk.'

'No, wait a moment, Freya, please. You need to know, and Aminah needs a friend to support her.' He turned back to Aminah, 'What about your family? Your mother and sister? Will they be able to help you?'

'No,' Aminah shook her head emphatically. 'I cannot tell them; it is better they don't know. We don't see each other very often and I don't think they will understand. I am a Muslim girl; it is not good to have a baby with no husband.'

Jack put his hand under her chin and lifted her face up to look at him. Gently he said, 'I can't marry you, my dear. You know that?'

Aminah nodded, 'I ask for nothing, *Tuan* Jack'.

'I know, I've already promised to marry someone else in my own country. But I want to help you. Will you let me help you?'

'Yes,' the girl nodded, lowering her eyes.

'How many months are you?' enquired Freya, practically.

'Five already.'

'So you're due around January?'

'Yes, Mem.'

'We must tell Roger, as well,' said Jack, 'and I'll arrange for money to be paid to you each month. Is there anything else I should do, Freya...to help?'

173

Freya regarded the unlikely pair on her sofa, the beautiful Malay girl and the handsome planter. She was full of curiosity as to how the two had met. Instead she said, 'Don't worry, Jack, Aminah will always have a home with Roger and me. Now I think I'll leave you two alone for a while. I'll be down at the pool if you need me. Please, Jack, call us at any time, and as for you, Aminah, we can talk later.'

The two women smiled at each other. The fine balance of their relationship had suddenly been altered irrevocably. They would now be friends.

After Freya left, Jack turned again to Aminah and again lifted her chin up so that she could look into the intensity of his kingfisher-blue eyes. 'You look tired, have you been sick?'

'So sick, *Tuan*, every day; Cookie made me fry the eggs at breakfast and I had to run out all the time. Oh, the smell made me so sick. Now I am better, the sickness has stopped, but look! Now I get fat!'

'Does Cookie suspect?'

'I think so, he makes a tutting noise, "Tch tch tch" like that all the time, but he doesn't make me lift the rice bin so maybe he is a little bit kind.'

Gently Jack moved on the cushion so that his arm went around the girl's shoulders and with his other hand he pressed against her swollen belly. Aminah could feel the fluttering, almost like a small bird trying to escape as the baby responded to the pressure of the man's hand. Jack's eyes crinkled into a smile. He could feel the small beginnings of life. He bent over so that his cheek rested on her abdomen. Shyly Aminah touched his hair. Softly she traced the outline of his profile and smoothed the black fringe from his brow. He raised his head and looked at her swollen breasts.

'Oh God, Aminah, you are so beautiful.' He took her face in his hands, and leaning over, he placed his lips on hers.

Chapter 11

Malaya

'*Merdeka, Merdeka, Merdeka...*'

The tumultuous cries of freedom filled the air as the British flag was lowered for the last time and the new flag of independence was raised. It was 31 August 1957 and Tunku Abdul Rahman, the prime minister-elect of the Federation of Malaya, had just proudly announced the independence of his country, in what he described as the greatest moment in the life of the Malayan people.

The Emergency, however, was not yet over. Guards were still necessary on the estates and the managers still needed armed escorts to accompany them on pay day. Although incidents were rarer, it did not pay to be complacent.

It was late in December of the same year that Alex attended a meeting with the chief of police in Taman Minyak. Michael, Jack and Callum were together for the last time in their bungalow. It was to be their fifth Christmas in Malaya. Michael had finished his acting manager position at Bukit Hijau Estate and now the three were reunited before going home on leave.

'I hope the *tuan besar* hasn't forgotten he said he'd call in and take us to the club,' said Michael, running a comb through his hair. 'Wonder what's keeping him.' He was still wary of Alex since the incident at Freya and Roger's dinner and felt sheepish about the spectacle he'd inadvertently caused. Freya had tactfully withdrawn, and whilst relations had cooled between himself and Roger, his evening tennis sessions with Lois had developed into something more meaningful. He sighed, looking towards the driveway. 'Alex had better get a move on; the kids are singing carols and Dorothy will be mad if we miss that. She's spent ages rehearsing with them.' He knew it was Dorothy who'd encouraged his attentions to Lois, her sister-in-law, and they were now writing regularly to each other. Michael believed that he would marry her when he went back on leave. The New Year was full of promise; a manager's post at last and his very own estate. He stood up and turned to Callum. 'Come on old boy, are you going to give that gun a rest? It's cleaner than a whistle. You should get yourself into the shower before Alex arrives.'

'Aye aye, I'll be on my way. Just want to put a wee drop more oil down the barrel. You can't be too careful, you know, where guns are concerned,' and he agitated the cleaning rod vigorously. 'Where's Jack, anyway?'

Jack was getting ready. He buttoned his best blue shirt and tucked it into a pair of white slacks. His hair, still wet from the shower, was slicked back off his forehead. Before washing, he'd nipped out to get a glass of whisky and soda which he'd then enjoyed lying back on his pillow, cooling off under the fan. He couldn't wait to see Estelle and bring her back; this clandestine marriage had been a hell of a strain on them both. Never mind, he thought, he'd be the manager of his own estate in April, and he'd have all his home leave to reacquaint himself with his pretty young wife. He'd a notion to climb some of those mountains in the Cairngorms so he hoped she liked walking.

Now with the empty glass in his hand Jack stepped out of his room, humming *We Three Kings of Orient Are*. He was tired. They all were. They had all served longer than the three years required, but owing to the troubles, the estate managers had wanted to preserve some feeling of stability, and had opted to stay on in their estates. The assistants had little choice but to accept an increase in their salary and await promotion after their next home leave.

Entering the lounge, Jack sunk down into his chair. '*Lagi satu*,' he signalled to Hassina, who was hovering at the door. 'You're not still playing with that pop gun, are you?' he asked Callum, 'I thought you'd finished cleaning it last night.'

'Aye, I did, but I was out an hour ago shooting flying foxes, didn't you hear me?'

'Maybe, I was having a snooze and the fan was making a racket; I had it on full pelt.'

'I told him to get a move on,' Michael cut in, 'Alex will be here any minute.' He finished off the beer he was drinking and put it on the tray that Hassina was taking out to the kitchen.

Jack put his head back and closed his eyes. He let his mind wander to his recent visit to see Aminah in Anak Kamsiah Estate. She was now heavily pregnant, the baby due in just a few weeks. He remembered how she'd held his hand, so trusting, her black eyes wet with emotion. 'It's going to be all right, Aminah, I promise. You won't want for money and Freya has offered you a home for as long as you want.'

'I know,' she'd said, 'I know and I'm so lucky. You are good man, *Tuan* Jack.'

Michael looked at his watch. Six forty-five, where the hell had Alex got to? No sign of headlights approaching.

Outside the air was humid and still and the perpetual droning and humming of insects filled the darkness and reminded the men of the ever-present reality of the life that coexisted alongside them: the life that stirred and stalked in the dark wet humus of the forest floor, the blind, unseeing creatures that gnawed on fungi and rotting vegetation and tunnelled amidst the spirally roots of fresh, sinewy seedlings. They couldn't hear the pad of the panther's paw, placed with such stealth and precision, heralding the sure death of the unsuspecting mouse deer. Nor could they hear the scratchy scrape of the giant python manoeuvring its coils around the freshly strangled corpse of a fallen monkey. The moon slipped behind a cloud and the cicadas fell silent. The night claimed the garden in a thick sheet of black. Suddenly an ear-splitting crack shattered the steamy silence of the night. Immediately the mouse deer bolted and the panther froze. The *jaga*, the armed guard, who had been sitting morosely, picking his toes and contemplating the boredom of the long night watch ahead, jumped up like a scalded cat. He ran to the open veranda doors, for the shot had been fired not by an unseen assailant lurking in the jungle but from within the white men's bungalow. Unthinking, he burst into the room, his wild eyes flying from one man to the other, and there he saw *Tuan* Jack. He started screaming and babbling in Malay. *Tuan* Jack's body was thrown back against the chair, his head and face red with blood. It was Michael who reacted first.

'What the hell? Jack! Oh Jesus! Callum, what have you done?'

In two lightning strides he was at Jack's side, and with urgency born of panic, tried to locate a pulse in his friend's neck, his fingers slipping in the blood from the gaping wound above the right eyebrow. 'There's no pulse, I can't find his pulse, he's not breathing. Jack, wake up, Jack! Christ, he's not moving, he's dead. You've killed him! Jack! I can't believe it. He's dead!' Michael stared down at his friend in disbelief, and too stunned to know what else to do, he ran his hand over the staring eyes to close the eyelids. He walked over to Callum and took the gun. 'What the hell happened? I thought you were cleaning it?' He stared at the rifle in bewilderment.

'There must have been a bullet lodged, I was just aiming randomly at that wall and suddenly the damn thing went off. I didn't mean to do it...' He pointed to his left and saw the crease in the plaster where the bullet had been deflected on its fatal journey. 'It must have ricocheted. What have I done? God, Michael, help me, what have I done?'

They looked up and saw the *jaga* and Hassina, both standing transfixed as the realisation of what had happened started to sink in.

Hassina started to wail, 'Oh, *Tuan* Jack, *Tuan* Jack, oh, Allah, Allah!'

'It was an accident, Hassina, *Tuan* Jack had accident.' In a daze Michael walked out to the hall and picked up the telephone.

'Hello, hello, get me the police station in Taman Minyak, *chepat chepat*, quick as you can and send a doctor to the house, yes, the assistants' bungalow, Bukit Bulan, *chepat*, please hurry!'

'Oh God, what have I done?' Callum's shoulders were shaking. He paced the room, wringing his hands. 'Oh my God, what have I done?'

'Make tea, Hassina, with plenty of sugar.' Michael followed her into the kitchen and poured out two large whiskies. 'Drink that, come on, Callum, get it down you. Christ man, it was an accident, an accident. It wasn't your fault, it just happened. Come here and sit down.'

Callum collapsed in the chair and drained the glass in one swallow before shuddering uncontrollably as the enormity of what he had done engulfed him. The jungle noises of the night were joined by his wracking sobs as he lost control.

The following week passed in a blur. Since there would be a police inquiry, Callum was briefed by an English attorney recommended by the embassy in Kuala Lumpur. The situation was exacerbated by Christmas falling two days after the shooting. Government offices were closed and the autopsy results were delayed. Telegrams were sent to London, but no advice was sent back as the country had come to a halt for the festive holiday. Jack's body lay in the morgue in Kuala Lumpur. A funeral would have to be organised, but only after the coroner's report and the wishes of the family were known.

Alex sent telegrams to Jack's mother and he chewed the top of his pencil while he struggled to compose a similar message to Estelle. Finally he wrote: 'Tragic accident. Jack Dunbar fatally shot. Deepest sympathy. Letter to follow. Alex McIntyre'. He then thought of Aminah. He would have to go and see her. He had already rung Freya and Roger of course, but asked Freya not to tell Aminah just yet as her time was so close.

Three months later in Scotland, Alex and Callum were sitting together in the lounge of the hospital at Creachan, Inverness. Converted from a Victorian castle, it was a retreat for people suffering from addiction or depression or trauma. Some of the patients were on suicide watch, some needed protection from themselves; others had text book symptoms of mental illness. And there was Callum. The two brothers sat looking out over the beautiful grounds. Callum wore a green paisley robe over his blue-and-white striped pyjamas. He felt nervous and awkward.

'They say you're doing fine,' Alex commented.

Callum sniffed, 'Whatever that means. They've got words to describe everything here, trying to make us all sound normal, I suppose. I'm quite a placid patient compared to some.' He chewed his already raw fingernails. 'I'm relatively easy to look after. You see some sights in here, I can tell you. There's no dignity in this place.' Callum fell silent. He wanted to return to the sterile white enclosure that was his room, his oasis, his escape from the world where his memories tormented him.

'You'll soon be your old self again and back with us where you belong, you know. It's just a matter of time. You are getting better. Remember when you came here, those first weeks in January with the snow on the ground and the bitter cold? The doctor told me you're making good progress.'

'That's true, but the guilt will stay with me for ever. I felt so deserted when you first brought me here. All those weeks I spent just sitting in an armchair by the window living in my private hell, I hardly spoke to a soul. I can cope with the days now, but it's the nights that are the worst. It's the dreams. I'm haunted by his staring eyes and the blood. Remember the blood on the wall?' I wake up shouting, "No, No, No!" until the nurses come and give me a jab. Then it's blessed oblivion.'

'This is my daddy,' Anna told everyone when they went walking. 'My daddy knows all about birds. He tells me their names.'

Alex was spending his compassionate leave in Glengrianach with Eilidh's parents and his little daughter. A simple walk along the street seemed to take forever as Anna proudly showed him off to her friends.

'Do you know what a sparrow looks like?' she asked the lady in the bakery.

'I've just seen a pigeon,' she announced to the postman. 'Have you ever seen one?'

'No, I'm not sure I have, they must be really rare,' chuckled the postie.

'My daddy lets me ride my horse all day if I want, not like my granny,' she boasted to Mrs Wiseman in the sweet shop.

'I didn't know you had a horse, pet. Is it a wee Shetland pony then?'

'No, my horse is a rocking horse, and he's a Malayan horse and he crossed the sea in a ship. Not like my daddy, he crossed the sea in an airy plane, didn't you, Daddy?'

Alex laughed, though the pain was still acute. After all, it was only a year ago that he'd shipped home the toys and the dresses. Now he watched Anna struggling through the snow beside him. His thoughts were soon interrupted by a loud wail.

'Snow in my boots, Daddy, it's making my socks wet,' and she started to howl.

'Come on then, up you get, you can ride on my shoulders and tell me what you can see ahead of you. Can you see any parrots from up there? Parrots like to fly high in the sky.'

'Not yet, Daddy, but I'm looking.'

Towards the end of January, Alex telephoned Jack's widow. He left Anna with her granny and drove south to Perth where he had agreed to meet Estelle for lunch. After parking his car he buttoned his woollen overcoat and walked over the bridge that spanned the River Tay. The cold was bitter but the sun shone, and he was full of trepidation as he gazed down at the chunks of ice swirling about in eddies in the fast-flowing water. What would she be like, this red headed woman whom he'd met so briefly a year ago when she'd joined him and Eilidh on holiday on the West Coast? When he arrived at McEwans, he climbed the stairs to the restaurant, bypassing the subdued hush of the carpeted department store. They looked across the room at each other. Estelle was sitting at a table by a window, the winter sun on her copper curls forming a pre-Raphaelite halo around her head. She smiled and raised her hand in welcome. Grinning, Alex strode towards her and she rose to meet him. He inhaled the scent of compressed powder on her face, and the faint trace of something familiar as he kissed her cheek. She looked into his eyes, always so shrouded with pain, and her own eyes filled in compassion.

Before returning to Malaya in early April, Alex dropped in to see his brother again. Although making good progress, Callum was not yet ready to return to manage a rubber plantation. 'You know I've been seeing quite a bit of Estelle?' Alex asked, watching Callum's reaction.

'Aye, you did say you'd seen her, and I think you're quite taken with her. Am I not right?'

Alex chuckled, 'If the truth be known, I am. She's quite special and when you meet her you'll understand why Jack was in such haste to marry her!'

'I don't know that I can see her,' Callum's eyes registered fear. 'I don't know what I'd say. It's enough knowing what I did, but having a responsibility towards someone he loved...'

'You didn't know he was married, nobody did. Estelle will be fine, she's a strong woman and I think it would be good if you let her visit you. I know she wants to; might be good for both of you. Just think about it. I've got her telephone number here and you can contact her whenever you want. She said she'd wait for your call.' Alex looked around at the almost empty room. 'But there is something else,' he paused, unsure of how to proceed. 'I don't know, maybe it would help you if you could do something practical?'

'Anything, you know I'd do anything if I could help somehow.'

'Well, there's this child...'

As Alex drove down the winding driveway of Creachan and saw in his rear view mirror the warm red brick walls of the old building sheltered in the lee of the high beech hedge, he pictured again the face of his brother when he told him about Aminah. 'She had a boy, Callum. He's fine and healthy, and Freya and Roger are happy for her to stay on. I went to see her just before we flew back. He was born in the last week of December, a little early. Maybe the shock of everything brought it on; she heard unexpectedly through the *amah* telegraph. Freya and I thought it better to keep it quiet but these things have a way of getting out, so there we are. He's a fine little lad, she's calling him Suleiman. Apparently Jack promised he'd pay her a monthly sum. Perhaps that's something you could take on? If you took over that commitment maybe it would somehow appease your conscience. Of course it would be our secret, no one else need ever know.'

Callum had readily agreed, and for the first time his eyes lost the dead look of a drug-induced lethargy. Alex felt that perhaps Jack's life would go on after all. 'The Lord works in mysterious ways,' his mother used to say. What Alex didn't know was that when Aminah was handed her newborn baby, the first thing she did was to turn over his tiny hand and examine the delicate pink lines that ran across his palm. She'd hugged him close and her tears had fallen on to the soft beating pulse of his temple.

PART TWO

Chapter 12

May 1960 – Malaya

Estelle stepped on to the tarmac and squinted into the fierce sunlight. Never before had she felt such heat. Looking down at her bare arms, she half expected to see drops of perspiration dance about and start to boil. Impatiently she joined the flow of people making their way towards a wooden shack, its corrugated tin roof reflecting yet more heat into the dense blue sky. She turned and looked back at the BOAC Comet that had transported her through the skies, the huge plane shimmering as though caught in a mirage of vapour. Thank God I changed my clothes after Bombay, she thought. I'd have died if I'd stayed in that suit I left Dundee in. It was good foresight to have packed a dress for my arrival.

'I'd take your nylons off as well, if I were you,' the stewardess had advised her when she emerged from the confines of the lavatory.

'Are you sure? I've just been wriggling and twisting to get out of my outer clothes, I left my slip and stockings on.'

'Believe me, madam; you won't need them where we're going!'

Now she was glad of the girl's advice, for she looked as fresh as a flower in a bright yellow-and-white polka dot dress and peep-toe sandals. Estelle adored fashion and the couture magazines displaying the latest collections in London and Paris. In her small way she tried to emulate the mannequins she saw on her shopping sprees. She hoped she would get a chance to dress up in her new life. After immigration and the long wait for her suitcases, she finally arrived at customs where her case was marked with a white chalk cross and she was free to make her way to the arrival hut. Her head flicked from side to side as she absorbed the activity around her. Faces of every colour, race and gender surrounded her, voices rose and shouted, people pushed and surged. Estelle shrank back, her eyes wildly taking in the crowd as she frantically searched for her husband amongst the sea of humanity. Alex saw her at once and ran forward, lifting her up and swirling her around, completely oblivious to the sniggering glances of the native porters. Her small frame was lost within the exuberance of his embrace and she was conscious of his smell, the wetness of his shirt and the slipperiness of his arms.

'You made it!' he exclaimed, stepping back to look at her. 'What a bonny sight, you're just a picture to behold. Why is it that I never look as fresh as that after a twenty-four hour flight?'

Estelle laughed, pleased that he admired her, 'I just put on my eye mask and slept, then woke up to eat and slept again. I was so glad to have brought some fresh clothes to change into!'

'Well, now you know how I felt when I first came out here! I had my vest and suit and woollen socks on. I had no idea what to expect and nobody took the trouble to tell me. Ah well, here you are and you'll be impatient to see everything. Stay close to me, lass, and we'll get through this rabble.'

'Taxi, *Tuan*? I give you good price. Where you go, sir? I take you, I have good car.'

'Over here, *Tuan*, you come with me. I know everywhere!'

'You want souvenir, Mem? You buy from me, I give you good price.'

'I carry your case, *Tuan*, no problem, where your car? I take your case.'

'Over here, Estelle, hold tight, my car is over here.'

Estelle again screwed up her eyes and marvelled at the brightness, the vibrancy of the emerald greens and fluorescent reds and pinks that made up the exotic foliage and flowers. She had arrived.

Alex opened the passenger door with a flourish. 'Come, Mrs McIntyre, you are home!'

Cookie, Amah, and the gardeners were lined up, all smiling warmly. Cookie stepped forward and bowed his head and said, 'Welcome, Mem, welcome to Bukit Bulan Estate.'

Estelle blinked and smiled and her eyes filled with tears. She swallowed hard and tried to smile more brightly. She leant over and patted the white dog with the black eye. 'And you must be Sinbad.'

He wagged his tail and hurtled off to greet Alex with wet-tongued enthusiasm. Estelle stepped on to the polished wooden floor and looked around her. Here was the house that had been described to her by so many. She took in the high ceilings, the arched doorways leading into the dining room and the airy sitting room. She walked over to the French windows and the veranda that faced on to the garden. Her eyes rested on the dry stone walls of the water fountain. She'd seen photographs centred on this particular construction. Jack had once sent her one of himself and Eilidh sitting just there, dangling their feet into the water. Estelle blinked and turned towards the brightly flowering shrubs. Cookie ushered her into the sitting room and she sat down on the white cushions on the rattan sofa. Her eyes took in the rich colours of the Bokhara rugs under her feet. Eilidh, Eilidh, Eilidh…and then she glanced out to the veranda and her eyes rested on the table and chairs where Jack had once written to her. A white cat came and sat and stared at her impassively…

'Come, darling, you must see everything. Cookie and Amah have been cleaning and scrubbing especially. Don't forget I've lived alone here for three years, so it's conceivable that I may need a wee bit of retraining, and I think you are just the woman for the job!' He whistled happily as he led the way upstairs and opened the bedroom door. 'Well, how do you like this? Admittedly it's not as plush as our honeymoon hotel in Paris, but I'm sure you can make it into anything you want!'

Estelle gazed at the large room, the stark bareness of the walls, the windows around two sides giving breathtaking views of the garden and the surrounding dark presence of the rubber trees. She looked out and in the distance she saw the rounded hills, thick with the tangled life forces of the virgin jungle. She looked down into the bright oasis of colour that was the garden, the citrus-green shoots of young banana trees growing alongside gangly palms with pendulous orange fruit hanging precariously from the thin trunks. 'What are those, Alex?'

'Those are papaya. I like to eat them for breakfast with a squeeze of lime juice. Look, the lime bushes are over there. They always attract those speckled butterflies. When you pick the fruit, you'll find that each stem has a fat green caterpillar with a funny face. Over there are pineapples and we also have mango trees and rambutans.'

Together they surveyed the view and Estelle stole a look at his sharp, aquiline profile. Well, she thought, it was only a house; she would just have to make it theirs; that was all. She went to shower, and when she

185

came out Alex had gone downstairs and Amah was unpacking and examining her clothes.

'*Banyak chantik*, Mem! Very beautiful, you wear this today?'

Estelle nodded, 'Yes, Amah, *terima kasih*, thank you.'

Cookie served Scotch broth and minced beef with carrots and potatoes for lunch. Estelle couldn't help smiling; she had travelled thousands of miles to eat what had been her staple diet for the last thirty years!

'I know,' laughed Alex, 'but it's what I like, and Cookie is an expert now. He makes a damn good stew as well.'

Estelle took a bread roll from a basket in the middle of the table. 'Mmmmm, this is delicious, it's still warm. Where do you get them, I mean you're so far from KL?'

'I make them, Mem,' Cookie replied as he refilled her water glass.

'Ah,' she smiled, 'of course!' Her eyes looked away and for a moment she drifted back to the dreary hotel where once there had been no fresh bread until Wednesday.

After lunch, the couple lay together enjoying the peace of siesta time. Noises drifted through the window and Estelle listened to the sound of a latex truck returning to the factory. Close by came the sharp chirrup of a mynah bird and from far away she heard the call of a monkey. Beside her Alex slept, his hands folded on his chest as though in prayer. She couldn't sleep. She watched the hypnotic turning of the ceiling fan and her mind flew unbidden to Jack. He'd lived for a while in this house and she knew that the assistants' bungalow down the road was where he'd died. She turned her face to the wall where she screwed up her eyes, trying to blot out the images of that awful morning when she'd received the telegram.

She'd been peeling carrots, she remembered. She'd read the words, 'Tragic accident...fatally shot...' and she'd stared at the everyday things around her: the Christmas cards hanging on the wall between her mother's Wedgwood plates, the chopping board and vegetables. Carols were being sung on the wireless. How could this be? Estelle let out a soft moan at the memory of that moment, albeit that it was three years ago. Being here in Malaya was rekindling a lot of suppressed feelings. She remembered the storm of indignation that came from Jack's family as well as from her own, for as Jack's legal wife and next of kin, she'd been left a considerable sum of money. This she had quietly invested. Somehow she'd got through it all, continuing her unassuming lifestyle, until one snowy winter's morning she received a telephone call from Alex McIntyre. Estelle turned to lie on her back again, a feeling of warmth suffusing her body. She stretched like a cat, remembering their initial meetings, reserved at first, but then on his return, the passionate flowering of romance.

'There's a dance in Dundee, shall we go?'

'I'm not much of a dancer,' warned Alex, 'but if you're happy to shuffle about, I'll be careful of your toes.'

The room was smoky and she held his hand chastely as he encircled his arm round the small of her back. Softly he caressed her cheek with his rough, unshaven chin. The intimate gesture and the smell of his skin ignited her passion and she pressed her body closer to him. Alex responded and they swayed in each other's arms, lost in the new beginning, savouring the precious moment.

Was it fate, Estelle wondered, or Lady Luck? Whatever, it seemed it had been decreed that she would become a rubber planter's wife. She rolled to her side and stared at her second love. They would be fine, she decided, they had weathered the storms and she had crossed the seas to be with him. She was determined to overcome any obstacle, for after all she had been given a second chance.

The weeks that followed passed in a blur of heat for Estelle. Nobody had prepared her for the sensation of living in an oven. Each day the heat fell on her like a physical force, the humidity enveloped her and she found that she had to succumb to having a lie-off, the Malay equivalent of a siesta. The heat drained her energy, and only in the early morning was she able to pursue her chores with her usual vigour. Her days took on a rhythm where she and Cookie battled for domestic domination. He dusted with a feather duster, Estelle preferred to stand on a chair and wipe with a damp cloth. She was a fiend for cleanliness and her sharp tongue caused great loss of face in the servants' quarters.

'Cookie! I thought I told you to take the rugs out and beat them on the washing line and then let them stay in the sun for an hour?'

'Yes, Mem, I will do that, but first I have to make the cakes for afternoon tea.'

'And I want all the chairs moved into the centre of the room so that you can brush the spiders' webs from the back. Oh! I can see that I shall just have to do it myself.'

She started to haul the heavy chairs about and Cookie's mouth compressed into a thin line, not at all pleased with this unwarranted criticism.

'I've been invited to play golf this afternoon, Alex. Are you still playing with Callum? Can we go together?'

'Aye, I am, and who are you playing with, may I ask?' He was slightly amused at his wife's sudden prowess on the course. She'd only had about six lessons and that was when the course was deserted. Just as well, he thought, for the balls were flying about like missiles.

'Well, there's a competition for the ladies and I want to take part. I'm a bit nervous about it, but it should be good fun.'

Later that day Estelle and her fellow competitors teed off first while the brothers watched in trepidation.

'We'd better give them half an hour,' chuckled Callum. 'By the time they've whacked the ball into the car park a few times and taken great chunks out of the driving range, it might be safe for us to get started.'

'There's nothing like enthusiasm,' agreed Alex, grimly. 'Talk about the new broom. She's rearranged the furniture again! I never know where my chair is going to be when I get in for breakfast. And cooking – we're having all sorts of strange menus: **Chicken à la King** and goodness knows what else.'

Callum could relate, having just got married himself. 'At least Kate sleeps late and doesn't come out on my early morning rounds with me.'

'You're lucky there, I can tell you. Estelle is up at six with the account books, and now she's a committee member for the club, she's planning to be the Ladies Golf Captain, never mind that she's only just learnt to play.'

'She's a good housekeeper, Kate tells me; she's been teaching her how to keep a tally on the household bills.'

'Oh, no argument there; if she doesn't make Ladies Captain, she's certainly the captain of our ship. Poor Cookie doesn't know what's hit him.'

Alex looked out to the fairway. 'Come on, I think it's safe now for us to tee off. They should be well on their way to the second hole.' Collecting his golf cart he made his way to the first tee. He reflected how well Estelle had taken to her new life and as much as she longed for the airmail letters from home, she was seldom melancholy. Her latest passion was learning the intricacies of *mah jong*. 'I won two dollars today, I can't believe it,' she crowed, 'I was convinced that Nancy Fung was going to win as usual, she always saves up the honour tiles. By the way, I've invited some people for dinner on Thursday, is that all right?' Their house had suddenly become a social hub; people came for drinks and barbecues, and Alex marvelled at his new wife's easy charm and confidence as a hostess.

The following Sunday, Callum and his wife Kate joined them for a curry lunch.

'How is everything, Kate, are you coping with the heat? I was just a soggy heap for weeks when I first came out, but I found a really good tailor in KL who made me some skirts and short-sleeved shirts...' she gossiped easily, leading the other woman into the lounge and sitting close to her. Her warmth permeated the group; even Cookie flashed his golden grin as she complimented him on his coconut mousse.

'That was excellent, Cookie, we must give the recipe to Mem Kate. Cookie is such a natural you know, he's learning how to make the dishes from my French cookery book.'

Callum and Alex exchanged a look. 'We'll have two more beers, Cookie.'

'Yes, *Tuan*,' and Cookie sidled out of the room, almost resisting the temptation to smirk.

At the end of the day, after much beer and gin had been consumed, Alex opened the car door for Kate and then turned a little woozily to shake hands with Callum. Suddenly a very flushed Estelle pushed in front of Alex and put her arms around his shy brother. The pair stood together for what seemed like a long time until Callum stepped back, still holding her shoulders. No words were needed. He then got into the car and drove into the dark shadows of the rubber.

'How's married life, Michael?'

'It's pretty good, Alex, in fact very good indeed. Lois is a lot better company than that motley crew I used to live with, I can tell you! She's got some good ideas in the kitchen as well.' He patted his stomach in appreciation. 'Mind you, I still prefer a drink in The Dog with you lads to being dragged around the Globe Silk Store.'

'I know, those places help the ladies keep their sanity, but I've never been one to get excited about reels of cotton and bolts of cloth. It was easier before in many ways; at least the house was free of paper patterns and what not all over the place. Callum's saying the same thing.' Alex laughed and looked around the bar. 'I see Gilbert Dawson is out again; I wonder who he's promoting now. How are you finding your new estate? Not too isolated away up there in Perak?'

'It's a good estate and I'm enjoying the challenge, but to be honest Lois is finding it a bit lonely. She's making the best of it though. Callum was lucky getting a place so close to KL.'

'Born with the moon shining out of his rear end, that one,' Alex said, before remembering the tragic history the three men shared. A minute passed before they spoke again.

'A lot of changes in the air, not just on the estates but in Malaya generally,' Michael eventually said. 'And it's only for the better.'

'One more beer and a stengah,' Alex shouted over to the bar boy. 'I saw Dorothy Bathgate at the Jacaranda Club the other day. She and Sam are still our neighbours but of course we don't see much of them. You know how things are...women have different interests.'

'And Lucy, how old is she now?'

'She's six, the same as Anna.' Alex's eyes turned away from the other man and gazed at the bottles lined up behind the bar. It was only last week that he'd bumped into Dorothy and Lucy. His brows bristled. Dorothy had snapped at him, 'Anna didn't die as well, Alex, but she seems to have become an unwitting victim.' Alex had turned from her and walked away, his fists screwed up tight and his teeth clenched. How dare that woman suggest such a thing? It was not his fault that Eilidh's parents had taken the child, he argued with himself, just as he'd done every day since December 1956. He was alone; how could he have cared for a child when the country was still in the grip of the Emergency? Dorothy and Estelle were not friends; the two women had little in common and Dorothy was unwilling to let go of the past. When Estelle was with him, Dorothy would merely nod as they passed, but still Alex read in her eyes her silent questions. Each time he saw Lucy, he wondered what his own daughter was like now. He knew that Estelle was desperate for them to have a baby and that a child would put a seal on their marriage. He understood how insecure and vulnerable she felt when confronted with the ladies of the club who were mothers already. She also had to cope with the older set that had weathered his years as the sad widower. These were the well-meaning matrons who had hosted dinners for him, mothered him and later tried to make love matches for him. Eilidh had become a small icon in this world. She was perceived as the beautiful, tragic heroine who had left Alex bereft. He'd played the part and over the years he'd dated several single ladies that had passed through his life and had the odd dalliance with a few that were not. Estelle had come into this set of well-intentioned women, some of whom disapproved of her frank honesty, but she held her head high, and just as she had done with Cookie, she played the game her way. She was not going to fill anyone's shoes. She was perfectly happy in her own.

Just the previous year, Alex had bought a brand new two-toned Jaguar Mk IX car. It was as beautiful and powerful as its name suggested. He loved its smooth six cylinder engine, its power steering and luxurious leather interior; he loved the feeling of achievement it gave him and he loved to drive it fast. It was his pride and joy. Thundering back home in the Land Rover for lunch one Thursday afternoon, he was horrified when he found the porch empty and his precious car gone.

'Cookie! Where's my car? Cookie!'

'Mem go to KL, *Tuan*.' Cookie looked at Alex quizzically, just a flicker of a smile causing a tic on his right cheek.

'What!' Alex roared. Estelle was tiny, she could barely see over the walnut dashboard. How would she be able to reverse, overtake, park and just cope with the lawless traffic in downtown Kuala Lumpur? He spent the afternoon pacing up and down and vented his frustration by chopping down an unruly hedge of bamboo. At last he heard the crunch of gravel and the scattering of stones on the drive. He ran round to the front of the house.

'Where have you been and what the hell did you think you were doing?' He looked at her, his eyes cold pieces of flint, his mouth drawn in a tight line.

She gazed back at him solemnly and then she smiled. Cookie had come to witness a mighty battle and hopefully to see his headstrong mistress being suitably chastised. He held his breath while she opened the door and clambered out.

'Hello, dear, I bought a plastic blow-up cushion to sit on after I killed the chickens.'

Alex and Cookie walked to the front and sure enough there were the remains of the dead birds. Alex grimaced at the feathers trapped in the radiator grill, at the blood spots spattered over the bonnet. In trepidation he walked around the car, minutely inspecting the bodywork, disdainfully noting the red mud caking the previously pristine white walled tyres.

'Oh my God, did you go so fast...were you out of control?'

'No, dear, I hardly went over forty. Even the trishaws were overtaking me and I got the security guard at Chotirmalls on Batu Road to park it for me; he didn't seem to mind. So I was fine! Cookie, I stopped at Cold Storage, if you could unload for me. There are a couple of crates of beer, and some soda. I could do with a whisky soda. First, though, I need a shower, my dress is drenched with perspiration. What a heat! Did you have a good day, dear?' and with that she breezed up the stairs.

Alex took a very deep breath to calm himself, and then he started de-feathering his prize possession.

The next morning, just after Alex had left for his rounds, Estelle came downstairs dressed in white shorts and a green sleeveless shirt. She jumped into the car and started the engine. Cookie ran through the house and Amah leant out of the top window.

'Mem! No, you cannot!'

Estelle drove round to the gardeners' shed and jumped out. She gathered soap and a cloth and attached the watering hose to the tap and started the mammoth task of washing the dust and laterite from the huge car. The heat was relentless and she had to stop continually to wipe the sweat from her neck and push her wet hair from her forehead. Sinbad padded back and forth leaving a trail of wet paw prints on the track. Finally he settled down and sat panting in the sun, his mouth drawn back in a big grin, his tongue dripping dollops of saliva. Estelle carried on until finally the bodywork was gleaming with crystal droplets and the red clay was washed from the tyres and hubcaps. The great car was a picture to behold.

'Now, my boy, you next; I have to wait until this dries, so I shall do you!' She took the dog by his collar and tied him to the metal pole that held the tap. 'Sit, Sinbad!' She began massaging the soap into his back and around his ears, and noted the ticks swollen with blood around his neck and between the pads of his paws. Gently she rinsed him and let him go. Immediately he bolted across the grass and shook himself and rolled about waving his legs in the air. Estelle laughed, then went into the gardeners' shed and found a tin of kerosene oil. She poured some into an old latex cup and then marched back to the house and called for Amah to bring her the tweezers. Sinbad raised one ear and watched her with growing interest. He sensed that his ordeal was not yet over and sure enough she came for him and he felt his collar being pulled as he was unceremoniously dragged towards the shed. Estelle commanded him to sit, and then she rolled him over and began removing the ticks from his body. The big ones floated white and bloated on top of the kerosene. She had squashed one that had escaped and had been appalled at the amount of blood that it had sucked from the poor dog. The smaller brown ones resembled little starfish attempting a strange swimming stroke across the surface of the liquid. Sinbad lay resigned to this new indignity.

Cookie brought out a glass of iced lime juice which she drank thirstily. Her final chore of the morning was waxing the car and brushing out the inside and polishing the woodwork. Eventually she staggered inside and climbed the stairs and showered then lay on the bed damp and naked under a towel. The stillness of noon lulled her to close her eyes so she didn't hear her husband come back for lunch or feel his presence as he lay down beside her. When she opened her eyes, she gasped in surprise.

'Well, well, my little tornado, are you totally worn out? Perhaps you should take the car out more often if it gets such wonderful treatment afterwards! And I don't think I have seen Sinbad so white since he was a puppy!'

He lay down beside her and for a while there was just quiet and the rumble of rubber trucks in the distance. Somewhere from the distant jungle came a scream followed by a further cacophony of hysterical screeching.

'We'll go to KL at the weekend and see about getting a smaller car for you, how would you like that? Then you'll be able to get about and not feel so confined.'

'Thank you, darling,' she giggled as she hugged him and she slipped her leg over his hip. She felt him responding to her, and he shifted his weight until he was over her and his breath was hot on her brow. Estelle held him tight and squeezed her eyes shut.

'Please, God, make it happen this time, please.'

At the end of July 1960, the Malayan government declared the Emergency to be over. Since the announcement, there was a general air of optimism and confidence was slowly returning throughout the country.

It was now October. Kate was sitting on the veranda of the Selangor Club, idly watching the pristine white-clad cricketers form and reform. The bat cracked and the players scattered to make runs or retrieve the little ball of leather. She smiled at the sight of the bowler vigorously polishing the ball on his private parts. She had once asked Callum why he thought that was necessary, and he had been quite severe with her, pointing out that it was not the private parts actually but the thigh that got such a good rub. Kate squinted into the sun and studied the man performing the debatable ritual. 'I am not convinced,' she muttered to herself and leant over to pour what remained of the pot of coffee into the thin china cup. She looked about her but saw no one she recognised. She was waiting for Estelle and Nancy Fung. They were to go to the Globe Silk Store on Batu Road to select fabric for evening dresses for the Planters' Ball in November.

Kate also wanted material for a dress to mark her first wedding anniversary, for she and Callum had married the previous November, almost a year after his mental breakdown. Time had begun its healing process and their relationship had blossomed after he'd been discharged from hospital. She was what her gran would describe as 'homely', and although she hankered to be tall and elegant, she had come to terms with her more generous proportions. She remembered how awkward she used to feel when Callum insisted she ride on the bar of his bicycle. She felt huge and ungainly but she hung on tightly while he deliberately wobbled his way along the grassy verges.

It was Kate's father that finally prompted them to take the next step in their relationship. He'd watched the routine of the bicycle rides and the trips to La Scala in Inverness for the Alfred Hitchcock thrillers; he noticed how his daughter would rush to the window at the sound of footsteps on the path or the tinkle of a bicycle bell. 'I think he's recovered, lass; does he still need nursing?' his eyes twinkled over the top of the Gazette.

She smiled back at him. 'I know what you're thinking, Dad, but I don't want to rush him.'

So the summer had turned to autumn and it was not until a cold day in November that she stood outside the small church with her posy of yellow and white roses and held her husband's arm.

'Mrs Kate McIntyre,' she said aloud, smiling happily at the memory of her wedding day.

Estelle's voice broke into her reverie as she and Nancy strolled towards her. 'All set! Nancy thinks we should do the market first, while it's not so hot, then get our hair done, have some lunch, and go to the Globe afterwards. Is that OK with you?'

Kate nodded in agreement and called to the boy to bring her chit. Nancy's husband, Winston, was a solicitor in town. Estelle had first met them soon after she arrived in the country and needed visas and official documents written for proof of her marital status. Since then, Nancy had taken the two women under her wing and become their guide and mentor. Together they explored the narrow alleyways off the main shopping streets. She made them climb rickety staircases up to lofty studios where tailors lorded over their pattern books imported from France and Italy and ran up creations seen not long ago on the catwalks of Europe.

Nancy led the way to the market as planned. Passing a marble slab laden with crushed ice and every variety of silvery-grey fish, she turned to them and said, 'Good when popping eyes are bright, no good when skin doesn't jump back when you push, see like this, don't jump back then not fresh.' She then pointed to a red plastic basin filled with a writhing black mass. 'This very good! Very fresh, you like eel?'

Kate pulled a face and shook her head. They moved on to the trays of prawns, all lined up like soldiers. There were the big generals, the tiger variety, with their striped black abdomens, long waving whiskers and menacing black marble eyes. On the next tray were the more ladylike specimens with mermaid tails that curled seductively out of armoured breastplates. Finally there was the platoon of regular soldiers. They had broken ranks and were lying all over the place, their whiskers intertwining in an intimate manner.

'You like?' Nancy asked Estelle.

'I love them but I hate shelling them, I'm afraid I let Cookie do that!'

'Very good you steam in beer, also very good on barbecue, you want buy today, we could get three *katis?*'

'No, I don't think so,' said Kate, ever practical. She had visions of the proposed trip to the beauty parlour with a bagful of smelly prawns at her feet.

They moved on to the vegetables and Nancy selected three types of parsley, lemon grass, lumpy pieces of ginger and four bulbs of garlic. They passed duck, chicken and quail eggs and they held their noses as they passed Ali Baba-style dragon pots packed with one hundred year-old eggs, a delicacy from China. Dried creatures, fish and seaweed lay alongside beans, peas and lentils. Alley cats prowled in their search for rats, and beady-eyed live chickens stared out from open-weave baskets. Corpses of freshly butchered geese and ducks hung on hooks above the chattering poultry. Kate and Estelle selected a watermelon and some succulent grapes. Their own gardens already yielded a steady crop of many of the fruits on sale, and so they took their purchases and made their way out of the gloom of the covered market into the glare of the midday sun. They hailed trishaws and were pedalled by elderly stick-like men wearing coolie hats to protect their leathery skin. The men shouted at each other companionably as they wove through the haphazard mêlée of traffic on their way to Jalan Bukit Bintang.

'Now we buy *laksa*, then get our hair done, what do you think?' and Nancy was off, darting through the bustling lunchtime crowd of pedestrians. She made her way into a local restaurant and promptly commandeered a marble-topped table with curvaceously tapered legs.

'*Tiga laksa, tiga* 7UP.'

'You're amazing,' Kate laughed. 'You make it all so easy!'

They savoured the delicious curry-based noodle soup and then relaxed on their backs in the beauty salon while their heads were shampooed and massaged. Later they sat under domed dryers, tended by two handmaidens sitting on stools on either side of them, filing and painting their nails into pointed, lacquered weapons. The results were immediate and each of the three women left with curled hair and exquisitely manicured hands.

'I may not have the shapeliest of bodies, but I do have good hands,' said Kate, proudly admiring her painted fingernails.

'Come on! Two o'clock already; we take taxi to Batu Road and then we have more time to choose.'

Kate never ceased to wonder at the sheer proportions of the Globe Silk Store. Lining every surface, wall to wall and floor to ceiling, were bolts of cloth in every shade and type of fabric. She gazed about her at the tables laden with swathes of cloth spilling over as others stood rigid and to attention. Three floors made up this emporium of silk, satin, rayon, georgette and cotton. There was material for bedding, soft furnishings, uniforms, pyjamas and parties. Assistants tirelessly chalked and marked, measured and cut, ripped and snipped, their long rulers flying like musical batons.

'I think I like this.' Kate fingered the citrus-yellow raw silk. 'What do you think, Nancy?' she asked tentatively.

'*Oi yo*, you look like lemon tree, no good for hair like you, no, no, you take this one!' and she handed her a bolt of soft green, lacy material and then carried over a roll of oyster silk. This will go underneath and shine through; very lovely!'

Kate let the two fabrics run through her fingers and sure enough the effect was almost translucent. 'Perfect. They'll go beautifully with the picture that I like in the Vogue book.'

Estelle selected a deep aquamarine green for a gathered full skirt, and a complementary shade of the palest blue that would form the strapless sheath of the bodice.

Nancy picked up a piece of crisp silver organza from the remnant basket and handed it to Estelle. 'This can make a rose to put at the side, I think very nice!'

'And what about you Nancy, what are you going to buy today?'

'I have some black satin here; I'll have a *cheongsam* made.'

'I wish I had your figure, Nancy,' said Kate mournfully. 'I'd love to wear a *cheongsam* but I'm afraid I have to stick to styles that are less figure hugging. I also want to get something for our anniversary, something that I can wear for dinner at the club. What do you suggest?' She fingered the soft silks and then Estelle came over with a deep midnight-blue Thai silk. 'Yes, that's beautiful! We can look for a pattern when we get to the tailor.'

Within minutes the assistants had taken their scissors, sliced the required lengths and folded the material up into parcels. The three ladies made their way out of this emporium of opulence and stepped once again into the glare of the afternoon sun. The shopping trip finished with the visit to the tailor, where the three stood with arms outstretched while they were measured from top to toe and their statistics recorded in Chinese characters.

Nancy turned their shopping trips into an adventure. She instructed them on how to bargain, which shop was superior for different types of goods, what food was good for different types of ailments and which Chinese medicines were beneficial for headaches or for indigestion. As well as guidance in the practical, she taught them about Buddha and fatalism. Over the next few years it was Nancy that guided them through the dark days of their marriages, when Kate suffered her first miscarriage, and when Estelle was confronted with the difficulties on becoming a stepmother. She kept their secrets and shared with them the wisdom acquired from her ancient Chinese culture and a very different set of beliefs.

Estelle had carved herself a strong place in the rubber estate community since she'd arrived two years ago. Her passion for achieving excellence drove her in all her interests. Cookie muttered when he saw Mem strut into his kitchen armed with Mrs Beeton's *Book of Household Management*, knowing that she would be fired up to concoct a banquet and he would be relegated to the position of sous chef, a job that he did not relish. Equally, she terrified the gardener as she marauded the garden, her nose poking and sniffing into hibiscus and orchids while she snipped and pruned in order to create an 'arrangement' for the centrepiece at her dinner party. Estelle aspired to the characteristic three flower study that represented perfect Zen lines in her Ikebana endeavour.

Alex felt like a rock washed and battered by the waves of Estelle's latest enthusiasm. 'You would be a formidable opponent if you ever took up business. Indeed, I think that might be a good idea. Maybe we should start some venture. You could be the boss and I shall be your minion. I have no doubt that you would have us rich in no time, and then, my fiery whiz kid, I shall lie back and let you take care of me. We could go and live in Hawaii and have hula girls to watch every night by the palm trees. How does that sound?'

198

Estelle continued humming, not really listening to him, for she was painstakingly writing the weekly airmail letter to Anna, in Scotland. 'What, big business? Hmmmm, could you just add your bit here please. Remember she's just been to stay with Molly. Maybe you could say something about that?'

Alex took the pen and immediately drew a rectangular dog, with four stick legs and round circles for feet. The head was a smaller rectangle with one eye and a pointed ear. There was no mouth. He moved over the page and drew a series of circles within circles which he turned into a pig. He added arched eyebrows to the dots he gave for eyes. The pig looked surprised, so he drew some inverted eyebrows beneath the dots. This now gave the pig a look of having been burning the candle at both ends. He decided to add a smiley mouth. Finally he added a cat. It had no face. Finally he signed it. 'Be a good girl, Love Daddy xxx'.

Estelle groaned and looked at him sternly. 'You didn't give the cat a face. It looks a bit odd.'

'No it does not,' retorted Alex, taking up his paper. 'It's a drawing of the cat's back; can't you see its tail coming out?'

Estelle didn't deign to reply. Instead she just signed the letter 'Aunt Estelle' and licked the edges of the blue aerogramme. 'You know that Hellen is failing, Alex? I think we should think about Anna's future. Should I get the spare room ready, just in case?'

Alex sighed and looked up from his newspaper. 'What's there to do, there's a bed there and a cupboard. What else does a small person need?'

'She's not that small, she's seven now. I think I'll go into KL and see about some rattan furniture. I shall make that room fit for royalty.' Estelle continued humming, going through a medley from her latest favourite film, Rogers and Hammerstein's *Oklahoma*.

Alex grunted, lowered the paper on to his chest and let the afternoon heat wash over him.

Estelle continued her mission of transforming Alex's quiet life into one of constant change. The floor of the spare room was polished till it glimmered, darkly emitting the heady smell of beeswax. The twin beds were bedecked in matching lemon spreads with frills and crisp white pillows. A cane headboard framed the two beds, and there was space for books and a lamp. A matching dressing table with a full mirror was placed on the side wall facing built-in cupboards with white sliding doors. A circular blue Chinese rug finished the room that Estelle now deemed fit for a princess. Alex carried in the cured skin of the panther that he'd shot on Bukit Bulan when he'd first come to Malaya.

'It'll give her nightmares,' said Estelle, crossly. Her voice acquired a faint whiny tone when she did not get her own way.

'Nonsense, it looks good there, next to the wooden elephant.'

'That's all very well, but you did promise to make a swing. All children like swings. Will you make a start soon?'

There was now some urgency in their preparations because only four days previously, they had received a telegram informing them that Hellen Matheson was seriously ill. The end would not be long and Estelle would be required to go back to Scotland to make arrangements to bring Anna out to Malaya. Alex had asked his office clerk to buy some timber and some steel posts and chains from one of their contractors. This swing was going to be strong enough to hold an elephant, and wide enough for it to sit down if it so desired. Watching the construction, Cookie and Amah were wide eyed.

'Very big, *Tuan*,' observed Cookie one evening as he brought a bottle of beer out to the work site. Alex was pouring cement into the holes that supported the frame.

'Aye, swings have to be built well. This one has a grand wooden plank for the seat. Anna will have a lot of fun on this when she gets out here.'

'Yes, sir, very good, very safe, sir.'

Chapter 13

Glengrianach, Scotland

Anna's world was turned on its head one snowy day in December of 1961. Hellen Matheson passed away in the night. Anna knew that her grandmother had been ill; she'd stroked her hair and told her she would get better soon, she'd arranged flowers for her and brought her ice lollies to suck. The wild ranting that she heard from the bedroom when the nurse called round had frightened her, but even so, she was unprepared when she awoke to find the house full of men in black suits, and the doctor talking in whispers to her grandfather. Mrs Ross, her grandmother's oldest friend, was there as well. This was very unusual. She normally came for tea and a Rich Tea biscuit, not for breakfast. It transpired that she had come to take Anna away for a few hours. The kindly woman took the small girl by the hand and led her out of the house.

'I don't understand,' said Anna, 'she wasn't very sick, why did she die, Mrs Ross?'

Mrs Ross smoothed Anna's hair back off her face. 'Look at you, pet, when I first saw you, you were just a tiny wee lass with the whitest hair I had ever seen. All that sunshine in Malaya must have bleached it. You'll be going back there now, I expect.' She looked down at the wide green eyes staring at her questioningly. 'Yes, dear, she was sick, very sick and she had to take a lot of medicine, but last night she was just too tired and she just went to sleep. She's peaceful now, and she'll have no more sore places. She's in heaven now with your mummy.'

'But what about me and my granddad? What about us? Oh poor Granddad! He will have no one to make his tea.'

'Hush pet, everything will be all right. Your Aunty Molly from Druimfhada is coming today and she'll take care of you. I'll make sure your granddad is all right. Don't you worry, Anna.'

Estelle's preparations for the possible death of her stepdaughter's grandmother had been well advised. For several weeks she'd been expecting the telegram to arrive and when it did, she was ready to make the journey back to Scotland to collect the child.

Two years had passed since Estelle and Alex were married and in the intervening years they'd been relocated to Satu Senga Estate. Both were sad to say goodbye to Bukit Bulan, it was as though an era had ended, and they felt that a new chapter of their lives was just beginning. Now, with the death of Hellen Matheson, Alex knew the time was right for his seven year-old daughter to join them in Malaya. Consequently Estelle flew back to Scotland in April. She hired a car and drove up through the glens and into the mountains. When she arrived at Druimfhada she was met like royalty by Molly.

'Come in, come in. Oh my! Let me take your coat, and what a beautiful scarf! Oh well, you just sit here and I'll get the tea. You'll want to drink out of my fancy cups, won't you, Estelle? You must have lovely things out there in Malaya?'

Estelle was bemused by such attention, and was conscious of the framed photographs of Eilidh and Alex that still adorned the sideboard.

'Hello, Anna; are you going to come and say hello to me?' she asked tentatively.

'Hello,' said Anna.

'Are you looking forward to flying on a big aeroplane and seeing your daddy?' Estelle persevered.

'Yes…he's quite a good drawer, you know. He can only draw pigs and cats though, oh and dogs, but they aren't very good.'

'Have you packed your special toys that you want to take? Not too many though, because we can buy new ones when we get there. There are some big shops in Kuala Lumpur. There are lots of toys there.'

'Did you hear that, Anna?' Molly bustled in with her best tea pot and cups on a silver tray. 'You'll be given any toys you want.' She sat on the edge of her chair, her eyes darting about as though she had been wired to a socket. 'Anna has prepared a song for you, Estelle. Are you going to sing it for her now, dear?' She gave Anna a push, 'She's been practising for hours, and even did it for the people at the funeral. Come on, dear, let's hear you.'

Anna stood primly in front of Estelle. A tall girl with chestnut hair cut short and with the front parts tied severely into a bow at the side of her head, she wore a neat green tartan kilt and a home-knitted cardigan. She looked straight at Estelle and broke into a high treble, 'My bonnie lies over the ocean, my bonny lies over the sea, my bonnie lies over the ocean, Oh bring back my bonnie to me.' She sang the chorus and then repeated it all again. Finally her face broke into a smile, and Estelle almost warmed towards her.

'That was very good, Anna; you have a good voice, I think you will like some of my records. We can play them together when you come to the estate. I have *Oklahoma*, and *South Pacific* and *The King and I*. Do you think you would like that?'

'Maybe,' conceded Anna doubtfully. She had no idea what Aunt Estelle was talking about. Instead she thought she might like to see how her packing was going. 'Would you like to see what I am taking with me?'

'Of course, dear, why don't you show me?'

Estelle was unprepared for the jumble of toys that were laid out in Molly's spare room ready to be packed.

Molly laughed, 'She won't part with any of them. Most of them arrived in the crate when she came back to Scotland when she was two, and I don't know what to say. The poor lassie has had to contend with so much loss and disruption in such a short time, I haven't the heart to say no.'

'Well,' said Estelle grimly, 'I shall simply have to start out as I mean to go on. She can take old teddy here, and that monkey and the cat, but the rest will have to be stored away.'

'No!' wailed Anna, 'I need my dog that walks and barks, and my blue rabbit that my granny knitted. I want to keep my Bunty dolls and all their paper clothes. I took ages and ages to collect those.'

'You see!' said Molly, 'easier said than done!'

Eventually they packed up the car, but Anna was too preoccupied with trying to spirit the dog and its batteries into the car to give much thought to leaving the little Highland village that had been her home for the last few months since her grandmother had died. Davey Matheson had asked Estelle if he could travel with them to London, so that he could finally say goodbye to them there. His life was suddenly full of empty spaces. He had lost his three most precious people in the last five years.

Just as the car door was about to slam, Estelle spied the dog. 'Sorry, Anna, we can't take this. It will have to stay with Aunty Molly. I know she will look after it for you.'

It was then that Anna started to cry, and as the car sped off down the old road she opened her window and yelled as loud as she could. 'Guard my dog, Aunty Molly, don't forget to guard my dog!'

The next six months in Malaya witnessed many changes in Anna's life. She experienced a whirl of new beginnings. She learnt to sit and take her meals at a long dining room table. She became the owner of two kittens and a tortoise. She listened to stories read by her stepmother in the afternoons, until, inevitably, Estelle would grow drowsy and fall asleep before she had finished the tale. On one such afternoon, Estelle did not open the book of *Alice in Wonderland*. Instead she looked at the little girl and said, 'You will call me Mother.'

Anna glanced into Estelle's green-flecked eyes and her mouth dropped. 'I can't, you are Aunt Estelle!'

'You must, this is how it is now, and we must all try to get on with our new lives together.'

Anna looked away and the word seemed to stick. It sounded unnatural even when whispered into the quietest place inside her head. She couldn't imagine saying it out loud.

'Say it!'

She looked down and muttered 'Mm...oth...er.'

'No, no, no; loudly, MOTHER!'

'I can't.'

Anna didn't want her lovely Aunt Estelle to turn into anyone else. She'd always been glamorous and smelled like a flower and worn beautiful dresses. Her tiny feet slipped into dainty fashionable high heels, and her slim ankles didn't look strong enough to support her body. She was like a vibrant butterfly, her hair a tangle of soft red curls. Anna loved to stand and watch her as she made up her face. She loved to lie in bed and hear the clip-clop of her high heels on the wooden floor when she swished in to say goodnight, on her way out to some party. Estelle would bend down and listen to the childish prayer: 'This night when I lay down to sleep, I pray the Lord my soul to keep. If I should die before I wake, I pray the Lord my soul to take.' Estelle would then lean over and kiss her cheek and Anna would be engulfed in a cloud of perfume. Anna did not want any more changes. Aunt Estelle was just fine being Aunt Estelle.

'Why do you not have babies, Aunt Es...? I mean, Mother?' Anna asked one morning as she played with an ornament on Estelle's dressing table. The figurine was of a young mother dressed in blue, bouncing a baby on her knee. 'Is it because God sent me to you instead? Is that why? You're lucky really, you know, because you have me and Santosh and God really loves missionaries and kind people who take care of children that no one else wants, isn't that true?'

Estelle continued brushing her hair whilst watching the child in the mirror.

'Santosh is lucky to have me to teach him things and to give him new shorts. He really likes the green ones that we got for him in KL. Being just the gardener's son, he doesn't know anything about detectives or anything. I've had to teach him everything. Did I tell you I'm going to be a detective when I grow up? It's very important to make notes about what you see. You might come across clues and then you have to write them down. We both have notebooks and pencils, and we keep a lookout for anyone following us. It's a really good game and maybe some bandits will come into the garden and we'll see them.'

'Well, I hope you don't just write down their names, young lady. I hope that you would come and tell me or Cookie,' Estelle said grimly.

'Of course, but I must borrow some of your talcum powder for fingerprint testing. That's important too. We can get a lot of clues from that, but Cookie just keeps polishing all the fingerprints off. It's really annoying. Did you know that when I am nine, Daddy said I can go and pick up rubber seeds in the field just outside the garden and get real money? I'll need a big bag to collect the seeds, and I'll have to be on my guard against giant spiders' webs. Maybe I can make Santosh walk ahead of me. He knows about them, anyway I am so excited about that. When I've collected a hundred he said I'll get a dollar. I expect I'll make hundreds of dollars as there are seeds everywhere and then I can buy anything I want.'

'Oh, and what would you be spending your money on?'

'Well, I might get a torch for my detective work and some invisible ink. Santosh will have to get some too. I'll have to save for other things that detectives need. I'm already an expert on tracking. I can tell who has walked around the house, and I know all the footprints. I can tell if it's Sinbad or a chicken or even a real live person.'

Estelle turned as the child left the room and went off into her own, no doubt to assemble her dolls for yet another tea party. The only person that did well out of that arrangement was the hostess who gobbled up the Iced Gem biscuits that Cookie always managed to find her.

Anna sat on the floor, busily organising her little family around their feast. Of course, as always, Teddy was the imposing authority at these parties, even though his ample rump never fitted into the rattan furniture that had been specially designed for the other dolls. He was propped up against the head of the dead panther which perpetually snarled his yellow teeth and gazed wickedly out of his marbled eyes. Anna knew that he'd been shot on the other estate that they'd once lived on, before being transferred. This estate they were on now was much better, her dad said, as it was much closer to Port Dickson, and it meant they could go to the sea and play at the Yacht Club every Sunday. Anna liked this, she liked splashing with the other children that she'd met there, and she'd made a new friend called Julia who shared a mutual passion for cats. Their idea of happiness was to have sleepovers in each others' houses, and to lie in the fitted wardrobes, one on the top shelf and the other on the bottom, with the doors closed, imprisoned with the cats. Anna's life was full of discovery. She loved her swing in the garden, and her box of colouring pencils that had every hue of the rainbow and more. For hours she drew ladies, and twisted stories and fantasies around their pretty heads and colourful gowns. She read the tales of Heidi and Louisa M. Alcott and in all these stories she tried to imagine that she too was one of the golden girls of fiction. On the whole Anna had adapted well to her new life and only sometimes did she long for her granny and granddad and a part of her childhood that was gone forever. Her new 'mother' did not condone any conversation about her dead mother, indeed no one spoke of her. It was such a contrast to her life in Druimfhada and Glengrianach where she'd always been reminded of how lovely and happy Eilidh had been.

Now it was as though she had never been.

Estelle had her reasons for trying to obliterate any memories of Eilidh. She believed that their new family could not survive with ghosts. The past was gone and it was not healthy to try to live with what she could see was a perceived icon. She knew that her attempts at motherhood would be judged by all. Thus, she was determined to mould this thorny young rose, so that she would be a credit to her.

'Now, Anna, I am having Nancy Fung over for coffee tomorrow and I want to you to behave nicely. You will clean your bedroom, and when it's done I shall come in and wipe everything down with a white tissue to see that you haven't missed anywhere.'

'But you said that Julia could come over. We can still play Rapunzel, can't we? We won't bother you and then we were going to practise our high jump with Santosh.'

Cookie, who was laying the table for lunch, interrupted this conversation with a reminder to Mem that Anna should not jump over the bamboo hedge.

'What on earth do you mean? I thought they were jumping over the brushes at the back?' Estelle asked sharply.'

'No, Mem, they pretend they are horses and jump over the hedge that goes around the house. Not good idea, as big snakes go in there. Cobras hide and already Kaboon has killed three this month. They want the chickens I think.'

'Thank you for telling me, Cookie. Also, would you make sure that Anna does not climb? I saw her up the water reservoir when I came back yesterday, and don't you deny it, young lady.'

Anna scowled. She didn't like this conspiracy to curtail her plans in the garden. She was convinced that if any snake was asleep in the hedge it would soon move when she and Santosh came thundering towards it pretending to be wild stallions. 'You just spoil everything, and you just want me to clean all the time. Julia's mother never makes her clean her room, and we're allowed to climb in her garden.'

'That is enough of your cheek; just go to your room and Cookie will give you a cloth and you can start right away.' Estelle sighed and resumed reading her magazine. It was not easy trying to home-school Anna as well as to discipline her. She had very little knowledge of children and dreaded the hours of sums and writing just as much as Anna did. Her attempts to perform a Pygmalion transformation were blighted with tears and rages.

Later that afternoon Julia arrived with her dad to stay the night with Anna. The two girls immediately ran round the back to where Amah was doing the ironing. They squatted down by the drain and began to torment the column of ants that were marching to salvage the breakfast remnants from the dog's bowl. They spread about like the marauding army they were, then each would capture a piece of white rice in his jaws and haul it back home, stopping only to tell his fellow soldiers where these treasures were to be found.

'Let's pretend we're God,' suggested Anna. 'We'll make something happen, like moving this big stone here so they can't cross. It will be like a catastrophe for them. Oh look! The soldiers have to go back and tell their regiment there's been a landslide. This is fun. We can reroute them any way we want!'

That night, after they had played two games of whist and two of rummy with Alex and Estelle, they said goodnight and ran off into Anna's room.

'Are we going to listen to your transistor, like we did last time?' asked Julia, just a little fearfully.

'No, the tales of mystery and suspense are over now. That last story was scary, wasn't it?'

'What was it called again?'

'"The Fall of the House of Usher,"' Anna said in a rasping, whispery tone, her voice rising theatrically. 'They were all crushed, and he fell and then the house fell and that was the end of the House of Usher.'

'Stop it, Anna; you're making me scared again.' Julia pulled the sheet up around her head.

'Let's plan an adventure tonight instead; let's go and see the King Wa.'

'King Wa?' Julia was still hiding beneath the cover.

'Mother's beautiful King Wa plant that she never lets me see.'

Julia was intrigued in spite of herself, 'What's so special about it?'

'Well,' whispered Anna. 'It's a magical flower and it only comes out at night, and only when the there is a full moon. I only get to see it if Mother cuts it for me and puts it in the fridge. It is so pretty. But guess what, there is a full moon tonight and we could sneak out and see it for ourselves.

Let's wait till they go to bed then we can get out the bathroom door and run round to the front!'

'Yes, let's! Gosh, I hope Sinbad doesn't bark at us!'

The girls waited for the house to fall silent.

Estelle had arranged for trestles to be built on either side of the front porch. On these, her pot plants were set out in tiers and her beautiful collection of tropical blooms competed in colour and exoticism. The most elusive of these was the King Wa. Its thick, succulent but rather ugly stems gave no indication of the flower that it would produce. Tendrils grew randomly up towards the sky, and large flat leaves hung as though the weight was too much for the plant to bear. For weeks the tiny dormant pink bud grew tantalisingly bigger and more engorged.

'When is it going to open?' Anna had enquired of Estelle the day before.

'Only when the moon is full.'

Anna had nodded sagely, already planning a night-time marauding mission. She wished she had a torch though, for when the garden was inky black and all the flowers had closed their dewy petals she knew the King Wa would open up like a fantastic white ballerina swan. She imagined its petals like a silvery-white tutu dancing towards the moon, the frilled edges forming the ruffles of its feathery petticoat. Estelle said that the smell it emitted was as strong and sweet as any perfume.

At last the house was quiet and Anna led the way down the steps to the bathroom. There was a hole in the wall that ran out to the open drains, and Anna always made sure it was stuffed with paper to prevent unwanted visitors like king cobras coming in. Although she loved the story of Rikki Tikki Tavi, she was not so sure about it when the house was dark and only the noises of the night whispered outside her window. The girls slid open the bolt and stepped out of the house. The moon was full and silvery and the concrete that their bare feet stepped on was still warm from the day's heat. The garden looked suddenly scary, with bushes that were black and ominous.

'Don't be afraid,' Anna said bravely, 'it's just past these flower beds and then round to the front of the house. Be careful of the drain, we don't want to fall in.'

Julia was very unsure about their adventure, and wished they were doing their normal things, like dressing up, or polishing the tortoise, but she tiptoed gingerly behind her friend. As they turned the corner they could smell the glorious perfume.

'Oh, look! Oh, it's so pretty!' Anna exclaimed, forgetting to whisper. 'I have never seen anything so perfect! Let's cut it off and we can draw it in the detective book and I can show it to Santosh tomorrow!' She scrambled on to the trestle, but as she leant over to the King Wa, she lost her balance and plunged down, knocking the pot off the stand. They both heard the sickening thud as it hit the ground. Earth and petals and stems lay in a tangled mess.

'Quick, Julia! Run!'

The culprits retraced their steps and arrived breathless into Anna's bathroom. They bolted the door, ran up the steps and into their beds in record time. The only sound that could be heard was their breathing, coming in great gasps of fear, and muffled by their pillows. Sinbad, ever the guard dog, was alert and barking, but otherwise the house remained silent.

'We did it! We got away with it!' whispered Anna triumphantly. In all her excitement she failed to notice her skinned knee and the nasty scratch on her thigh.

Estelle was on the warpath the next morning. She had Nancy Fung arriving for coffee and she was not amused to discover the broken pot plant. The girls had eaten breakfast at the back of the house with Amah and then had disappeared into the wardrobe.

'Anna, come out at once! I told you yesterday that this room had to be clean and you have deliberately disobeyed me.' Estelle looked aghast at the pieces of clothing and abandoned toys scattered about the bed and floor. 'Have you seen what has happened to my King Wa? I thought at first it might have been those cats prowling at night, but I think something heavier was up on that trestle for it to break like that.'

'Did you break it?' whispered Julia, her eyes wide and questioning.

'Maybe, I did hear the wood creak when the pot fell off,' Anna whispered back.

'Did you hear me? Come out at once!'

Sheepishly they opened the door and the cats darted out as fast as lightning.

'And what is that blood on your knee, Anna? Have you been climbing? There will be big trouble if you have. I shall find Cookie and that gardener and I shall find out what you've been up to.'

'No, I just slipped, that's all. We've been in here. Shall we get changed then?' Anna asked quickly, hoping to distract her.

But there was to be no respite, for Estelle had spied the blood on the sheets. 'When did this happen?' Her face was drawn tight around the mouth and her eyes narrowed into slits.

'We were just playing Rapunzel escaping from the witch's tower, that's all. The sheets are good for making the pretend rope,' she added knowledgeably.

'Oh, that Rapunzel!' exclaimed Estelle furiously. 'I need a cup of coffee, and you had better get this room into some kind of order, or else!' She clip clopped out, her footsteps full of determination.

'Oh help! I'm so glad you're here, Julia, otherwise she would kill me. We can go and hide with Santosh when her friend turns up and they start jabbering on about my latest crimes.'

Later that afternoon, after Julia had gone home, Anna found Santosh round by the gardener's house and persuaded him to go over to the compost heap with her. Together they sifted through the day's collection of tea leaves and potato peelings until they found the broken King Wa.

'Look, Santosh, we must save the flower, even though the petals have all closed up. We can stick it in our book of things we found as detectives.'

'Everything there nearly gone, ants eat everything.'

'Well, we drew around things too; remember that precious stone we found, and that key? We still have to solve that mystery.'

'Yes, but I think Mem not happy she find Anna with flower.'

'Don't be silly, Santosh, she'll never know it was me!'

During the next few weeks Anna gave up horse jumping, but she and Santosh continued to prowl around the garden. They had butterfly nets made of bright yellow gauze and would run and chase the elusive fluttering creatures. Specimens of jade green and black, scarlet and dark imperial purple ended up in their sweating palms, and for a few hours they referred to the books and tried to match their prey against the illustrated samples with unpronounceable Latin names. As the children ran for the swing that had been constructed between two flame trees, and where Santosh was tutored to be part of *The Great Flying Trapeze Act* that involved very complicated ballet moves, the abandoned butterfly corpses were gobbled up by the voracious army of ants.

'You have to do the same as me at the same time,' Anna ordered.

Santosh hung on to the chain and they bent their knees simultaneously and soared higher with each bend.

'Lift your leg to the back, just like arabesque and now hold my hand! Now face me and we will just hold on with our hands and swing around the chain and back on to the seat. Right, now we really are a flying trapeze...but higher, we must go higher!'

Santosh did not like to interfere with Anna's choreography. He had never played such games in his own home where the estate workers' children passed the time harmlessly with sticks and marbles, and he had no idea of *The Greatest Show on Earth* shown at the Cathay Cinema in Kuala Lumpur. Anna's vision was of sailing up to the feathery branches above her and flying higher and higher, right up to the sky, so she worked and shrieked to obtain a certain routine that was at least symmetrical. Santosh was commanded and cajoled to perform daring acts, never before witnessed in the history of garden swings. Their exhilarating game continued in many forms over many months.

Anna's days as a trapeze artist contrasted greatly with those spent indoors with Estelle. The days and weeks became arenas of confrontation. Both were strong willed; both were determined to get their own way. The attempts at home-schooling were the final straw. Alex watched the tantrums; he listened half-heartedly to the litany of sins that his daughter committed daily, shrugging his shoulders helplessly but doing nothing. These dramas did not fit in with his idea of a quiet life so he separated himself from the domestic fray. He was the middleman sadly lacking in the Wisdom of Solomon. Anna grew more confused and angry as the months passed. She had no ally in that house. Things had started to change. She felt that her world was plagued by the black spider that lived in her head. Her new home, admittedly beautiful and sunny, was a place from which she needed to escape into her fantasy land. She made new friends in the swimming pool and she knew there was the unknown spectre of boarding school looming up, but for the present, she fled into the imaginary lives that she depicted in her drawings.

Her new home was very different from the bleak railway cottage that she had left behind, with its small patch of grass that grew near the platform, and the old stone dyke that ran up to the shinty playing fields which were surrounded by dark, looming mountains. After a previous way of life where her playmates lived in the adjoining houses, she was now introduced to friends who could only be met by arrangement. The remoteness of the rubber estates and the distances between the main towns and golf courses and swimming clubs meant that there could be no spontaneous meetings. Her new life centred in the yellow bungalow with the red-tiled roof. The house was isolated, as was the child.

'Can I stay with Julia?' she pleaded.

'You stayed with her on Sunday, wouldn't you like her to come here for a change?' Estelle was pinning the tissue of a dress pattern on to some batik material.

'We haven't finished our game and she said she'd leave everything just the way it was until I could come back.' Anna sat down on the recliner chair and pulled her legs up.

'Put your legs down, Anna. That's not how young ladies sit. Cookie might come in and see your pants.'

Anna scowled. She dreaded the times when Julia came to stay. Estelle always tried to humiliate her in front of everyone. It was much more fun at Samudra Estate where she and her friend became invisible amongst Julia's noisy family. Her elder brothers and sister entertained their own friends and Julia's mother was often out playing bridge. Her father was oblivious to all the noise and confusion, so the two girls, draped in sheets, had the run of the veranda and bedroom to recreate 'The House of Usher' or 'Rapunzel' or whatever story they were re-enacting. Julia's *amah* would giggle at their antics but Cookie would scowl at the improper use of Mem's good bed linen.

'*Ai Ya!* Better to play in the cupboard like before. Better for Cookie.'

The next few months and subsequent years saw Estelle become even more of a driving force. Her reign of tyranny was seen through her own eyes as sainted martyrdom. Her duty was paramount as she stretched her skills and talents to match the various commitments that made up her life. She was a woman of passion and her passion was now turned to bricks and stone and mortar. She and Cookie were locked in their daily war of cleanliness. Not a mote of dust was permitted to lie; *chichaks'* eggs were gouged out of unused key holes; cleanliness was next to godliness: everyone knew that. The club was her refuge, and the small white ball was hit with gusto around the eighteen holes of the golf course. Her lady friends supported her on her mission to reform Anna.

'Have you considered boarding her in that school on the top of Penang Hill?'

'Well, she will be going back to Scotland for high school,' Estelle countered. 'Alex and I thought it would be nice to have her with us, but it's proving to be a struggle.'

'I think you should consider it, really. It would be better for the child as well.'

Estelle reflected on the advantages. With Anna gone, her life might regain some peace and Alex would be truly hers once more. The school in Penang would be excellent for the interim period and would prepare Anna for the Common Entrance examinations she would need to sit in order to get into the boarding school of their choice in the UK. Hmm… she decided to broach the subject with her husband. Penang would give them the breathing space they all needed.

Alex sat alone on the veranda. He wore only a pair of slacks, and the cool rotation of the fan was refreshing after the hot, deep bath that he had just enjoyed. He was grateful to the light breeze as he wriggled his toes luxuriously, free at last from the confines of his woollen socks and heavy boots. He relished this quiet time of day when his work was done and he could relax with a beer or two before Cookie called to say that dinner was served. Alex took a drink from the chilled glass; some drops of condensation fell onto his chest and he absentmindedly wiped them away. Lazily he gazed into the darkness of the garden and reflected on how his job continued in the same daily rhythm as during the early years, commencing with coffee and a game of patience, then out in the Land Rover through the still black dawn to inspect the new saplings and the various grafting projects. He liked to peep his horn to acknowledge his tappers going about their early morning routines before veering off the road and parking on the top of a small *bukit*. Alex's favourite view was from that hill; he would stand and survey the shimmering blue haze that rose from the acres of meticulously laid-out rubber. In the distance was always the brooding presence of the jungle, always the screeching of millions of scurrying, whirring insects as the new day greeted the dawn. He swallowed some more beer, stretched back into the rattan lounger, closed his eyes and let his mind wander. He drifted back to the time in his life when he still had Eilidh. So many pictures and images of her flashed in front of his eyes. How would things have been had she survived? He let his mind take him back to the late afternoons on Bukit Bulan when he sat on the edge of the fountain while Anna played in the water. He could see Eilidh laughing, her head thrown back as her eighteen month-old baby sprayed her with a jug of water: 'You've soaked me, you little horror. Do you think Mummy needs a bath? What about Daddy? Shall we give Daddy a bath too?' Alex let out a little laugh, reliving the moment when Anna splashed the water over his freshly pressed slacks. Aye, Eilidh lass, we'll never know what might have been. And what about poor Jack and the effect it had on Callum's sanity. There was no doubt about it, they had all been through difficult times, yet now, just when he thought he was eligible for a quiet life, he found himself caught between the fiery temper of his current wife and the stubborn nature of his daughter. Every day brought more domestic upheaval. Alex hated addressing conflict. Instead of offering diplomatic solutions, he would retreat and hide behind his newspaper or take the Land Rover out to seek peace in the silence of the trees and jungle clearings of the estate.

'Daddy, what are you thinking?' Anna enquired brightly.

'Oh, just this and that.'

'But what? You can't just lie there and not think of anything,' she persisted.

'Well,' sighed Alex, 'I was just wondering if you'd like to come out with me to inspect the fields and the tapping in the mornings.'

'Me?' she said incredulously.

'Well, why not? I don't see much of you these days. You're away for three months and then you get home and you're off with Santosh or Julia.'

'I would like to come. Will I have to wake up very early?'

'Yes, you will. Half past five and we'll be out the door by six. Maybe we can take Sinbad. Poor old boy, he's getting a bit stiff, but we won't walk too far.'

'Wow, Daddy, I can't wait.' Then she chewed her finger and asked quietly, 'Will Mother come too?'

'No, it will be just us and the dog. I'll give you a shout in the morning.'

He closed his eyes once more and Anna went over to the radiogram. She selected his favourite record, and put it on the turntable. It was Acker Bilk. The house seemed to melt into the warm, plaintive tones of the clarinet. He sighed and closed his eyes once more. Outside he could hear the squawking of birds in the distance, and the gentle throb of the generator. For forty winks he dozed, then woke to the sound of Estelle's shoes as she crossed the hallway to the veranda.

'Cookie is serving dinner now, Alex. Will you two be coming in?' She handed him his batik shirt.

Alex hauled himself out of his lounger and buttoned up his shirt. He winked at Anna, before draining the last of his beer. 'On my way, darling, I'm on my way.'

The holidays were a mixed blessing, allowing the trio time to interact and create an illusion of family life. Anna feasted on girls' classical literature and longed to emulate her heroines who lived on high mountains in Switzerland. She delighted in drawing pictures of ladies and girls, and in her mind she would weave stories around their make-believe lives. The illustrations filled the long hours alone on the estate, where she whispered all her longings to her imaginary friends.

The swimming pool at the Tanjong Aru Club became a focus for mothers and children during these holiday periods. Boys and girls who were schooling on top of Penang Hill, or others who had been flown out from the UK, paraded their pale torsos around the normally deserted pool. At first it was awkward and children were shy when they met up again after the intervening months, but soon the pool became the scene of shrieking and laughter and nut-brown arms and legs thrashing and splashing. Tables were soon cluttered with bottles of ice cream soda and cherryade, and discarded plates of chips. Batik-clad mothers with Parisian-styled dresses copied from the glamour magazines in Kuala Lumpur sat with wing-tipped sunglasses and an air of Rita Hayworth or

Ava Gardner. Such was the fading glamour of a fading empire.

'Kick your legs, Anna, and breathe!' Estelle leant over the edge of the pool in her attempts to coach the finer points of the crawl. She shook her head, stretched and walked back to her plastic lounger where she took up her discarded tapestry. Both she and Anna had been enthusiastic at the beginning of the holiday but now Anna's half-finished horse lay untouched at the bottom of the basket.

'You are so lucky you're such a good swimmer,' remarked Kate. Her skin was pale and freckly and although a redhead like Estelle, unlike her she had no tolerance for the sun at all. She disliked swimming and golfing and preferred the company of other women playing either bridge or *mah jong*. Today she was here at the club to play *mah jong*. She looked at her hard, lacquered fingernails and said, 'How is it all going? Is she any easier?'

'Boarding school was definitely the answer.' Estelle looked over her glasses and surveyed the cauldron that was the pool. 'She talks less of her past and seems to have stopped comparing me with her grandmother. Alex takes her out in the morning and they drive around the estate then after breakfast she goes to her room to draw her pictures. It's good that Julia is out for the holidays too and they seem to have moved on from incarcerating themselves in the wardrobe. It's all nuns now. They parade around in sheets singing about what they are going to do about Maria!' Estelle laughed and picked up her scissors to cut off the piece of green wool that she was finished with. 'She wants me to take her to see *The Sound of Music* again when we go to KL on Sunday. It will be the fourth time! Alex is playing in the men's championship at the Royal Selangor Golf Club, not for him the delights of the stinking lavatories of the Cathay Cinema!'

Kate looked down again at her coral-coloured nails and then took out her compact and pressed her matching coral-coloured lips together. 'Time to go; Ming and Liz and Maggie Seatton are making up the four. I'll see you at the Jacaranda Club next week. The men have got their monthly medal the following Sunday. Alex and Callum are thinking of getting a practice round in beforehand.' She waved at her sister-in-law and disappeared into the dark interior of the club house where the ladies had been allocated an air-conditioned room for their weekly game.

Estelle mused on the irony of their situations. Both were childless.

It was five years since Estelle had married Alex and she was now resigned to the fact that no child would come from their union. Instead she bore her disappointment with her inner reserves of strength and lavished her pent-up maternal instincts on Alex, on the house and sometimes on Anna. Poor Kate had lost her twin sons at birth. She and Callum had been devastated and the funeral had been one of the saddest many had attended for years. The poor little bodies had been buried in Batu Gajah alongside other infants that had passed away. The day had been dark and ominous black clouds had gathered over God's Little Acre. As the earth was sprinkled on to the twin white boxes Alex had taken his brother's arm and Estelle had held Kate. The past had become the present; the soil was once again claiming more of their lives, bones and blood. They had walked out of the lonely little graveyard, leaving behind loved ones to the enduring earth and darkened, rain-filled skies.

The Jacaranda Club, a ramshackle collection of wooden huts connected by narrow covered walkways, was a club for the golfers. The bar was the high altar, and the walls were adorned with plaques engraved with names of previous champions and presidents. On the far side was a snooker table with its attendant rail of cues. The dining room was inlaid with a small parquet floor for dancing. The shower and locker rooms gave an air of a school gym, and the utilities seemed at odds with the rather grand signs on the doors. 'Ladies' Powder Room' suggested something sumptuous, but inside, attempts had been made to add jolly frills and swathes of rosy fabric around the rather plain stools, and little skirts had been made to hang around the dressing tables. The pity now was that the paint was peeling, the walls had ugly smears of damp and only an unprotected sixty-watt bulb illuminated the sadly jaded elegance. Running along the front of the complex was a spacious veranda, on which cane chairs with bright red and blue cushions were arranged around glass-topped rattan tables. From this point the golf course swept ahead and the manicured perfection of the putting green at the eighteenth, directly in front of the gallery, gave the viewers prime seats to watch the final shots of the tournaments. In the distance the course meandered like a bolt of emerald felt which swirled around the kidney-shaped bunkers and ruffled in coarser hues where the shadows deepened near the casuarinas. The recesses were moist and dark and soothed the eyes after the harsh sunlight blazing down upon dazzling flowering shrubs at the centre of what felt like a verdant motorway.

Kate and Estelle sat sipping tea as they waited for their husbands to finish their round of golf. It was close to sunset and the bar boys were going around depositing mosquito coils at each table. Anna was sulking. There was no one to play with and nothing to do this afternoon. Why couldn't they have gone to the swimming pool instead? Just then the Sandersons drove up and their three boys tumbled out of the car, so Anna immediately cheered up and she ran off to play with them. At the same time, the golfers clattered into the club house and naturally made straight for the bar.

'Two gunners and two Anchor beers,' Alex wiped his forehead with his Good Morning towel. 'Phew! That was good. That putt at the seventeenth was a grand shot and that birdie at the fourteenth was just what I needed.'

'Ach, my putting is off.' Callum shook his head and downed half his gunner to slake his thirst before getting started on the beer. 'Aye, I'll have to play better than that on Sunday.' He got up off his stool and walked over to where the ladies were sitting. 'Not my day! And how was your afternoon, ladies?'

Alex followed and dropped a kiss on Estelle's head. 'Are we eating, dear, or what? I'm starving.'

Estelle laughed and shook her head, 'I'm not surprised. Look at you; you're as lean as a bean. I wouldn't be surprised if you haven't got one of those tape worms inside you!'

'I'll have you know that this fine physique you see before you needs a constant supply of good Scottish beef to keep it like that. Talking of which, how about club sandwiches? May not be Scottish beef, but Australian cows are said to be the next best thing.'

The night fell suddenly. The trees surrounding the course seemed to close ranks, forming a wall around the group of buildings. The generator hummed and in the more modest dwellings of the servants' quarters paraffin lamps gave off ghostly shadows. Fireflies flickered and Anna and her fellow golf orphans rushed about trapping the little creatures in an old mayonnaise jar. An owl swooped across from a mango tree and alighted on a telephone pole where it puffed itself up and surveyed the ground below for suitable snacks. Bats feasted on the wing, their aerial circus wild and death-defying; the night was alive with the constant shriek and trill and buzz of the insect and animal worlds hunting for their evening meal.

Anna and her friends ate hamburgers and chips. It was obvious that the McIntyre brothers had no intention of going home. The children slunk through the bar and watched the men playing snooker for a while. They watched the balls being smashed and pocketed, the religious recording of the scores, and they giggled at a player contorting his body in gymnastic manoeuvres across the green baize to hit a particularly elusive shot.

Much later Anna sat hunched on the floor with her jar of fireflies. Most people had gone home and now only her father and his brother and their old friend, Michael Parrish, were left. Aunt Kate had taken out her sewing and was peering at the cloth. Alex and Michael were still playing snooker but Callum was relaxing at the bar with Estelle.

'I wish I had seen you first,' he smiled at her.

Anna looked up, her ears alert. She pressed herself closer into the shadows.

'You're a lucky man, Callum McIntyre, so don't you start sweet talking me!' Estelle grinned and added, 'That's one of the worst commandments that you can break. You must not lust after your neighbour's axe.' She took another sip of her gin, 'That's not quite right actually; it's an ox, not an axe, though it could be. You must not covet another man's wife, especially your brother's.'

'I still wish I had met you first.' He stared into his beer. 'She won't let me touch her, you know.'

'Ssssssh, Callum, it will take time. God knows you should be the first to understand that. She needs to heal emotionally and she's afraid of having to go through it all again.'

'I know that, I do. It's just that I remember being in that sanatorium and just wanting to die too. It was Kate that gave me the courage to go on with my life. I want her back; I want what we had before. She's so remote and it's as though she's blaming me. And why is it you never reproached me when you know I am responsible for your loss?'

'Stop, Callum, this is definitely not the time. That all happened a long time ago.' She leant over and gave her brother-in-law a soft kiss on his cheek.

'More drinks, boy!' Callum sat up straight.

'Well, just one for the road then,' Estelle agreed.

Anna crept out from their feet. She knew that there was a bond between these two and she screwed up her face and twitched her lips. She decided to go and talk to her Aunt Kate, who seemed quite alone on the veranda.

'Well young lady, it's another late night for you. Are you going to let those poor creatures free? You're such a marauder, dead butterflies and insects strewn about wherever you go.' She watched Anna take off the lid, and empty the rather dull collection on to the grass in front of the club house.

'Poor things! So what's happening in there, are they having another drink?'

'Yes, I think so. I just wanted to stay at home and play *The Sound of Music*. Do you know I got the record and the book when we went to the cinema in KL? It's not the book of the story, but the book showing all about the actors. There are photographs of Maria and Liesl and it tells you all about them in real life. I have decided that I'm going to be a nun, just like Julie Andrews. Julia always wants to be Maria because her name is nearly the same as Julie Andrews, it's not fair. I have to be the Reverend Mother and sometimes I have to be the captain as well, just because I'm taller than she is. Did you ever want to be a nun, Aunt Kate?'

'Never!' Kate replied, looking at her beautifully manicured hands. 'I did want to be a mannequin in a store like Draffens or Jenners. The mannequins used to strut out wearing beautiful clothes designed by Worth and Chanel in Paris, and as they wove around the luncheon tables the ladies marked on slips of paper the outfits they wished to purchase. I thought it would have been so glamorous.'

'Hmmmm, so you didn't become a dummy then.'

'Silly girl! Those are the mannequins you see draped in a shop window. No, I was never tall enough to be a model; my legs were on the plump side. I became a nursing auxiliary. Not a real nurse, but a nurse's aide if you like. I helped to arrange the flowers and sometimes I would sit with the patients and just talk to them. That's how I met your Uncle Callum.'

'I didn't know he was ill. Did he have cholera or leprosy or something fatal like that?'

'No silly, nothing like that.'

'Was he wounded in a trap in the Emergency?' Anna had heard terrible stories of those times.

'No, dear, he had a different kind of illness; it's called a breakdown, but he's better now.'

Anna nodded. She understood about things breaking down; it was easier to understand than dengue or malaria. 'Did Uncle Callum know Aunt Estelle, I mean Mother, before he knew you?'

'Of course, dear, they met in the hospital just before I met him. We actually got married before them but I couldn't come out here until your Uncle Callum was made a manager. But your dad and Estelle knew each other from before. Estelle was very good to me when I eventually arrived in this country.'

'Oh,' said Anna and she turned to look at the pair sitting at the bar. What on earth did it all mean? Her father and Michael strode over to the bar and everyone started making moves to go home. 'At last!' She jumped up; 'We're going. I never ever want to be a golfer in my whole life!'

'It's not usual for nuns to play golf,' her aunt smiled. 'Come on, Sister Anna, and don't forget to say your prayers.'

Chapter 14

2003 – Scotland

The cobbled paving of Edinburgh's New Town echoed as a black taxi sped past with late night partygoers. Anna fumbled for her key before letting herself into her house and carefully stepped over two days' worth of letters. First she filled the kettle, then went into the lounge and closed the wooden shutters before drawing the red velvet curtains and turning on various Chinese porcelain table lamps. Immediately the room with its white sofas and dark rosewood furniture felt warm and welcoming. It felt so good to be home and see the familiar detritus that made up her life. She made some tea and returned to where she had set the tin box on the coffee table. It rested there full of the fragments of past lives. Anna picked up some random photos, but was too tired and too confused, and her shoulders ached from being hunched over the wheel for so long. She lay back on the sofa, her feet resting on the coffee table, her hands cradling the mug of hot tea. It was good to savour the stillness, the quiet. She yawned, feeling overwhelmed with weariness. Eventually she pulled herself up, and methodically turned off the lights and climbed the stairs. She ran a hot bath, then surrounded by fragrant bubbles, she finally began to unwind. Her eyelids grew heavy. Eventually Anna fell into bed, and pulled the crisp cotton duvet around her. Tomorrow, she thought, she would go through everything in the box tomorrow, and she drifted away on a cloud of dreams.

The following morning, Anna settled herself on the red Chinese rug with the tin box, the photo album, the letters and all the photographs that had accumulated throughout the years. On one side she placed the pictures of people unknown to her. These she decided to store in a brown envelope. She was just getting into her task, and putting all the pictures of Eilidh in another pile, when the phone rang.

'Mum?'

'Hello? Jason! Oh how lovely to hear from you! How are you? Where are you?'

'Hi, Mum, I'm down here in Caen at the moment but I'm not so good; I broke my ankle. I was wondering...'

Anna rolled her eyes. 'How on earth did you do that? Are you all right?'

'I had a bit of an accident on my friend's motorbike. Some idiot driving on the wrong side of the road tipped me off! I'm OK, just a bit shaken up and my ankle is in plaster, but yes, actually I was wondering if I could come back and stay for a bit; it would be nice to catch up with everybody. I can get a lift to the ferry then I'll get myself onto the train home somehow.'

'You are awful, you don't get in touch for ages then suddenly you bombard me with news, disastrous news at that...but of course you must come home. You know you don't even have to ask.'

Thinking about the call later, Anna frowned and felt uneasy. Had she sensed remoteness in him? Oh, why was she so sensitive, always imagining things that weren't there at all? But still, there seemed to be an undercurrent. Maybe it was just a mother's intuition. She shook her head. Her foolhardy boy had suffered a long list of accidents over the years. Why couldn't he just ring to say that he was fine for once? Muttering, she returned to the tin box but could no longer concentrate. She tried to focus on Eilidh but her heart was no longer in it. Her mother was gone, she had been lovely and blameless and no one could have foreseen how her death would bequeath such a legacy of pain to so many people. Anna had been hoping to find the reason why her father and stepmother had ostracised her so suddenly all those years ago. There didn't seem to be any clues in the box, and Aunty Molly and John Sinclair only remembered their personal versions of the history.

Anna was about to replace the lid when a loose photo, a black-and-white picture of a family group, slid on to her lap. Written on the back, in the characteristic violet ink, were the words: Dorothy, Sam & Lucy – Fraser's Hill 1956. Maybe fate had decided to give a helping hand after all. Holding the photo, she walked over to the telephone. She knew that the Bathgates had retired and now lived somewhere in Sussex, but where?

Lucy was married and lived in East Africa, but apart from Christmas cards she didn't really keep in touch. She dialled the familiar number of her dad's house and spoke to the resident carer who lived with him. She asked Morag to look in Estelle's old bamboo telephone book for the number of Dorothy Bathgate. Anna remembered Estelle telling her that Sam had died of cancer about five years ago. Within minutes she had the number and suddenly the years rolled away at the sound of Dorothy's soft voice.

'Anna! What a surprise, how lovely to hear from you!'

It was all very simple. It was as though she was being prompted to follow the trail. She decided to drive down to the south coast the next day and then, after meeting up with Dorothy in Chichester, she would be able to collect Jason from Portsmouth when he arrived on the ferry from Caen, and then they could travel back home together. Anna rang his mobile and told him about her new plan.

Refreshed after an overnight stay in a nondescript motel after her long drive south, Anna followed the signs for Chichester and glimpsed the spire of the cathedral rising above its verdigrised roof, clean and fresh after the night's rainstorm. She turned the music off to concentrate better on the directions that Dorothy had relayed to her, and meandered at a slower pace through the streets of the ancient city where Georgian and Victorian buildings stood united against demand for change. The sun shone through a clear sky and the old couple she stopped to ask the way were cheerful as if they too were enjoying this break from the wind and rain. Kerb crawling along the tree-lined avenue, she found the wooden nameplate: Bukit Dosam. Anna smiled at the romantic blend of their two names, Dorothy and Sam, as well as the permanent and welcoming memory of their years spent overseas. The garden, like hers in Edinburgh, still had late-blooming roses. She pressed the bell and the door opened almost instantly; she was like a little jack-in-the-box spider. Anna giggled in spite of herself. Dorothy seemed smaller than she remembered, and as she reached down to hug her, Anna noticed that the old lady was flexing her fingers, as though she was about to pray, or maybe play some scales. Her head had a slight twitch.

'Come in, dear. Oh my goodness, it's been so many years,' and her eyes filled with tears. 'You look so like your mother.'

Dorothy led her guest through the hall and into her elegant front room, with a tall window facing on to the garden. Around the room was the rosewood furniture that had been shipped over from the Far East. A Buddha and a dragon stood to attention on the polished surface of the carved rain tree coffee table. Dorothy herself seemed out of place amongst all this elegance. In her nylon housecoat and pink suede slippers she looked like an assistant in an ironmonger's shop. The parting in her dyed hair revealed the snowy ridge of white roots, and her lipstick had clearly been applied in a rush.

'Old age, dear, it's a terrible thing. In truth, I don't sit in here much these days. Let's go through to the kitchen; it's cosy in there. This house is too big for me now, but it does have a little den at the back that I like to use for watching television and knitting and so on. Do you know I have a computer now? Can you imagine; me with a computer? Lucy insisted I should have one so she and Mark set me up with all the mod cons when they were here last Christmas. I'm still struggling to get the hang of it, but I manage to send them the odd email now and again. What do you think of that? Come on, dear, we shall sit through there. I've made us a nice quiche for our lunch, and we can chat about old times.'

The two old acquaintances spent the afternoon poring over countless photo albums, in which Anna saw her childhood companion in various stages of her life. Although the parents had kept in touch, Anna hadn't seen Lucy since they were both eleven years old. Now they were over fifty, and Lucy had three grown-up sons. She looked vivacious and tanned, with her auburn hair curling to her shoulders. Not that different, perhaps, from how her mother had looked at that age.

'How is your poor dad?' Dorothy asked; her hands now at peace, locked in prayer under her chin.

'He doesn't appear to know me. Since the stroke he can no longer swallow and has to be fed by tube; as you know, he still lives at home with his carer. Morag is a very strong woman, a retired nursing sister and she also gets a lot of outside support.'

'Poor Alex, he was such a great man; so good-looking.'

Anna stared at the wallpaper in front of her; it had vertical pink stripes in a texture that she wanted to touch, satiny and soft, like ribbons. Twisting the errant wisps of hair from her forehead, she tried to summarise the news that Dorothy craved. 'Estelle's in hospital with a bout of pneumonia. She's very frail; I don't know how she'll cope when she does get home. She never did like her world to be turned upside-down. It is all very sad. My father is so helpless, though some days his eyes do seem quite bright, whereas Estelle...you know how spirited she is, she'll find it hard to be immobilised. Goodness knows what will happen when she gets out of the hospital, for I doubt Morag will want someone giving her orders all day long.'

Dorothy appeared to be deep in thought, but her head continued to twitch, and as though Anna had not spoken at all, she continued her reminiscences. 'Of course I knew him better when your mother was alive. I'll never forget how he looked when he returned to Bukit Bulan after poor Eilidh passed away. He went so thin; his eyes seemed to sink back in his head. He'd lost everything, can you imagine? It was just heartbreaking. I was the one that packed up all her dresses and your toys and organised the shipping. It was all too much for him.'

'But you did see him after he was married to Estelle?'

'Yes, dear, of course, but I wasn't so friendly with her; she was quite different from your own mother. She had her own friends, but there was a sharpness about her that I found difficult to cope with, though I'm sure she was kind enough in her own way.' Dorothy thought for a minute, then went on, 'When you came out to join them after your grandmother died, we used to get together so that you and Lucy would have company in the holidays, but after your dad was moved to Port Dickson it was difficult to meet up regularly. I was closer to Lois, my sister-in-law who married Michael Parrish, and to your Aunt Kate of course; we used to play *mah jong* together. But as you know, I was always there for you and your dad when you needed me.'

Anna leant over and squeezed the older woman's hand. She liked this cosy and cluttered den, so different from the cool elegance of the front room. In here, the only sign that Dorothy had lived in Southeast Asia for many years was a black octagonal waste paper basket with a Chinese figure glued on to each section. Prints of English flowers adorned these walls and Hummel porcelain figurines pouted coyly on the mantelpiece. Anna pointed to the tin box at her feet. 'As well as coming to collect

Jason, I'm actually on a different mission. You see, I need to make sense of things that I never did understand. I was hoping you could help me?'

'Well, I can try, dear. What is it you need to know?' Dorothy's eyes lit up, her fingers started to flex alarmingly.

'Well, you see, I've been given this box by my Aunty Molly. It's full of pictures and letters and memorabilia from my mother's days in Malaya. I know how she died, and I know that my father married Estelle, but I don't know much about Jack Dunbar. I was hoping you could tell me how he died, Dorothy. Was he killed in the Emergency?'

The older woman suddenly lost her bird-like brightness and seemed to sink into herself. She took a deep breath. 'You wouldn't have known, would you, dear? Poor Jack was shot dead.'

Anna nodded. 'I did hear, actually, just the other afternoon. I always thought he'd been killed in the Emergency, but John Sinclair, an old flame of my mother, told me that Jack had been shot, but he didn't tell me why or by whom.'

'No, I suppose there was no need to tell you, tragedies happen and poor Callum was not to blame. It was just a terrible accident, the poor man suffered for years afterwards.'

'What? Uncle Callum? But that can't be right?' Anna couldn't form the words in her confusion.

'It's true, dear. Callum had been cleaning his rifle and it went off somehow. He was cleared at the inquiry, but the poor man completely broke down at the funeral. Jack was buried at Batu Gajah together with a young soldier who had been fighting in Pahang. He was from Scotland as well, Bill Ripley I think his name was. After the bugle player played taps at the end, a Ghurkha piper stepped forward and played an old Highland lament as we all filed out. Oh, my dear, it was such a sad, sad day. Callum was in a terrible state. He just fell apart and had to be sent home on compassionate leave. He was so distraught your dad travelled back with him.'

The two women sat quietly for a moment, Dorothy lost in her memories, and Anna silent, struggling to process this unexpected revelation.

'I can't believe it. All those years and I didn't know.'

'Well, it was in hospital that Callum met Kate.'

'Yes, I do remember her telling me when I was little that he'd had a breakdown. Goodness knows what I imagined that was!' Anna laughed at the memory, 'But how could such a thing have happened, Dorothy? And what about Estelle?'

'Oh, what a scandal that was! When the news of Jack's death was broken, so it came out that he'd been secretly married to Estelle all that time. His poor mother was so shocked, and of course Estelle came into not just all his money but the proceeds from the farm sale as well. You can imagine the unpleasantness over that.'

Anna studied Dorothy's face, trying to read her thoughts and wondering what images from another world were flashing in front of the old lady's eyes.

'In fact,' Dorothy resumed in a rather clipped manner, 'I think Callum himself was quite sweet on Estelle; they met when she visited him in the hospital.'

'Yes, I remember they always seemed close.' Anna vaguely recalled how they seemed to share a bond during her childhood. 'But my dad, how did he come to marry Estelle?'

'I believe he went to see her after settling his brother into hospital in Inverness. Maybe they had dinner together or something. They'd both been widowed so there would have been a mutual empathy, and then after Alex returned to Malaya, they corresponded and became quite friendly. All that letter writing must have achieved something because they married on his next home leave!'

'I was there for that one,' Anna laughed, 'five years old and a flower girl! But I see it now, and I suppose I understand why they wanted to close the book on the past. I just wish I had known my own mother.'

'You do already, dear. If I knew Eilidh at all, I don't believe she's ever been far from you.'

Anna looked down, her eyes suddenly feeling hot and weepy.

'It's all right, dear, I think you've been kept in the dark far too long. I have something to show you.'

Dorothy shuffled over to the bookcase and brought down a dusty old album. Perching it on the younger woman's knees, she riffled through the black pages covered with small photographs affixed with silver corner fastenings, soft tissue separating the leaves of the book. Anna recognised so many faces and places; her dad and mother in a garden, another of Michael, Callum and Jack leaning against the bar of The Dog in the Selangor Club.

'That's Jack! You were just about to go to Fraser's Hill for Eilidh's TB cure.'

'Oh! It wasn't a row between Callum and Jack, was it?'

'No, dear, it was as I said, the shooting was just the most awful accident. I'm sorry; it's been such a shock for you.' Dorothy stood up and replaced the album back on the shelf. 'But why don't you tell me about yourself now, dear, you've just let me natter on about Lucy and her family and now here we are full of the glooms about what happened over forty years ago. Let's have a pot of tea and you can tell me what you have been up to all these years. I'll go and see what I can find.'

They both wandered through to the kitchen. Dorothy fussed around in cupboards and back they came with a tray loaded with biscuits and a very welcome pot of Earl Grey. Still chattering away, Dorothy poured the tea. Anna looked at her bright eyes and the hands that she could not keep still. Her head did have a decided twitch. It was quite disconcerting, Anna thought; hard to hold her gaze.

'You're quite right,' Anna finally said, 'we have been a bit glum, but I'm stunned by what you've just told me. What an appalling thing to have happened, and to think they all just carried on with their lives somehow. There are so many things I've never known about.'

'I'm sorry, dear; maybe I shouldn't have said anything.'

'No, I'm glad you did. Anyway...' and Anna put down her cup, 'moving on, you wanted to hear about us. Well, Duncan is really the one that travels; I mostly stay home and look after the shop we have in Edinburgh. He is in Cambodia and Thailand just now and is very excited about a shipment of silks and teak screens that he's had made. They're rather like that miniature triptych lacquered screen you have over there. His are full size of course. When I go with him on his buying trips, I tend to select jewellery and lamps; I love the filigree silver bracelets, and they sell well here.' Anna prattled on, but as she talked she wondered how Uncle Callum could have behaved so normally after what happened. Her brain was reeling with the discovery she'd just made, but she tried to keep her voice normal while she talked of her own life. 'Duncan is lucky, he is gregarious as well as a natural linguist so he's made a lot of friends and good business connections over the years. Oh! I forgot to mention that he's taken on Luke as a partner. Do you remember Kate and Callum's son, and how we all played in the swimming pool when we were young?'

'Of course I do, dear; he was like an angel, that child. Blond curls and blue eyes, he looked like a cherub that might have been painted by Fra Angelico.'

Anna laughed at that, 'Luke has preserved his cherub looks; he still has a round chin and an ample stomach. He never married, though he was engaged for a long time. He lives with his parents in Scotland and I'm afraid he's showing signs of his mother's roly-poly pudding diet!'

'And what news of your boy; you said you're going to meet him tomorrow?'

'Well, apart from a broken ankle, I suppose Jason's fine. He's been in Perpignan, in the south of France these last three years. Did you know that Duncan's brother Hugh married a French woman? Well, Jason teamed up with his cousin Raoul who has a carpentry business down there. He's always been good with his hands. He just loves France and, like his dad, he has a flair for learning languages. I'm glad of course, but...'

'But you miss him, dear, I can see that,' Dorothy nodded, her eyes wide with sympathy.

Anna couldn't go on, for how could she explain the sense of loss she felt? Her only son gone and her husband away so much of the year. She looked over at this lonely old lady in this beautiful house and saw how her life had been reduced to one room. All they both really needed and craved, she thought, was a bit of company. It didn't seem such a lot to ask. But compared to others she knew who had lost so much, perhaps she should really count her blessings. And Estelle, she was a poor soul. Old age and pneumonia had reduced her to a thin shadow, and Alex was a sad shell of the man he had once been. Anna closed her mind and tried to blank the image of him as she'd last seen him: dribbling and being spoon fed. Her whole being had revolted at the suggestion that she might have to care for him. Instead, Estelle had employed Morag. Let him have the pity of strangers. They certainly had made it clear that she was not wanted in their world.

*

231

Later that evening, Dorothy decided to open a bottle of wine.

'You've made my head spin, girl. There are bees buzzing in there and all the stories and faces of long ago are just whirling about.'

'Tell me, Dorothy, tell me about Callum, and please tell me more about what happened to Jack and everything. I really want to know.'

'I will, dear, but before I go into all of that, did you know Freya well?'

'No, just from my childhood and odd snippets of news from Estelle at Christmas; I do know they went to live in Collioure, close to where Hugh lives with his family, but that is all. Why?'

'Well, you may not know this, but Roger and Freya took their *amah* to live with them in France. That was unexpected, but apparently they had always been close. I know you knew Suleiman, Freya's *amah's* son… forgive me for talking about him, Anna.'

Anna lifted the wine goblet up and buried her face into it. 'No, it's all right, please go on.'

'There were rumours of course that Suleiman might have been the son of someone we knew. Rumours only, but there's never smoke without fire, and there was definitely a look of the European about him. I doubt he could have been Roger's but you never know.'

'So Freya and Roger are still in France? I always imagined that the *amah* went home to her family.'

'No, it was most unusual, and caused quite a stir in the club, but they took the girl with them, and she's still there. Not a girl now of course, both she and Freya must be close to seventy! Poor Roger died quite a few years ago. A dicky heart, they say.'

Suddenly Anna felt weary and needed a break from the revelations and memories that Dorothy had evoked during the course of the day. Taking her leave from an equally tired Dorothy, she climbed the stairs and prepared for her second night in a strange bed. Lying propped against the pillows, her eyes fell on the shape of the object that had started her quest. She was only trying to find out about her mother but it was becoming more like Pandora's Box. How many more secrets would fly out?

Chapter 15

December 1965 – Malaysia

The Emergency had been over for five years, and the McIntyre families were celebrating Christmas together on the Tuaran Tinggi Estate.

'I love your house, Aunt Kate, 'Anna declared rapturously.

'Do you, dear, and why is that?'

'I feel I am a grand lady in the bedroom. It is so huge! I've been practising my ballet. Have you heard of Anna Pavlova? Well, I'm going to be like her when I grow up.'

'I see, and is this before you become a nun, or after?' Kate was copying a recipe into her book. Rich pudding with brandy butter sat heavily on all their stomachs, so Estelle had gone out for a walk with Callum and Alex.

'Well, I might be a nun after because it's important to start training straight away for ballet. I have to do my exercises every day. Anna Pavlova was selected out of millions of girls, you know.'

'What else do you learn at that school, apart from balancing on your toes and giving yourself premature bunions?'

'What's a premature onion?'

'It's what premature ballerinas get on their toes.'

'Well anyway, this is first position and this is second position and this is *plié* and this is *grand plié*.'

Kate regarded her niece's thin legs and knobbly knees. She imagined the great Pavlova might have looked a bit like this gangly swan once upon a time herself. 'And apart from dancing, what do you do?'

'Well, we don't dance actually, Aunt Kate, we just do positions. And in piano we don't play, we just do scales. Madame Chin hits me with a ruler if I do it wrong, especially the B flat one and then she makes me massage her shoulders because she says she's tired. I hate piano.'

'I see,' said Kate, struggling to conceal a smile.

'And,' continued Anna, warming to her subject, 'I also hate Latin; it's dead, you know. I just get kisses all over my translations. I do know my declensions; shall I say them to you? OK, nominative, vocative, accusative, genitive, dative and ablative!'

'And what does that all mean?'

'Well, I don't know really, but you have to say things like *amo amas amat* and *bellum bellum bellum* and they all mean I love, you love, he, she, it loves and things like that, but I prefer French and I am really really good at running. Do you know I saw a whole family of monkeys when I was learning my French vocab on the path behind the classroom? It was so scary when they trooped past me. The mum had a baby on its back and the dad showed me its teeth. I told the teacher, and she said we mustn't go near the jungle paths on our own. Mrs Lily found a black cobra sleeping on the clean towels in the laundry cupboard. She screamed and then so did we and we all ran out into the playground.'

'So you like school on the top of Penang Hill?'

'I suppose so. It's quite exciting sometimes.'

'And what about sums?' Kate asked.

'Some sums are good, like long division and long multiplication but some are bad, like decimals and fractions. Do you know, we had a test, and if you got them all right, you could go to choose which colour material you wanted to make an apron with? I got five wrong, and by the time I got to choose, all the good colours like red and blue and yellow were gone so I was stuck with lilac. Ugh!'

'It's not so bad,' said Kate kindly, 'lilac is a pretty colour. Have you enjoyed Christmas, Anna?'

'Oh yes, I've loved it, I love being here. Thank you for the bath salts and the back brush and the books. I hate bath time at school. Do you know we all have to stand in line on the stairs and watch as everyone showers? There are four cold showers, so four girls go under at a time. I hate it, as everyone watches and the matron shouts at us not to forget our private parts. I don't think it should be allowed, do you, Aunt Kate?'

'No, dear, it sounds quite awful. Well, you enjoy the holidays and have lovely warm, deep baths and don't forget to scrub your back!'

*

After Alex, Estelle and Anna left on Boxing Day the house seemed echoing and empty. Callum drove into the office and Kate stood alone in the middle of the room that had been Anna's. The chairs were still lined up facing the mirror where the child had been doing her exercises at the barre. It seemed *The Sound of Music* had been relegated as the tutu and the pointe shoes had beckoned more strongly. Kate went to sit on the single bed and reflected that it had been three years now since she had lost her twins. Three years since she'd allowed Callum to share her bed. She shivered with revulsion each time she thought of what she would have to endure if she wanted more children. She had been unprepared for the intimacies of marriage. Brought up by a widowed father, she'd felt from a very young age that her role was to nurture, thus it was easy to carry that persona to her work. Patients were drawn to her warmth and her patience. Her gentle demeanour and the ability to listen and accept without giving judgement attracted Callum and led him to fall in love with her. He'd mistaken her compassion for genuine warmth, and was to find out that he'd been deluded.

They had been married in a simple service and she had looked the part as the innocent, blushing bride. Callum had drunk whisky with her father and they had toasted each other for being so lucky to have such a prize as Kate. The new bride had remained detached and aloof as the hour approached when she would have to submit to her new husband's drunken, pawing advances. As it turned out, it was everything that she had been led to expect. She had listened to the chatter of her nurse colleagues while they giggled and related their own intimate stories around the tea urn at the hospital: 'Dinnae worry! It's just in and oot, in and oot, a big bore and then a snore, nothing to get your knickers in a twist about, love!' And it was: exactly that. He had rolled off and then the bed had heaved rhythmically with his snores until morning. Then there had been the months of waiting for her first baby, only for the pregnancy to be cruelly terminated by untimely cramps at the end of four months.

Kate got up and walked over to the mirror. She studied her face and sucked in her cheeks, then turned sideways to see if the pounds gained over Christmas were very evident. She looked to see if the pain etched from the searing loss she had endured after her second pregnancy was physically apparent in her eyes. She squeezed her eyes tight in an effort to block the vision of her beautiful twin boys. She remembered the long, thirty-six hour labour, the panic when the doctor found the cord had strangled the first, and the mad rush to try and save the second, all to no avail and she had lost them both. She knew that, as a result, she and Callum had reversed their roles. Now it was he who was caring and solicitous towards her, he who cared for her every need. He never pressed himself on her, and for that she was grateful, but it had been three years and her body ached for the fulfilment that she believed she would find in motherhood. Her whole being was made for caring and love, and without a child she felt starved. She looked over to the dressing table where she remembered painting Anna's bitten fingernails. 'Have I left it too late?'

While Kate sat up in the spare bedroom, Callum walked through the rubber, inspecting the trees that were just coming into maturity. He too had enjoyed the Christmas break and the time spent with his brother. The two men had sat up together on Christmas night, rather like the old times before they were married. The tree lights had twinkled and remnants of nuts and raisins and toffee papers littered the small table tops. They had both been feeling replete and garrulous. Alex had requested an LP of Frank Sinatra to be played before Cookie retired to his room.

'Another year almost over; Malaya as we knew it has gone, now it's the brave new Federation of Malaysia. And a very good thing it is too. Thank God there's also peace between Indonesia and Malaysia, but what a tragedy that men like Angus Robertson and Tim Bradley and all the others that were shot down could not have lived to see it all.'

'Aye, and Jack and Eilidh too,' added Callum quietly.

They raised their drinks and clinked their glasses together, not verbalising a toast, both lost in their own reveries while Frank crooned about *Strangers in the Night*.

Finally Alex spoke. 'Do you remember that curry lunch we had at Roger and Freya's back in '57?'

'I do that,' smiled his brother. 'They knew how to hold parties, that pair. I believe old Rog is due for retirement next year. He was telling us about the property they'd bought in the south of France. In Collioure, I think he said, right on the Spanish border.'

'Well that should suit them, hot and sunny weather with vineyards to keep up their wine supply!' laughed Alex. He coughed and tapped his index finger rhythmically on the arm of his chair. Clearing his throat, he enquired, 'What of Aminah? I've often wondered what became of her. I heard Freya was trying to settle her somewhere. Do you still send her money?'

'Yes, I got an address from Freya so I send the money to Petaling Jaya. I've only seen the boy twice since he was born. Once, when the kid was about three, Freya had him swimming in that pool of theirs; the second time when he was five.' Callum took a drink and looked up at a moth flickering round the shade of the standard lamp, intent on burning itself to death. He went on, 'You know, things are not so good with Kate any more. She has never got over the death of the twins, and blames me. Sees me as the cause of all the pain.'

'Aye, it's a terrible thing. It's hard for Estelle too, knowing she can't have any. She was talking about adopting, but I don't know. I see us fine the way we are, we have our golf and Anna in the holidays and God knows we're getting on! We're in our forties now! It's all right for you young ones!'

The brothers gossiped companionably as the night deepened, talking of rubber and politics and planters who had been transferred and promoted. It wasn't until an owl hooted that they remembered the lateness of the hour and made their way to their respective bedrooms.

On Boxing Day, with the visitors gone and after enjoying a simple meal together, Kate and Callum sat watching their new television set.

'It's quiet now.'

'I know,' Kate looked up from her sewing, 'I was just thinking that. I miss Anna. What a lassie! She's got so many notions of what she's going to be when she grows up.'

'Is she still planning on being a nun?'

'Oh no, that's gone, it's a ballerina now. You should see all the drawings she left in her bedroom. They're all of girls standing on their toes in tutus. So funny,' and Kate chuckled, 'the bodies and heads are in reasonable proportion but the legs, oh my goodness, they take up three quarters of the page!'

Callum grunted and took another sip of his whisky soda. Although his eyes remained on the screen his thoughts were going over his conversation with Alex about them not having any children. It was so unfair. Estelle was sexy and flirtatious. He loved the way she teased him and kissed him and he was drawn to her warmth. Callum couldn't help feeling jealous of his brother. He looked over at his own wife pensively, then swallowed the rest of his drink and called to Cookie for another. He was bitter and fed up with this situation. To make things worse he couldn't shake off the image of Estelle laughing uproariously at a joke that even he thought was a bit risqué. What did he have in comparison, just a frigid wife who wouldn't let him touch her?

Kate went upstairs early, and he could hear the splash of the water running into her tub. He asked Cookie for one more whisky then told him that he too would be calling it a night. Alone he sat in the silent house, and as he drank he grew more and more convinced that he had a right to Kate's body. It had been three years, for God's sake. He mounted the stairs and walked into the sacrosanct interior of her bedroom. He found her standing by the bed, brushing her hair, her body covered in a long cotton night dress. He lurched over and encircled her in his arms. Instinctively she pulled away from the red-rimmed eyes and the reek of whisky fumes.

'Bloody hell, woman, what do you take me for? You were the one who told me I had to move on and get over my grief. Don't you remember all your wise words? Can you not apply them to yourself...can you not love me a bit?'

'I do love you,' Kate sobbed. 'You know I love you, but I can't. It hurts. It always hurts.'

Callum steamed and his face became redder with frustration, 'Is it going to be another aborted attempt?' he sneered, 'another night of hysterics? Sex is not taboo, woman. You're my wife and I have rights.' Swaying, he leant over to grab her and tried to kiss her, his hands fumbling at her breasts. She drew away, repulsed by his wet mouth and his leery eyes. He backed off, his eyebrows raised and his voice lowered. His tone was threatening, 'Everything hurts, your bloody head, your neck, your back, well I'm fed up with your cold shoulder. I've had it with all your whining, you just need sorting out.' In rage he pushed her back on to the bed, and with one hand on her shoulder he used his other to force her legs open. Struggling with the buttons of his shirt and frantically pulling at his trousers he was impervious to her cries.

'No! No! Please, Callum, please don't do this.'

He pushed past her resistance and lunged into her. She felt as though she had torn and dreaded the coming friction, but mercifully he had no control and it was all over in seconds. He rolled over and suddenly felt bone tired and disgusted with himself. Vaguely he heard her choke back her rage and indignation but he was past caring. He shut his eyes and soon all she could hear was the inevitable rumble of his snores. Trembling, Kate staggered to the bathroom and surveyed her stricken face. She wet some towels and pressed them to her thighs where the tender flesh was red and already beginning to bruise. She squeezed some toothpaste on to her brush and scrubbed her teeth, desperately trying to rid herself of the taste of whisky and animal lust that had pervaded her body.

Over the next few days the couple formed an icy truce. They were polite and merely coexisted. Callum reinstated himself in the marital bed and a nightly pattern soon established itself. Kate lay like a corpse on a morgue slab waiting for him to raise her cotton nightgown. He would heave himself on and then off, the ritual lasting only a few ticks of the bedside clock. He had won a victory of sorts but somehow there was little pleasure in the spoils.

Two days after Hogmanay, Callum drove to Kuala Lumpur's new Subang airport to meet his planting adviser, Vincent Taylor, an elderly planter who had come out of retirement to take up this position. He commanded great respect owing to his exaggerated limp as he manoeuvred his wooden leg, a result of an exploding mine in the troubled times of the Emergency.

'Just take me to the Railway Hotel, old boy. There's been many a night that I've stayed there. We'll have a bit of tiffin and then I shall turn in. We'll meet up again tomorrow; bloody buggered from being cooped up in that damned sardine can for so long.'

After spending an hour with his mentor, Callum was unexpectedly free. It was only four o'clock so he walked down to the Selangor Club and into The Dog where he ordered a beer at the Long Bar. There were a group of Australian tin miners down from Ipoh but there was nobody that he knew, so he finished his drink and left as quickly as he had arrived. He took a taxi and gave the driver the address that he always carried with him. It was folded tightly and hidden in the back of his wallet where no prying eyes were likely to see it. The taxi pulled up in front of a block of flats in Petaling Jaya. Fruit vendors and street hawkers were plying their trade and they ignored Callum as he squeezed past. His attention was caught by a sugar cane seller and he watched for a moment as the man turned the wheel of the mangle that crushed the sticks of raw cane, the yellow juice dripping into the bowl. Some schoolgirls giggled while they waited to give him some cents, and in return the juice was poured into a plastic bag already containing a few spoonfuls of crushed ice and a straw. With their freshly squeezed drinks, the girls sauntered off to join some friends. Callum watched them as they made their way down the pavement, then realised he was blocking the alley where two young Malay boys were trying to get out.

'*Tabik, Tuan*,' they grinned at him, and he noted their bright eyes, their clean white shirts and the navy blue velvet *songkok* hats that they wore.

Callum felt conspicuous in this neighbourhood that was inhabited mostly by Malays and Indians. Eventually he found the number on the paper he was clutching and he climbed the stone steps, passing piles of rubbish until he reached a landing with a blue door. He rapped the knocker and glanced about him, noticing the cleanly swept floor and the colourful potted plants.

'Hello, *Tuan* Callum.'

He spun round and there she was. 'Hello, Aminah, it's been a long time.'

'Please come in, I not expect you, is everything all right? Your wife, she OK?'

'Yes, thank you. I just collected my planting adviser and couldn't think what else to do, and then I thought of you and the boy. How is Suleiman getting on?'

Aminah's face softened. 'I think you may have passed him just now. He has gone out with his friend.'

'Those boys in white?'

'Yes. He's a big boy now, eight years old! Leman I call him, all his friends call him that at school. But please, come in.'

She led the way inside and Callum's eyes took in the modest room.

Three armchairs were clustered around a coffee table that had been draped with a red and yellow velour cover with a picture of a mosque on it. A bead curtain separated this room from a small kitchen, and next to that was a further room, presumably either the bedroom or the bathroom.

'We sleep in here,' Aminah smiled as she watched him looking about. 'We lay down our mats on the carpet. The apartment is very small, very different to the estate house but we are lucky to have it. And we are lucky to have you to take care of us so well.'

Callum coughed, and looked away. He felt embarrassed about the whole situation and preferred not to think about this woman having had an involvement with Jack. He accepted her offer of tea, which she served as efficiently as she had always done on the estate. She sat with him and he found her easy to talk to, answering all her questions about the people who had once been in her life as well. He told her about Alex and Estelle, and Michael and Lois Parrish, and then suddenly the boy was back.

'*Tabik, Tuan*,' Leman said politely, recognising this European man from outside the alley way.

'Hello, Suleiman, or should I say Leman, do you speak English?'

'Of course, *Tuan*, Mem Freya taught me and she taught me how to read as well.'

'How do you like living here, then?' Callum asked.

Leman smiled, showing strong, even teeth. 'It's OK, I have friends now, and school is not too far and we can buy Chiclets. Do you know what they are? They are chewing gum, and I can get bubble gum too. My mother only likes me to eat *assams* and Malay sweets but I like bubble gum best.'

'Are you doing well in school?'

'Oh yes, *Tuan*, my best subject is geography. Do you know I can tell you all the names of the islands that make up Indonesia and do you know it was Francis Light who founded Penang?'

Callum grinned, for Freya had obviously given this young lad a good foundation as he was articulate and exuded confidence. He looked over at Aminah and noted how proud she was of her boy. Her eyes were soft as though she was caressing him, and she seemed unable to refrain from touching his arm, his shoulder, or smoothing back his glossy black fringe from his eyes. He studied the boy's face, but saw little resemblance to Jack. The eyes and hair were dark; his skin was pale as powdered cinnamon;

perhaps the tilt of his head or the arrogant self-confidence? It was too early to say.

'Have you married, Aminah?' Callum asked, although there seemed to be little evidence of another male presence in the house.

'No, *Tuan* Callum, I am happy as I am. I do some sewing for a dress shop and the money you send helps us to live. I have everything I need,' and she smiled and leant over to kiss Leman on the forehead.

'But we need a radio and a television,' Leman reminded her. 'Don't we need those things, Mum?'

'Leman! Enough!' Aminah spoke sharply to her son.

Callum grinned at her over the boy's head. 'Well, I'm very pleased to see that you are both managing so well. Might I come to see you again?'

Callum found himself driving to see Aminah every Tuesday. Their initial meetings followed a polite decorum, sharing some tea while Suleiman entertained them with his stories of school. On one such Tuesday, Callum drove through heavy monsoon rain to get to her apartment. The water rushed down the drains in a minor torrent and he ran to her building, his shirt soaked in the deluge.

'Oh my goodness, you're so wet. Please take this towel; maybe you should take off your clothes and they can dry?'

Callum shook his head, water spraying out, and he pulled at the wet cotton of his shirt clinging to his body. 'Where's Suleiman?'

'Leman is now attending afternoon school,' Aminah explained. 'Before he attended the morning session but now it has changed. I'm sorry you won't see him today. He will be disappointed that he has missed you.'

'I could come back later?'

'No, you are so wet. Stay. I'll make some tea.'

Callum was conscious of his body draped only in a thin towel. 'You're very kind, Aminah.'

'You think so? Maybe I'm glad to see you too. It's lonely here for me.'

Callum blew the hot liquid, not sure if the pounding he heard came from the rain outside or the blood coursing through his heart. He replaced his cup on the table and shyly reached for her hand. Her dark almond eyes were almost black, her lips were moist, and he noticed her cheeks were flushed. Studying the slim fingers, he massaged his thumb over the soft palm, before lifting it to his lips and kissing the impossibly thin wrist. Immediately she knelt before him, pressing her body between his open knees. Callum was at a loss. Sensing his reticence, Aminah took his face in her hands and lowered it towards her own. Gently she nibbled his lips, caressed his eyes with her mouth, and gently rubbed her hands down his bare back. Callum was aware of sensations he had never felt before as his body was teased by those long fingers. He arched his back as he felt her breath on his neck and around the soft lobes of his ears, and her eyelashes flickered on the firm flesh of his shoulder. He heard the rain, and silently thanked God for the wetness that had brought him to this place. He kissed her, gently and softly, bringing his lips down to the soft places round her breasts; the robe she wore parted easily and he heard her sigh. Gently he pushed her back on to the floor, where they rolled like the breakers on an ocean whilst outside the storm raged, and the afternoon was dark.

Two months passed and Callum counted the days until he could see Aminah again. His eyes frequently caressed the calendar, willing time to pass. The minutes ticked and the hours took an age. Each time it was the same. He found himself smoothing his hair as he ran up the steps to her apartment. His heart was pounding and his mouth was dry while he waited for her to open the door. As soon as she saw him, she pulled him inside away from prying eyes and threw herself into his arms and covered his face and neck with kisses. Her exuberance and joy and unconditional love brought warmth to his starved heart.

As the afternoons passed, he explored her body with the same slow and sensuous technique that he'd learnt from her. She taught him to play and caress, to withhold the ultimate of pleasures and now he felt the joy of giving and watching this beautiful woman eventually scream out in ecstasy. For the first time in his life he held a woman, damp with perspiration and limp from the pleasure that he had given her. He paced the days that he was not with her; his behaviour became erratic, his whole demeanour became that of a man obsessed.

Kate was relieved. He was so often distracted it meant that the couple actually spent less time together. Thus her days resumed the old pattern of chatting on the telephone and arranging bridge and *mah jong* dates with Nancy Fung and her other girlfriends. Callum's initial lust that had begun on that horrible Boxing Day seemed to have burnt itself out and she was grateful that she was spared the indignity of the nightly huffing and puffing. So it was a shock to both of them when she realised that another child was coming, conceived during the cold, brutal union on that drunken night.

'It's lucky the poor mite will never know how it came to be,' she sniffed bitterly into her handkerchief.

'It's on its way, Kate, and I'm sorry. I'm sorry for everything. But it is wonderful, isn't it? Another chance?'

'To end in the toilet or to be born dead?' She glared at him and choked back the sobs. 'I hate you, I hate all that; you know I do. Why did you make me?'

'Sssssh, come here, Kate. I'm a big oaf, I know, just come here, my wee darling.'

Callum pulled her reluctant body into his arms. She stood like a board, suffering him to run his hand up and down her back. Slowly she responded to the hypnotic movements and she relaxed and allowed him to soothe her. He felt the soft, lumpy figure and he inhaled the familiar scent of her perfume. As the wiry texture of her hair tickled his cheek, his thoughts turned to Aminah, evoking the memories of her fragrance. Unbidden, he recalled images of his lover, the silkiness of her hair, the lithe shape of her narrow hips, the beads of perspiration that formed on her forehead and breasts as they made love. He blinked and brought himself back to the present. 'It'll be all right, Kate, this time we shall take good care of you. You will rest and you'll live like a lady with your feet up until the wee bairn is born.'

She blew her nose noisily, and walked over to the mirror in the hall.

'Oh God! What a mess.' She examined her tear-blotched face, her swollen eyes and she took in the image of her dumpy figure. It was going to blow up like a football again, complete with varicose veins and swollen ankles. 'Perhaps I should go home to see the gynaecologist in Raigmore Hospital in Inverness?'

'Whatever you want, my dear; we'll go to KL tomorrow and see the doctor and take his advice.'

*

Callum resolved to end the affair. He made a stern promise to himself that he would stop seeing Aminah, but each time her door opened he was lost in her arms and when he kissed her throat and felt her hands pulling at his shirt he would be overcome, lost in the intimacy of their passion. Holding her later, he would try to compose words to tell her it must end, but then she would rush them both into the shower and afterwards she would make tea and before long Suleiman would come barging in, full of his day's adventures.

'Hello, *Tuan* Callum, I am now the King of Marbles in my class. Look!' and he spilled the contents of an orange drawstring bag on to the carpet. 'These are all of the marbles that I have conquered!' The shiny balls of coloured glass clustered and twinkled like precious jewels, some battle weary and chipped, others in pristine condition clearly lost to their previous proud owners soon after their purchase. 'I won them all, I only started with this one here, this is my lucky blue one, and look! I have now *satu, dua, tiga,*' and he counted in Malay up to *tiga belas.* 'I have thirteen!' Which one do you like best?'

Callum sighed and smiled. He couldn't tell her today. He would tell her next time.

But the next time he got a surprise. Aminah and Leman were both dressed as though they were going out.

'You don't mind, Callum? Today Leman is not well. His ear is giving pain. I must take him to the clinic. It is only open at 2 p.m. You could wait, we won't be long.' Her eyes were like liquid chocolate.

Frowning with concern, he ushered them outside. 'Come, we'll go together in my car. Where is the clinic?'

When he opened the car door and slid into his seat, he caught sight of Kate's sunglasses. Feeling a twinge of guilt, he quickly hid them in the glove box, away from Aminah's inquisitive eyes. Arriving at the clinic, Callum parked the car and then went round to help Aminah and Leman to get out. As the boy straightened up, something in his manner made him think of Jack. He looked again; yes it was in the tilt of the head, the profile. There was something there that suggested his Scottish father. He was also going to be tall. The three walked down towards the clinic and to any casual observer they looked like a typical mixed race family. Callum had his hand on the boy's shoulder and there was an easy intimacy between himself and Aminah. But unknown to Callum, a more astute observer had seen the trio pass by. Nancy Fung was sitting behind the wheel in her car. She had been visiting a friend in the area and could not believe what she had just witnessed. She bided her time, waited until they emerged from the clinic, and then keeping her distance, she followed the car back to Aminah's apartment.

Kate decided not to go back to Scotland after all. She had no one to take care of her in Inverness, and she knew that if she moved back in with her father, she would have to resume caring for him, so she resigned herself to staying. She would just have to stay on at Tuaran Tinggi and she would have the baby in Kuala Lumpur. From thereon, she established a regime of resting and taking proper care of herself. Cookie and Amah helped her with ordering from Cold Storage, her friends came to visit her, and the days passed by with her *mah jong* mornings interspersed with bridge and sewing. Nancy Fung was her main confidante and she trusted the Chinese woman's advice for drinking body cooling concoctions, and accepted special lotions and liniments for massaging the stretched skin on her belly. Of course she also loved Nancy's chatter and the delicious gossip that she brought from town.

One morning at the end of September, with the baby's arrival due in less than three weeks, Amah was washing down the bars of the cot and airing the mattress of the small cane Moses basket.

'Where's Callum?' Nancy asked her friend as she helped her fold small shirts into the wicker case that would be going to the hospital.

'He's in KL; it's Tuesday. He likes to play golf in the afternoon. He leaves in time to have lunch at the club, but he is usually home by six. Should I take pink and blue booties or just the white? What do you think?'

Nancy's eyes took on a hard glare. 'Who does he play golf with?'

Kate shrugged unconcernedly. 'Alex, I think, different people. Why? It's good for him to get a break from me and the estate. Men need a change of scenery and I must be such a sight at the moment. Just look at me! The classic cliché of the beached whale.'

Nancy accepted the invitation to stay for lunch, and the two women sat down to plates of mushroom soup. During the meal, Kate complained of heartburn, and fidgeted uncomfortably.

'What is it, Kate? Are you uncomfortable sitting up at the table?'

'It's my back, I know it's silly, it's too early but I seem to remember... ow!' Her face creased up in pain, and then she relaxed. Her bump had gone hard and as taut as the skin of a drum.

Nancy could see the beads of sweat on her friend's upper lip and called to Cookie, 'Come quick, go upstairs and get everything, Mem needs to go to the hospital. I will take her, get towels as well for the car, the water will break soon. Come, Kate.'

'But what about Callum? It's only two o'clock; he'll be on the golf course.'

'I'll sort out Callum, don't you worry about that.' Nancy grimly put the car into gear with a dramatic flourish.

'Good luck, Mem, *Selamat Jalan*.' Both Cookie and Amah waved from the top step, their faces showing the grave concern they both felt, for they remembered the sad homecoming after Kate's last confinement.

Callum and Aminah started at the sound of someone banging on the door.

'Who is that?' asked Callum, 'Are you expecting someone?'

'No, of course not, maybe it is something to do with Suleiman? I shall go and see.'

She slipped on a yellow satin 'happy coat', her black hair falling loosely down her back, and stepped towards the door. Callum jumped up and rapidly rolled the mattress away to the side of the room, then backed into the small bathroom where he struggled into his trousers.

'*Selamat Malam?*' Aminah said, her head peering around the door.

'Where is he? Where is your rat of a boyfriend?' Nancy pushed the door open and confronted Callum as he emerged from the bathroom.

His eyes grew round in shock as he identified this menacing friend of his wife, here in this room, his sanctuary.

'You had better get to the hospital. Kate is in labour and it won't be long.'

Callum stood speechless, a million questions and emotions rioting round his brain, and his tongue lay inert; he could only stare. Finally, after what felt like an age, he gathered himself together and returned to the bathroom where he pulled on his shirt and shoes.

'Did you know his wife was pregnant?' Nancy asked Aminah, a cruel gleam in her eye.

The girl shook her head. She turned her face away in shame.

Estelle and Anna had found Kate's room at the Lady Templer Hospital.

'What are you going to call him, Aunt Kate?' Anna sat perfectly still and as upright as a statue. She clutched the newborn baby in her arms, and peered at the small beetroot-coloured face. 'And why is he all bandaged up like a mummy?' she continued critically.

'It's called swaddling, and it makes the baby feel secure. Otherwise they throw their arms around and get frightened. After being in such a small space for so long, too much freedom is scary,' said Kate, smiling at her niece.

Suddenly the baby opened his eyes and a puzzled frown creased his already wrinkled little face.

'Gosh! What blue eyes. He's looking at me!' exclaimed Anna excitedly.

Estelle came and took the baby from her and she too studied the miniature features intently.

'Why are you still fat, Aunt Kate?'

'Ssssh,' cautioned Estelle. 'The tummy takes time to shrink back to how it was.'

'How do you know? You haven't had a baby,' retorted Anna.

'I know lots of things, young lady, and just you mind your manners.' Estelle looked over at Kate and raised her eyes and let out a loud sigh.

'I doubt I'll have far to shrink, Anna, I was not really thin to start with,' Kate said matter of factly. She patted her belly and then looked down at her inflated breasts. 'Oh dear, I do feel a bit huge!'

'What are you going to call him, Aunt Kate? Have you given him a name already?'

'No, dear, not yet, but I wanted something from the Bible.'

'Oh no!' said Anna, her eyes wide with disbelief. 'Not Moses, or Isaac or Jeremiah or names like that?'

'No, you silly, I was actually thinking about Luke.'

Just then Callum walked into the room carrying a basket of flowers.

'Hello, darling, a present from the estate clerk and all the office workers.'

'That is nice of them, but maybe you should have left them at home? I should be getting out of here soon.'

'Two weeks, the doctor said, so that is the advice you must follow.' He smiled at her and leant over and kissed her forehead. 'What have all you ladies been discussing?'

Anna was staring at the baby, who was now lying in the bassinette beside Kate. She had a very owlish expression on her face. 'Aunt Kate wants to call the baby a Bible name. I was thinking about Samuel who was given to Eli in the temple. That would be nice. We could call him Sam; or what about Solomon?'

Callum coughed and bumped into the dresser by the bed. 'Er, not Solomon. I don't think so.'

'But why not? He was a very, very wise king, you know. He had to decide between two ladies who were arguing about which of them a baby belonged to, so he advised that the baby should be cut in half and then he would know who was the real mother.'

'That is enough!' Estelle spoke sharply and Anna turned away sulkily and folded her arms. She had only been trying to assist.

'I want him to be called Luke,' said Kate. 'He was a good man, a writer and a doctor. What more could I wish for our son?'

'Luke it is then,' said Callum, 'Luke Callum McIntyre.'

'Luke Callum Solomon McIntyre,' muttered Anna under her breath. Estelle glared at her so she turned away dramatically and resumed her intense study of the freckle on the back of her hand.

An uneasy truce prevailed between Nancy Fung and Callum. They each played their part in giving support to Kate, but the two had tried hard to avoid each other during the days following the birth of baby Luke. Callum's days were divided between the estate work and the drive to the hospital in the late afternoon. He knew he should try to resolve the issues with Nancy but he felt he had been such a cad to everyone concerned that it was better to stay away. He had not been to see Aminah since his undignified departure on the afternoon that Nancy had barged in on them, and felt cowardly and foolish about the whole affair. It was Nancy that finally approached him. She was sitting in the reception area of the hospital, and she stood up to confront him as he stepped out into the tropical night.

'Can we talk, Callum? I think better we talk now before too much time passes.'

He nodded resignedly, and feeling chastised by her brisk manner, he fell into step with her to where he had parked his Rover. 'Have you eaten? I was going to the Coliseum; perhaps you would care to join me?' He glanced at her before putting the car into gear and reversing out of the parking space.

'Thank you, I would like that very much,' and she sat primly holding her crocodile handbag on her firmly closed knees.

Sitting opposite Nancy across the white-draped table, Callum felt uncomfortable and looked longingly over to the bar, where men were nursing cold pints of beer and passing the hours discussing cricket scores and politics. He took in the coat stand that stood like a denuded tree by the side door, now holding just one umbrella. Only ten years ago, planters had slung their rifles on its curved branches, before settling down to drink their beers and swap stories of atrocities that had occurred. How times had changed, he mused. Nancy's clipped vowels broke into his thoughts and he was brought sharply back to the reason they were together.

'Who is she, Callum? Is the boy yours?'

She was certainly direct. Where was the classic Asian preamble? He looked up in relief as the plates arrived and the steaks continued to sizzle and splatter on their skillets. The ancient Indian retainer hovering nearby came forward and fastened large white bibs around their necks. Callum immediately sliced through the succulent meat, and raising his fork to his mouth, he held it suspended momentarily.

'The child is Jack Dunbar's.'

Nancy stared at him, round-eyed in amazement. She put down her knife and fork and patted her lips with her napkin.

'Jack Dunbar! The planter you killed?'

'Yes, I have been paying for the boy's maintenance ever since he was born. I suppose it's been my way for atoning for Jack's death. I never thought I would get involved with the mother. It's just that Kate and I...'

Nancy nodded and said kindly, 'I know, Callum. Actually we women do talk a lot, you know. It's been hard for her with problems of being pregnant, *Oi yo!* What a to-do.'

'I was lonely,' went on Callum. 'She just cut me out of her life after she lost the twins. She blamed me for that. She never wanted to be intimate with me again. She was always so kind to everyone else but yet she always rejected me. I just felt that I was no good at anything. She didn't want me to touch her; she just wanted me to be the husband figure. When I first met her at the hospital she mothered me, I suppose, made me feel loved and helped me get over the shooting. I had killed my best friend; it was the worst nightmare, an accident with gigantic repercussions and, knowing that I had taken that man's life, I had to learn how to carry on somehow. Then later she blamed me for the death of our twins; it was so unfair. I went to see Aminah totally out of curiosity. I didn't know anything about her really, just that she had worked for the Grants, and when I heard that she had had Jack's child, I somehow didn't even question it. We're all human after all, and who am I to throw stones? When I met her, she was so gentle, so giving. She gave me physical love such as I had never experienced before; she loved me with her whole being. I shouldn't be talking to you like this, Nancy, but perhaps you won't think so badly of me if I explain a little. Aminah taught me not just about love, but also about making love. Her generosity was alive and vibrant. I had been so lonely – I know that sounds so pathetic – but so was she and it just seemed so natural. I had no idea that it could be like that between a man and a woman and after the first time I couldn't help myself. I just had to see her again, and again, and so it continued.' He took another bite of his steak and chewed silently. 'I know it was wrong, I should have stopped it. Every time I went there I meant to put an end to it. And then you arrived at the door.'

'What are you going to do now?'

Callum shrugged and signalled to the waiter to bring another beer.

'It's over, Nancy. I love Kate and now I have little Luke, I won't be seeing her again.'

Nancy smiled weakly. She was not so sure. She could see that his resolve came from honourable intentions and she understood his feelings of guilt and duty, but he was a man and she had seen the pair together. She knew that it would be difficult for Callum to remain faithful to Kate with Aminah so close.

'I can help you, Callum. Do you want me to help?'

He nodded and asked her to continue.

'I have family in Singapore. I ask them to find place for Aminah there and get the boy enrolled into the Raffles Institution. He will get best education, and you continue to pay monthly maintenance, yes?'

'Of course I shall. Would you do that, Nancy? I know I don't deserve it. You have every reason to despise me.'

'I will do it for you and for Kate. You are my friends; Kate will not be told of your...er...indiscretions. You men are only human, you know, not the big gods you all seem to think you are. We women understand men more than you give us credit for!'

He raised his beer, and she her glass of water, and they sealed their pact as their eyes met and a feeling of relief flooded over him.

'Health, happiness, long life and plenty riches to you, her, him and your family too! Good Chinese wishes to you. Come, you drink up!'

Freya returned to the estate, hot and cross. The city traffic was particularly bad and the combination of the congested streets and hooting horns aggravated her already pounding head.

'Hello, old girl, did you get my gin at Cold Storage?' Roger looked up as his wife climbed the three steps from the porch into the sitting room.

'Yes, dear, I did, as well as the Angostura bitters. Oh God, what a day and I didn't even get the chance to go to Petaling Jaya to visit Aminah. I had planned going after seeing Kate and the baby but the traffic was vile.' She flopped on to the reclining chair and theatrically tossed her head back against the cushion.

'How are the mother and child?' Roger asked, not really caring for a response. He rang the bell to summon their new maid. 'Pink gin when you've finished unloading Mem's car; no hurry of course!' and he winked at the young Chinese girl.

'Bring me a gin and tonic, Ah Ling, thank you.' Freya smiled, watching the girl walk gracefully through the dark hallway to the swing doors of the kitchen. She then regarded her now quite frail husband. She noted how thin he had become and how short of breath he was. She did wish he would go into KL for a check up, but he promised he would get himself seen to once they returned to France where they had recently bought the beautiful hillside home in Collioure, overlooking the Mediterranean. It was only a couple of months now until he retired. 'I saw Estelle McIntyre and Anna at the hospital with Kate.' She turned away from him and positioned her face so that it was directly under the overhead fan. 'I have a feeling that child is quite a character. I believe Estelle finds it hard to cope during the holidays.' She laughed quietly to herself as she continued to mull over the events of her day. 'Both must run rings around Alex. It seems a pity that pair never had children themselves.'

Roger grunted and took the proffered glass from the linen-clad tray that was presented to him by the soft-footed maid.

Freya played with her glass, glistening with frost from the ice cubes, and smelt the tang of the lemon slice. 'Mmmm, how delicious!' and she sipped at the first alcoholic drink of the evening. 'That is so good, and just what I needed.' She enjoyed the stillness that came between herself and Roger, both lost in their own reveries. She thought of the son that Jack had had with Aminah, and the daughter that Alex had had with Eilidh. There seems to be no rhyme or reason, she mused, why Estelle should not also bear children. She smiled softly as she remembered the unspoken choices that she and Michael had made. He was happy with Lois, and she of course was content enough with her trusting friend, husband and companion. Silently she made a toast to the wild, passionate rendezvous with her one-time lover. Taking another sip, she broke the silence. 'I also met Nancy Fung, just as I was leaving. She suggested that I meet up with her at the Selangor Club on Friday; very odd, as we've never been close. Do you mind if I take the car, dear?'

'No, by all means; you beetle off and I'll be happy to read my French newspapers that arrived this morning.'

Friday saw the temperature in the mid-nineties with the sky a scorching blue. Kuala Lumpur at midday was broiling in heat and humidity exacerbated by traffic congestion, noise and squalor, a living cauldron of brightly clad humanity. Freya decided to walk from Batu Road to the club, and was caught up behind some Indian children heading for their afternoon session at school. They were immaculate in their starched white shirts and dark shorts and tunics. Freya, by contrast, felt frazzled and uncomfortable. The back of her red cotton dress was dark with perspiration and her blonde hair had escaped from the chignon and now hung limply, straggling down her back. Her feet were sore and bleeding where the too-tight high-heeled sandals had scraped her heels. Constantly being shouted at by trishaw drivers and beckoned by hawkers selling noodles and satay on the pavement, she at last made it across the busy road and entered the hushed interior of the club house. Nancy's face was enigmatic as Freya gushed up to her on the veranda.

'So hot! I so need a fresh lime juice with a bucket load of ice.'

The Chinese woman smiled. 'Better you have green tea: more cooling for body.'

Freya screwed up her nose but politely agreed. 'All right, but it's not my favourite taste. It is so bitter.'

'You try, then tell me how you feel.'

Freya studied her companion, sitting so composed and elegant, her ankles crossed and showing off her patent leather shoes. Her navy shirtwaister dress was set off to perfection by a jade-green silk scarf at her throat. Above her heart was a brooch depicting a dragon made entirely of tiny emeralds and rubies. The conversation started with the usual safe topics such as the weather and prices of meat, but after sufficient polite chitchat, Nancy came to the point.

'Small problem with my friend Kate and your old *amah*.'

'What do you mean?' asked Freya, slightly bemused. 'What small problem? They hardly know each other.'

'Lucky, still don't know each other. Problem is Callum. You know Callum pays for boy's welfare?'

Freya nodded, not sure where this conversation was heading.

'Now I think he too much involved with boy's mother. Already too much jig-jig.'

'Oh my goodness!' exclaimed Freya. Her eyes had grown round in surprise, the blue irises dancing about in confusion as she absorbed the Chinese woman's words and their implication. 'Is this common knowledge?' she ventured to ask.

'No, but must stop now. Big promises from him it will end. I said I will see to the boy getting a place in school in Singapore. Maybe better for Aminah to leave KL. If she stays, maybe too easy for Callum to visit again. You know what I am saying?'

'I know,' sighed Freya, 'I know; it's never easy.' She took a sip of the hot tea. 'So why did you tell me?'

'I think the girl needs to talk, maybe have a friend. She knows you.'

'Of course; you are kind, Nancy. Thank you. I will go and see her this afternoon. Maybe she could come back to the estate with me for a while. It would be nice to have Suleiman around the house again. You know that we are retiring soon? Roger only has two months to go; that's why I made the arrangements for Aminah and Suleiman to set up home in Petaling Jaya. Oh my goodness,' she looked out to the *padang* in front of her, 'I didn't expect this to happen.'

'Buddha says we must try to control our human desires. Not so easy for everyone. Hard if people are alone, or lonely as you English people say. I think Callum and Aminah were both lonely. Opportunity comes when there is a knocking at the door. It happened before. Now we must stop it happening again. Agree?'

'Agree!' and the two ladies clinked their white china tea cups in unison.

'Secret is to keep drinking good Chinese tea,' she laughed at Freya. 'No hot passion: keeps body nice and cool!'

Freya knocked on Aminah's door. She had given no warning that she was coming, so when the door opened an inch, she was unprepared for the wan, spiritless young woman that confronted her. Although she was only a few years younger than Freya, Aminah's soft rounded Asian features belied her true age. Her long black hair also conspired in giving her the look of a girl. In truth she was now close to thirty.

'Come in, Mem,' and she stepped to the side to let Freya enter.

Freya looked about and saw the room, as pristine as always. She wondered what Aminah had been doing, for there was no sign of any ongoing activity.

'I sit here and wait for my son. Leman will be back soon.'

Freya nodded, realising that Aminah was suffering from some sort of depression. 'I've missed you both so much, *Tuan* Roger as well. We want you to come back and spend two weeks with us; is it possible? Suleiman is on holiday now, isn't he, so you could both come?'

'I cannot, Mem, you want some 7UP?' and she made to get up and go to the cordoned-off kitchen.

'You can, Aminah,' and very gently Freya moved over and put her arm around the girl. 'I think you need a friend just now, don't you?'

Aminah's eyes were dark as molten tar. Understanding flickered and registered in her serene face. 'You know about Callum? Nancy Fung has spoken to you?'

Freya nodded.

'She is very kind to us. Wants us to go to Singapore and stay with her aunty. Leman will go to school there.'

'I think it's a wonderful idea and Callum is a kind, kind man. I know he'll do the right thing and protect you and Jack's son. We have kept this secret a long time, eight years already and we can continue, but now you need to be looked after too. Please, will you come back with me today?'

Aminah let a tear escape from the fringe of lashes. It ran fast and streaked her lovely face. 'Thank you, Mem. Always you are kind.'

Suleiman was ecstatic to be back in his old childhood home again. He toured the garden in a proprietary manner. He ran and splashed into the pool and went fishing with the gardener in a rough flowing river on the estate border. He rediscovered all his old haunts and befriended the new Chinese maid who let him have some of her joss sticks to stick down ant holes. Only Cookie frowned at this activity. The house had been very peaceful without the small boy's presence. Suleiman's world had been tilted on its axis by the move to Petaling Jaya, but his confidence and sunny nature had helped him to adapt to his new circumstances. Now he was back and again had access to Freya's bookcases and record collection.

'Come and sit with me, Suleiman, and listen to some Mozart. You always liked *The Magic Flute*. Do you still draw well? You used to love copying the pictures from the big encyclopaedia.'

'Very well, Mem Freya.'

She smiled at his almost condescending manner. He had developed quite a sense of his own importance.

'I do prefer playing marbles now. Did I tell you I am the champion? No? Well I have two bags of marbles and I won them all! Oh, look! Behind your head, a giant praying mantis! See? It's so green and its eyes are as big as pip squeaks and it's looking right at you. Maybe I can draw that. You sit and I will draw it. Just like a portrait.'

Freya shuddered and scowled at the boy. This was not how she wanted to be remembered for posterity. She begged him to hurry up.

'It's OK, Mem Freya. It won't jump on you.' He carried on drawing, the tip of his tongue protruding from his parted lips. Slowly the picture took shape and he proudly presented it to her.

'Oh my!' she exclaimed. 'What a likeness! You really do have so many talents, but as an artist you must sign it. Here, dedicate it to me.'

Suleiman looked at the picture, his brows drawn down in concentration. After much deliberation, he eventually wrote on his picture, asking how to spell each word: Mem Freya and praying mantis by Suleiman aged 8.

'Wonderful!' she laughed. 'A man of few words,' and she thought again of Jack, so quiet, funny and charming.

Later in the afternoon the harsh bell of the telephone broke into Freya's siesta. It was Estelle McIntyre. Freya was naturally disconcerted, for although the women knew each other and met occasionally at social functions, they had never taken the casual acquaintance any further. With a sense of guilt, Freya looked around the deserted hallway for signs of Aminah or Suleiman. She had long protected the identity of Suleiman's parentage and she lived in fear that one day Estelle might stumble on the truth and find out that her first husband had fathered a child whilst she had been waiting for him in Scotland. She remembered Nancy Fung's words, just the other week, about fate and chance and how life had a habit of throwing things in one's path. She collected her thoughts and smiled into the mouthpiece, 'Hello Estelle, what a surprise! What can I do for you?' her tone giving no hint that she was massaging a knot of tension in her stomach.

'I've been made the chairwoman for the club's social fixtures. Can I come over this afternoon and get some ideas from you?' Estelle rattled on enthusiastically, 'I know you have been in the East for years, so you are the perfect person to give me advice.'

'Of course,' Freya was about to prevaricate, but could think of no reasonable excuse to delay the inevitable, 'yes, why don't you come round this afternoon?'

'I'll bring Anna if that's all right, she'll be no trouble.' Estelle rang off without waiting for a response.

Anna stood glowering in the sun. This had not been part of her plan for the afternoon. She watched the two women settle themselves around Freya's coffee table, and being utterly ignored, she felt herself at liberty to wander about and explore.

'You want to swim?' a voice broke into her mutinous thoughts.

'Who are you?' Anna asked rudely.

'I am Suleiman. I am an artist.'

'How can you be an artist, silly, when you are only a boy?' Anna said meanly, for she prided her own rare skills in colouring.

'Mem Freya said I have a gift. I am only eight years old and I am a prodigy. That is like Mozart you know.'

Anna frowned; she knew that the word was familiar but was not sure of its exact meaning. She decided she would save face and look it up later. She herself was not too familiar with Mozart. Her father preferred listening to *The White Heather Club* and Jimmy Shand music and of course, Mantovani and his orchestra.

'I am also the champion at marbles. Do you play? I could lend you some. I have loads.'

'Of course not, marbles are only for junior boys. I am a senior now, you know. I am eleven and we play much more sophisticated games. At the moment I am collecting animals to study, as I plan to be a vet when I grow up.'

'Oh,' said Suleiman. 'What kind of animals? Do you have cheetahs or bears?' His eyes were round and impressed.

'No, I prefer studying lizards and scorpions. Once I had a flying fox that Daddy shot, and it wasn't quite dead, so I had to nurse it. Then Mother got really mad as it was full of fleas, and the cat dragged it in across the Persian rug. Anyway it died.'

'So are you really going to be a vet?'

'I haven't decided yet as I also plan to be a famous trapeze artist. Santosh and I are putting on a show. I could invite you if you like.' She added regally, 'I could make you an invitation.'

During this exchange, they wandered down to the pool, which glistened blue and inviting. Anna glanced at the attap-covered pool house and bar beside it. The shelves held neatly folded striped towels, and in the fridge she found bottles of Coke and 7UP.

'Can we really swim?' Anna asked with a new brightness. 'I do have my costume. It's in the beach bag in the boot of the car. I can get it. Gosh! How amazing. You are so lucky to have your own pool. You can be my third best friend, after Julia and Santosh of course.'

Chapter 16

August 1966 – Malaysia

'Please, Mother, I promised him that I'd invite him. I made him an invitation and everything. Please telephone and ask them to come.' Anna was in a fever of expectation. She stared at Estelle beseechingly. 'Please, please, I promise I'll be good for a year.'

Estelle exhaled volubly and strutted over to the telephone. She tapped her nail on the receiver as she listened to the ringing tone. 'Hello, Freya? Estelle McIntyre here: I have a very insistent young lady standing here beside me. She is hoping that you and Suleiman will come over this afternoon to attend a 'Command Performance'. Yes I know, it is usually the Queen that issues those invitations, but I think this is a little along those lines. Our Anna has aspirations to grandeur I'm afraid.' Estelle smiled at a response that Freya was making then went on, 'I believe the invitation was issued verbally last week when we were over at your house. Would you and Suleiman care to call over this afternoon, around two? Perfect! We shall look forward to seeing you then.' She replaced the receiver and looked down into Anna's eyes that were as wide and questioning as flying saucers. 'They're coming. You'd better get some more crates out for your extended audience to sit on.'

'Thank you, thank you! And can I borrow some lipstick and some of your shiny eye shadow? I shall wear my blue leotard and my ballet shoes. Santosh will have some Christmas tinsel round his head and T-shirt. It is going to be the most fantastic show. Are you sure that Daddy is coming... and Cookie and Amah?'

'Well, you invited them. Good gracious, I think the invitations took longer to make than the rehearsals did. I just hope you know what you're doing.'

At a quarter to two, Anna burst forth from her room, a vision of grace and poise. Her hair had been scraped back off her face by a pink-toothed Alice band. Her skinny legs strutted duck-like, her toes pointed outwards in exaggerated imitation of Miss Tan, her ballet teacher. Her face was a mask of scarlet lips and accentuated blue glitter around the eyebrows.

Meanwhile, Santosh waited at the appointed place, nervously pacing up and down and feeling very self-conscious because of the green tinsel that he'd draped around his body and the slightly too large matching green shorts that Estelle had bought him. He looked at the chains of the sturdy swing with its heavy wooden seat, built by Anna's father and wide enough for two children. He was full of misgivings about the whole idea of a public performance. He did not relish doing acrobatics in front of the estate manager. At twelve he felt he was growing too old for such childish games. It was one thing humouring Anna in the privacy of the garden, but quite another performing for an audience. 'I wish I invisible and big, big hole come and I jump in. That's what me Santosh wants,' he muttered to himself, grimacing again at his gaudy attire.

At last the waiting was over and Estelle led Alex, Freya and Suleiman out to the flame trees at the bottom of the garden. She was intrigued at the familiarity shown by Freya to this Malay boy. She couldn't imagine herself taking Santosh to visit friends on another estate. After all, she wondered, wasn't he just her *amah*'s son?

During the show, Estelle took her eyes off the performers and studied Suleiman while he fidgeted on his beer crate. He held his personal invitation in his hand and his eyes were alight with interest and brightness. She conceded that he was a very good-looking boy, typical of his race. Beautiful eyes, wide grin, and when he turned to her, sharing the moment, she had a vague feeling that he reminded her of someone. She gave herself a shake and turned back to the proceedings. Anna and Santosh were now on the swing together and were piling rhythmically, as one, in order to achieve the desired momentum. Cookie and Amah sat at an angle opposite Freya and Suleiman, whilst Alex and Estelle closed the little gallery by facing directly towards the swing. The grown ups politely applauded each act.

Alex cheered loudly when Anna managed to haul herself up by the arms, clutching the chains and performing an awkward aerial somersault. 'Bravo, Bravo!' he called out.

Beside him, Estelle slapped her ankles and shoulders. 'Is anyone else getting bitten? I've just had two whopping big mosquito bites, Oh look! There's one attacking me again.' She took aim and slapped hard at her lower leg, squashing the insect and leaving a bloody mess where it had been feeding.

'I hope you're still taking your Paludrin?' Freya asked, her eyes still giving the flying duo her full attention.

'She does better than that,' Alex joked, 'the gin and tonics that she imbibes so regularly give her a good daily dose of extra quinine!'

Cookie and Amah politely clapped at each elaborate bow given by Anna and Santosh, but their faces remained impassive to their employers' comments.

The penultimate act involved Santosh doing a headstand on the seat, with Anna giving his legs only minimal support. The swing moved gently back and forth. Suleiman watched wide eyed and for a second forgot to breathe. The Indian boy's legs trembled as he retained his balance and then finally he rolled down and jumped off and took an elaborate bow.

Suleiman stood up and clapped enthusiastically. 'That was quite amazing, wasn't it, Mem Freya? I can't even stand on my head on the grass. Can you?'

Freya smiled at him fondly. 'No, Leman. I could do when I was your age but I haven't stood on my head for quite a few moons! Oh look, here comes Santosh again. What on earth? I think they are going to do something blindfold. I'm not sure I can take all this excitement!'

And then suddenly Suleiman was dead.

The aftermath of the accident was a blur. How had it happened? The afternoon was supposed to be fun, just a show but there was screaming and people running to and from the house. Frozen in shock, Freya knelt on the ground with the poor child's head lying twisted at a horrible angle on her skirt. Cookie came with cold towels, Amah with wet cloths. Anna seemed to see it all in a haze as though she were a long way away and not really part of the scene. Her father disappeared into the house to telephone the estate doctor. Fearful and confused, tears flooding down her face as she sought reassurance, Anna turned her eyes to Estelle.

Her stepmother turned to her with unconcealed contempt in her eyes. She walked over to where Anna was standing and hissed at her.

'You stupid little show-off: always wanting to be the centre of attention. Well, look what's happened now, thanks to your silly performance!'

Freya looked up, her eyes full of tears. 'Go inside, Anna, take Santosh…' When the children moved away, she looked at the other woman. 'He's dead, Estelle, Suleiman Dunbar is dead.'

'What? What did you just say?' Estelle's breathing turned into a silent pant and her pulse rate increased alarmingly. Her lips felt as though they'd turned into rubber and her tongue appeared to have swollen in her mouth. The world grew dark and thousands of pin pricks like stars flashed in front of her eyes. A feeling of nausea overwhelmed her at the sight of the boy's still form. Estelle swayed.

'OK, Mem, you come now, come and lie down.'

Amah put an arm around her waist and supported her weight. Somehow they staggered back to the house and Estelle fell onto the white sheet on her bed. She was conscious of a cold, damp flannel being placed over her eyes. Amah held her up as she took a sip of water before flopping back again. For a few minutes she was free from having to confront the reality. She lay inert.

'Are you all right, Estelle?' It was Alex. She was aware that for once he hadn't removed his outdoor shoes in the house. He entered the room, closing the door behind him, and came to sit on the edge of the bed. 'I've rung the police and the hospital, though it's too late for the boy. They'll know what to do.'

Estelle groaned and turned on her side away from him, wanting to block out his words. Alex sighed; he considered staying, but instead he stood up, and shrugging his shoulders, he left her and went outside to inform Freya that the authorities were on the way.

Freya had not moved. Her body was bent over the child and Alex felt that he'd seen a similar pose in religious paintings, those that depicted the *pietà*, when Mary held the crucified body of Christ. Tears were running down Freya's cheeks and Alex looked on with compassion as she rhythmically stroked Suleiman's face. His body was so pitiful, so young. Alex tried to calculate his age. She became aware of his presence and looked up, her eyes swollen with grief and unknowingly answered his silent question.

'Oh God, Alex, how am I going to tell Aminah that her little boy is dead? He was only eight years old.'

Suleiman's body was lifted on to a stretcher and placed in the back of the ambulance. Freya cried more tears as his small body, now wrapped in a blue sheet and looking so alone, was finally driven away. Alex stood with his arm around her shoulder.

'What a tragedy,' she sobbed, 'he was so good at drawing and he loved to listen to Mozart.'

'I know, it's hard, but you must be strong. You must help the mother to get over this. It's a strange fact of life, is it not, that secrets, no matter how well kept, have a way of getting out…in the end?'

The three police officers set up a temporary inquiry base at the dining room table and took formal statements from Alex, Cookie and Freya.

'Where is Anna?' Alex asked, looking at Cookie expectantly.

The white-clad servant was for once dishevelled, his normally smoothed black hair falling across his eyes. 'Don't know, *Tuan*. Mem sent her inside, maybe in her room?'

Alex felt a pang of remorse. He realised that he'd not given his daughter a thought during the drama of the last hour. She would be distraught at what had happened. He knew that she might be required to give a statement to the policemen as well. He also knew that there would be a formal inquiry. He mused about the possible outcome. He was sure it would be classified as just a tragic accident, but what would the repercussions be? And what of Estelle? How was he going to cope with the situation of which she'd so abruptly and cruelly become aware? He felt as though his head was being attacked by a swarm of hornets.

Amah padded softly across the hall to Estelle's room and knocked before letting herself in. 'Are you feeling better, Mem? Can I get you anything?'

'I need to rest, I still feel faint. Have the police gone?'

'Not yet, Mem; only ambulance go with dead boy. Policemen want to talk to you. They wait in dining room. You come now?'

'Yes, Amah, you go down. I'll be there in a few minutes.'

Meanwhile Freya sat sipping tea, her tears an unstoppable stream as memories of Suleiman ran like a kaleidoscope turning across her mind. So many images. How could his young life have ended so suddenly, like switching off a bright light? She stood up and made her way to Anna's room. In a daze she looked around at the pretty shades of yellow and white lace that Estelle had so painstakingly picked out. She went over to the dressing table and picked up the child's comb and slowly ran it through her own long tresses. The action was rhythmic and soothing. Suddenly she heard a creaking sound and spun around to see the wardrobe door opening as though by magic. 'Who's there?' Freya stuttered. 'Is someone there?'

'It's only me.' Anna slid the door along the runner and presented herself. She'd been lying along the middle shelf of the fitted cupboard and Freya could see the terror in her face. There was more scratching and Santosh's dark face suddenly looked down from the top shelf.

'Come out, both of you, are you all right? Oh you poor things. Come here, Anna.'

The child's lip trembled as she looked in fear and uncertainty at this adult who had every reason in the world to turn them over to the police. She had just finished telling Santosh how they would most definitely be hung or even guillotined for murder. 'Are the police going to take us away?' she asked; her voice high and quavering.

'No, dear, of course not, but they do want to talk to you. They have to talk to all of us. We are called witnesses, and it's important that they know what happened. It was an accident, Anna. You only invited us; you couldn't have foretold what Suleiman would do.'

'But it's my fault, you heard Mother. If I hadn't wanted to put on the trapeze act, he would be home safe and playing and practising for when he became an artist.'

'Sssssh, of course not, come and sit down here, both of you.' Freya gestured towards the bed. She made sure that they sat together on Anna's bed and she sat on the spare one opposite. 'There are many things that happen that we can't foresee, like people falling off ladders, or being thrown off a horse, or tree branches snapping and then some poor soul underneath getting hurt or killed. People might drown at sea or get killed in a plane crash. Now would you say that was murder or an accident?'

'An accident,' muttered Anna.

'Yes, an accident and it would be nobody's fault. Now, listen to me, you cannot take the blame for what happened today. Do you understand?'

Anna and Santosh stared back at her. Two sets of eyes, wide and troubled, but comprehending her words. Both were reassured by her soothing voice and gentle tone.

'Anna and me Santosh go to jail?' Santosh asked tentatively.

'No, I promise you won't go to jail!' Freya smiled and reached over and held their hands.

'Anna!' The strident tones of Estelle broke into the gentle ambience that Freya had created. 'The police are waiting and want to talk to you. I though you might have tried to run away.' She paused as her eyes flicked over the touching scene in front of her then continued, indicating with her chin that she was addressing Santosh, 'And after they've talked to you, you can go back to the labour lines. You should not be in Miss Anna's room.' She folded her arms and watched Anna and Santosh walk out of the beautifully decorated room to give their statements. Estelle turned and finally confronted Freya. 'Just now you called the child Suleiman Dunbar...an odd name for a Malay child, is it not? I presume he is, or should I say was, your *amah*'s son?'

'Yes, I did say that,' concurred Freya, 'and yes, he was Aminah's beloved child.'

'And the father?'

Freya sighed. 'It was a long time ago, Estelle. You know how long it is since Jack died.'

Estelle fixed her with a steely look. 'And did you know that I was married to Jack Dunbar?'

It was Freya's turn now to look visibly shocked.

'Married? Estelle! I didn't know, I promise you. I had no idea. Jack never told any of us that he was married. He certainly never disclosed any of this to Aminah.'

'Was it common knowledge, this liaison he had with your...' Estelle pursed her lips, 'your servant? I feel quite sick. There I was waiting patiently for him to send for me and all the time he was philandering with a native girl. Does everyone know about the boy's parentage? Oh my God, I suppose everyone in the club has been laughing at me behind my back.'

Freya swallowed and looked at the irate, deeply upset woman in front of her. She knew that Nancy, Callum and Alex knew of the brief affair between Aminah and Jack, but she calculated that a small white lie might be in order, considering the circumstances. 'Why would they be laughing, Estelle? No one knew that you had a connection with Jack. Please, I know this whole afternoon has been shocking.' Freya blew her nose. 'I'm in no fit state to cope with any more just now. I want to get home, and I have to break this awful news to Aminah. How on earth am I going to do that?' Freya got up, and made to cross the room, but at the door she turned and looked at the stiff form of Estelle, still standing, her arms crossed over her chest. Was it a protective gesture or a forbidding one? 'Estelle, I hope you will find it in yourself to show some compassion towards your stepchild.' Freya watched Estelle's eyes narrow and came back into the room. She was afraid that their voices would carry across the hallway and she had a feeling that Anna should not hear the venom that was about to be spat out.

'Compassion! To her? She's done everything in her power to make me look useless and a failure in Alex's eyes. She deliberately tries to make me lose my temper so that it looks as though I can't cope with her wily ways. Oh, I can see through her; a manipulative little bitch, that's what she is. All I ever hear is how wonderful Eilidh was, what a model mother, what a saint. Even this so-perfect room that I planned for the child, she defiles with her felt tip pens and her stupid games in the cupboards. Food gets left lying about and armies of ants are all over the place. It's so unfair. Here's me with no chance of having a baby, yet Alex seemed to have no problem in producing a child, and now I hear that my beloved Jack was casting his seed about while I pined alone. I can't live with that girl. I've tried, but she's determined to get her father away from me. I hate her, I hate her.' Estelle sat down, as though the furies had left her sail, and she collapsed and crumpled, looking wan and pathetic.

Freya stood aside as Alex briskly stepped into the room, and instantly put his arms around his wife and soothed her, smoothing her red curls, crooning into her neck. Freya watched, momentarily mesmerised until she felt a tug at her arm. It was Anna. Wearily, Freya smiled down at her. 'Has Santosh gone?'

Anna nodded and looking past Freya she too saw the tableau, framed in the doorway, of her father comforting her stepmother.

'Come on, dear, I shall sit with you for a while, then perhaps you can see if Amah has anything for you to do...'

266

Half an hour later, Alex led Freya out to her car. 'Will you be all right, Freya? Can I drive you home and we can send someone over to collect your car?'

'No, Alex, thank you, I'll be fine. I have to keep my head clear, but one thing you could do? Please could you ring Roger for me? Tell him what has happened so that I'll have some support when I have to face Aminah.' The tears began again and Freya blew her nose. 'I hope I can find the words. There are no good ones, are there? No set phrases that might cushion the blow?'

Sadly Alex shook his head. 'I wish I could say there were. The boy is dead; nothing at all can make that easier to bear.'

Freya hesitated before tentatively asking, 'I didn't know that Estelle had been married to Jack. Oh God, Alex, how are we all going to get through this? And what about poor Anna?'

'As you say, Freya, there is no script for us to follow. God knows that I had a tough time after I lost Eilidh. Because of that I could empathise with Estelle's feelings during her widowhood, but on top of the dreadful tragedy this afternoon, she's now discovered that her perfect Jack was maybe not so perfect. I foresee a very bumpy ride ahead.'

Freya nodded, gazing with unseeing eyes at a dragonfly flitting about before landing on the succulent leaf of a banana palm. The jerky movements mesmerised and soothed her into an almost hypnotic trance. She shook herself back into reality and turned towards Alex. The two stepped closer and embraced. 'I expect there'll be an inquest; please let's keep in touch,' and she leant forward and kissed his cheek then climbed into the front seat of her car. Sadly she backed up and headed out of the sunlit garden into the gloom of the rubber trees perpetually shaded by the crown of dark emerald leaves.

All through the next day, the telephone network crackled with voices, questioning, sympathising and condoling. Aminah, after the first reaction of muted disbelief on seeing Freya return alone, sat stunned. Her reaction was almost stoical as she listened to Freya's account of the unbearable news. From then her emotions had broken through like waters in a dam, weeping and weeping. Disbelief gave way to horror and dismay at the injustice of life. Freya called for the local Imam to come and sit with her, and she watched as the holy man said gently, 'You should try to be patient and remember that Allah is the One who gives life and takes it away, at a time appointed by Him. It is not for us to question His wisdom.'

Aminah keened by her bed, rocking with her head in her hands, crying, 'My son, my beloved son, my Suleiman, my baby.' Eventually the doctor was called and obediently she swallowed the two small pills that he gave her, releasing her from the jagged edges of reality. Since being given the repeat dosages of medication, Aminah sat cosseted in what felt like a wad of foam rubber. Seeing and breathing, slipping in and out of dreamless naps, she showed no resistance to any suggestion.

Freya came to her and urged her to sip some hot tea. 'Drink this, dear, and let me wipe your face with this towel.' She gently soothed Aminah's brow with the cool, damp cloth until she was calm. 'We have to talk, and I must ask you what you would like us to do. The Imam has told us a little of what your Muslim traditions demand in such a circumstance, and I think we can arrange for Suleiman's body to be prepared for burial by the ladies of the community. Do you want to be part of that?'

Aminah shook her head, but raised her eyes up to her friend's. 'Jack was a Christian. After the ceremony of our Muslim prayers, I want to have him buried with his father. Can you ask the Imam if that is possible?'

'Of course, my dear; Roger will ring the authorities in KL and arrange for the burial to take place at Batu Gajah. Would you like me to accompany you, or would you prefer some of the Muslim ladies to go with you?'

Aminah shook her head, and said, 'I want you with me; please don't leave me.'

The following morning Roger travelled with representatives from the mosque to Kuala Lumpur where the police released Suleiman's body. After the dead child had been washed he was gently wrapped in a simple, white cotton *kafan*. Meanwhile back on the estate, Cookie helped the sedated Aminah into the back seat of the car, where she slumped against Freya. Alex drove the sad little group to Kuala Lumpur and then on to Ipoh where they were met by Roger and members of the estate's Muslim community who had already travelled by bus earlier in the day.

'Do you want me to stay with you, Aminah?' Freya asked. 'For the service? Is it like ours, I wonder? I am so sorry, for I really don't know what to do.'

'Please stay, Mem; I don't want to be alone.'

Following the other women's example, Freya covered her head with her black pashmina and entered the courtyard of the small mosque on the outskirts of Ipoh with Aminah, Roger, Alex, Callum and Nancy Fung following behind. All of the Muslims that Aminah knew had gathered for the Janazah Prayer. The Imam stood in front of the body of Suleiman, facing away from the worshippers. Aminah clung to Freya's hand and mouthed the holy words, numb with grief. By tradition Suleiman had to be buried straight away, so immediately after the prayers ended, the entourage made their way to their cars and drove the short distance to the awaiting newly reopened grave. It was very unusual for a Malay boy to be buried in the same lair as a European man, but as that was what Aminah wanted, Roger Grant and Alex McIntyre had acted upon her wishes. The boy was buried alongside his father. Freya held Aminah's arm tightly throughout, swallowing to ease the constriction in her own throat as tears flooded from her *amah* and friend's brown eyes. God, Freya thought, how can you be so cruel to this woman? Overhead a single puff of cloud broke the blue expanse, and she felt an overwhelming emotion as the Imam completed his recital from the Qur'an: 'May Allah have mercy upon us all. From Him we come, and to Him we all return.'

Freya waited until Aminah walked back to the car with Nancy before taking Roger's arm and whispering softly to her husband, 'I want to take her with us to France. We could all start a new life there, for what has she here? A mother and sister in Johor she hardly ever sees and who knew nothing about Suleiman. We are her family, and God knows, we've all been together through some very rocky times. Please, Roger, say yes?'

Roger smiled down at his pretty wife, 'Of course, old girl, the sooner the better. I've only got six weeks to go, but I'm sure that after nearly fifty years of service, no one will quibble if we leave a few weeks earlier than planned.' His skin was clammy and the brown spots stood out alarmingly on his neck and forehead. She held his arm protectively and led him through the mounds that marked the graves. 'Don't know how long I've got left for this life,' he went on. 'No, don't you tut-tut like that, cemeteries should always remind us of our own mortality. I think it would be good for you to have Aminah with you; in fact it would be good for both of you. I'll see what needs to be done and how long it'll take to get her a passport and so on. It's a sorry, sorry business, this; we'll all miss the little chap.'

It had been six days since the afternoon of *The Great Flying Trapeze Act*, during which time Anna had been banished to her room or sent to Julia's or Lucy Bathgate's house. Estelle seemed to be living on a diet of pills and had withdrawn to her room, leaving the running of the house and the answering of the telephone to Cookie. Today, Alex had left early on a business trip to the north, leaving Estelle and Anna at home. Estelle lay on the cane settee on the veranda. Anna, who was drawing and colouring in her room, heard the tinkle of Estelle's bell summoning Cookie, and sure enough, she soon heard his footsteps padding across the wooden floor of the hallway. Anna was startled when she heard him run back the way he had come. This was unheard of: Cookie was a pillar of decorum and never ran. Her curiosity fully aroused, Anna decided to investigate.

Estelle was groaning in pain, her face flushed, her eyes squeezed shut. Leaning closer, Anna heard her mutter, 'I'm so hot, my arms and legs, they're so sore. Get me water, please, I need water.' Estelle opened her eyes, but they seemed unfocussed.

Anna darted through to the kitchen 'Cookie! What's wrong, why are her legs covered in red spots? What's happened to her?'

Cookie was wrapping ice in some Good Morning towels. 'I take them to Mem. You run, Anna, you find Amah. Tell her come quick and phone doctor. Go, Anna, you hurry!' He returned to Estelle's side and pressed the cold towels on her aching joints. He set the fan to its fastest speed and helped her drink some water. Cries of anguish filled the air as the pain wracked her body. Amah appeared with more wet towels and mopped Estelle's face and neck and soothed her until Dr Rajaratnum arrived.

'Not good; her fever is too high and look at this bruising. Already blood is coming from her mouth. Has she complained of mosquito bites recently? This is a severe case of dengue fever. We must get her to hospital. I will ring the Lady Templer Hospital in KL. Mrs McIntyre must be treated there at once.'

He went to make the call while Cookie considered how best to get her

270

to Kuala Lumpur. It was Amah that suggested the Bathgates, so another phone call was made. An hour later, Anna watched fearfully as Estelle was carried out to Sam's car, screaming in agony from the unbearable crushing pain in her limbs. Amah wrapped some ice in one of Alex's handkerchiefs and Estelle weakly sucked the liquid that she so desperately needed.

As the invalid departed, Dorothy called to Anna, 'Come on, dear, let's pack up your things and you can come and stay with us. What do you need? Pyjamas? Toothbrush?' She helped the child to pack her baby-doll pyjamas into her cane travel case, along with her colouring books, and then drove her back to her house in the estate Land Rover. Anna wished she could go to Julia's, but thought gloomily that she wouldn't be allowed.

When Alex returned to the estate at eight o'clock that night after the long journey back from the north, he was emotionally drained and not prepared for the further dramas awaiting him. Instead of seeing Cookie holding the long cold glass of beer that he'd been relishing, his servant was wild eyed and excitable.

'It's Mem, *Tuan*, Mem very sick. She gone to KL. Dengue fever!'

With a feeling of *déjà vu*, Alex closed his eyes and rubbed his fingers hard over his brow. Was he going to lose another wife? He forced himself to take long, slow breaths. 'OK, now tell me, slowly. When did she go, and who took her?'

'*Tuan* Bathgate come and take her at two o'clock. Dr Rajaratnum tell her she must go to hospital, she go to Lady Templer Hospital.'

'Good, Cookie, good. I shall telephone now and find out how she is. But please, bring me a beer. Oh! And where is Anna?' He looked around as though he expected her to appear.

'Mem Bathgate take her. She stay with Miss Lucy.'

For the next few weeks Alex's days revolved around his work on the estate and his long drive to Kuala Lumpur in the late afternoon. He sat by Estelle, willing her to fight the fever that was ravishing her body. A saline drip ensured that her liquids were kept topped up, but bruising and bleeding prevented her from having any aspirin to dispel the bone-crushing pain that was so typical of the illness. Nurses swabbed her aching body and she lived in a twilight zone of consciousness.

Once she whispered through her dried, cracked lips, 'I was bitten on that hateful afternoon, Alex, do you remember?'

Yes, Alex did remember. He would never forget that afternoon when all their lives had changed. It seemed imperative in his mind that his daughter should return to Scotland immediately.

'I do appreciate everything you have done for us, Dorothy, but Anna must go back to Scotland. We'd already arranged for her to start at St Leonards School in St Andrews in the autumn and Estelle was going to take her. God knows what I'm supposed to do now.'

'It's not a problem, Alex, Lucy is going home too. She's due to start at Roedean School. Anna could travel back with us. Have you a relative that could help her to buy the uniform and get the other things on the list? I somehow can't see Estelle being able to do that now.'

'Yes, there's Molly, but good God, it's a lot to ask.' He wrung his hands. 'I'm in no position to offer any other solution and I'd be eternally grateful to you. Molly is Eilidh's cousin and I know she would meet her and take care of her. Poor Anna, she's had a rough couple of weeks.' He compressed his lips, 'I haven't been much of a support to her. I don't know what I would have done without you and Sam.' He smiled, rather abashed, at the woman who had been Eilidh's best friend. 'You've both been such good friends to me. I just hope that Anna will get over it all; she's young and resilient, and the school will be full of new diversions for her.'

Dorothy weakly returned his smile and gave him a hug. All she knew of the affair was that Anna had been present at the accident that had resulted in the death of Freya Grant's *amah's* son. 'Probably best she goes home, Alex, then you can concentrate on getting Estelle better.' She patted his arm. 'By the way, did I hear that Freya and Roger were leaving early, for their retirement in France?'

'Yes, they're leaving in a few weeks. They're taking Aminah with them. They just have to wait for the papers to come through.'

It was a chilly October morning, and London was grey with drizzle. Molly pushed down the window of the train and leant out to survey the platform, her eyes squinting in the murky gush of air. When the train came to a shuddering halt, she jumped on to the platform and walked towards the exit. As the crowd dispersed, she saw the stricken figure of Anna waiting to meet her. She was standing with another woman and a girl of a similar age. Could this be the same child who had left Druimfhada four years ago? She looked so young, so thin and forlorn on the platform of Kings Cross Station.

Anna ran forward and hurled herself into the waiting arms. 'Oh, Aunty Molly, I said I was sorry. It was an accident but she hates me, she really hates me and Daddy just wants rid of me.'

'Ssssh, it's all right, Anna,' soothed Molly. 'Shall we go and find some hot chocolate and you can tell me all about it.'

'Yes, let's. Do we have a long time before our train leaves?'

'We've got an hour or so, but I think you'd better say goodbye to your friends,' and Molly looked over at Dorothy who was standing back, her face a picture of concern.

'Goodbye, Lucy. Goodbye, Aunty Dorothy, thank you very much for looking after me.'

'Oh come here, my darling girl, give me a hug,' and Dorothy pulled Anna to her and squeezed her tight, unable to suppress the welling tears. 'We're going to miss you so much, but I'll write and I know Lucy will too. You can compare notes on your new schools!'

The two children repeated their goodbyes, and Molly thanked Dorothy for all she had done, and took her farewell. Over the girls' heads, Molly mouthed to her, 'Is she all right?'

The other woman shrugged her shoulders, 'Would you be?'

PART THREE

Chapter 17

2003 – Scotland

It was a dreich December morning. Jason and Anna sat in the outpatients department of the Edinburgh Royal Infirmary. The waiting room was antiquated as befitted the old Victorian building with its forbidding walls, turrets and high windows. The floor was covered in shiny linoleum, the walls painted a dull shade of green. Anna looked around at the other patients and noted perversely that they all looked remarkably well. The wailing of sirens and the frantic pushing of trolleys created a voyeuristic sense of tension. Beside her, Jason thumbed through a car magazine, seemingly unaffected by the whole experience. Anna looked at his queue number and checked it against the screen. 'We shouldn't have long to wait now. Every time we're in one of these places all the mishaps and accidents you had as a child flood back to me. I'm surprised you're so calm.'

'Mum, relax; I'm only getting my cast cut off. It's no big deal. But I will be glad to get rid of my crutches, I can tell you that.'

She fidgeted and re-crossed her legs, then picking at a thread coming from the strap of her handbag she ventured, 'Will you go back to France, do you think?'

'Not now, Mum, OK? Not now.'

Anna sighed and made a show of rummaging in her bag for her diary. What a mess it all was, what a painful mess, and she was not referring to the contents of said bag.

Mother and son had weathered a stormy few weeks since Jason's arrival in Portsmouth in October. The journey north had been straightforward until they'd approached the Scottish border. Driving through the rolling hills and grazing ground of Galloway, they were both conscious of the autumnal bleakness of the season. The random clusters of stark trees gave little shelter to the groups of stoic sheep. Farm cottages stood on bluffs of hills or cowered in the valleys, each guarding its burden of human secrets and frailties.

Anna remembered the conversation they'd had in the car, and Jason's scathing observations. 'I'd forgotten how depressing it is, how empty. All slate and grey stone, the same unimaginative row of houses in every single village and town. There's no warmth or colour here.'

'It's October, Jason, just look at that sky. Those fat rain clouds look ready to burst.'

'In France, well in the south of France, there's always light, and colour where you least expect it. People paint their shutters bright yellow, or blue. They might even paint some old farming implement and grow ivy over it. There's not the same uniformity you see here; the houses have more character, they're more individual.'

'You're lucky to have the chance to work in such a lovely part of the world. Do you like the work? You must be learning a lot.'

'Yeah, I enjoy working with Raoul and I've made some good friends in Perpignan.'

'Anyone special?' Anna took her eyes off the road and looked at him with a mischievous glint of expectation. 'No girlfriends?'

He didn't answer; he just leant forward and twiddled with the radio. For several miles he remained silent with his jaw clenched, a sure indication that he wouldn't be pressed. They listened to the mundane chatter and newsflashes.

'I don't suppose you met a woman called Freya down there, did you?' Anna kept her eyes on the road, concentrating on overtaking a lorry.

'Funny you should ask that, Mum: I did. She said she knew you when you were a child. She took me out for a meal one night and was really keen to hear about you and Granny and Granddad. She said you used to swim at her house when you were a girl, and she told me about a time she threw ice at Granddad's nose!'

'Well, fancy that! Tell me more.'

'Raoul and I did some work for her. She has four chalets that she lets out to artists, and she needed some renovations done on the kitchens, so we actually spent quite a bit of time in Collioure. It's such a smart place. Busy as hell in the summer. The whole harbour area is jam packed with tourists and there are some good restaurants, but in autumn and winter it gets really quiet.'

'Well, what's she like? Is it a nice house? It's so funny because Dorothy Bathgate has just been telling me stories about those years and she mentioned Freya and told me she's living in France now.'

'Really, Mum, you should go down there yourself. Her house is in such a top spot, surrounded by vineyards and overlooking the town. In the summer there were sunflowers along one side, and honest to God, they were so bright I had to wear sunglasses just to look at them. She has decking at the front and has it set up with a long table with chairs. Raoul built a wooden trellis over the top some years ago, and she has pink and red roses growing over it.'

'It sounds so lovely,' his mother sighed, comparing the image with the rain falling on this grey winter landscape. 'Go on.'

'There's a beautiful blue wisteria growing up the side of her house. When you sit on the terrace you look straight out over the Mediterranean. It's fantastic; you should see the boats down there, they must be worth a fortune.'

'Where do her artists live?'

'Well, their chalets are on the hill, a little way down. They each have a balcony and a studio to catch the light. Sometimes they come up and share a glass of wine with her and Aminah in the evening.'

'Aminah?'

'She's a Malay woman. She's really nice. She's lived with Freya for about forty years, apparently. She remembers you as well, Mum. They're really quaint, the two of them. They're both about seventy, with long white hair tied up in buns, but they seem fit enough. Freya is thin and sparrow-like and keeps jumping about. She wears crochet tops and long dresses. Aminah is quite fat and wears a sarong all the time. She seemed pretty quiet; she's much slower than Freya, but she's quite comical. She looks like an owl with her big tortoiseshell-rimmed glasses. She powders her face and it sort of flakes off and lands on her blouse. She said she had a son once but he died when he was young.'

Anna concentrated on the road. Wishing to change the subject she asked, 'Do they have anyone to help them?'

'Yes, they do. They have two French girls who do the cleaning and a woman who cooks for them. Sometimes Aminah makes curries and her speciality, *nasi lemak*. She made it for us one night and it was fantastic.'

Recalling Dorothy's speculation about the possible parentage of Suleiman, Anna tried to make her voice sound casual. 'Do you think Aminah came from a wealthy family? What happened to her husband, do you know?'

'I've no idea, Mum. I don't know if she was ever married. She didn't discuss it with me. I mean, why would she?'

Content for the moment with what he'd told her, Anna pondered the information that she had gathered in the last couple of days. The miles swished past. Rain and dirty lorry spray kept the wipers on full, hypnotically linking sunflowers and wisteria with dark rubber plantations. Images, long repressed, were stirring and resurfacing into her current consciousness. When they finally reached the rain-washed cobbled streets of Edinburgh, she could see that Jason had cheered up. His head craned at the view of the castle above them.

'It's good to see it hasn't fallen off its perch since I've been away. Look at all these gloomy taxis hurtling through the puddles like Black Marias.'

'Yes, and look at the umbrellas bobbing about on a sea of raincoats; our very own Scottish Mediterranean.'

They were hardly in the door before Anna heard the deep voice of her son on the telephone arranging assignations for later in the evening. The only appointment she wanted to keep was with the bath. It had been quite a week and her brain was reeling from the information that she'd acquired. 'Jason, get off the phone, can't you see the answering machine flashing? It's probably your father.'

It was. Six messages, all from Duncan: Hello, are you there, hello? Hello? Where are you, sweetheart? I'm calling from Bangkok...

His gruff, terse voice filled the flat and Anna smiled as she imagined him sitting in his hotel room thousands of miles away. She could picture the deep-ingrained lines that had formed round his mouth, the leathery creases that etched his forehead. She laughed softly, and was glad that he still thought of her as his sweetheart after so many years.

Jason grinned as well, 'Hope he calls back soon. Do you mind if I go out, Mum, I just want to catch up with a couple of the lads?'

Anna eyed his plaster cast and his crutch and raised her eyebrows.

'I'll be careful. I'll get a taxi down to Stockbridge, don't worry.'

Later that evening, Anna was alone again, but she didn't feel alone. The past was crowding the present, and with the help of Aunty Molly, John Sinclair and his daughter, Catriona, Dorothy Bathgate and now Jason with his news of Freya and Aminah, her head had been transported to another time. Gingerly, she eased herself into the steaming bath, slowly lowering her legs and submerging her upper torso. Immediately the delicate skin of her breasts turned scarlet, and just as she closed her eyes and let her mind drift away with the feather light foam of bubbles popping and fizzing against her face and neck, the jarring of the telephone interrupted her reveries. Damn and blast, she thought, it had to be Duncan. Couldn't he just wait for another half hour, for goodness' sake! Still the wretched thing rang. Because she'd turned off the answering machine, he'd know she was home. She hauled myself out of the masochistically hot but blissful bath and padded wetly through to the lounge.

'Anna, is that you? Where the devil have you been? I've been phoning at all hours.'

'I know I know, but I've only just got back and I was in the bath.'

'Aye, and what about the other ten times I called?'

'Yes but...When are you coming back? Is everything OK? Duncan, I have so much to tell you.'

'Yes, I know, you always have so much to tell me! I am coming back in maybe three weeks, it's hard to say. I have the chance to go to Laos; I'm waiting for my visa. I've already sent forty boxes in a joint container. It'll take about eight weeks before they arrive there.'

'Duncan, I have Jason here. His ankle is broken.'

'Good God! What's happened to him?'

'Oh, he says it was a motorbike accident, but it's not too bad. I drove down to Portsmouth to meet him; in fact we only got home about an hour ago. Can you call again tomorrow? I know he'd really like to talk to you.'

'Of course, sweetheart, I'll call about ten in the morning your time, OK? Make sure the reprobate is up and about! Now, get back to your bath, my darling, we'll speak tomorrow. Goodnight!'

It was so good to hear his voice, his concern, his love. She padded back to the bath and gingerly lowered herself into the cauldron, exhaling luxuriously and blowing soft froth from her shoulders. She thought of the early years of their marriage, when she was still insecure and disbelieving that anyone could possibly love her. He'd always been there for her; he'd never made her feel second best. Anna scowled, rather as she'd done as a child, and thought of her dad, and the choices he'd made. She could hear Duncan's words, repeated so often over the years. 'Let it go, Anna, you've turned out well, in spite of everything. God knows how, but you have. With the splintered childhood you've had it's a bloody miracle, but there you are, you're a survivor.' He used to laugh and hug her then, and the moment would pass.

During the next few weeks Jason and Anna sifted through the tin box. He laughed aloud when he read through a bundle of his mother's letters written from boarding school in Scotland.

'Listen to this, Mum!' He read from a letter:

Dear Aunty Molly,

Thank you for sending me the home made tablet. I ate it all with my friend Debbie. Then I was sick. It was very nice though.

It is cold, and the matron is a monster. She refuses to put on the central heating. Instead she says we can have one bar of the electric fire. I don't think that is fare do you? Specially as all the parents are payeing. I have saved up three shillings and I can't decide whether to buy wool (blue) to knit a scarf, or buy the French perfume I saw in the chemist for two and six. It's called Aimee. That means Love in French. I feel more sofisticated now that I am twelve. Matron says we have to wear our berets all the time, and we can't wash our hair before going out as it gives you meningitis. That is really really bad and life threatening.

I have decided to be a missionary when I leave school. I don't think you need to sit many exams so I shall leave school early and probably go to China.

I hope you are well and please write to me.

With love from Anna

'I can't imagine why Molly kept all that nonsense.' Anna grimaced, trying to recall what she'd been like at that age. But as she watched her son chuckling over her old ink-stained epistles, she could see that he was trying to piece together his mother, just as she was trying to do with hers.

*

In early November, Jason and Anna paid a visit to Estelle at the Athol House Nursing Home. On the way, they decided to take a detour and drove about fifteen miles up into the more remote farmlands away from the main road. Anna parked the car in a lay-by and they made their way along farm tracks and across desolate fields. Jason's ankle was stronger now and he was able to hobble with the aid of his crutch across the rough terrain. A few brown doleful-looking cows raised their heads in acknowledgement as they trudged past. They climbed up the gentle rise that led to the boundary of the farmland. A sturdy wire fence stretched around the perimeter of the field to keep the cattle in, but behind it was an old dry stone dyke that had withstood the ravishes of time and weather and, although in places it had tended to wobble, it still held its own with dignity. Here was the very heartbeat of history, the stones that separated one man's land from that of another. Above it the spiny fingers of the gorse scratched the pitted surface of the stone. Anna caressed the rough surface and let her finger trace the long tapering tendrils of green moss. Absently Jason lifted a fallen boulder and replaced it into the rough-hewn bed from where it had become dislodged. His hands were large and strong, the characteristic shape of his fingers the same as his grandfather's and his father's before him. What he had done unselfconsciously had been done for generations in that family. He had bent and chosen, weighed and balanced and finally placed the rock perfectly into the intricate jigsaw puzzle that his forefathers had built. Together they gazed over the fields stretching before them and Anna told him of these lands and how his grandfather had worked here during the war. From the dark forest of pines they could hear the harsh caw of a raven. Above them, they watched a flock of gulls soaring up in the invisible currents of the cold and bitter east wind.

'Do you know, when I was a child, I would stare up at the sky like this – look there, where the sun is filtering through those clouds – I would imagine that was a sign from God. I spent my life praying and getting ready and waiting for Jesus to make his second coming and I was so sure it would be on a fluffy cumulus, like in the illustrated Bible stories. I was incredibly worried that because of all my sins I would be damned to hell. I felt so jealous of all my Catholic friends; they seemed to have an easier time of it; they only had to say sorry and that was that!'

'You're mad, Mum, you really are. What great sin did you ever commit?'

And somehow, leaning on that dry stone dyke with the November wind whipping at the ends of her scarf, she told him.

'I committed the very worst kind. I was a selfish, self-centred brat. I thought the whole world revolved around me. That's what Estelle told me often enough and she was right. Since that day, I've carried this black burden around knowing that I can never make up for what I did.'

'Tell me, Mum, what burden?'

Anna looked away and instead focussed on a gull that had separated from the flock. It seemed to hang motionless in the sky. 'When I was eleven I had a swing. It was the biggest, most magnificent swing ever built. It had chains hanging from a steel beam and the seat was a huge plank of solid wood. I used to play on that swing every day with my friend Santosh – he was the *kaboon*'s son – that was the Malay word for gardener. We thought we were amazing and I had visions that one day we would be good enough to join a circus and be *artistes* on the flying trapeze. I was quite a headstrong girl, and probably quite bossy, but also full of enthusiasm. I remember being taken to see the film *The Greatest Show on Earth,* so no doubt that was instrumental in my idea of putting on a show. We invited all the adults, Granny and Granddad, Cookie and Amah, and some other people – actually people you now know. I'd met Aminah's son, Suleiman, when I visited Freya's house with Granny. I remember we played and swam together, and I-oh-so-graciously invited him to see *The Great Flying Trapeze Act.* Freya brought him round to our house to see the show and he was so thrilled and he clapped at all our great acts.' She looked down at her feet and could feel her voice breaking.

'Go on, Mum, what happened?'

'He was so excited...but there was an accident...'

He put his arm around his mother and squeezed her. 'It's OK, Mum, just tell me.'

'Santosh had just completed the act where he had to run in front of the swing blindfolded. Everyone was clapping.' She looked up again at the brooding Scottish sky, taking in the bleakness of the grey winter's day. Anna felt her throat swell with the pain of unshed tears. 'He died. He died, Jason. He was only eight years old...' She felt the tears run down her cheeks and swiftly wiped them away. 'All these years I've tried to shut it out. It's just that you met her, you met Suleiman's mother. I never did. I never knew where she was. I only found out from Dorothy Bathgate that she was in France and now you tell me that you've seen them both. She cooked a meal for you. Did she know you were my son?'

'Of course, Mum, she was so kind and she asked about you. There were no bad feelings. For goodness' sake, it had nothing to do with you. You just organised the show and there was an accident. End of story. And you've been beating yourself up about it ever since?'

'I know, I have, but I was sent away almost immediately. My parents sent me away. They sent me to Scotland, to boarding school. I was only eleven years old. My mother had died. My grandmother had died. My father had married another woman. Suleiman died and I was responsible. I had to live with the guilt and the fear that I was going to hell. Every church service I attended in that boarding school for six years underlined the fury of the Ten Commandments, the promise that sinners would burn in hell.'

'But what about Granddad and Estelle? Why did they send you away?'

'I still don't understand why. I know that Estelle got very sick with dengue fever shortly after the accident. Perhaps my dad was just extra protective towards her, afraid he might lose his second wife. Estelle was never fond of me anyway, so she just let it all happen. Enough, Jason, I don't want to talk about it any more. We'll go and visit her now, but keep all this to yourself. I can't explain, but it's as though parts of a puzzle are finally falling into place. I couldn't believe it when you told me about visiting Freya and Aminah in France, and so soon after Dorothy telling me that the Grants had moved there many years ago.'

'Do you know who Suleiman's father was?' Jason asked, as they tramped down through the thistles towards the main road.

'No, Dorothy didn't know either. I imagine there was plenty of speculation about that!'

Somehow they got through the visit with Estelle. They sat beside her in the visitors' lounge while she ate the grapes that Anna passed to her. Jason refilled her glass with Lucozade and held her frail shoulders and helped her to take each small sip.

Estelle was subdued, the drugs keeping her in a state of sedation, but she was able to mutter softly to Anna, 'He looks good. Has he got a lass yet?'

Anna just smiled weakly.

Jason shook his head and said, 'Not yet, Gran, still looking!'

It was always like this, there was little to say any more. Anna looked at her and recalled all the stories she'd heard, the stories she'd pieced together from the threads that had come from the tin box. Could this be the red-haired woman that had so besotted Jack, Alex and even Callum? The room was too warm. There was a stuffy smell that made Anna long for the fresh air outside. There were other visitors this afternoon, and she gazed casually at the small huddles of family groups fussing over their relatives. Perhaps the insecurities that came with being a second wife and stepmother had blinkered Estelle from seeing the child in her care as a vulnerable victim. After an hour, they left Estelle and drove back to Edinburgh. Both silent, both lost in their own thoughts.

'Are you OK, dear?' Anna asked when they got home.

'Sure, but I've got my own goblins, Mum, things I've done that I'm not that proud of. You're not the only one eaten up with guilt.'

Jason then announced that he was going out. He didn't come back that night or the next, and eventually, when he did return, it was late and he was drunk. Anna was kneeling on the rug, going through the tin box, when he towered over her, his demeanour menacing. He lifted his plaster-clad foot and tapped the box, causing it to spill photographs and letters over the rug. Bending over, awkwardly holding the side of the armchair to keep his balance, he picked up the album that Eilidh had once sent to her mother and flicked through it.

'What are you bothering about all this ancient history for, Mum?

She struggled to stand, but her legs were numb and she lost her balance. Jason lurched forward to catch her. His breath stank of stale beer but his arms held her tight and together they swayed precariously amongst the scattered papers that had formed as a random collage at their feet. Holding him, Anna squeezed her eyes shut as the tears welled up. A million images of her funny little boy came dancing in front of her. Pictures of his eyes as they had been, shiny brown buttons lit up with happiness and enthusiasm. For two days she had fretted about him.

Something was wrong; something was eating into him, making him so resentful and angry.

'Come and sit with me, Jason.' She beckoned to him and he flopped down heavily beside her. A million accusing eyes seemed to stare up at them from the debris of photographs.

'It's my turn to confess.' Jason leant forward, holding his head in his hands.

'What is it?' His mother stroked his hair.

'I've done a terrible thing.'

Anna stiffened but said nothing.

'But it's worse than you, Mum, for what you witnessed was an accident. My sin was premeditated.'

'Oh Lord,' she breathed, 'I don't think I can take this.' Her heart was beating too fast. She struggled to keep her breathing normal, silently praying: Oh God, please, please…

He sat up and hugged a cushion against his body. In a subdued voice he continued, 'I forced my girlfriend to act against her will and have an abortion. She didn't want to do it but I refused to listen. I dropped her off at the clinic and I left her there. It was after that on my way back home that I broke my ankle. I was feeling so bad I stopped off at a bar and got drunk, then stupidly tried to drive my motorbike. I swerved into a car and the impact sent me skidding over the road. I was bloody lucky it was only my ankle that broke.' Jason turned to her, his voice matter of fact. 'So you see, I'm no good, Mum, I've hurt the only girl I've ever cared for and now I've ruined everything!'

'And your girlfriend?'

'I don't know.'

'Jason, have you not been in touch, doesn't she know that you're in Scotland? '

'No, she's better off without me. She'll get over it.'

'Well, you don't sound as though you have. Why did you want her to have a termination?'

'I told you, I loved her. I just didn't want us to be tied down; I'm just a selfish bastard. I don't deserve her.'

'Write to her, Jason; if you don't want to telephone her, write. The poor girl must be feeling devastated.'

*

So on a grim morning in December they sat in the outpatients department of the Edinburgh Royal Infirmary, waiting for someone to come and remove Jason's plaster cast. Anna just wished the doctor could wave a magic wand and remove the pain in their hearts at the same time. As she morosely mulled over her dark thoughts she returned to the present with a jolt, for suddenly a door opened and a disinterested voice announced, 'The doctor will see you now.'

Chapter 18

December 2003 – Scotland

'God, it's good to be back!' Duncan's eyes scanned the familiar pictures and knickknacks. 'I can't tell you how good it is to be home. I've seen enough bars and lonely hotel rooms to last me for many a month. I was getting as depressed as a lyric from a Leonard Cohen album. I must have looked like a real sad old git, sitting at breakfast with my novel and all the hotels punting out *Rudolf the Red Nosed Reindeer.* Next time I'm definitely not going for so long. What are our plans for today?'

'Shopping, of course! It's Christmas and I want to collect the turkey I ordered.' Anna hugged herself whilst watching him circle the sitting room. Today she was dressed in a long red woollen dress, her hair wound up in a French roll. She felt warm and affectionate as she listened to him ranting about his travels.

'Hmm, I'll come too. I need to supervise what you're going to buy to feed us all. Have you got parsnips on the list?'

Anna laughed, 'You just worry about your own department, and leave the kitchen to me. You need to do the tree. Jason insisted we wait for you, so perhaps after the food shopping you and he could go and collect it this afternoon?'

'Fine, that all sounds fine,' and he whistled as he walked over to the window and moved the poinsettia a little to one side so that he could peer out at the weather. 'I think I'll put on my Russian hat; it looks cold enough to freeze my ears off!'

After battling through the crowds on Princes Street, Anna was glad to be back in her warm kitchen, preparing dinner to the sultry tones of Bing Crosby. How could she not be cheered at such a time? Duncan had only been home a day but always his sense of optimism lifted her mood, and she noted how cheerful Jason had become as well. Together father and son had gone on their mission to buy a tree, and had now decorated it with the familiar glitter and ornaments that had been stored year after year.

'Oh that is so beautiful!' Anna inhaled deeply, her eyes scanning the looming fir, its branches heavy with small dolls that had been collected from all over the world; little hand-sewn embroidered representatives of nomadic tribes of China, Tibet, Vietnam and Thailand. Funny wooden carvings, so small and so intricate, that had been bought from dusty markets for just a few pennies. Now they hung side by side, uniting the cultures of the world in a blaze of pretty lights and tinsel.

'Oh my darling, you always create a masterpiece!' and she walked into his open arms. Looking over her husband's shoulder she met her son's eyes; they were warm, and a shy smile played around his lips. She extracted herself from Duncan's embrace and went to Jason.

They hugged each other tight, and he whispered, 'What shall we put on top of the tree, Mum, a star or an angel?'

Anna considered for a moment: 'Why not a star? Something bright and cheerful!'

Duncan and Anna attended the midnight service at St Giles Cathedral. They sat with the hundreds of others who had braved the chill December night to come out and celebrate the true message of Christmas. Anna suppressed a smile, listening to her husband singing *Gloria in excelsis Deo*, his voice joining the swell of the packed congregation. The familiar words of the prayers that followed came back hesitantly, and then all too soon the singing was over and they rose to leave.

Anna laced her fingers through Duncan's and said, 'We should come to church more often, it's really quite uplifting. Oh look, Duncan, look! It's snowing! Merry Christmas, my darling, Merry Christmas!' and they shook hands with various strangers whilst making their way out to the ancient Royal Mile. 'It's like being in a snow ornament, with all the old buildings and the spires of the church caught in a whiteout.'

'Come on,' Duncan pulled her hand, 'we'd better run before it settles and gets too deep; be careful now, this slope by the castle is steep. Maybe we should hold on to the rail.'

The wintry streets grew more silent the further they moved away from the centre. They could hear the muffled sound of their footsteps as they passed the yawning alleyways of the wynds and closes. Around them were the shadowy shapes of trees silhouetted in the parks and they felt a frisson of fear at the sound of a skeleton branch scraping in a silent churchyard. Laughing self-consciously, they picked up the pace as the snowflakes fell in flurries about them.

'I'm so glad you invited Uncle Callum, Aunt Kate and Luke for Christmas dinner,' Anna said as she climbed into bed. She pulled the crisp duvet around her and watched Duncan toss his dressing gown on to the chair. 'It will make the meal more of an occasion.'

'Aye, I think so too. But we'll think about all that in the morning, I'm much more interested in giving my wife her usual Christmas surprise. Come down here beside me.'

Anna giggled in spite of herself. 'Surprise! Is that what you call it now! Surely it's not been that long!' His arm snaked out from the cover and switched off the light. Outside, the soft flakes of snow continued to flit across the sulphuric glow of the street lamps.

And so it was, with candles burning bright on the sumptuous table and branches of holly dropping scarlet berries in protest at the heat, the extended family sat together on Christmas night, surrounded by walls adorned with strings of cards in a mix-match of Madonnas and robins, kings and babes. The normally muted tones of the dining room had run riot in an orgy of red and gold depicting the festive cheer. Callum, at seventy-three, was rounded and jovial. His eyes twinkled as he teased Kate and made elaborate toasts to his 'wee darling'. Duncan and Luke talked animatedly about their successful buying trip to the Far East and the talk flowed easily around the table. Kate demanded news of her old friends, Freya and Dorothy, so Jason and Anna were able to give her all the information that each had gathered. Kate, in return, told them of her and Callum's visit to Estelle and Alex, on their way to Edinburgh that morning, for the care authorities had kindly arranged for Estelle to be allowed home for Christmas day.

'Have you any plans to visit them, dear?' Kate asked her niece, a touch hesitantly.

Anna looked vague, so Duncan stepped in. 'We'll be visiting them at the New Year,' and then to stop any further discussion he ushered everyone away from the table and through to the sitting room. Anna noticed Kate latching on to Jason and imagined the incessant questions about Freya: What had she been wearing? Did she look old? What was her house like? Anna cleared the plates and made towards the kitchen, Callum following closely at her heels. He peered out of the window at the frosty picture. The frozen snow glittered and the stars were bright within a clear night sky. He came away from the window and sat down at the kitchen table. Anna looked at him expectantly.

'What is it, Uncle Callum? Would you like some tea or some water? Can I get you anything else?'

'No, lass, well, maybe I'll take a wee drop of brandy if you have it?' His eyes lit up with a hint of the old mischief. When she gave him the glass, he talked at first as though to himself. 'It's a funny thing, isn't it? Years go by and I hardly give Malaya a thought, then suddenly it's as though it was yesterday and I feel as though I'm back there. I suppose it's all this talk of people we knew, and getting cards from folk I don't give a thought to from one year to the next.'

'Isn't it nice though, to hear how old friends are?'

'Aye, lass, that's true. I got a terrible shock when I visited your dad and Estelle this morning. I doubt this may be his last Christmas. They are both struggling with the inevitable, I suppose. I just hope I go in my sleep, and failing that I might give Kate permission to push me off a cliff! I don't want all the indignities of lying around with my mouth open, and people feeling sorry for me. I didn't like seeing my own brother so lost to himself like that; he used to be a fine-looking man, a bit like myself yet!'

Anna smiled weakly and assured Callum that they were both being well cared for. Then he got up and walked through to the hall where his winter coat was hanging in the vestibule. He came back and handed her a brown envelope.

'Estelle gave me this, Anna. She'd been keeping it in her purse. I think I know what it is, but I'm not so sure that you do.'

Anna looked at the envelope, and immediately recognised the loopy, almost indecipherable script, but when she made out the inscription, her eyes opened wide in surprise.

'Aminah? Why is Estelle writing to her, and what could be in that envelope?'

'It's a long story, pet; a very long story.'

Whirling images of the last two months swept past Anna's eyes. Names that had previously meant nothing to her had been introduced and were now forming a shadowy cast of players. It was as though a drama that had taken forty years to be enacted was finally reaching its natural denouement. She had been an unwitting audience, had witnessed so much, but had understood nothing.

'Tell me, Uncle Callum. No, why don't you tell us all, please?'

He nodded resignedly, 'Aye, perhaps you're right, lassie; perhaps it is time after all to clear away the old cobwebs'. So carrying his glass he led the way back to the sitting room and sat down beside his wife. Duncan and Jason both looked at her quizzically. Anna just shrugged her shoulders and indicated for them to sit down near Luke. She then pulled a cushion onto the floor and sat down against the settee near Callum.

He began his story, and talking at first slowly and hesitantly, he gradually warmed to his subject and swept them all away with him to a Malaya that many had only ever heard of. He described the country as it was when he and his friends had first gone out in 1948, when rubber planters lived in grand bungalows, hidden away by acres of rubber and jungle. He painted a graphic picture of the fear they'd all experienced in their isolated estates during the Emergency. Finally he took a deep breath and looking over at Kate, he told them about Estelle, and how she had once been married to Jack Dunbar. Quietly he told them about the part he played in the man's death. How he accidentally shot him one tragic night. Luke and Kate were familiar with this part of the story, but not with what came next. Bit by bit, the whole story came out and he told them about an affair that Jack had had with a Malay woman called Aminah. About the son she had borne him, and how Freya and Roger Grant had given the young woman a home right up to the time that Roger was due to retire. He then went on to admit his part in the affair. How he had paid for the boy's education and had taken over the responsibility when Aminah had moved to a place of her own outside Kuala Lumpur. He explained that it was his way to atone for the death of Jack. Anna suddenly felt faint, as realisation slowly sunk in. At last she knew whose child Suleiman had been. How Estelle must have suffered when she realised that it was her first husband's son who had been killed in her garden, a son she hadn't known existed.

Kate interrupted here, a look of utter disbelief on her face. 'How did you keep this so secret? Did Estelle know about the boy?'

'No, she didn't know until Suleiman was accidentally killed. Nancy Fung was a huge support to Aminah through that time and obviously Alex and the Grants wanted to keep it all hush hush. Poor Anna here was the victim; she has lived with the blame for organising that tragic afternoon. I know it's been on her conscience her whole life.' Callum bent over and affectionately patted his niece's shoulder. Anna lowered her head and said nothing. 'If it hadn't been for Dorothy Bathgate I don't know how she would have got through it all.'

'Yes, Uncle Callum,' Anna murmured, almost inaudibly, 'it hasn't been easy to live with.'

'Oh, Anna!' exclaimed Kate, 'I never knew; if I had known, I would have done anything for you.'

'I know, Aunt Kate, don't worry, it's all in the past. I'm just in shock, for now I'm beginning to realise why my parents treated me as they did. It was actually nothing personal at all. It was all related to events that happened long before I was born.' She looked over at Jason and their eyes locked as they remembered her revelations to him by the old wall in November.

'Nancy Fung!' went on Kate. 'What on earth did she have to do with all of this? I thought she was my friend. Why did no one tell me?'

Callum continued, 'Nancy looked after Aminah for a while in KL. She had plans to find her a place in Singapore; I think she had quite a few relatives there, and she got the boy a place in a good school, the Raffles Institution. Unfortunately he never lived that long. Nancy was just that kind of person, some might say nosey and interfering, but at heart she was good to us all, wasn't she, my darling?'

Kate sighed and looked down at her hands. From habit she turned them over, bending her fingers in order to admire her freshly painted nails.

'Well, talk about dark horses and skeletons in the cupboard! That's quite a story,' interrupted Duncan.

'And I met Aminah, just last year in France,' said Jason. 'She lives with Freya, has done for years. Gosh, I wish I'd paid more attention to the pictures she had up. So let me get this straight; Granny's first husband that nobody knew about had an affair with that old lady now living in France?'

Anna nodded. 'Yes, that seems to be the story in a nutshell.' She pondered the conversation. How funny. She and Dorothy had a very similar discussion in October. Dorothy suspected the boy's father to be someone she knew. Estelle, when she talked about him coming home in the car all those years ago, suspected that he was half European.

Kate turned sharply to her husband and demanded, 'And is that the whole story now, Callum McIntyre? Is there anything else you might be missing out?'

'And what more could there be, my wee Scottish dough ball?'

'Are you sure? I don't want any more shocks that might just send me off to my grave. Was it only the education that you paid for?'

'Education?' Callum's eyes looked over at the curtains as though they were the most fascinating curtains he'd ever seen. 'Aye, it was that, just an education,' and he took his wife's hand and gave it a loud smacking kiss. 'Och, I'm sure, sure, sure, now stop your nagging, woman!'

Anna interrupted their little domestic ritual and, pointing to the brown envelope, asked, 'So what's this?'

'I don't rightly know, Anna, but I have a fair idea.'

'What do you think might be in there, Dad?' Luke asked. He had been silent throughout the revelations.

His father sighed. 'Och, I'm tired, son, it's been a long day, no doubt we shall find out all in good time.'

It had been a long day, and it was not till after ten that they gathered up their presents and their coats, and Jason helped Luke to get Kate and Callum safely into the car. Suddenly the day was over, and the house seemed to sigh when the tree lights were switched off. Only the hum of the dishwasher disturbed the silence as they made their way to bed. Waiting for Duncan to finish in the bathroom, Anna looked out at the snow-clad city streets. Only the pavements were hard packed with sheets of ice, for the roads had been salted and were black. The street lights gave off their yellow glow and somewhere in the distance an ambulance siren wailed through the night. Anna pulled back the curtain and thought again of Estelle. In spite of herself, she felt pity. Poor lady, for so many years she had borne the knowledge that her first husband had had a son, conceived presumably whilst she waited back in Scotland. Anna brought herself back to the present and, picking up the envelope from where she'd placed it on the edge of the bed, she walked over to the wardrobe. Beneath the silks of her mother's dresses that she'd taken from Molly's house lay the tin box. Anna bent over and lifted the lid. The black and white photographs seemed to be staring at her. She covered the face of Jack Dunbar, and placed the brown envelope containing yet more secrets on the top.

Chapter 19

Spring 2004 – Scotland

Duncan Maxwell knew his wife too well. He knew how tantalising the envelope in the tin box was to her and he guessed she wouldn't be content to leave it there for long. 'Why don't we go to France, in March or April,' he suggested, 'and we can deliver it to Aminah in person. Can you wait till then?' Anna's eyes lit up immediately. 'First though,' he continued, 'I have to stay here until the shipment arrives, then after we have the shop shipshape again, perhaps we could fly to Perpignan and visit Freya and Aminah. We'll be able to catch up with Hugh and his family as well. We'd better pop up north to spend a couple of days with my mother before we go away, though. What do you think of that as a plan?'

'Yes, France! Oh, Duncan, What a lovely spring we have to look forward to. We'll have the next couple of months free, and I'm sure that Luke will be able to take over the management of the shop whilst we're away.'

Duncan's shipment eventually arrived and for the first time Jason was showing an interest in his father's line of work. The years spent in France had given him more than a skill in woodwork, and he worked well alongside Luke, unpacking the crates and boxes and exclaiming appreciatively at the exotic carvings and screens and panels.

'Wow, these are pretty cool,' Jason marvelled, fingering the fine workmanship produced by Thai, Burmese and Chinese craftsmen. 'It must have taken months to carve these. Look at these inlaid pieces, all individually painted.'

'Yes,' agreed his father, 'but without the trade those people would have little means of making a livelihood. Just put them over there; your mother likes to organise them in her own way. Our job of collecting and transporting is over now, the selling and arranging is all in the hands of the Boss.'

Anna blew him a kiss, and with a flick of her duster moved towards the new delights. She so loved the chaos of the shop at such times. It resembled a wonderful bazaar when the silks, cushions and carpets were piled with glossy lacquer ware, brass and silver pots, bells and dragons. Anna and her two assistants did nothing at first except finger each piece and admire and dangle semiprecious stones up to the light. It was important to find the right place for each treasure so that customers coming into this Aladdin's Cave would see each article as though cast in a carefully prepared mosaic, or like leaves on a tree, she thought whimsically, each having its own place in the puzzle to best catch the sun's rays.

By March the shop was restocked. Customers opening the door set off a tinkle of small bells, and immediately inhaled the ingrained aromas of distant lands while being transported to a lush semblance of a palace of the mystical East. They were drawn to the colours and textures of rich rugs and smooth, silky embroidered fabrics. They stared with fascination at beaten silver and bronze trays and, under the strategically placed lights; they saw the colours of the stones reflect deep blue hues that would drop like raindrops from their ears or smoulder around their throats. It was more than a shopping experience; just for a short while, these casual buyers had flown with their senses to the lands from where these treasures originated.

Outside, the city was grey, trying to shake off the cold mantle of a late winter. Crocuses and daffodils were bravely following the snowdrops' appearance, but the chill, biting wind gave little of the warmth that the spring flowers promised. Nevertheless, Anna was excited at the prospect of the forthcoming travels. Jason had promised to keep an eye on everything, and as well as working in the shop and the renovated garage where furniture was repaired and restored, he had got some casual work in the Playhouse and Lyceum theatres building sets for forthcoming productions. Anna watched her son go about his business, appearing so mature and in control, yet she knew he carried the burden of guilt and could imagine his pain. She just wished she could persuade him to go back to France, and find the girl again. Maybe they could patch things up.

'It is good that you keep yourself so busy,' Anna said to him one morning. She was stirring the porridge with the old spurtle that she'd used since she was married. 'But for some reason, I think you're avoiding thinking, my boy. You've been back here in Edinburgh since October and here we are in March already. I haven't once seen you out with any of your old girlfriends. Are you not planning to move on?'

'Leave it, Mum,' he replied, his manner abrupt. 'I don't want to talk about anything, OK?'

Anna shrugged and deftly ladled out two helpings of porridge. 'I was just curious, that's all. Have you not had any contact with her? Did you write as I suggested?'

'No, Mum, I didn't and I don't think you're such a great expert here. As I've just discovered, you're not exactly the greatest communicator in the world, are you?' He blew on to the spoonful of porridge. 'You've managed to keep your secrets to yourself, just as your mother and father did before you. Can I not keep my life private?'

Anna frowned, making a show of pouring tea and passing the sugar over to him. 'I was just wondering, Jason, that's all. It's quite natural for a mother to be concerned and to want to know. You led me to believe that you didn't want anything more to do with this girl, and yet you seem to be obsessed in keeping busy and cutting yourself off. You certainly don't look happy.' She feigned a casual interest in rearranging the napkin on her lap. 'So...I was just wondering, you know, if you'd tried to make contact with her?'

'The girl you keep referring to is Michelle,' Jason finally volunteered. 'She's twenty-two years old and I met her in Collioure. She's a sculptress and was a friend of an artist that lived in one of Freya's chalets.'

'Michelle? A French girl? Of course! She must be French, living in France.'

'She's half Singaporean actually; her father met her mother just after the war. He was a foreign correspondent I think. So, there we are. It's all over, and now I have to get away to work. Thanks for breakfast, Mum. Now please, just leave it.' He looked at her, his brow wrinkled, and turning to him, Anna met the pleading look in his eyes.

'Fine,' she smiled over her glasses and pulled the *Scotsman* towards her. 'Have a good day, dear.' After she heard the door slam, she sat on, cradling the mug of tea in her hands and letting her thoughts take flight.

Whimsical images of France and of Singaporean girls flitted around her head, but she returned to earth with a jolt when the sharp ring of her mobile phone interrupted her pleasing reverie.

It was Duncan. 'Are you coming in to the shop today? I have to go to Glasgow and would appreciate it if you could get here fairly soon?'

'Of course, dear, I was just leaving.'

Chapter 20

Spring 2004

Far away in Kuala Lumpur, Nancy Fung was dressing for dinner. Her husband, Winston, was downstairs answering the telephone. 'Always talking talking talking! That man has the most energetic tongue in Malaysia, maybe even in whole of Asia. I think he could win a prize for talking!'

Her Chinese *amah* passed her the black silk dress that she would be wearing this evening. 'You wear diamonds, Madam, or pearls tonight?'

Nancy considered, for although now seventy years old, she was still as elegant and minimalist as ever. She pursed her carefully painted lips into a questioning moue. 'Terence Chong is bringing his wife, so I think the diamonds. Yes, and you come here and help fasten them. You got white orchids from the market?'

'Yes, Madam; Ah Lai has steamed the dim sum and has the sea bass steaming with chopped spring onions and ginger, just as you tell me.'

'Good, now I get that husband off the phone and into evening trousers. Talk talk talk. Better when he plays golf, then I don't hear his talking all the time.'

'Nancy!' Her husband bellowed up the stairs. 'Nancy! Come down!'

'Big shouting now, what is the reason? Maybe Asian stock market collapse and we are out on our noses.'

'Yes, what is it, Mr Big Shouting Person?'

'It's a call from the UK, from Callum McIntyre's son. He has just rung to tell us that his father has passed away.'

For once Nancy was silent. She blinked at her husband, trying to absorb the news. 'Callum? He's dead?'

'You better go to funeral,' Winston said. 'Luke said it happened very fast, no warning. One minute sitting reading paper and the next...*kaput.*

Kate has had a big shock. Me too, I think I'll have a whisky. What about you?'

Nancy's thoughts were spinning. Whirling plans for travel were interspersed with the dinner that was under preparation. Guests were expected in half an hour. Her husband was only wearing his undershorts beneath his white dress shirt.

'It's OK, I get some Chinese tea, and you get dressed. Terence Chong will be coming soon. I think of everything after dinner.'

The next morning Nancy decided to call her old friends in Collioure. 'It was big shock, Freya. Winston got the call last night. I still don't believe it. Aminah will be upset, too. I know you two would want to hear straight away. I've booked a flight to Edinburgh tomorrow to be with Kate. I know she has Luke and other family with her, but I think it's good to have a friend at a time like this.'

'Of course,' Freya said into the phone, 'you two were always close. I'm so sad, Nancy, it's just so unexpected. He wasn't ill, was he?'

'No, just gone, no warning. Good for him, bad for us, no?'

After the call, Freya and Aminah sat together, stunned and saddened by the news. No words were necessary; both were lost in their own reveries of the years when Callum had been in their lives. Freya wondered if Michael and Lois Parrish would have been notified, and whether they would attend the funeral. She tried to picture what Michael might look like now, dreamily imagining him in a smoking jacket and striped cravat. 'Oh dear, just look at me,' she said to herself and blinked away a tear before removing her reading glasses. 'What a sentimental old biddy I've become.'

Aminah too seemed lost in thought, and eventually she said, 'I liked Callum very much, he was so good to my Leman.'

Freya nodded and patted her friend's back as she went to the phone. She adjusted the golden chain that held her reading glasses around her neck, slipped them on and screwed up her eyes while she flicked through her Monet address book. She rang Dorothy in Chichester and told her the news. Dorothy in her turn gave her Anna's number in Edinburgh.

'Jason! It's Freya from Collioure, hello again. I know you weren't expecting to hear from me.'

'No, but it's good to hear your voice. How are you and Aminah? Both well, I hope? I expect you've heard the sad news about Callum?'

'Yes, Nancy Fung rang from KL and told us. I was just wondering about funeral arrangements. Is your mother there, Jason?'

'No, I'm afraid not, they're spending a few days in the West Highlands with my gran. I've been trying to reach them all day. As soon as I know what Kate and Luke decide about the funeral, I'll call you.'

'Please do, dear boy, we're both looking forward to meeting you again.'

Thus it was from Jason that Anna received the news of her uncle's death. She and Duncan had just returned from a walk when his mother summoned her inside to take the call. They watched her reaction as she listened to the bad news that it was very clear that she was receiving. Eventually she turned to Duncan, and with a look of disbelief she said, 'It's Uncle Callum, he's dead.'

Aminah sat alone on the terrace of the house, perched on a hill top overlooking the sprawling fishing town of Collioure. It was a house built of stone and painted a warm shade of ochre. The wooden decking swept around the front, giving the impression of being in a tree house suspended within the branches. Roses climbed and snaked their tendrils through the overhead beams and fat globules of wisteria fell in blue clusters along the edges of the walls. It was a magical place, for although the inside of this elegant house was shady and filled with rich furnishings and oriental rugs, the two ladies preferred to spend their days sitting on the rattan furniture that had been shipped over from Malaysia so many years ago.

Aminah was visibly distressed by the news of Callum's death. She was sitting as she did every day, but for once, she was unable to concentrate on the needlework that she had on her lap. Her eyes swept over the hypnotic, interchanging shades of green sea in front of her. Instead of the ocean it was the laughing face of Callum she saw bursting into her small house in Petaling Jaya, his eyes full of warmth as he listened to her son's chatter.

'Excuse me.'

Aminah heard a cough, a polite cough. The old woman was reluctant to leave the gentle memories of the past. She turned around, looking quizzically to see whose it was, this voice breaking into her thoughts. 'Yes, can I help you?' she tried to focus, and fumbled for her glasses.

'I'm sorry, I was looking for Freya. She said I was to come round when I'd finished the piece I was working on. She said she might be interested in buying it.'

Confused by the intrusion and talk about pieces and buying, Aminah informed the interloper that Freya was out. 'She's gone shopping,' she said tersely. Then, when she remembered where she was, her usual good humour returned. 'I'm sorry, why don't you wait, I don't think she'll be long. What is this piece that you have made, then?' Aminah smiled at the girl, exuding her gentle charm, and beckoned her to pull up a chair.

'I made a horse. I was in the Camargue watching the wild horses there and I got the inspiration and took lots of photographs, and I set to work. I think it's quite good.'

'If you made a horse, you must be very good. I cannot even draw a horse. Once my son loved to draw horses but that was a long time ago. Is your horse a big horse?'

'It's about a metre high. I've been busy with it all winter. It's been cast in bronze.'

'My goodness! That must be a very expensive horse. I seem to know you, my dear. Did you not stay with us for a while?'

'No, I didn't stay here, but I did have a friend who was renting a chalet. I met you back in July. My name is Michelle.'

'That's a pretty French name, but forgive me asking,' Aminah peered at the girl through her large spectacles, 'are you not Asian?'

'My mother's from Singapore, but my father is French. We live in Perpignan. I met Monique when we were studying in Paris, and she became a painter and I a sculptor.'

Aminah's eyes lit up; another link with the past. 'I am from Johor Bahru,' she informed the girl, 'but I spent a long time on a rubber estate near Kuala Lumpur. Do you know Malaysia?'

'No, I'm afraid not. I've only been to visit Singapore twice. My mother took me back to visit her parents, but since then they have both died. Why are you here with Freya?'

'I live here. I used to work for her.'

'I hope she buys the horse.' Michelle arched her back and stretched her neck. It was then that Aminah could see the girl's condition.

'You need money, is that it? Can your parents not help?' Aminah leant over, and gently patted Michelle's rounded bump.

'I haven't told them. I've been with artist friends in Montpelier who let me use their studio, and I've been so absorbed with my work that I somehow lost track of time. I seem to have created two masterpieces, but one I have to sell in order to feed the other!'

'And the father?' Aminah asked tentatively.

Now it was Michelle's turn to gaze out at the rolling waves of the Mediterranean. 'He made it very clear that he didn't want a child.'

'So he knows you are pregnant?'

'No, he doesn't,' said Michelle.

Aminah studied the slender neck, almost as skinny as a lotus shoot, and the soft almond eyes and long waves of blue-black hair. She thought that the girl should look in the mirror sometime and paint what she saw before her.

Freya was in her element. Returning from the market where she had haggled for the best snapper and mussels that the fishermen were selling, she was intrigued to find Aminah and Michelle cosily exchanging their life histories. 'What a wonderful surprise, you are like a gift, my dear, turning up like this on a day when Aminah and I were so melancholy. You must stay for lunch, I insist. No no, you just sit there and I'll get a cushion for your back, heavens you look ready to pop!' She bustled about, calling through from the kitchen, 'I'll just nip back down to my vegetable man, I won't be gone long and then we shall feast! Callum has gone, but I want this meal to be a tribute to him and to the memories that we shared from another lifetime.'

Aminah and Michelle smiled at the flurry of scent and silk as Freya exited with a trilling goodbye, and in no time at all she returned with fruit and flowers, baguettes, peppers, courgettes, olives and tomatoes and all the other produce that had caught her eye. Stunned at such spontaneous generosity, Michelle leant back on the soft cushions and inhaled the aromas emanating in whispers from the kitchen. Just when her stomach was beginning to growl, Freya appeared, flushed and triumphant with a platter containing a chargrilled red snapper on a bed of sliced tomatoes drizzled in olive oil and fried in rich double cream and black pepper. The effect was piquant and rich.

Aminah winked at the girl and pulled herself up from her chair. 'Come, my dear, shall we taste this wonderful fish?'

Tossing a mixed leaf salad, Freya pointed to the batons of crunchy bread. 'Soak up the juices with these, dear, and help yourself to the olive oil and lemon juice.' She looked around the table, and then exclaimed, 'Wine! Of course! How can we have a celebratory lunch without some wine? You just sit there and I'll get some for us.' She dashed off again and returned holding a bottle carefully wrapped in a white linen napkin. 'A little for you, Michelle? Not too much, I understand, but just a soupçon, *oui*?'

The alcohol made the girl smile and her chocolate brown eyes sparkled.

Aminah, feeling warm and mellow, couldn't resist stroking the raven hair that spilled down Michelle's back. 'She is such a beauty, Freya, and she is going to be a mother soon. Isn't that good?'

Freya laughed, 'Yes, I'm sure it is, and I must say, I do like the photographs of the bronze horse. It's magnificent. I shall telephone Marcel to collect it and bring it round. I think if you attempt to lift it, my dear, you will be in labour by nightfall!'

'You are so kind, both of you. I had no idea I would be treated to such a lunch, and such hospitality. I am so grateful to you both.'

'It is serendipity, my dear. You chose today to visit, and as I said just now, both Aminah and I needed to have a special lunch to commemorate the life of a very good friend. Your turning up has made it extra special.' Freya surveyed Michelle's enlarged bump. 'Can we not help at all? Maybe get in touch with your parents, or your boyfriend? Is he a local chap?'

'No, he's not. Actually I met him here last summer. He was working for you. Do you remember the Scottish boy? His name was Jason?'

'Oh, this is the day that we are being sent messages from above, Aminah! First we hear of poor Callum, and now we find out that Anna's child has come back to visit us, in more ways than one. Can you cope with so many strange coincidences, my old friend?' Freya poured some more wine into her own glass, then taking a piece of bread she soaked up the juices of the fish and olive oil. 'Mmmmm, delicious!' she exclaimed,

'Just heavenly food that's been kissed by the sunshine.'

'What on earth do you mean?' broke in Michelle, looking from one old woman to the other. 'Messages from above? What are you talking about?'

'It's a long story, my dear, but we might keep that for another time. Today we want to know about you. An artist, a mother and an angel just dropped in on us. Tell us about Jason.' Freya smiled beguilingly and poured just another small splash into Michelle's glass, then filled it up with sparkling water.

Michelle looked over to Aminah, who nodded encouragingly.

'There's not much to tell, really.' Michelle faltered.

'Try,' prompted Freya. 'Where did you meet?'

'Well, it was last summer and I was here visiting my friend, Monique. She was renting a chalet from you. We were just catching up really as we had drifted apart after our student days in Paris. Jason was here fixing up one of the chalets and we got talking, you know?'

'Yes,' sighed Freya, 'we both know, but go on.'

'He had a motorbike and he offered to take me exploring. We ventured up and down the rough trails around the area of Argeles. When we weren't on the motorbike, we went swimming and ate barbecue. Once we made our own, and cooked lobster and drank wine. Every day I waited until he finished work and then we would go and eat and dance and walk. He used to meet me with flowers; he loved the sunflowers and once we sneaked into a field and lay underneath the canopy of yellow heads. It was amazing. You know?'

'Yes, we know,' acknowledged Freya quietly. She was far away on the rough tracks in the jungle, where the sound of the cicadas shrieked in the hot midday sun. 'We know...'

'At weekends,' continued Michelle, 'we sometimes drove up into the foothills of the Pyrenees and sat on rough boulders and ate peaches dripping with juice and smelt the pungent aromas of thyme and tarragon and rosemary. He told me stories about Scotland and the house up in the Highlands where his grandmother lives. He loved my sculptures, and I loved his passion for wood. He was so creative.' Michelle went quiet, and gazed down at the bump under her stretched jumper. She gasped as the baby inside her seemed to turn a somersault and a small foot or fist punched into the stretched skin.

'So what happened, why did you two part?' Freya prompted impatiently.

'The old story,' Michelle sighed. 'I found that I was pregnant and he panicked.' She looked away. 'He thought we needed more time to get to know each other. He thought we would be trapped and not be able to achieve all the things we had dreamt of. So he drove me on his motorbike to the clinic, and that was the end. I never saw him again, never heard from him. He just disappeared.'

'What did you do?' asked Aminah. 'You obviously didn't have a termination.'

'I went in, and got as far as taking off my clothes and putting on a gown, but then I was left to lie in a room alone. It was a blue room. It was very nice and had white curtains. Everything was clean and I lay looking as the white curtains blew in the breeze. I heard people walking outside, normal people going about their business. Going shopping or to the dentist or maybe to an interview. They didn't know that I was lying just few feet from them, about to end a life. Before that moment, I was quite OK with everything. Of course I was sad, and of course I was angry with him for making me do this, but in my heart I accepted that I'd been irresponsible and as Jason said, there was plenty of time in the future for children. But then I heard a woman walking with a baby. She was singing to it, soothing it perhaps, and suddenly I heard it cry. Just a small cry and I knew I couldn't do it. It was that simple. I got up and put on my clothes and stopped at the reception and explained to them. I walked out and went to have a coffee. Do you know, I felt quite sick? For three months I suffered with sickness, every day. I thought it was God's way of punishing me for what I nearly did!'

'And now, Michelle?' Freya asked. 'What will you do now?'

'Now that I have finished the sculpture, I suppose I'd better make amends with my parents.'

Freya glanced over at Aminah, and raised an eyebrow at her old friend.

'Michelle, we have had some very sad news today; our old friend Callum McIntyre has died in Scotland. He would have been your Jason's great-uncle. There is to be a funeral, and I was just wondering whether...'

'Perhaps she cannot fly?' commented Aminah, eying the active state of the bump in Michelle's middle.

'How many months are you?' demanded Freya.

'Seven; I'm due in June. Are you suggesting that I go to Scotland and try and coerce Jason to acknowledge my child? You couldn't have been listening to me. He didn't want this baby. He took me to the clinic and left me. How plain is that? He hasn't even tried to contact me.'

'But how could he?' interrupted Aminah. 'You've been in Montpelier. Perhaps he wrote to your parents' home?'

'Do you want us to tell him that we have seen you?' went on Freya. 'He does have the right to know.'

'He has no rights; he gave up those rights in October.'

'Very well,' said Freya, 'but please give us an address for you and a telephone number. We don't want to lose you now, just after finding you, do we, Aminah? I also want you to choose where I should put your horse. It needs to have pride of place!'

Later that evening, the two elderly ladies took a stroll around their garden. They loved this time of day when the sky darkened and the sea turned to ink. Shortly after Michelle left, the phone rang.

'Hello! Jason!' Freya laughed just a little too loudly, 'What a coincidence, we were just talking about you this afternoon.'

'You were? Is everything all right with the chalets?'

'Of course; no, we were talking about Callum and remembering happier times, and we were wondering about the arrangements for the funeral. I presume that's why you're calling?'

'Yes, and to let you know I've booked you into a hotel in Perth. Perhaps I could show you around when you arrive?'

'Thank you, dear boy. We'd love that, thank you for thinking of us.'

Aminah giggled softly at Freya. 'I hope it's not too cold in Scotland. You know I don't like the cold. I wonder how it will be, seeing all those faces from long ago, Callum's widow and her son Luke, and Nancy Fung from KL. I wonder if Estelle and Alex will be there.'

'I don't think so; I think they have both been quite ill. Anna will be there. Are you all right about that?'

'Yes, Freya, my good friend; that poor girl, I have always wanted to meet her.'

Chapter 21

May 2004 – Scotland

It was a grey spring day in Perth. The funeral service was over and now the guests were gathered in the Royal Hotel to complete the final ritual in saying goodbye to Callum. Anna felt as though she was part of a theatrical production; the characters were all present and so many of them she felt she knew, even if it was only through relayed histories.

'Honestly, Anna; in all the time I've known you I don't think you have ever stopped asking questions.' Kate blew her nose and adjusted her glasses. 'Come, dear, let's sit over there. I suddenly feel so very tired.' The older woman led Anna over to a window seat and together they looked at the groups of people who had flown to Scotland especially to be at the funeral. 'He went peacefully; he was just sitting reading the paper, then he put it down and suddenly he was gone. No pain, just peace. Awful for me and Luke of course, it's always worse for those left behind, but he had a good long life, and he seemed to retain his boyish sense of fun all the way through.' Kate looked down at her fingers, and she twisted her wedding ring. 'I met him in the hospital nearly fifty years ago as you know, when he was so low after that terrible shooting business, but he was a good husband and father and I am sure he made up for any mistakes he made.'

Nancy Fung had walked over and stood by the two women. She heard the last part of what Kate had said. Now she said softly to her old friend, 'He certainly did, Kate, and you were a good wife to him too. He very lucky man.'

'I forgot that you and Callum were so chummy,' Kate replied. 'He told me that you knew about his helping Aminah's boy.'

'Did he now? So what did he tell you?' Anna watched the Chinese lady making a fuss of polishing the lenses of her glasses.

'Well, just that he felt he should continue where Jack left off, so to speak, and help raise the child.'

'Ah yes,' said Nancy, obviously relieved, 'he did that, and it was a wonderful thing he did, too.' Anna squeezed Aunt Kate's hand.

On the other side of the room Anna could see another elderly couple meeting for the first time in many years. The man stopped playing with his cigar when he heard a familiar voice call him from behind.

'Hellooo! Look at you, a bald head and a white moustache, but you are still the most handsome, debonair man in the room!'

'Did you know them, Aunt Kate, that couple over there? They seem familiar; let's go a little closer.'

'That's Freya Grant and Michael Parrish. Don't you remember Freya? They were on neighbouring estates at one time. Come to think of it, there was a little rumour, but stop your speculating, it was all a long time ago! You go over if you like, dear, I think I'll just stay here and maybe talk to Nancy.' Kate patted the now vacant seat beside her, and Nancy promptly sat down and the two put their heads together.

Anna chuckled to herself, remembering her childhood aspirations of being a great detective, with very little success as she recalled. Still, she couldn't resist sidling over to where the glamorous couple were animatedly renewing their acquaintance. She planned to eavesdrop and hovered just on their periphery.

'Freya! Good gracious, don't you ever change? Have you never heard of growing old? It's Scotland and it's freezing; don't you know they only have one hot day a year, and believe me it's not today! Look at you, wearing only a silky bit of handkerchief, and your hair still lovely!' He enfolded her into his arms, but their fond reunion was cut short by the clipped voice of Michael's wife. Anna almost choked on the cheese straw that she was pretending to enjoy. She sensed their discomfort.

'Hello, Freya, it certainly has been a lifetime, hasn't it?'

'Gosh, Lois, how lovely to see you and you haven't changed at all. You look as trim as a gym mistress. That blue dress sets off your pearls perfectly.' Freya had recovered quickly and kissed Michael's wife effusively on both cheeks, at the same time noticing Duncan standing nearby.

'I don't think we've met. I'm Duncan Maxwell, Anna's husband, and I'm very pleased to meet you.' He leant over and kissed Lois, who flushed at his Gaelic charm. 'Why don't you come over here and tell me all about those days, and what the pretty ladies did to amuse themselves all day on the estates. You must have been like beautiful birds locked up in golden cages.' Duncan led Lois away, leaving Freya and Michael to themselves. With his hand pressed firmly on her lower back, Michael escorted Freya to the bar, where she demanded champagne. Anna made a play of refilling her plate with vol-au-vents, studying the platter with interest.

'You are incorrigible, Freya,' Michael continued, 'but I think Callum would have approved somehow.'

Freya took a sip from her drink, and looking about her, she replied, 'Yes, I think he would, but this is such a gloomy hotel, with the waiters gliding about and just wanting us to leave so that they can clean up and go home. Callum deserves a better wake than this horrid, stuffy room. Look outside; it's supposed to be April after all, and where is the promise of spring? France is glorious at the moment; warm winds blow in from the sea, and there is colour and light and promise. Spring always makes me think of Solomon in the Bible, you know? There's a wonderful verse in the Song of Solomon, Chapter 2, verse 11.' She quoted:

For, lo, the winter is past, the rain is over and gone;
The flowers appear on the earth;
The time of the singing of birds is come,
and the voice of the turtle is heard in our land;
The fig tree putteth forth her green figs,
and the vines with the tender grape give a good smell.
Arise, my love, my fair one, and come away.

'Well well, Freya, you never cease to amaze me. From shooting guns in the Emergency, running schools for tappers' kids, rescuing *amah*s and providing artists with studios to create masterpieces, and now here you are quoting the Holy Book at me!'

'Silly man!' She smiled fondly; looking into the same laughing eyes that Anna guessed had once entranced Freya as a much younger woman. 'And wasn't it you that used to sing hymns when you went on your patrols through the rubber, scaring the tappers half to death?'

Anna moved away, feeling like the intruder she was, listening to things she shouldn't have, but it was all so quaintly romantic. Dorothy caught her eye and scuttled over to offer her condolences. 'I'm so sorry,

Anna, it's so very sad when our dear ones are taken from us. We just have to be grateful that we have known such fine people. He always thought the world of you, you know.'

'Thank you, Dorothy. I'm so glad you were able to come. Look, here's Duncan. Come and say hello to him as well.'

Duncan bent down and gave the old lady a kiss and a hug, then said quietly to his wife, 'Look around you, Anna, I think your search has come to a natural conclusion. You don't have to look any more, your characters are all here; they have found you!'

Kate hugged Freya before turning to Nancy, Dorothy and Lois. 'Is it possible? I can't believe we're all together again; why have we never done this before?' and then she remembered. One person was not there, and she started to cry. She let the sobs take her and Luke held his mother until she had released this bout of grief.

'It's OK, Mum,' and as he held her, he became aware of another person standing beside him, and he turned to look into two owlish eyes. It was Freya's *amah*, Aminah.

'Better she drink something. Can I get some brandy or maybe tea?'

Anna watched this exchange and felt her eyes prickle with the threat of tears. She had only smiled at the old Malay woman, and had nervously managed to avoid her throughout the service.

Duncan took his wife's hand and said, 'You have to talk to her, Anna, this is ridiculous. Why don't you invite her and Freya to stay with us for a day or two?'

Anna looked aghast, but she knew he was right. She hadn't seen Freya since she was eleven, but the effervescent charm of the older woman was perhaps what they needed. She remembered Freya as a gay butterfly, warm and so different from Estelle, and she also remembered her on that fateful day that had so scarred her childhood. If anyone could, Anna knew she would be the one to help her make amends. Now, taking a deep breath, Anna marched resolutely round to where Freya was still standing with the other ladies, and gently manoeuvred her over to the window. Looking over her glass of white wine, Anna asked, 'Where are you both staying? What are your plans after today, will you go straight back to France?'

Freya shrugged. 'I thought we would stay on here for a short holiday.

I've never spent much time in Scotland and we have a room at the Isle of Skye Hotel. Why, dear? Why do you ask?'

'It's just, I was wondering if you and Aminah would like to come and stay with us? We had planned to go down to France to visit you and also Duncan's brother and his family, but now that poor Callum has passed away and you have come to Scotland, there is no point. Duncan and I would love it if you could. You would be able to see more of Kate and Nancy and I believe Michael and Lois are staying on in Edinburgh as well.'

'Anna, that is a marvellous idea, and yes of course we would be delighted, if you're sure we wouldn't be too much bother. I know Aminah would love to explore Edinburgh. We'll have to get her a warm sweater, however, for as you can imagine she doesn't like the cold at all.'

'Oh I'm so glad, Freya, I'm looking forward to spending some time with you.'

Anna scanned the room, her eyes searching for her son. He was not too hard to distinguish, with his dark hair and his tall, slim frame in the dark suit. She had always imagined he was a mix of herself and Duncan but seeing him now, dressed formally in this unfamiliar setting, he suddenly reminded her of Alex. She could just imagine her poor father as he might once have been. Just then, Jason looked up and caught her gazing at him. He whispered something to his father, and the two men separated. Jason crossed the room and immediately fell into easy conversation with Aminah, while Duncan walked over towards Anna and Freya.

'Hello, ladies, I could see you with your heads together. Always means a plot is being hatched!'

Anna laughed. 'I've just invited Freya and Aminah to stay. I thought we could invite everyone for a curry lunch this Sunday; Freya is going to help me. It's Tuesday today so that will give us time and it will be a proper send off for Uncle Callum, what do you think?'

'Good gracious,' whispered Freya, 'would you just look at those waiters, that one over there is poised with his vacuum cleaner, how outrageous is that? I think Anna's idea is wonderful, a proper send off for Callum, a leisurely farewell from his Malaysian friends.'

Eventually the gathering came to a close. Luke ushered his mother to the door where he, Kate and Nancy shook hands with the many guests as they left the hotel. It had been a long and sad day, yet there was a poignant piquancy in meeting up with so many old and loved faces.

'Poor Callum would have loved seeing everybody today,' Kate sniffed as more tears started to fall.

'It's better to see people when we are alive, better than when we are dead,' concluded Nancy Fung in her matter-of-fact voice. 'Good idea that we all meet up on Sunday again for curry lunch; very good idea of Anna's. Maybe you and me, Kate, we can prepare some *gula Malacca* for pudding. Can we buy the sugar here?'

'Yes, we can. There's a very good Asian supermarket near me. We can get almost everything there.'

Anna's invitation for Sunday lunch had lifted their spirits, for it meant that this would not be a final goodbye. They would meet again soon.

Edinburgh glowed in a blaze of May sunshine. It was as though the city, with its dramatic backdrop, wanted to mesmerise its visitors. The reunited friends made excursions to the castle and the surrounding wild areas that provided walks along rivers and up high volcanic rocks. Michael and Lois tramped the hills, whilst Nancy, Kate and Dorothy enjoyed the shady tearooms in some of the more elegant stores. Jason appointed himself as Aminah's official guide, and the unlikely duo borrowed Anna's car and toured the Fife coast and St Andrews.

On Friday, Freya and Anna began a cooking frenzy. Anna ferried her guest from spice stores in Leith Walk to delicatessens in Bruntsfield. They selected fish from a shop near the Meadows and vegetables and meat from Tollcross.

Eventually, worn out from selecting plump aubergines and peppers, Freya announced, 'Lunch, Anna, please, let's have a drink! I am worn out!'

They sat outside the Golf Tavern overlooking the Links. The soft, rolling expanse of green was soothing to their eyes after the harsh pavements and city concrete. Idly they watched people of all ages pitching and putting across the parkland. The tables around them filled up with students with frothy flagons of beer, and some elderly gentlemen sat dipping their moustaches into a lunchtime gin. Anna wore her hair in a loose pony tail down her back, and fiddled with the stray silver streaks, fancying that they intertwined like fine embroidery through the remaining chestnut. She felt like a girl again, laughing constantly in the company of Freya.

'Just white wine spritzers and a goat's cheese salad I think, my dear. We don't want to be wheeled home this afternoon. You have a lot of chopping to do, and I must be there to supervise.' Freya chortled gaily at this picture that she was construing for herself. She went on, 'We have everything now for five different curries. I shall make the samosas with a mint and yogurt dip for starters; if we can get all that done today and tomorrow we shall be on target. Then of course it will just be a matter of flowers and fruit. I so love entertaining, and I do as much as I can in France. I'm always persuading my artist guests to come and eat with us in the evening. Poor things had hopes of starving in an attic and producing masterpieces, but they never get the chance to be hungry and desperate with me! When Roger was alive and we lived in Malaysia we used to have such wonderful parties.'

Anna was intrigued to hear references to Freya's artists. Her mind was also distracted by the unlikely friendship that had sprung up between Jason and Aminah. The meal preparation with Freya was the perfect antidote for her inner tensions. Butterflies, bees, moths and bats were going mad inside her head; she was afraid that she might have a hysterical breakdown if she didn't keep herself busy.

Sunday came at last. Duncan and Jason pulled the extendable kitchen table into the walled garden. Anna covered it with an Indian cloth that was red and rich with embroidery. White plates, dishes and cutlery were brought out. The weather was perfect. Anna walked around her neat flower borders, bending down to remove the odd shoot of ground elder, and Jason came up behind her.

'Those red poppies must have known, Mum. They've opened specially to match your table.'

'Yes,' she smiled, leaning over to feel the soft tissue of the red petals, 'they always make a good show. Soon it will be the peony roses; look at those fat buds just waiting to burst open. But talking about flowers, you and Freya and Aminah sound as though you had a good day out yesterday at the Botanic Gardens?'

'Well, it was quite slow. Freya wanted to look at everything, then she spent about an hour in the Glass House ooohing and aaaahing, and remembering this fern or that tree. She and Aminah were clucking about Malaysia the whole time. To be honest I could have done without it, Mum.'

Anna laughed and patted his cheek. 'Well, there's another crowd of wrinklies coming this afternoon. Maybe you can slip off after lunch. It's different for me, and special, for all these people knew me as a girl. I feel transported into another time zone when I hear their voices!'

'OK, Mum, you enjoy them, and I will definitely enjoy the curry.'

Anna went upstairs and heard Freya humming to herself in her bedroom. She decided that she would indulge herself today by wearing the earrings that Duncan had brought back from Burma. There were not many occasions when she could wear the exquisite droplets of rubies that fell like dragon's tears. Today, however, the ladies that were coming would appreciate the perfect workmanship of the Far East, and she suspected that they too would be adorned in sapphires, emeralds and diamonds. Anna gave herself a critical look. Creases of fine lines had etched themselves around her eyes and mouth. So much for all the expensive creams and lotions, she thought, her skin just marched on towards old age regardless. The opal green of her eyes seemed more shadowed than usual, a reflection she supposed of the silent pain that was gnawing at her heart.

'Are you ready, Anna?' Freya was calling from the landing. 'The smells coming from the kitchen are transporting me back fifty years! How do I look?' She burst in and twirled around, showing off a lime-green caftan on which were hung two strands of black pearls. Her hair was softly styled into a chignon, held in place by what looked like half a chopstick. Her lovely face was powdered and rouged and she looked as expectant as a girl.

'You look like a lady and you smell divine. I'm afraid I just look a fright. Jason is always calling me an elderly hippie. He might be right!' Anna stared ruefully at the mirror.

Freya came up behind her and surveyed the pair of them. 'You are so different from your mother, dear; maybe you have her eyes and her smile, but you have the height and slimness of your father. How is Alex?' she asked gently, 'I hear he isn't well?'

'No,' Anna lowered her eyes from Freya's bright, inquisitive gaze. 'He's not the man he once was. Did you know him well, Freya?'

'Actually I didn't. Not really. Of course he was in our social circle and I saw him with your mother at the club but we didn't start socialising until Michael was transferred to the neighbouring estate. By then of course your mother had died. Somehow I never really hit it off with Alex. Perhaps he thought I was too frivolous, which I'm sure I was. Then of course I hit him with some ice and nearly broke his nose.'

'You did what?' Anna exclaimed, turning from the mirror. 'That is outrageous, why on earth did you do that?'

Freya patted her shoulder and reached up and kissed her on the cheek. 'Another time, I think. I did meet Estelle at the Selangor Club. We got together a few times when you first arrived. I remember you came and you swam with Suleiman, do you remember? I think Estelle took up with her sister-in law-and Nancy Fung. They were all into *mah jong* and bridge. Anyway, enough of all this, let's get the poppadums done then we can have a glass of champagne and congratulate ourselves before everyone arrives.'

The afternoon sun shone down into the garden, and people dispersed from the table and took themselves to different parts of the house. Plates were filled and refilled as chicken, vegetables, meat and fish were devoured in sauces of coconut and tamarind, hot chilli and ginger. Kate's cooling sago dish with molten brown sugar brought back memories of curries eaten on other Sundays long ago at Port Dickson where the Straits of Malacca lulled them into a post lunch siesta.

Freya helped Anna load up the dishwasher. 'We've filled them up and now they're ready to snooze like portly pythons for the rest of the afternoon.' Freya sipped a glass of water and noticed her friend, Aminah, sitting quietly on the patio of crazy paving. 'Aminah has the right idea, she loves observing people, and look how they keep drifting in and out of the garden. Your flowers are beautiful, Anna.'

Anna nodded in agreement, and came over to stand beside Freya. Together they regarded the old Malay lady peering comically through her owlish spectacles at the crochet work on her lap. From the sitting room window, Anna could see Nancy Fung was also looking out at the garden scene; she seemed to be quietly chuckling to herself, perhaps at her own memories of this shy grandma figure.

Kate had rung Anna earlier in the day and asked if she would mind if she brought her *mah jong* set. Duncan set up a card table in the upstairs lounge and there Kate, Nancy, Lois and Dorothy sat together around the tiles like high priestesses at a well-known ritual. They had picked up their friendship, and although the years had separated them and had brought so many changes to their lives, ultimately they were the same though just a little older. They took their places around the table and resumed their game, remembering the hands with all the different winds and dragons and honours. Their voices could be heard from the terrace as they announced who was saving the wriggly snake, or the unique wonder or the red lantern. Periodically a voice would call *'Pung'* or *'Kong'*, or question 'Who is East Wind?'

'Are you sure they're not members of some Chinese Triad group?' laughed Michael to Duncan as they passed through the hall. With Lois so happily occupied, Michael found the afternoon was mostly his own. Inevitably he found his way out to the garden and sat with Freya, sniffing the scent of sunlight on the fresh herbs growing in pots, and squinting at the riotous colours of the scarlet and orange poppies. As with the *mah jong* group, Michael and Freya slipped into the easy relationship that apparently they too had once enjoyed. Idly watching them, Anna wondered at the liaison they might have shared in the clearings of the rubber estates so long ago. Of course she'd never know.

After lingering over their coffee, Duncan and Jason excused themselves to check on the shop, leaving Anna sitting alone in the lounge, lazy and sleepy. It was warm, even with the French windows open. There was the promise of summer days in the sun; clematis had opened into baby pink clusters of star-shaped blossom and rosebuds were bursting with expectancy. She closed her eyes and savoured the blue whorls of smoke from Michael's cigar.

It was not till late in the afternoon that she was finally able to approach Aminah. Anna hauled herself out of the deep sofa, and yawning sleepily, made her way through to the dining room. There, she encountered the old lady sitting alone. She was sifting through the photograph album that Dorothy had brought up from England. Anna smiled nervously and sat down next to her. For a few seconds she tried to gather her thoughts. Dust motes danced in the afternoon light, her finger followed the swirl of the polished wood. 'It's been a funny few months for me,' Anna finally ventured. 'Do you know that I visited Dorothy at her home in Chichester in October? She showed me those photographs then. I was trying to make sense of my past, and didn't understand why so many things happened the way they did.' Anna indicated the album: 'Those pictures must bring so many memories back to you?'

Aminah nodded in agreement, and turned back a few pages. 'I like this one of your father, Callum, Michael and Jack all standing holding their beers in the garden of Freya and *Tuan* Roger.'

Anna took the album and studied the faces closely, noting the sunburnt arms and wide grins. 'I imagine that they were all quite mischievous. They have a look of being in collusion, don't you think?'

'Collusion,' Aminah asked, 'what is that?'

'Well, as though they all knew a secret and weren't going to tell.'

'Yes, maybe that was right. There were a lot of secrets at that time,' agreed Aminah.

Tentatively Anna walked over to the sideboard where she had left her handbag, and came back to the table. She took a deep breath and said, 'Please forgive me, Aminah, but actually I have something for you and I've been waiting for the right moment to give it to you.' She delved into her bag. 'Last Christmas, Callum asked me to give this envelope to you. Duncan and I were going to make a trip to France in order to give it to you, but then poor Callum died. Please, would you take it now?'

The old lady took the brown envelope and peered at the unfamiliar handwriting. She looked at Anna enquiringly. 'Do you know what it is?'

'No, but I do know who it's from.'

Anna stood up in order to allow Aminah to open the envelope in private.

'Don't go, Anna, please stay with me and we'll look at it together.'

'Are you sure you want me here? Should I not get Freya?'

'No, I want you. Please you stay.'

Anna raised her eyebrows and resumed her seat to watch Aminah open the envelope. The Malay woman's eyes were screwed up tight as she peered through the thick lenses of her glasses, valiantly attempting to read the almost indecipherable script that Anna knew so well. Eventually she sat back and looked at Anna in total amazement.

'What is it?' Anna asked. 'Is everything all right?

Aminah shook her head then with her hands shaking, she took out her handkerchief and wiped her brow. She motioned for Anna to read the letter to her.

'*Athol House, Scotland, July 2003…*' Anna interrupted the script at once. 'But that was just last year, and not long after she'd been diagnosed with pneumonia. Sorry, I'll go on.' She read on:

Aminah,

When my first husband, Jack Dunbar, was killed in Malaya in 1957, I had no knowledge of the existence of you or your son at that time. I shall never know, nor shall I ever want to know, the circumstances of your liaison with my late husband.

Some time ago, I received a letter from the Chartered Bank in Kuala Lumpur. The bank had tried to contact you at your previous address, c/o Freya and Roger Grant at Anak Kamsiah Estate, but of course you had moved from there several years before. A letter was sent to me, as Jack's next of kin, informing me that he had left a trust fund for a child born to Aminah Binti Musa. They thought perhaps I knew of your whereabouts.

You have been on my conscience for many years. It is only now that I have had a brush with mortality that I feel I should act while I still can. I would like to put right this matter which has been troubling me.

I enclose the letter from the bank in Kuala Lumpur. Perhaps you will be able to use this money to honour a cause that would befit your son's memory.

Sincerely,

Estelle McIntyre

When Anna had finished reading, they both looked at the letter from the Chartered Bank and were silent. For Anna the threads of the past were now slowly unravelling and she was sure it must have been the same for Aminah, for the old lady was at a total loss for words.

Eventually Aminah spoke. 'Do you know, when you gave me the envelope, I actually thought it might have been from Callum himself.

I never dreamt that Jack might have set aside money for the child's future. Leman wasn't even born when Jack died. Jack must have planned it all secretly with the bank. He was such a good man; he didn't have to do that.' Her eyes filled with tears, and she removed her glasses and wiped them with her already damp handkerchief. She went on, almost apologetically, 'You would not know this, but Callum and I, well, we were close for a while. He used to visit us when Leman was quite young. I think he was sad, maybe things were not so good with Kate at the time. He was a kind man. He paid for Leman's schooling and he gave me an allowance to live in my small house in Petaling Jaya. He said it was his way of making up for shooting Jack. I really liked him but then his visits stopped. It was just for a very short time. You must think I am such a bad woman.'

'No, I don't.' Anna smiled. 'I can see why people are drawn to you. You have a quality that is almost magnetic. I've been so jealous of Jason spending so much time with you. You have no idea how much I wanted, no, needed to talk to you, to say how sad and sorry I am, how I wish I could turn the clock back and make everything good again.' And suddenly Anna lost control and choked on the already flowing tears. Her face crumpled and her hands rose up to cover her distressed features.

'Ssssh, child, don't cry. Come here, sit close beside me. You know that there is nothing we can do about the past. I wanted to see you after the accident, but they sent you away so fast. It was terrible, for we both needed to talk together, and I want you to know that through all these years my heart has been sore, just thinking of you and knowing how you must be suffering.'

'I wish I'd never invited him. I'm so sorry, Aminah,' and sobbing, her face wet with tears, Anna knelt down by the old lady's chair.

Aminah pulled Anna's head down on to her lap and soothingly caressed and smoothed her hair, pushing the wispy strands back from her forehead. For a long time they stayed like that, the letter forgotten on the table beside them. It had only taken forty years, but thank God, finally they'd said the things they needed to.

Chapter 22

May 2004 – Scotland

Early next morning, Anna kissed Duncan goodbye and let herself out of the house. She ran round the corner to the newsagents and bought some grapes and mixed freesias before settling herself into her car. She drove east, away from the capital, and without much thought, took the road she knew so well, the road to see her stepmother. An hour and a half later, she turned into a curving driveway lined with mature copper beech and chestnut trees. She drove slowly, avoiding the pot holes in the uneven surface, and pulled up at the Athol House Nursing Home. She walked straight to the reception office.

'Good morning, Mrs Maxwell, so nice to see you again. Your mother's in the day room; just go through, or Sister Duthie's in her office if you want a word first.'

'Thank you; I'll just go through if you don't mind.'

Sunlight streamed through the bay windows of the airy room that was decorated in light oatmeal shades. Winged armchairs were arranged in clusters around occasional tables bright with vases of fresh flowers. Estelle was sitting alone, reading the newspaper in a quiet corner of the room.

'Hello, Mother, how are you?' Anna leant over and kissed the delicate papery skin, so reminiscent of her garden poppies.

'This is a surprise, Anna, I didn't expect you today. Oh, what lovely freesias! You know I love them, don't you?' She sniffed them appreciatively. 'Just get a vase from that cupboard over there and you can get water from the pantry. You're looking very tired; are you all right?'

'It's you that's sick, Mother, not me. I'm just sad after Callum's funeral, that's all.'

'Oh, I know. I got a terrible shock hearing that, but I got a visit from

Kate and Nancy Fung. I enjoyed that, even though it was not in the best of circumstances. Nancy is looking as spry as ever, but what's wrong with you? Is there something the matter with Duncan and Jason?' Estelle bit into a grape and looked up. 'We should get morning coffee soon. I expect you'll be gasping for a cup after your drive. Have you been to see your father? Morag rings me every day, so I get a full report of his menu and so on, and if anyone has been to see him. I seem to have made a good recovery, so I should be allowed home in a week or so.'

'I'm glad you're on the mend.' Anna paused, not sure how to continue, still feeling the old fear and inhibitions that arose whenever she had contact with her stepmother. 'Actually, I've come here today to ask you something and to tell you something. None of it's easy, so perhaps I'll see if we can get that coffee.' She walked over to the door and had a word with one of the nursing staff. In just a short while, a young girl came in carrying a tray with cups of instant coffee, milk and sugar. Anna assisted Estelle and then herself. After a few tentative sips of the hot liquid, they both sat back.

'Well?' enquired Estelle. 'What's this about?'

Anna took a deep breath, conscious that her heart was beating rapidly. 'Mother,' she began hesitatingly, 'why did you never tell me any of your history? Why did you not tell me that you had been married before and that your husband had been shot by Uncle Callum?'

'Oh, I see.' Estelle looked down and picked at the balls of lint on her sleeve. 'It seems that Callum's funeral has turned into a real hotbed of gossip. No doubt that Nancy Fung has been badmouthing everyone and spreading stories that she had no right to do. If you want to know why I didn't tell you anything, you were a child, and frankly speaking it was none of your business,' she snipped brusquely. 'I don't choose to talk about my past life and that's all there is to it.'

'But that's not right,' Anna protested, 'there is more to it, and it doesn't just affect you. Nancy Fung said nothing, by the way; she was a proper lady and was very nice to everyone. I actually found out about it all from an old friend of my mother who knew you as well. Do you remember John Sinclair?'

'Of course I remember him. He had no right telling stories about me.'

'But don't you see it might have explained so much? All my life I've lived in my own private hell. I thought I was precious to my father because I was all he had left of my mother, and I imagined that you were jealous of the relationship that I shared with him. After my mother died, it was you I needed. I needed you to treat me with affection and not as a rival for his love. If I had known that you had your own secret grief tucked away, having lost your first husband so tragically, I might have understood why you were so blind and totally lacking in empathy towards me.'

'What are you talking about?' Estelle responded sharply.

Anna stared hard at the older woman, and finally said, 'Did you not have any feeling for me at all?'

Estelle's eyes widened, and then she looked away at the centre of the room. 'You were always a very difficult child.'

'Yes, and when that accident happened, and you got dengue fever and nearly died, my father chose you. He chose you over me. I was the one he sent away, his own daughter, eleven years old. Did it never occur to you to comfort me, to be kind?'

'I was in shock,' countered Estelle, acid lines forming around her mouth, 'and why are you dragging this up after all these years?'

'You sent me away. Did you not know how terrified I was? Suleiman was dead, and no one thought to comfort me. It was my show, and I was made to believe I was a sinner, a bad person, and that I would go to hell. I was only eleven years old, for goodness' sake.' Anna took a sip of coffee, trying to calm herself, then continued, 'It's been a nightmare; I've tried so hard to behave normally, because I so wanted to look normal, as though I came from a proper family. I just wanted my friends to like me. I didn't want anyone to know what had happened, so I kept the secret for years and years.' She stopped then, her throat constricted with unshed tears, and looked at the hard glare in Estelle's eyes. Anna took a deep breath. 'But you never spoke of it; when I saw you in the holidays you acted as though I was a distant relative. All through those teenage years you never asked me how I was, or how I was coping.' She broke down and took some tissues from her bag and blew her nose. Estelle sat immobile as a statue whilst her daughter tried to restore her composure. The freesias on the table and the grapes beside them gave the impression of a normality that had now gone from the room, and had never featured anyway in their strained relationship.

'As I recall, I had dengue fever, the worst kind, haemorrhagic fever, and your father thought it best to give you stability and a sense of normality, so he sent you home to boarding school, albeit a little earlier than planned. You were a child; there was no need to tell you all the details of the past. We acted in the way we thought best.'

Anna had a fleeting thought of the previous afternoon when she had sat with Aminah, and how they had crossed the chasm of years. She recalled the warmth, the gentle wisdom that had emanated from the simple Malay woman. Now, blinking back the tears, she brought herself back to the present. She studied Estelle, sitting with her hands now still and clasped in front of her, and realised that there had never been any love shown. She sighed, a touch wistfully. She was certain that if Eilidh had lived, she would have been a friend as well as a mother. But then a wave of compassion swept over her. Anna could see the loneliness in Estelle's eyes, the self-imposed exile that the old woman had committed herself to, and Anna longed to cross the gulf. She had learnt a lot of things over the last few months. It was easy to take sides and condemn without understanding. Now she felt a little more qualified to stand back from making judgements. Sometimes it was good to imagine oneself in another's shoes.

'I met Aminah,' she said quietly. 'We talked.'

'Good,' countered Estelle, 'so with Callum gone, and you knowing everything, perhaps we can let the past rest now?'

Her heart was still racing. It had not been her intention to hurt Estelle, but she reasoned that it was not right to hide these secrets any longer. She looked over at the proud old lady then gently took her hand, and said quietly, 'I would like that, Mother. When you get home I shall come and see you and my father. Maybe it's not too late to start again?'

Estelle nodded, and looked down to the carpet, studying the flecks on the pile. 'What about that boy of yours? Has he got a lass yet?'

'No, Mother, not yet, but I have a feeling there may be someone on the horizon.'

Chapter 23

May 2004 – Scotland

The next day Duncan suggested that they all take a walk along Salisbury Crags and up to Arthur's Seat.

'It's a volcano, but they tell us it's extinct now,' added Jason with a grin.

'Me? You want me to climb a volcano?' exclaimed Freya, in disbelief. 'I think not; I would rather explore the antique shops in St Stephen Street and potter about in Stockbridge. Don't let them persuade you, Aminah, I can think of much nicer things to do,' and she resumed flicking through her magazine with renewed determination.

'Are you going to climb, Anna?' Aminah asked, a little hesitantly.

'Yes, perhaps I will. I like to get away from the pavements and shops every now and then, and it isn't too steep if you walk behind the Crags; how about you, Jason?'

'Yes, I'm up for it. Come with us, Aminah, I'll treat you to an ice cream if you make it to the top!'

The day proved perfect for hill walking. Puffy clouds dotted a blue sky and only a soft breeze brought the smells of new bracken wafting up through the moist grasses. No hint of traffic noise or angry voices spoiled the serenity of this idyllic place. Jason and Duncan led the way along the beaten path, keeping to the lea of the imposing rock above them. Gay coloured broom festooned the lower tracks leading up to Arthur's Seat.

Aminah mopped her brow with her handkerchief, and stopping for a moment, gazed back towards the glinting waters of the Firth of Forth. 'It reminds me of one of Freya's silk scarves,' she sighed, 'same shimmery blue colours. Very lovely, but I'm too old for climbing. Would you mind, Anna, if I sit here for a while until you come back?'

'Not at all, you guys carry on; I'll catch you up in a minute.' She tipped the water bottle into her mouth, and wiped her lips with the back of her hand. 'Aminah, I don't know how to ask you this, but has Jason talked to you at all about what is bothering him?'

Aminah looked serious and turned towards the Bass Rock in the distance. 'Yes, he told me about the girl in Collioure. I said I knew her, and he wanted me to tell him about her, but I didn't know what to do. You see, Michelle confided in me; she asked me to keep her secret.'

'Oh no, not another secret! Jason has been upset ever since he got back from France. His father and I are at our wits' end. I just don't know what to advise him. Did he tell you the whole story?'

'Perhaps you could persuade your son to return to France. I think that is the best advice I can give. I must not betray the girl, but,' Anna thought Aminah smiled enigmatically, 'he should go to France, and quickly.'

'Mum!' Jason was beckoning from the ridge above. 'Are you coming? Dad's coming down, his knee is playing up. He can sit with Aminah; come on, there's hardly a soul up here.'

Anna turned to the old lady. 'I'll see what I can do! We won't be long, just a quick clamber up, and you and Duncan can make your way back to the car park and we'll meet you there.'

Anna caught up with her long-legged boy and together they scrambled up through the gorse and bracken, then higher still to where spongy moss gave way to thin grasses clinging to the windblown rocks. Short of breath and damp with perspiration, they arrived at the summit and stood there gasping as they took in the panorama around them. Below them lay the city, a maze of roofs and spires, streets and parklands. Ancient monuments huddled together, jealously guarding a thousand years of gory history, and from the famous castle, the Royal Mile ambled its way down to the baroque splendour of Holyrood Palace. To the east were rolling fields and sweeping hillsides with white fluff balls of sheep and lambs, and away in the distance the sequined sea lapped against the Fife coast. Jason leant back against the stone indicator and began to peel the skin off a tangerine. Anna sat down beside him and felt the peace of it all wash over them.

'Mmm, isn't this glorious? I could stay up here forever.'

'Pink lungs, Mum, that's what you get up here, pink lungs and a flushed face. But you look sad. Are you upset about Uncle Callum's death? Has Granny's letter to Aminah brought old wounds to the surface, especially since you've uncovered so many dark secrets?'

Anna took a breath and stared in front of her. The wind had loosened her braid and tendrils of hair had escaped. She raised her face to absorb the rays of the sun. 'It's you I'm worried about, dear.' She kept her face averted. 'What are your plans? You're helping your father and doing the theatre work, but I get the feeling that you're here only in body, if you know what I mean.'

'I know, I know, it's true. I do want to go back to France. It's just I feel so guilty. What do I do if I see Michelle?'

'So, you see her, you talk to her. Nothing can be resolved with you here and her over there.'

Jason fidgeted and tossed some stones into the air. 'I'll think about it, I will. I do need to sort myself out and I do need to find out what's happened to her.'

'Well, that's a start, but don't leave it too long.'

'Yes, I know. Anyway, what about you, Mum, have you finished your searching about in that tin box?'

'Yes, I have. It's been a very strange time, and so weird how it all worked out. I'm just sorry that it was Callum who gave me so many of the answers that I was seeking, and his death that brought so many of the people that were involved back together. I miss his cheery face.' As she stared out across the city, her thoughts drifted back to that last visit to Estelle, just a few days ago after Callum's funeral. She could still see the frail form of her stepmother sitting defiantly in her chair. Anna squeezed her eyes shut, wanting to block the image. 'Come on; let's make our way back down before my joints seize up. I think you said you're buying the ice creams!'

On the way down the hill, Anna suddenly turned to Jason and said, 'What do you think? Aminah has invited me to accompany her to Kuala Lumpur. She has some business there with the Chartered Bank. Freya is unable to go for some reason, so she's asked me to go. And do you know? I think I will.' Anna smiled up at her son. 'What about you, my boy? Do you want to come with me?'

'No, Mum, I think it's good for you to go with Aminah. It will be good for you both. As for me, maybe you're right. I think, if Dad can spare me, I'll head back to France.'

Chapter 24

June 2004 – France

Whistling tunelessly, Jason fished in his pocket for some euros and paid off the taxi driver. 'I'll walk from here,' he told the man, and he set off along the road that wound past the old harbour. He wanted to savour the fresh fragrances of France in June, to take in the new leaves on the plane trees and the irises amongst the grassy verges, to listen to the shouts of the fishermen and the cacophony of traffic noises that threatened to choke the congested streets. He decided to stop at a pavement café where he ordered café au lait and a croissant. It was good to be back, and he inhaled the rich aroma of coffee and cigarettes, and listened with amusement to the furious chatter of two housewives as they fortified themselves before going on to the market. Other customers exhibited the slow, almost lazy, ambience of people with no need to rush, of having the luxury of passing time in the sunshine and viewing the world through creased eyes and pursed mouths. Looking up at the stone villas nestling like small birds in a bushy beard, his eyes settled on the one that he remembered. Suddenly impatient to get on, he drained his coffee and made his way up the hill, enjoying the morning sun burning into his back. He pulled out the crumpled letter from the inside pocket of his jacket and re-read the simple message, then squaring his shoulders, he unlatched the gate and walked up the drive, past the tracks that led to the chalets, and up the path to the warm yellow stone of Freya's house. He rang the bell, nervously running his fingers through his hair. What on earth had she summoned him here for, he wondered; he hoped Aminah wasn't sick.

The door burst open and there was Freya: 'Hellooo!' He was immediately clasped in a tight embrace and kissed noisily on both cheeks, 'My dear boy, how lovely that you came. Aminah! Look who's here, it's Jason! We couldn't believe that you were able to get a flight so quickly. Come in, come in!'

Aminah hurried through to the hallway. 'I knew you'd come!' She took his hands in her own and her face was alive with excitement.

'So what's the urgent news you had to tell me, could you not have just telephoned?'

'Oh hush, boy, plenty of time to talk. Do you want a drink? Some cold water?'

'Please,' replied Jason, 'I'm quite thirsty after walking up that hill; it's a lot hotter here than in Scotland, as you can imagine!'

He gratefully accepted the glass of water from Aminah but before he could finish drinking, Freya impatiently took the half-empty glass back and ushered him along the corridor. 'Come this way, I have someone I want you to meet.'

'Gosh, it must be urgent,' Jason protested, looking ruefully at the glass. 'Why! This is your bedroom, Freya. Who do you keep in here that you want me to talk to? I hope you haven't got a gigolo that's giving you bother!'

'Just go with her, and stop talking; there will be time later,' Aminah responded, pushing him gently before her.

Jason followed Freya into the bedroom that had been decorated in a dark colonial style. The wooden floors were buffed to a deep gloss, the walls were white, and the bed was canopied in dark blue velvet. On the white, crisp sheets Jason could make out the shape of a cane Moses basket. Freya walked ahead of him, leant over the bassinette and gently lifted out the tiny form of a newborn baby.

'I want you to meet your daughter, Jason. This is Coco Camille.'

Jason stood frozen to the spot, his thoughts a jumble, his eyes taking in the shapes and forms before him, but it felt as though the connection to his brain had been severed. Nothing in his past experiences had prepared him for this. He had no idea of how to react, or what was expected of him. His mouth hung open as he gaped at the tiny face, like a crab apple with a soft fringe of black hair. He noted the tiny ears, the tiny nose, the eyes closed into tight slits. The rest of the body was swaddled in a pink flannel blanket. Jason looked from Freya to the baby then back again to Freya. At last, there came a flicker of understanding, like a tiny light in the fog of his brain. 'Michelle?' he finally mouthed the name that suddenly had turned on a great floodlight in his befuddled mind. The need to know became an urgent quest. 'Where is Michelle?' A million fears caught hold of him. 'Where is she, Freya, has anything happened to her?' His mouth was dry; had he missed his chance to put right all the wrongs of the last nine months? Panic seized him as he searched Freya's face for answers. He wanted Michelle; he wanted to hold her, bury his head in her arms, tell her that he loved her and would never leave her again. 'Where is she, Freya? Where is Michelle?'

'Hush, hold out your arms,' Freya admonished, 'gently now, hold her gently, make sure you have her head. She is only a week old, you know.'

Jason held the baby and sat with her on the edge of Freya's bed. He held her as though she was a hollowed-out thrush's egg, so fragile that she might crack or splinter if he dared to move. It was with alarm that he suddenly noticed her eyes had opened and were regarding him with an all-knowing look; eyes the colour of black onyx. Suddenly her face screwed up and a tiny tongue peeped through the red, blistered lips. She squirmed in his arms, and he was amazed at the strength in the small body. Nervously he looked around for Freya, hoping to gain some reassurance, but he realised he was alone. Tentatively he stroked the soft strands of silky hair. 'Coco Camille,' he whispered.

'Does this mean you like her?' A voice broke into the silent room.

'Michelle! Oh my God, Michelle! I thought...you know? I thought...'

'You thought I didn't go through with it?'

'Yes, but no. Just now, I thought...' Jason stammered incoherently.

'Oh I see!' smiled Michelle. You thought I'd died in childbirth! Well it felt like it, you can be sure of that, but no, I survived, as you can see.'

Michelle sat on the chair facing Jason. She looked beautiful. Her hair was loose around her shoulders, and her denim smock hung over her bare legs. She was barefoot and her face was pale. Jason watched every nuance of her expression as she chastised him for the long, enforced separation. 'Aminah told me she'd seen you in Scotland and that she had talked to you. She told me that you regretted everything. Do you?' Jason's eyes grew misty as he nodded. Michelle went on, 'She seemed to think we both needed a little help. I'm glad they played Cupid, aren't you?'

Jason looked deeply into her eyes, and said quietly, 'I was so ashamed. I was such a coward and when I broke my ankle I just scarpered. I'm so sorry, Michelle, I can't tell you how sorry I am.'

She came and knelt by his side. 'There's been too much time wasted already, too many things we didn't do. I should have called you; you should have called me...enough recriminations. I think we have been miserable enough these last few months.'

Jason held his newborn babe in the crook of one arm and with the other he encircled the pliable body of his sweetheart.

She looked up at him with her liquid eyes and said, 'I don't want to be apart from you ever again.'

Jason smiled down at her. 'We'll be a family and we'll still follow our dreams, after all we've already proved we can be creative! Coco Camille, where did that come from?'

'Don't you like it?'

'Yes, I do, it's just unusual that's all.'

'Well, Coco is after a very artistic and inspired French woman who is better known by her second name, Chanel. Camille is from the composer, Camille Saint-Saëns, who composed *The Swan*. I have always adored that piece, and all winter I played the music as I sculpted. It is so haunting.'

'You are unique, and I do like the name. I can't believe this miracle has occurred. Isn't she exquisite?'

Michelle unwrapped the baby in order for Jason to be able to hold the tiny star-like hand that had automatically clasped itself around his finger.

Aminah and Freya tiptoed to the entrance of the room and silently peeked in. What they saw warmed their hearts and they smiled at each other, pleased with their matchmaking efforts.

Chapter 25

2004 – Malaysia

It was late September, a time of year she always loved. The golden colours of the bracken echoed the violent orange of montbretia. Autumn crocuses grew in violet clusters amidst the more flamboyant array of dahlias, violently coloured as a child's paint palette. Apples and plums fell from overburdened trees, and smells of burning leaves permeated the suburban gardens of Edinburgh. So it was with a tinge of regret that Anna boarded the plane. The invitation from Aminah had been reiterated, and after much excited speculation, she and Duncan had settled on a convenient time for Anna to make the journey to Kuala Lumpur.

'I'd come with you, dear, you know that, but this is for you. It's a continuation of your quest and your personal odyssey.'

The aircraft taxied down the runway and rose smoothly through the layers of mist up to where the air was clear above the clouds. As the plane circled over the capital city, Anna peered down at the castle bathed in a ray of golden sunshine. Her eyes followed the Royal Mile down to the Palace of Holyrood, along the ridge of Salisbury Crags and on towards Arthur's Seat. She thought she could make out people standing like stickmen on the top, and smiled at the memory of so many walks over the years up those very same slopes. They had been a refuge from the city, a place where there was a sense of freedom and wildness amongst the coarse grasses and whin bushes where small birds took their first tentative flights. Her gaze traced the line of the road over the Forth Bridge north to where the A9 snaked its way up to the Highlands. She thought of Molly sitting alone by her electric fire and promised herself that she would visit again soon. How did that old lady get through her days with so little to look forward to? It was as though the pilot could read her mind, for he dipped the wing of the plane and turned so that in the distance Anna could see the hills that held the small towns that were home to her father and stepmother. She imagined them both staring unseeing into the distance. She pulled her handbag towards her with her feet, and leant over to retrieve the photographs inside. She opened her spectacle case and put on her glasses to view the glossy pictures of her little granddaughter. There was herself and Michelle, grinning delightedly for the camera, sitting under a spray of summer roses on Freya's terrace, and Anna smiled foolishly at the pictures of Duncan holding the tiny pink form of Coco Camille.

Sleepily Anna made her way through Kuala Lumpur airport, where thankfully she was met by Aminah and Nancy Fung. She gave them both a hug and walked between them to the car. Nancy insisted on calling a porter to push the luggage trolley, and the boy obligingly loaded the cases into the boot of Nancy's Toyota. Anna was bemused to note that both ladies wore tropical lightweight jackets and seemed quite comfortable, but it was not until they drove away that Anna understood why, for she couldn't stop shivering in the chilly air conditioning.

'I thought it was going to be really hot,' she commented, looking out at the already darkening sky. She could make out the black shapes of the oil palms as the car whizzed along the motorway.

'Don't you worry about that, Anna; it is hot, very hot, and humid. Believe me; it's more comfortable to travel in this aircon than without. Do you see all these oil palms? You know this estate used to be a neighbouring estate from Satu Senga where you were brought up. The new airport where you just landed now covers all that land. I'm afraid your old house has gone.'

'Oh my goodness, I wasn't expecting that. But where are all the rubber trees? Are there none left?'

'No, gone now, though some estates are still as they were, but further north. The big companies found that changing over to palm oil production was more lucrative in today's market.'

'I used to spend my days with my friend Julia and her cats on that estate, closed up in a cupboard with sliding doors. Then we moved on to playing endless games of *The Sound of Music*.'

'I remember that!' Nancy laughed. 'You knew all the words of all the songs. Estelle wished you would erase all that clutter from your brain and make space for some academic facts, but no such luck! She said that your generation would end up as senile old women sitting in old folks' homes with no memory other than the full score of *The Sound of Music*!'

Anna nodded in agreement and smiled wryly at the picture Nancy painted. Kuala Lumpur was a maze of roads and flyovers. Huge twin towers dominated the skyline and the flashing neon portrayed a fast-growing market economy. It was obvious that this was a country that had shed its colonial past. Only the majestic architecture remained as a legacy of the various powers that had once seen fit to build and rule this beautiful peninsula.

For the next two days, Nancy and her husband propelled them around the city.

'It hasn't changed in half a century,' Winston informed them as they entered the Selangor Club, 'but nowadays Malaysians have the majority of membership'.

'First time for me to visit this place,' Aminah whispered to Anna as they gazed at the sprawling colonial haven.

Anna did recognise the *padang* and the long veranda which triggered so many childish memories. She could only begin to imagine the lives that had gone before hers, and the dramas that might have unfolded within these walls.

Later Nancy and Winston took them for a meal at the Coliseum restaurant where they were served by the oldest waiter Anna have ever seen. There was a rumour that he was over eighty, and on a good evening, if he felt so inclined, he might treat some of the guests to stories of long-gone days, when planters frequented the restaurant for a good meal and a beer during the Emergency. Unfortunately that evening he was looking quite glum and morose. Around the bar the little group read faded framed snippets from newspapers of the 1950s. The grainy photographs were still clear enough for Anna to study the faces of those who had been contemporaries of her father, and she realised that Jason was now about the same age as these men were at the time the pictures were taken.

Seeing the walls and the unchanged décor, she couldn't help commenting to Nancy, 'I don't think this place has seen a coat of paint since the good old days!' She smiled at the elderly pair and said, 'You've both been so kind to us, and we don't know how to begin to thank you for your hospitality.'

'We're very happy to see you,' Winston replied, wiping his spectacles on his napkin, 'and after Nancy takes you both around KL and you see to your business, Aminah, please I want you to use my driver and he'll take you wherever you want to go. Nancy says that you wanted to search for Bukit Bulan, Anna? I don't know if you will be lucky. So much development has been carried out in that area over the years. If I didn't have to fly to Hong Kong, I would take you myself. Still, Mr Joseph, my Indian driver will be a good guide. He has perfect English, and he'll know where to go.'

The next day, Nancy insisted that her two guests should visit Chotirmalls and the Globe Silk Store on the street Anna remembered as Batu Road, since renamed as Jalan Tunku Abdul Rahman. When she stood opposite the shop, she was transported back to another time when she and Estelle shopped there to buy material for her school uniform, and on a later occasion, for the soft yellow silk and green georgette for her first dance dress. She must have been so sophisticated in a made-to-measure Vogue original, though she couldn't have been much more than fifteen or sixteen.

Nancy broke into her thoughts. 'Estelle liked to shop here. For myself I prefer Robinsons.'

Anna walked into the dark interior of Chotirmalls and stood looking at the old-fashioned glass counters. An Indian assistant manned the one closest to the door and started nodding and gesticulating towards the displays of men's ties and cuff links, and then he indicated the bottom drawer of the cabinet.

He leant over conspiratorially, 'Briefs, Madam?'

Anna laughed, shaking her head, 'Not today, thank you.' She turned to Nancy, 'It's a very different experience from shopping in Marks & Spencer!'

They walked back up the street to the Globe, but Aminah hung back, unwilling to be tempted by the delights inside. Instead, she glanced back to the busy pavement. 'I'll just stay here and watch all this noise and confusion. Oh my! Look at that man carrying all those plastic things on his bike! You can hardly see him!'

Inside the emporium of silks and cotton and every material known to man, Nancy and Anna fingered and smoothed the bolts of fabric. Eventually Anna selected a pale green silk that shimmered like water. 'I have no idea what to do with it, but it reminds me of a dress colour my own mother had. It still hangs in my wardrobe. Perhaps I can have a blouse made?' She watched enthralled as a sales girl pulled the material out like a shiny river, and with a long ruler and giant scissors she expertly snipped and ripped the cloth. It was folded up and parcelled neatly then just before leaving, she shouted, 'Look, Nancy, Good Morning towels! I remember they featured in every house and bathroom on all the estates, and even afterwards my dad kept them for his golf or as dusters. Oh my goodness, I must buy some!'

That evening, Winston Fung unfolded a map of the northwest of Kuala Lumpur and presented a plan to them. 'Nancy has to chair a charity function, as you know, but as I said, Mr Joseph can take you on your safari. Perhaps you'll find the estates of your childhood. I know both your hearts are in Bukit Bulan. For you, Anna, it's the estate where you were born, and for you, Aminah, it's the estate where Jack Dunbar worked as an assistant. So much of your history began there. Would you be interested in doing this, Anna?'

'Yes, that's perfect.' She smiled at Aminah. 'We would love to do that, but first Aminah has some business to attend to at the Chartered Bank.'

'Yes,' said Winston, 'I know that, and I've made an appointment for tomorrow with Mr Ricky Lee. He'll be able to help you, Aminah, with your business.'

The next morning Anna accompanied the old Malay lady into the frozen halls of the marble palace that was the Chartered Bank. A lift whisked them up twenty floors in seconds and when the doors parted to the sound of melodic chimes, they found themselves deposited on to thick grey carpets that muffled any strident noise or footstep. Green potted plants and portraits on the muted tones of the walls suggested the neutrality of this enclave of the bank's inner sanctum. Aminah was led into an office by a slim Chinese girl wearing a black pencil skirt and long sleeved blouse in a shade of plum. She beckoned Anna to join them. Anna hesitated, and made to go and sit on a sofa outside the office.

'Please, Anna, I want to you to come in with me.' Aminah looked enquiringly at Mr Lee, who had arisen from behind a desk the size of a ping pong table.

'Good day, Miss Aminah.' Mr Lee signalled for his secretary to leave. 'Of course,' he graciously ushered Anna to an adjoining chair, 'your friend is most welcome to sit in on this meeting.'

'Hello, my name is Anna Maxwell,' and they shook hands. Mr Lee then returned to his padded chair behind the expanse of polished teak. 'I believe I have some very good news for you today, Miss Aminah.' He smiled kindly whilst opening the file in front of him. 'We've been trying to contact you for some considerable time, so it was fortunate that at last we were able to find you.'

Aminah nodded. 'I have been in France for many years. I only got the letter in April of this year.'

'Quite.' Mr Lee shuffled through the papers in the file. 'Now, we have here a trust fund set up for a child that you had with the late Mr Jack Dunbar, but I note that you wrote to inform us that your son Suleiman died in 1966. I am sorry about that.'

Aminah acknowledged his words by lowering her eyes.

'However,' the banker continued, 'the sum of money that has since accrued is now quite a sizeable amount and it is eligible to go to you, as your son's next of kin. His father must have been quite a gentleman to have had such foresight as to provide for him.'

Aminah nodded, still keeping her eyes averted.

'What are your instructions, Madam, to the bank? How do you wish us to proceed? Do you want the money transferred to an account in France?' He passed her the statement showing the monies due to her.

Aminah gasped. Clearly she was stunned at the figures in front of her. At this point Anna did feel she was intruding, so took the opportunity to excuse herself. Smiling inanely, she retreated out of the plush office and left Aminah holding the bank statement. When she eventually stepped out of the office, Aminah squeezed Anna's arm and whispered, 'It's a fortune! I have asked that Mr Lee to first do something for me here in Malaysia, and then to transfer the rest to France, but I also asked him to give me some money for spending here. I want to get my hair done. Shall we go and eat some *laksa* to celebrate, and have our hair washed?' She was positively gleeful.

Anna laughed, enjoying her exuberance. 'Yes, what a good idea; I haven't had *laksa* for years, and come to think of it, I haven't had my hair done for a while either.'

The next day Mr Joseph arrived with the car. He was a burly, thick-set Indian man with white grizzled hair that curled on to the collar of his dazzling white shirt. He was deferential and polite and seemed enthusiastic about the forthcoming journey. 'You must see a lot of changes?' he enquired. 'How many years is it since you lived here in my country?'

Aminah and Anna made polite conversation with him whilst he manoeuvred his way out of the city. Anna thought of Santosh and imagined he would have been about the same age as the driver. She wondered what had become of her childhood friend and fellow conspirator. Had he married? Was he well? She doubted she would ever know. As the day wore on they made good progress in their journey, travelling north along the coastal road of Kuala Selangor and threading through the back roads to join the main road north of Taman Minyak. Periodically Mr Joseph pulled up at some local shops where they bought cold drinks and asked for news of Bukit Bulan, but all to no avail. They feared the bulldozers had already done their work and that the new developments and country parks now covering so much of the surrounding areas had claimed the old rubber estate.

Eventually, Mr Joseph drew up outside an Indian temple and stepped out of the car to talk to the priest. 'He's a real old timer,' he observed. 'He's probably lived here all his life and might even remember the estate.'

Anna stepped out into the sunshine. The holy man certainly appeared ancient and leathery, and she was intrigued with the long, straggly tresses falling about his shoulders in iron-grey ropes. A white ash mark was smeared on his forehead, and his gaunt body was naked to the waist, with only a dirty white sarong draped around his middle then slung up between his legs. Speaking Bahasa Malay, Mr Joseph addressed him, and to their surprise the old man replied to the question in perfectly articulated English.

'I am very sorry to inform you, but the estate once known as Bukit Bulan has gone. A new country park has been built over the hills and a small township has been erected. Only my temple here has been spared.'

Mr Joseph sprang back as though he'd been struck. 'I wasn't expecting that you could speak such first-class English, sir; where did you learn?'

'At school, of course; I used to be a clerk for a tin mining manager. That was before I retired and took over my temple duties. I take it you have memories of Bukit Bulan?'

Anna nodded. 'I was born there and spent my early years there, and my friend here knew the families that lived around these estates.'

The priest nodded sagely, and pressed his hands together in prayer. 'All gone, my friends; the old Malaya is gone and with it all the wars and tensions. Today we strive on and make a new history.' He drew his clasped hands level with his chest, and bent his head in a farewell greeting. 'Forget the past, good ladies; just live for today and look only to the future.'

Anna couldn't look at Aminah. As they retired into the shade of the car, they both felt a deep sense of loss. They had resigned themselves to the inevitability of this news, but now the words were uttered, they realised just how much they had been hoping for the chance to revisit and savour again the essence of the place. Anna was surprised when, instead of driving towards the city as she expected, Mr Joseph turned north. Ignoring her questions about where they were heading, he drove on, only a flicker of a smile acknowledging her questioning. Eventually he pulled up at a little shack by the roadside and, with a huge grin on his face he ushered them out of the car, 'Please, ladies, will you join me? Please follow me.'

They entered the dark interior of the hut and Anna was appalled when he ordered lunch. 'Good heavens, Aminah, what on earth will we get?' she whispered, looking aghast at the dirty floor and the huge basins of bright red curry with dubious chunks of unknown substances lurking beneath the surface.

Mr Joseph calmly sat down on a child-sized plastic chair and gestured for them to follow suit. Sitting in the middle of nowhere, looking out on the tar road, Anna was conscious of the quiet. Only the beat of the cicadas broke into the absolute silence of the afternoon. A haze of heat rose from the verges made up mostly of *lalang*, grasshoppers leapt high and randomly across the long grasses, and from within, a dirty yellow dog appeared, and as if too weary to stand, it flopped down on to its side and stretched its legs and promptly fell asleep.

When the meal appeared, Anna's face lit up. There was *murtabak*, freshly made and chopped up, with a yellow dhal sauce to go with it. She inhaled deeply and the aroma made her nostrils twitch. 'Mmm, that smells heavenly. It takes me back to when I was a child!'

Aminah's eyes crinkled into a thousand laugh lines. 'We shall drown our disappointment in the best possible way.'

Immediately they started to eat, and a young girl brought them a plate of rambutans and three bottles of rather warm 7UP.

'Well,' Mr Joseph said, 'that wasn't so expensive; it was only seven ringgit for all of that!'

As they drove on to Ipoh, Anna continued to plague him with questions: 'Where are we going now?' but then she saw the sign posts indicating Fraser's Hill. 'Oh, I'd forgotten that it was so close! Are we going to visit? Gosh, it's years since I've been here.'

The road twisted and turned, up and round impossible corners, where tree roots twisted down into the storm culverts at the road edge. Fat leaves dripping with moisture hung over the congested ground foliage, smothering the grasses where insect life swarmed and seethed. At what felt like thousands of feet up, Mr Joseph drew into a lay-by and Aminah and Anna got out to stretch their legs. Looking down into a deep ravine, their eyes scanned the deep, untouched jungle interlaced with whispery fingers of cloud lying like a coverlet on the branches of the canopy. Anna squinted at the overhanging creepers, and the familiarity of the hanging vines seemed to link the present to the past. The years slipped by in a blur of impressions. She thought of the letters that Eilidh had written during the months of her convalescence and confinement; her words conveying her fear of the communists hidden in the jungle, the potential death sentence of tuberculosis, and the pain of separation from her husband and family during her pregnancy. It was beyond her comprehension but she tried in vain to put herself in her dead mother's shoes. Malaysia was now a strong, thriving country. The threat of ambush from communist guerrillas had gone. A new generation was at the helm.

They spent two days on Fraser's Hill and Anna was glad of the opportunity to walk along jungle paths and admire butterflies and waterfalls. She relished the cool mountain air and the quiet of the resort. During the evening meals, taken at restaurants dotted into the recesses of the mountain, she and Aminah talked easily about their joint memories of the past.

Mr Joseph finally asked, 'Well, Miss Anna, are you ready to go? Tomorrow we must return to KL. Aminah has asked me to make one extra detour, but I shall not tell you about that until tomorrow.'

The following day, they set off after lunch, planning to return to Kuala Lumpur that same evening. After many miles of driving, Mr Joseph veered off the main highway and took a side road that led to a plot of land bordered by jungle. The entrance archway was similar to those leading into the rubber estates.

Anna was intrigued when they left the car outside and tentatively walked in, keeping clear of three mean-looking dogs that sat by the roadside. 'Batu Gaja! So this is God's Little Acre; this is the graveyard that I've heard so much about!'

Together they stood and read the inscriptions on the gravestones near the entrance then walked through the hushed afternoon stillness.

'Be careful, Anna,' Aminah warned, 'I think snakes are here; those logs and branches are places they hide.'

Anna took her advice and noisily slashed through the long grasses with a stick, inspecting the old stones and crosses on her way, each one telling a story. The cemetery was an oasis of sadness, yet there was also a sense of peace. A hushed stillness hung in the air. They read the obituaries etched on the stones: of planters killed in the Emergency, children who had died in infancy, young soldiers who had been on service in the jungle but had not reached their twentieth birthday, and young people cut down by tropical sicknesses. A few new graves had been dug, suggesting that those who had lived long overseas had died in this country of Malaysia and made it their final resting place. And then they found it: a new stone had obviously replaced an older version. The words had been freshly chiselled in black wording. Anna realised that this was what Aminah had spent some of her money on. Shyly she held out her hand and took Aminah's into her own. Quietly they read together:

JACK DUNBAR, RUBBER PLANTER, 1923–1957
ACCIDENTALLY SHOT AT BUKIT BULAN ESTATE
DECEMBER 1957

AND HIS SON SULEIMAN
ACCIDENTALLY KILLED AT SATU SENGA ESTATE
SEPTEMBER 1966

TO ERR IS HUMAN, TO FORGIVE DIVINE
RIP

Aminah gripped Anna's hand and her shoulders started to shake as the tears coursed down her old cheeks.

Anna turned and put her arm around her. 'What a fine thing you've done, Aminah, a memorial to remember them both. It's beautiful.' Anna's eyes were wet and her tears fell into the soil. They stood together in respectful silence, each lost in their own memories. 'Come,' Anna said gently, 'it's time to go. Let's get back now.'

By the time they left the graveyard, the sun had set and they heard the evening chorus of deafening insects compete with the loud shrill of the creatures of the jungle. Squawking birds and screaming monkeys shrieked as the night fell and the nocturnal animals awoke and prowled and threatened. Aminah sat quietly as they drove away, their pilgrimage over, and unthinkingly Anna pulled the grass seeds from the hem of her dress and cast them away.

Nancy met them at the door of the high rise apartment in the centre of Kuala Lumpur. She was clearly agitated, 'You must phone Duncan, Anna, he said to ring him as soon as you return.'

Anna could see by the expression on Nancy's face that it was serious, so she immediately placed the call. She heard Duncan's deep voice, and sat down as he gave her the news of her father that she had been half expecting.

Anna told Nancy and Aminah the news and then they sat quietly together. There was little to be said. Anna walked over to the balcony of the apartment and stepped out and looked down at the city lights spread beneath her. 'Do you know where the Bungsar Hospital is, Aminah? Can we see it from here?'

The old Malay lady pointed to a hill in the distance. Anna could see the silhouette covered in mature trees, and imagined the old-fashioned building, a rambling wooden colonial structure that somehow had been allowed to remain in this rapidly changing modern city. How ironic that it should be here in Malaysia that she would hear the news of her father's passing. She looked over the city, and imagined a young woman standing there on that hill, fifty years ago, looking out over quite a different landscape. In her arms she held a newborn baby.

'I'm so glad you're with me,' Anna said softly.

Aminah linked arms with her. 'And I am so glad that we had this time together. Life is a circle and we have come all the way around. We are here together, bound together by the past and I hope, as that Indian priest told us, bound together forever.'

Chapter 26

October 2004 – Scotland

Anna stared at the pine coffin resting on two trestles at the front of the church. She felt a tear slip down her cheek as she sang:

Abide with me; fast falls the eventide;
The darkness deepens; Lord with me abide.

She felt removed, as though this funeral was for someone else, not for her father. How could that box in front of her contain Alex McIntyre? How could his life be over? She looked up at the stained glass and focussed on the spiralling patterns of blues and reds. Anna travelled in the black limousine with Estelle to the cemetery. It was a crisp, cool day; rain had fallen during the night, and drips from the overhead trees sporadically fell on the sober colours of the mourners' coats. She gazed down at the hole in the earth, her face one of a ring of faces that stared while the cords took up the slack and the box was lowered into the ground. Each had private thoughts, and Anna couldn't help thinking that the play was almost over. Funerals are public rituals. Accepted forms of behaviour are expected to prevail. Grief is controlled, hidden, transferred to a widow with words of hushed sympathy. A flower may be taken and thrown to land randomly on the shiny wood of the casket. Following Estelle's lead, Anna bent over and plucked a bloom from her own exotic wreath. She shuddered as it fluttered down into the dark pit below. It was a white orchid.

Anna reflected that it had been October, almost a year ago, when she had first begun her mission to uncover what might have been if her own mother had lived. She remembered the people, the letters and the secrets that had come to light as a consequence of her attempts to unravel the past. It had begun when she had driven north, up through the Scottish Highlands, and come to a small village tucked into the rolling, peat-covered hills of the Grampian Mountains. It had ended when the cords dropped on to the shiny wood of the coffin. It was over.

An unseasonably icy wind threatened the carefully arranged bouquets of Cellophane-wrapped chrysanthemums and roses. Estelle stayed behind as the gravel crunched under the feet of the mourners scurrying back to their cars. Anna watched her stepmother reading the sympathy tags attached to the wreaths; knowing how she wanted to save them, together with the many cards that she had received. It brought her comfort, she said, as she placed them inside her handbag. Anna had been surprised that the twenty-third psalm had not been included; her father used to sing it so loudly and lustily, what now seemed a lifetime ago, when he towelled himself dry after his bath before padding through the house leaving white footprints of Johnson's Baby Powder on the polished wooden floors. She remembered him as he had once been, tanned brown as a piece of leather in his colonial whites, always full of fun, a man who had once gambled and taken on the challenge of the unknown. She tried to imagine his years with Eilidh, and the unspeakable loss that he'd borne after her death. Anna looked now at his widow, this old woman, small and frail, yet still showing the same indomitable spirit that had driven her all through her fateful life.

'Well, he was a wonderful husband to me for over forty years. It was just hard at the end when he seemed to look straight through me.'

'You were a good wife to him.' Anna's tone was sharper than she intended. She softened her voice and continued. 'Will you be all right?'

Estelle took a lace-edged handkerchief from her handbag.

Anna smiled. 'You are the only person I know who actually uses those. And look, it's so beautifully ironed.'

'Aye, if you let the small things go, you might just as well jump into the grave too. Folk are quick to judge, but they won't find me eating my dinner from a paper plate, or wearing clothes on my back that haven't felt the heat of an iron.'

Anna sighed. Estelle would never change. There was no point in trying. There was no point in raking over the past. She had uncovered enough in her search, enough to lay it all to rest. 'Come on, Mother, let's go and get ourselves a gin and tonic.'

Estelle nodded, and made to turn away from the grave. Then suddenly, for the first time in her life, Anna felt Estelle's fingers seek hers. Looking resolutely forward, Anna tenderly enfolded the small hand into her own and squeezed it tight.

The old woman's voice was very small as she said, 'It's all in the past, Anna, let it go.'

'I know; the trip to Malaysia was good. It was almost like closing a chapter, a final goodbye.' She hesitated then said quietly, 'I saw their graves, you know, they're buried together. I am so sorry, Mother; I didn't understand the significance to you of that afternoon.'

'How could you? You were only a child.' Estelle looked down at the coffin and wiped her eyes with the handkerchief. 'It's best forgotten.'

But Anna couldn't forget, she had never been able to forget, and now standing by her father's open grave she thought she heard his laughter. Was it the crows, sitting like black silhouettes on those twisted tree branches, or was it the sough of the wind whispering through the stones of the graveyard? She shivered, for from somewhere she could hear Alex's jolly laugh coming from the beer crate where he sat, like a king at a Command Performance. She heard him cry, 'Bravo, Bravo!' It was the *Grande Finale*. And she remembered; it all came rushing back as she relived that afternoon in her mind. She remembered standing alone on the seat of the swing, gazing up at the red feathery fronds of the flame trees, and the swing taking her higher and higher as she bent and pulled on the supporting chains. It had been thrilling, everything had gone so well. Marvellous acts on the 'flying trapeze' had been promised; the invitation had not lied when it foretold that the audience were to see 'death defying daredevils of the sky'. She remembered looking down and seeing Santosh, poised and ready at the side, his blindfold just a grimy bandage. She had counted aloud. One, and the swing pulled back. Two, and it flew forward. Three! Santosh had run across in front of her as she had swung backward again. She had smiled triumphantly and swung forward just after the boy ran by. Up and back again she went, encouraged by the clapping from the audience. Then she, the great star, with her face lifted exultantly towards the sky, no longer counting and so not concentrating, saw in her periphery vision the adults rising up, their faces frozen in horror. Suleiman dashed forward, his face alive with laughter and daring, totally caught up with the excitement and desire to emulate Santosh. She had been aware only of the blurred impression of his shirt in front of her eyes as the boy ran out in front of the swing. There was a gasp then a deathly silence as the dull smack of the wood splintered his skull.

No words would ever be able to appease the guilt, or erase the look on the child's face as he lay bleeding on Freya's skirt. Anna remembered wondering if she would be taken away and imprisoned for murder. She also remembered that the only kind words she received that day were from Freya. 'He ran out in front of the swing, Anna. Nobody could have stopped him, except perhaps me. I could have grabbed him, but it was so unexpected and he was so fast. We were all helpless. I want you to tell the policemen out there about the swing and how you could not control it. You were standing up, Anna, how could you have possibly made it stop?'

Anna held Estelle's hand, and together they made their way to the waiting black limousine.

Epilogue

Five years later

Coco Camille was in heaven. She was staying in her Scottish house, as she called it, where she could run free all day long. She had only been there for a week, but already the small cottage was littered with the treasures that she'd proudly brought back from her explorations of the woods and mountain tracks. The window sill in the sunny kitchen was cluttered with stones, cones and rocks. Jars held mashed petals of roses that were supposed to turn into perfume. There was a small cemetery beside the washing line where dead mice that Horace the cat brought back were duly interred. Molly was sitting ensconced in her orthopaedic chair, out in the back garden. It was early summer and the sun glimmered through the intermittent clouds that gusted down the Beinn.

Anna followed the progress of a buzzard as it soared lazily above the rocky outcrops. She and Duncan had arrived in Druimfhada last night, and were enjoying a short break with Jason and Michelle, who were escaping the heat of France for a couple of weeks. Anna noted the daisies dotted on the lawn and buttercups in clusters around the boundary fence. Her main focus, however, was the child at her feet and she smiled affectionately at the attempts made at dressing the cat in a doll's cardigan. Coco Camille had blossomed into a tall, bony five year old. Her legs were smeared in grass stains and what looked like angry scratches from the irate captive. She was dressed in yellow shorts and a white T-shirt that had been pulled on back to front. The face when it looked up at Anna was dominated by flashing black eyes and the small mouth was contorted with determination as she manhandled the struggling Horace. Michelle had plaited the long hair which fell down almost to her daughter's bottom.

'Granny, make him sit still. He needs to have the dress on.' She held the cat down, not heeding the low growl that was emanating from its tense body. Its eyes had taken on a fixed stare.

Luckily for both child and feline, the welcome voice of Michelle broke into the ominous deadlock. 'Coco Camille! Come and see! Come and see what your papa and granddad have made for you!'

Molly pulled her Zimmer frame closer and tried to raise herself. Anna seized the opportunity to lean down and pull the woollen sleeve from the offended creature. It shot off, no doubt to find some place free from further assaults. Anna stood up and stretched her arms above her head, before she too went to see what the excitement was all about. She helped Molly up, and together they followed the path round the side of the cottage. What Anna saw made her gasp. She stopped in her tracks, and for a minute she tried to control her breathing and contain the panic that was rising up inside her. Coco was clambering on to a swing that Jason had constructed for her. Anna's eyes searched for Duncan, entreating him to give her reassurance that this was not happening.

'It's all right, Anna, it's all right. Come here beside me.'

Suddenly Anna heard the harsh caw of a black hoodie crow. She looked up and squinted into the tree branches overhead. An unexpected dazzle of sunlight broke from behind the clouds and she saw not the twisted branches of the burgeoning sycamore, but two flame trees of long ago. She gazed up at the red feathery fronds. The swing took her higher and higher as she rhythmically bent her legs and pulled on the supporting chains. She saw in her peripheral vision the approach of the invited adults, their faces nervous at the sight of Santosh preparing his blindfold for the *Grande Finale*. The laughing voice of her granddaughter broke into her reverie.

'Look at me, Granny! I can swing!'

Tremulously Anna smiled up at Duncan and Jason. She mouthed the words 'thank you' to them, before gently pushing the child.

'Push me, Granny, push me! Higher, I want to go higher!' Coco Camille sat on the swing, gleefully feeling the wind against her face.

'You are wonderful, my darling, do you feel that you are flying?'

'Oh yes!' shouted Coco Camille. 'I'm the best flyer in the world!'

Lightning Source UK Ltd.
Milton Keynes UK
UKOW042319161212

203731UK00002B/25/P